Barb,

My partner in
literary crime... here's to
keeping Barbara on her
toes

Chantone

i

Annals of Wynnewood

Beneath the Cloak

by

Chautona Havig

The events and people in this book are purely fictional, and any
resemblance to actual "creatures" or medieval villages is purely
circumstantial. Two exceptions to this are William de Brailes and Simon
de Montfort, Earl of Leicester. Montfort did arrive in Oxford in June of
1258 and the resolutions he and the other barons decided on are
historically known as the Provisions of Oxford. De Brailes and his wife
Celena lived in Oxford around the same time at the site of what is now
the All Souls Chapel near the Church of St. Mary the Virgin and worked
as bookmakers.

Furthermore, while I kept the story as authentic to thirteenth century life
as I could, I there are deliberate inaccuracies. England was infused with
Christianity by the time of this tale, but I chose to keep the little corner of
northern England, fictionally known as "Wynnewood," free from
conversion by the Catholic Church for my own purposes. Furthermore,
Broðor Clarke's "heresies" would likely never have been tolerated.

In addition, the names of Morgan and Wynne are traditionally considered
Welsh, not English, and therefore are another stretch of my literary
imagination.

For Barbara—

    Your friendship means so much more to me than sneak peeks at Knightley or the corralling and subduing of my non-parallel phrases. I love your wit, your gentleness, and how the Lord shines in you. I am honored to call you my friend. Double Stuff Oreos will whiz across the water forthwith!

Craig—

    You surpassed yourself again. I just couldn't end this series without taking a moment to thank you for your generosity, your incredible talent, and for becoming such a good friend. I look forward to robbing you blind again in the future!

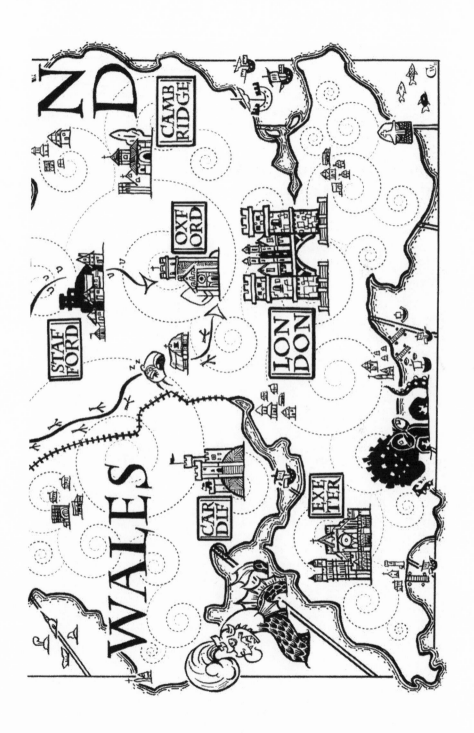

Broðor (BRO-thor)- brother
Ciele (CHILL-leh)- chill
Fæder (VA*-dare)- father
Ge-sceaft (jeh-SAFt)- creature
Wyrm (WEE-you-hrm)- dragon
Hælan (HA-lahn)- healer
Holt (HOLE-t)- forest
Heolstor (Hay-OL-store)- hiding place
Mæte (MAT*-eh)- small
Modor (MOE-dore)- mother
Nicor (NEE-core)- Sea monster
Sceadu (SAD-oo)- shadow
Scynscaþa (SKEUN-skah-thah)- demon

*æ is *a* as in cat or rat

Note: There is controversy over the correct pronunciation of certain letters. I found opposing pronunciation guides and chose to go with what seemed most consistent. I also found that "F" was pronounced like "V" since writing Shadows & Secrets. I apologize for any errors.

The Minstrel's Song

CHAPTER 1

Spring

On a sunny morning in late spring, strange sounds echoed through the forests near Wynnewood. A shadow seemed to float between the trees, pause, bend, and float again. It is no wonder that new tales of spirits haunting the fearsome forest spread across the village and even up to the castle. Some thought it was the mystical creatures of the Sceadu—terrifying beings with fiery eyes strong enough to repel the mesmerizing gaze of the dragons. In fact, only one in Wynnewood could do that. Just one cloaked little girl— a girl they feared more than anything you could imagine.

Everyone had heard of the Ge-sceaft's ability to resist the hypnotic eyes of the dragons of Wynnewood. The minstrels and bards told the tale of how she'd saved their local hero from a gruesome death at the claws of the mother dragon. Their songs and stories combined local folklore and a great deal of superstition until no doubt remained in the minds of the villagers that the small creature, the Ge-sceaft, drew her abilities from the devil himself.

Broðor Clarke's sermons, private rebukes and admonitions, and even his attempts to befriend the small girl had been completely unsuccessful. The people of Wynnewood remained prejudiced against the one sometimes known as Dove, and she against them. No amount of support from Lord Morgan himself was able to rid the fears regarding the cloaked child from the hearts of the villagers.

Accompanied by a mandora, a tenor filled the Great Hall with music as he sang his tale. Philip sat near the fire, listening as the song told of the failed siege on Wynnewood Castle. Only Philip heard Dove's disgusted snort as she hid behind a screen. Unbeknownst to him, Lord Morgan watched the amused expression on his face with curious interest.

Polite applause was followed by murmurs of the listeners' appreciation and, if you listened closely enough, a derisive growl from somewhere near Philip. Ignoring it, Lord Morgan smiled at their entertainer and gestured toward the kitchen. "Perhaps you'd like some supper and a glass of ale or mead?"

"Thank you, m'lord. I'd appreciate that."

"Follow John. He'll show you to the kitchens. Perhaps you'd sing a few songs for the servants as well. I'm sure they'd enjoy your talents as much as we have."

With a nod and a bow, the minstrel sauntered after John, leaving the silence in the room nearly oppressive as their footsteps echoed in the corridor. When John and the minstrel were out of earshot, Lord Morgan turned to Philip with a smirk on his lips. "So what amuses you this afternoon?"

"I don't understand," Philip said, confused.

"Something amused you as our guest performed."

Understanding lit Philip's eyes with a similar light of mirth. "Oh, that was Dove. She was getting irritated at the song."

"Come out here, little one. The minstrel is gone."

Rustling sounds behind the screen sent a fresh round of amused glances between the others as they waited for her to appear. The young girl, taller after a year's growth but still quite small for someone of twelve, stepped into the firelight, pulling on her gloves. She settled herself at Philip's feet, stashing her embroidery basket under her cloak.

"What irritated you, Dove?"

Aurelia shifted on her padded bench, lounging on the other side and pulling her rolled pillow with her. "Did you get that section done, Dove?"

"Nearly."

Visibly eager to avoid the subject, Dove jumped up and seemed to float across the room as she hurried to show Aurelia her progress. The two girls whispered about stitching and left the others to exchange smiles at her obvious attempt to divert attention away from her. "Since Dove will not share her feelings, Philip, perhaps you'd care to enlighten us?"

Philip glanced at his friend, and seeing the frustration in her posture, chuckled. "Dove doesn't like the way the song exaggerates her involvement—in her opinion anyway."

"You do not think you were heroic, Dove?"

Dove didn't respond, but her hood shook impatiently. A few seconds passed before Philip tried to explain. "You know that Dove has no false modesty about her, m'lord. She isn't ashamed to admit when she has done well, but you have to admit the stories are a bit exaggerated. Why, this man's song makes it sound like the mists whispered to her and told her that the kidnappers were coming."

"True, but she did come warn us—as did you," Lord Morgan added hastily.

"Dove's objection," Philip began again, "is that she did something anyone would have done, but the song makes her sound like she—we I suppose—did something extraordinary."

"She risked her life. She let those horrible men take her and pretended to be me!" Aurelia protested. "Dove, how can you say that is not heroic?"

Dove's hood turned toward Philip, and she nodded. He returned the gaze he couldn't see until at last he shrugged. "Dove doesn't think doing what anyone would have done in her position qualifies her as heroic. There isn't a little girl in the village who wouldn't have tried to do the same thing." Philip tossed an apologetic glance at her and added, "I disagree with her that any of them would have been successful, but the bravery is in the attempt, not the success, and Dove believes that she did what any girl would have attempted."

"Do you agree?"

"Father!" Aurelia's exclamation brought smiles to the others' faces, and even Dove's posture showed that she too was amused.

"I didn't say I agreed, dear heart. I simply want to understand their thoughts on the idea."

"To an extent, I agree, yes. Dove expects people to give credit where it is due, but she is a hard taskmaster. She isn't a master who would lavish praise on expected chores. She would reserve praise for truly outstanding work."

"And yet..."

"Well," Philip hesitated. "I just think that sometimes Dove forgets that her unique—um, situation—makes even simple actions heroic."

"Oh, Philip, really!"

"No," Lord Morgan agreed, "Philip seems to have put my emotions into words. If another girl, say Letty for example, had attempted to do the same thing, being caught wouldn't have put her in the same kind of danger as you."

"I think it is a whole lot of fuss about something that was more exciting than dangerous. How many girls get to do something so fun and thrilling?" Unaware she'd proven the others' point, Dove sat back, her entire body exuding the self-satisfaction she felt. Her smugness didn't last long. Just as the others couldn't hold in their laughter any longer, she threw her hands in the air. "Ok, so you think it was something extraordinary. I think the true hero was Philip when the Scots came from Bramburg. I had the easy job. Go get Aurelia and hide. Philip had to allow himself to be caught, beaten, incarcerated... He had to leave the more exciting and glory-filled tasks to others."

Nodding as she spoke, Lord Morgan turned to Philip. "I agree with Dove there. I don't think you give yourself credit for what I consider your bravest and most heroic deeds. Coming to warn us about the kidnappers couldn't have been easy. I know how gruff my guards are when they're wakened while they're supposed to be working." The twinkle in Lord Morgan's eyes nearly set everyone laughing again. "Had you allowed the men to brush you off, we might not be sitting here today."

"Father! Those horrible Scots were going to use me to gain control of the castle! I'd be dead if it were not for Philip and Dove!"

"That seems a bit melodramatic, dear heart. After all, with the heir alive, no one could question their right to the lands."

The young girl tossed her blond curls and leveled a scornful gaze at her father. "We both know that as long as the king gets his taxes and the church gets their tithes, no one cares who claims what land as their own. We'd be dead and the villagers would likely be driven like slaves."

Dove sat quietly through the exchange, listening even more intently than usual. When the conversation lulled for a moment, Dove turned her hood toward Lord Morgan and asked, "Was the first kidnapping attempt truly the original plan to take control of Wynnewood Castle?"

"Well, yes. I thought you knew that."

The young girl shook her head. "I think I'd heard it, but until just now, I never quite understood that the two things were so closely connected." The girl shoved her basket under Aurelia's bench and sought the warmth of the fire by Philip again. "So Lady de Clare was behind the original plot?"

"No, Dove. Lady de Clare was brought in when the first attempt failed. They simply took over her castle, and her only hope to regain it was to help them infiltrate mine."

Philip's voice sounded irritated—furious even—as he growled, "I still can't believe she was such a coward, leaving her own people to the mercy of those barbarians and using a cripple to betray a distant kinsman. Shameful."

"She did look funny when Father's men brought her in from the Heolstor all covered in twigs and mud." Aurelia sighed. "I still think she was not punished adequately."

"She had to go home to very angry people. As I learned by watching my father and grandfather, your people will serve you cheerfully and more productively if they know you will protect and defend them as much as you expect them to serve and honor you."

"Just like Jesus said," Philip mused under his breath.

Dove latched onto his words eagerly. "What did Jesus say, Philip?"

"He said that anyone who wanted to be a leader of people must first serve them."

To everyone's surprise, Dove laughed. "That sounds just like something I AM would say. He seems to delight in speaking wise things that sound foolish."

Broðor Clarke's voice joined the group from the door.

"'For the wisdom of this world is foolishness with God. For it is written, He captures the wise in their own craftiness.'"

"Are you saying that I AM deliberately allows us to think we're wise when we're truly foolish?"

The round minister settled himself and accepted the goblet of wine offered by the master of the castle. "Truly, I just threw out the first pertinent scripture that came to mind."

"I wonder if Philip will do that after he goes to Oxford. He already finds a Bible story for almost anything that happens."

The mood in the room became more serious—almost somber. Philip smiled at the realization that she noticed his attempts to interject the Word of I AM wherever he naturally could, but the reminder of his impending move to Oxford added a sting to his joy. There were just a few short weeks before it was time to make the two-week journey south.

"Isn't it exciting?" Dove seemed oblivious to the change in tone around her. "He'll come home knowing all the stories, all the verses, and even things like history of other places."

"I don't like to think about it," Aurelia confessed.

"It—" Philip began, but Dove interrupted him.

"Oh, but think of the things he'll see, the people he'll meet, the things he'll learn. Why, we'll be grown women by the time he returns!"

The discouragement on Aurelia's face slowly morphed into amusement. She exchanged covert glances with her father as Philip's face slowly fell. It seemed obvious to them that Dove had chosen to focus on all the advantages of Philip's university education and in doing so had left him with the impression that she wouldn't miss him at all.

"I promised my modor that I'd fill the wood pile

today," Philip said at last, dragging himself off the floor. "I'd best be going home."

"The dragon should be visiting his wife tonight. The clearing?" Dove seemed oblivious to the hurt she'd caused.

"I'll be there."

Aurelia latched onto the change of subject eagerly. "Hasn't that egg hatched yet?"

"Bertha says a dragon's egg takes fifty years to hatch."

"How would she know? She isn't even fifty years old yet."

"True, Philip, but that doesn't mean that she isn't correct." Broðor Clarke's voice seemed to rebuke the young man.

"I think," Lord Morgan added thoughtfully, "I remember my grandfather saying that they noticed the change in the caves about five years before he died. That would make the time close to twenty-five years since she laid her egg or eggs."

Philip stood listening for a few more minutes before quietly slipping from the room, shoulders drooped and footsteps dragging. A little while later, Dove stood, retrieved her basket, and left, turning toward the kitchen entrance on the opposite side of the castle from where Philip had gone.

"I think Philip is feeling a little rejected," Lord Morgan observed.

"Dove almost cried."

The two men turned toward Aurelia, but Broðor Clarke asked the question on both men's minds. "Why do you think that?"

"She wanted to finish that section of her embroidery. With Philip gone, she would have stayed to have me help her with the flower, but she's gone."

"Still—"

Aurelia shook her head. "If you knew Dove's voice, you would have heard it. Seven years is a very long time."

"Or eight, dear heart. Broðor Clarke has said seven or eight years."

"I prefer to be optimistic, Father. Philip will do it in six if he possibly can. He's intelligent, determined, and loves his home here. He'll do anything possible to return early."

"I think he is going to spend the first year studying various things, Lady Aurelia. He'll start with the Arts and then make a decision as to whether he wants to stay with the Arts, or if he wants Medicine, Civil Law, Canon Law, or Theology."

"He'll choose Theology."

"Why do you say that?"

"Oh, Father. This is Philip. He'll choose the most difficult task because he'll find it a challenge. He'll choose Theology because of his love for I AM."

"Your daughter is correct. Usually, he'd struggle within himself to know what to do, but in this case, the most arduous task is also his first love."

A Fæder's Wisdom

CHA
PTR
2

All the way home, Philip recounted the discussion in his mind, trying to eliminate the final words that now drove him from the castle. He'd known—the practical side of him, anyway—that Lord Morgan and his daughter appreciated his part in protecting the castle. Even as minimal as his efforts seemed at times, how many lads could say they had helped with anything in a castle—well, anything but polishing silver, scrubbing flagstones, or some other task that lacked any excitement at all? He'd helped foil an attempt to overthrow the Earl of Wynnewood—twice! He'd been part of the capture of the one thing the Earl wanted and couldn't procure for himself—a unicorn! He should be grateful.

Usually he was. He often thanked the Great I AM for being blessed with a man like Lord Morgan as a benefactor. Alas, there were times that it wasn't enough. He ached to do something brave—something important. In fact, that desire of his was what drove him to excel in his studies. He'd failed at becoming a fletcher. Oh sure, he sometimes admitted to himself that it wasn't his fault. Tom Fletcher had been a weak master. However, when his thoughts were already predisposed to think the worst of himself, he added that failure to his list of other perceived weaknesses.

Not only could he not make a simple arrow, his skill

with the bow was the result of hard work rather than natural talent. Even then, in the wrong conditions he could be more trouble than help. For some reason, his eyes saw things just a little off center from their actual position. Why couldn't he at least have had normal vision?

He had no desire to try his luck at sea. Instinctively, he knew he'd be a poor seaman. What else was he good for, save academia? According to both Lord Morgan and Broðor Clarke, he was a natural scholar. "It's not that I don't like learning," the young man admitted to himself as he kicked a stone along the road leading toward Wynnewood from the castle. "I just like to be active. Even a farmer can sleep at night with the comforting ache of well-used muscles."

Despite Broðor Clarke's hopes that Philip would choose the church, he had other plans—secret ones that he hadn't told anyone. Even Dove was oblivious to his intentions. Oxford was a large town. There were tanners, millers, tailors, gold and silversmiths, cobblers and coopers. Why, he might even make friends with a constable. He'd learn everything he could, but he'd try to learn a trade too. That's what Philip Ward wanted more than anything else—a useful trade of his own.

Philip passed Bertha as she checked on a first-time mother near the fishermen's quarters. The woman, hardly more than a girl, took every kick, every twinge, and even her sore back as proof of impending birth. The town teased her and joked about it incessantly—all but Bertha. The midwife came at every summons, as far as Philip could tell, and sat with Mary until the young girl realized that it was just another gas pain or stretched muscle. He had to respect her for that, but he would rather have been able to despise her for ignoring a terrified young woman's pleas for reassurance.

"How's Mary?" It galled him to speak casually to the

woman, but he was curious.

"Feeling a bit better now. I gave her some herb tea that should relax her."

Feeling compelled to ask, Philip jerked his head in the direction of Mary and James' cottage. "How much longer?"

"At least a month or a little over."

"She calls you three times a day!"

Bertha's smile infuriated him. "Yes, and I'll come five if it'll reassure her that all will be well."

With that, the tired midwife shuffled toward home, leaving Philip staring after her. Still smarting from Dove's apparent lack of concern about his leaving, Philip called after her. "It is a shame that you don't have the same compassion and care for the girl who keeps your home such a pleasant place to live."

He could hear her mutter something, but what it was, Philip didn't know. As he reached his yard, he took the axe from the pegs on the outside of the wall and carried it to the chopping stump. All the frustration and hurt that he carried in his heart during the long walk home was shattered with each stroke of the axe. Chips flew as he slammed the blade into the wood once more.

"Philip?"

His father called to him from the doorway. A glance up at the sea-weathered face told him that he'd have to explain the... intensity... of his efforts. Stalling, Philip filled his arms with the pieces of wood and dragged his feet through the yard to his father's side. "Yes?"

"There is something wrong."

"Yes." He wasn't sure how to answer the unspoken question.

John Ward took the wood from his son and carried it indoors. Philip watched from the doorway as he stacked it next to the hearth. He beckoned for his son to follow, and with his arm around Philip's shoulder, they strolled toward the seashore. "You're a good lad, Philip. You don't sulk, you work hard; what has brought about this anger I see in you? It's not like you."

Shame flooded Philip's face as he struggled to find the words to explain. "I feel as silly as a girl."

"I don't think anyone would mistake a tall young man like you for a girl," his father teased.

"Well, I feel like one. It was just something Dove said."

"Your little friend is usually very wise for someone so little. That must be hard to swallow when she grasps a concept before you."

"It wasn't that, Fæder. I—" He swallowed hard. How could he explain what happened without looking any more ridiculous than he already felt?

"Tell me, son, what is it?"

"Well, we were talking about Oxford—how I'll be going soon."

"Yes..."

"Well, she just sounded so—so—eager. It was almost as if she looks forward to me going."

"And you thought she'd miss you? Say she didn't want you to go?"

Hearing the words from his father made Philip feel even more ridiculous. "It sounds petty, doesn't it?"

"No. I would hope that you would want to know that your mother and I will miss you. I think that's a normal expectation. You would want the other lads or Broðor Clarke to miss your company. Why should you not wish for the same from your little friend? She's become almost a sister to you."

"Why does it sound so foolish when I say it," Philip asked, kicking a shell into an oncoming wave, "but when you—"

"Everything sounds wiser from an older voice. It's one of the advantages of growing old."

"You're not old, Fæder!"

"Compared to you, I'm ancient." Philip's father grabbed for the shell that tumbled about in the water and tried to skip it across the tops of the waves. "Philip, did you consider that your friend might not want you to see how much your leaving hurts her? She'll be all alone again. It'll be harder than before you met her—she's tasted friendship now."

Philip's head snapped up and he met his father's gaze—surprised. "Of course! I—"

"Go talk to her." John waved his hand toward the cliff near The Point.

"I will see her tonight. We're going to watch for the dragon."

"Then tell me something."

There was something in his father's voice. Philip knew that tone. It meant a serious talk ahead—one he might not like. All he could do was ask the obvious question. "What?"

"If you can do anything at Oxford that you want, what will it be? Law? Medicine? The Church?"

"It all sounds fascinating." A look on his father's face showed that John Ward didn't quite believe his son. "No, truly. I like learning. It is nice to be good at something when you've failed at so many other things."

"And what are your failures?"

"Well, I should be a reasonably competent fletcher, but I can barely repair damaged arrows. I cannot shoot well, and even when I've tried to help Lord Morgan, I've not done the kinds of things that truly help."

"Now you're just feeling sorry for yourself," his father admonished. "I thought you beyond that foolishness."

Once more, shame washed over him. He'd expected to hear contradictions much as Lord Morgan, Aurelia, and Dove had made. As grown as he was—a man now in the eyes of the village—he still wanted the approval and praise of his father. "I'm sorry. I think—" the temptation to excuse his behavior because of the impending removal to Oxford nearly smothered him, but Philip choked it back. "I think I have a lot to learn yet."

A smile crept toward the corners of John's mouth. "You're a good lad—a man already. I'm proud of you. You wanted to hear me tell you that your failures weren't your fault—that you could not have avoided them. Those aren't things to be proud of, Philip. Praise for a job well done has value. Praise for good character is something that no one can take from you. Commiseration, excuses, and sympathy will not make you into a better man."

They'd almost reached the jetty where the rocks jutted into the ocean giving them access to the caves. John turned and began strolling back toward the village. "We've veered from the topic, Philip. Why does it all sound fascinating?"

"Because I like knowing things. I like succeeding at something. I'd choose the law because it's a good and interesting vocation, but what would I do with it? I want to live here—raise a family here. I don't see a use for that."

"What about Medicine?"

"If I hadn't met Dove, and I still had this same opportunity, I would have chosen medicine. I may still. I don't know. But now that I know how often Bertha differs from the Hælan and how she has saved lives that Biggs would have lost had she not interfered..."

"You would choose the midwife's ways over those of the Hælan?" Philip's father stopped midstride, stunned.

"Yes. I saw what his methods did to Liam. Had Dove not told me what Bertha recommends for fever, I think Liam would be dead."

"Interesting. And why not the Church? I know how you love your Bible stories and your lessons with the minister. Why do you not want to become like Broðor

Clarke?"

"The Church would be my first choice. It is more difficult—the challenge..." He ducked his head at the arrogance he heard in his voice. "I didn't mean it like that—really. I just meant that if I am going to be given this opportunity, I'd like to take full advantage of it."

"Yet you hesitate."

He nodded. "Broðor Clarke is a minister, Fæder. I don't want to be a minister."

"Why not? Wynnewood already has one? You want to return here and this village is too small for two ministers?"

"A minister doesn't marry."

"But you told me that Broðor Clarke said—your little friend heard him—a minister can marry."

Red crept down from his forehead and up from his neck. It took several minutes for Philip to formulate what he wanted to say, but at last, he blurted it out. "I know it sounds impertinent and a bit arrogant, but I think I will find at Oxford that the priests will prove marriage is not allowed for a minister of God. I—" he swallowed hard. "I don't know if Broðor Clarke was teasing Lord Morgan, or if he really meant it. He also told the Earl that he was in love with someone. That's ridiculous."

"Why is it? Why should Dennis Clarke be immune to the very thing that you say you want so desperately?"

Philip shook his head. "It's not possible."

"Well, I think you should ask him about it. Before you leave, Philip, ask him. You need to make an educated choice when you are there. You will be gone for a very long time. I want to know that you will not be wasting your time. You spent six years with Tom Fletcher. Do not let this be another wasted apprenticeship."

As they reached the corner of their little house, Philip turned and smiled. "I won't, Fæder. I know this is a great opportunity. I will miss you, Modor, Will, little Adam—"

To his disgust, Philip's voice cracked.

"Your friend... Yes, you'll miss us all."

"But I'll see more of the world. I'll learn new things. And maybe..." He glanced over his shoulder involuntarily. "Maybe Dove will learn to rely on I AM rather than on my stories of Him. That would be worth the time away."

"And do you care if your fæder believes in this god of yours?"

Feeling like quite the little boy, Philip wrapped long, strong arms around his father and choked as he said, "Even more. Much more. I'd truly give anything for it."

Quarrel

CHAPTR 3

The spring night was cool—crisp. Philip and Dove sat, back to back in the old way, wrapped in blankets as they scanned the skies looking for signs of the dragon. They'd hardly spoken. Philip still mulled the conversation with his father over in his mind as they waited. Dove broke bits off a carrot and threw them into the forest, giggling as a rabbit crept closer.

"Have you decided what to study?" Dove's voice was quiet—reluctant.

He couldn't resist a grin. "I was thinking of becoming a lifetime scholar. Oxford sounds so exciting."

It failed. She snickered. "You'd go crazy being away for that long. You don't even want to make the journey."

"It's a long time. When I come back, Adam will be an apprentice to someone. Una's Adam will be learning what I should know. All my friends will have families. Will—" He swallowed hard.

"You don't have to go." Her attempt not to sound eager flopped. "Lord Morgan said you could become a guard at the castle. Maybe Broðor Clarke could keep teaching you when you have the time..."

"Thank you." There was something comforting about knowing he didn't have to explain himself. Dove knew that he appreciated her confidence in him.

Before she could respond, a familiar whooshing

sound reached them and the forest grew silent. The faint bleating of a frightened sheep slowly grew louder. The great wings of the dragon beat against the air as he flew overhead and then stretched his wings to their full span. They wouldn't hear him again until he returned to the Sceadu.

"I wonder that the knights do not try to kill the dragons," Philip mused. His mind immediately swung to ways to slay the dragon and earn himself a place among Lord Morgan's knights. How could the Earl resist after such an incredible feat?

"I hope they won't. How would the Mæte stay warm?"

Dove's question was a valid one. Suddenly, the idea seemed revolting. "I suppose even if he had ever considered it, Lord Morgan won't now…"

"I know you want to slay a dragon—even a metaphoric one—but you don't realize that you have already done it. You slayed your pride every time you had the chance to denigrate Tom Fletcher for his failure to teach you the craft you worked hard for the chance to learn. So many times you've forced yourself to admit you were wrong or that you couldn't do what you wanted to say you could. Your 'dragons' aren't visible like that enormous creature, but they are just as dangerous." She laughed. "How did you like my sermon?"

"I think you should go to Oxford."

"A girl learning French and Italian? A girl studying law or medicine? That's not likely ever to happen, is it? Particularly a girl like me—scary enough to send reason fleeing even the strongest mind."

"Ok, that's just silly."

"Yes. A female scholar is silly—and yet you've made me as close to one as you can."

"Aurelia is somewhat of a scholar. She has studied Latin and Italian at least." Philip interjected.

"Yes, and she's the heir to a large property and title,

as well as a cripple. It's hardly comparable."

"Do you think women will ever study at places like Oxford?" The idea intrigued him. Dove asking questions of a master... she'd drive him mad.

"To what purpose? All that time and money spent, for what? A woman has no use for it other than interesting conversation. She'd use her time better to care for a family and learn from her husband if he were educated."

"That sounds almost like something Broðor Clarke was reading last week."

"He's a much more intelligent man than people credit him. Some think he's been conditioned to spout stories at will, but I think he is wise. Even Bertha tries to hide her respect for him, and she respects no man, including his lordship."

Philip continued to mull over the idea of Dove at Oxford. As much as the concept of her as a scholar intrigued him, she had a point. No one would waste so much money to educate a woman when she had no use for the education. Oh, surely the princess of any country was well educated. Even girls like Aurelia had a reasonable use for some education, but the law, as interesting as it might be, would help no woman with tending a garden, baking bread, or nursing a sick child. No university was going to allow half a dozen women to attend their lectures no matter what their station.

"I think you're right, Dove. An education might be wasted on women. They certainly won't allow even a girl like Aurelia to go."

"I think," the girl added with a hint of mischievousness beneath her words, "the university knows that if they ever let a woman inside, the world would discover that men and women both have equal numbers of fools and wise ones."

"Another reason that you'll never see a woman at Oxford or Cambridge. Men couldn't handle a discovery like that."

"At least you speak sense. That's more than I can say for most men." Dove snickered. "I sound like Bertha, don't I?"

Philip laughed. "All right. I have criticized my brothers enough. I have some pride. Let's go see if we can watch the dragon fly from the cave."

The days flew into weeks. The full moon rose over the clearing once again on a bright mist-free night. A great shadow would appear when the dragon made his way from the Cliffs of Sceadu, over the Heolstor forest, and into the farmers' fields to snatch a sheep for his wife. He'd turn west from the pastures and soar over the clearing in plain view of Philip and Dove as they lay on the blanket, head to head, talking.

It was their last night before Philip's journey south. They'd spoken of nearly everything except the journey. Dove told of a project she hoped to begin. Philip listened to the high voice that he'd miss before he reached the first village on the way south to Oxford. He hardly heard her describe the careful way she expected to dig out the dirt and carry it deeper into the forest before spreading it under the trees.

As if unable to stop himself, he blurted out the question that seemed to consume him at times. "Before I go, will you lower your hood? I—"

"No. Don't ask, Philip. I won't do it."

Fury flooded his heart. "I've been understanding. I've tried to accept your wishes. I've proven that I will be your friend even after the Mæte called you a demon. Well—" his conscience ordered him to stop, but Philip seemed unable to obey. "I think it is time that you are a true friend too. Friends don't do this. They share secrets; they don't keep them from each other."

"I didn't think you'd define a friendship by what face it wore. If my face is necessary for us to be friends, then we can be strangers. I won't do it." She stood, tears choking her words as she gathered the blanket, dragging it out from under him.

Philip stood with his arms crossed, watching as she folded the blanket and threw it over her shoulder. Six feet separated two friends who had been as close as any brother and sister for three years. The hooded cloak barely moved even as the breeze tried to ruffle it in the night air. Time seemed to stand still as the young people stared at one another—one seeing the hurt in the eyes of her friend, the other seeing a black void in the depths of a hood.

At last, Dove turned and crept toward the edge of the clearing. As she reached the first tree, her hand curled around the birch bark and her head turned and glanced over her shoulder. Philip hadn't taken a single step toward or away from her. She stood watching him for a minute—maybe two—and then continued on her way to the cottage.

The young man didn't move. Nearly shaking with suppressed rage and hurt, he watched the shadowy cloak flit across the grass, much as it had that afternoon when the lads had challenged him to approach her. When the cloak was no longer visible, he turned, his heart heavy, and strolled through the now-familiar Wyrm Forest and onto the road that led to the village.

A voice called out to him as he passed the church. "One last night of dragon gazing, Philip?"

"I guess."

Broðor Clarke stepped outside and beckoned Philip to come closer. "I suppose you'll miss that."

He sighed. "I thought I would. Right now, it seems as

31

if I'd be happy never to see those awful beasts again."

Broðor Clarke pulled his young pupil into his cottage and poured a tankard of mead. "Drink up and tell me what's ailing you—maybe I should have offered you ale, eh?"

The joke fell flat. Philip didn't even crack a smile. Instead, he hung his head and whispered, "Why do I always feel as if I'm the one being unreasonable whenever Dove and I disagree."

"Careful there, son. You sound like an old, married, hen-pecked husband."

This time, the faintest hint of a smile twitched at the corner of Philip's mouth. "Wouldn't she be annoyed to hear that?"

"What happened?"

"I asked her to show me her face. I wanted to leave in the morning with a picture of everyone here in my mind. I see faces—Modor's, Fæder's, yours, Lord Morgan's, the lads..." He sighed. "And with her I see an empty hole in a hood."

"You knew that was a condition of your friendship. You want to change the rules; she doesn't."

"Shouldn't friends trust each other with these kinds of things?"

Broðor Clarke spoke quietly but firmly. "Shouldn't Christians trust the Lord when their friends hurt them unintentionally?"

The reproof did not strike the intended target. Rather than piercing Philip's conscience with an arrow of compassion, it struck the core of the young man's pride. "Again, we see that Dove can discard the basic rules of civility that even the common man must abide by. She believes she is above all laws and rules—no wonder she rejects the commands of I AM."

Had Philip glanced at Broðor Clarke, his pride would have been further wounded and scarred as the lips of the minister twitched with amusement. "That must feel good."

"What?" The lad didn't even raise his stormy eyes to meet the gentle gaze of his mentor.

"To have such confidence in your rightness that you need not worry about little things like compassion and understanding for a weaker person."

"Dove? Weak? She'd never forgive you for that."

"I disagree. I think she'd recognize that regardless of the validity of it, perception about her puts her in a weak position."

Philip stood and shuffled his way to the door. It seemed as though he was both eager and reluctant to leave. "I guess it doesn't matter. I'll be gone tomorrow, and she can be happy in the knowledge that I'm just as ignorant about her secret as the rest of Wynnewood."

As Philip opened the door, Broðor Clarke questioned him once more. "Are you angry because you believe it best for your friend to share this information with you, or are you angry because you feel as though you have earned the right to her privacy?"

With his hand still holding the door open, Philip paused. It seemed as though he would relent, but again pride won out over right. He shook his head and started to close the door behind him, but Broðor Clarke's next words stopped him once more.

"Do not allow yourself to go to bed angry with your friend. Work this out between you and the Lord, Philip. He has commanded it."

At last, a hint of humility entered the young man's voice as Philip nodded. "I will. No matter how wrong she is, I have to try to find a way to forgive her."

The door closed behind him as Philip strolled out into the night once more. In the quiet darkness of the minister's cottage, Philip would have been irritated to see the sad but slightly amused shake of Broðor Clarke's head as he muttered, "How magnanimous of you."

Journey South

CHAPTR 4

Summer

A shadow drifted through the trees, following the road a dozen or so yards away from the entourage that slowly made its way through Wynnewood, past the midwife's cottage, and around the Sceadu toward the road that led to their intended destination—Oxford. The horses stamped and danced, skittish at the fluttering that the others didn't seem to notice. Aurelia's litter jostled with each awkward movement until Lord Morgan stopped the procession and scanned the road and the trees for what might be causing the trouble.

Just as he was sure it was nothing, he saw the familiar flap of a cloak—white for summer—in the distance. It disappeared and reappeared for several long seconds, always growing farther away with each appearance. "I think it should be fine now. Our little cloaked friend was giving us a send-off, but she has gone."

"I imagine she realized the horses were unsettled by her cloak flapping in the breeze," remarked the minister, glancing at Philip.

Philip hardly acknowledged their conversation at all. He appeared surly and in bad temper but was actually struggling to keep his countenance. The sudden urge to weep choked him as he bounced along on the back of a horse. His inexperience with riding was something none of the party had considered when planning for the trip. He'd be sore inside of an hour.

Lord Morgan saw him struggling not to look around for his friend and frowned. "Philip, we can wait if you'd like to go find her."

"No, thank you," the young man choked, fighting back tears. "I saw her last night. Modor is watching. If we stand here much longer, she'll run up and—"

"Did you make things right with Dove this morning, son?"

Philip dragged his eyes across the backs of two packhorses and met the gaze of Broðor Clarke. "No. It's fine between us though. If it wasn't, she'd have been at my door when I awoke. She understands."

"Are you sure—"

"Yes." Without another word, Philip tried to swing himself down easily from the horse and found himself sprawled out on the road. The knights around him erupted in laughter, and even the snort of the animal seemed to mock him. He picked himself up, dusted off his clothes, grabbed the reigns, and began walking alongside the litter where Aurelia watched with compassion-filled eyes.

"I think you are right about Dove. She understands. I don't know what the disagreement was, but Dove understands everything."

"Not everything," he muttered.

"What happened?"

"Well," he glanced around and saw that no one paid them any attention before continuing, "I asked her to lower her hood."

"You didn't!"

The startled exclamation brought several eyes their way but the interest dissipated quickly. "Why is it so surprising? She's a friend. What kinds of friends keep such a silly secret from one another?"

"I thought better of you, Philip. You've been such a good friend to her—understanding and patient. I didn't think you were selfish."

"Selfish. I'm going to be gone. Who will protect her? If I knew—"

Aurelia scowled at him in a most unbecoming manner. He had no idea such a beautiful girl could look so hideous with a simple change of expression. "That's swine slop. She protected herself perfectly well before she knew you—"

"And often had terrible bruises where rocks from the village children struck her."

"Which she still gets. You think you have singlehandedly changed the opinion of Wynnewood, don't you? Do you truly believe that?"

"People still throw stones?" The surprise in his voice was unmistakable.

"You thought they didn't? Don't you see her limp or move gingerly at times?"

He nodded. "I asked her about it. She said that those with her condition sometimes have those aches and things. I—"

"Didn't consider that perhaps it is because those with her condition are treated abominably by those who are without it?"

Philip ducked his head, swallowing hard. "Why didn't she tell me? I could have tried—"

"And succeeded where Broðor Clarke and my father have not?"

"But she's just a girl. People shouldn't persecute her simply because she's different. Who cares what she looks like?"

Aurelia's answer came swiftly—firmly—but gently. "You obviously do."

The miserable look on Philip's face pricked Dove's conscience. Maybe she should have waited for him near his home that morning. She thought he would know—would understand that she wasn't angry, but maybe not.

"Oh, don't be a ninny," Dove muttered to herself. "He's leaving his home, family, and all of his friends." She smiled at the realization that she was one of those friends. "Of course he is going to be miserable—maybe for months."

She turned toward the edge of the Wyrm Forest. It was time to make one of her dreams come true. For a moment Dove paused, wondering if she should return to the cottage for a shovel, but kept walking. She'd plan her project and then return home. There wouldn't be time for actual work on it today. They needed fresh meat. With all the things that Letty did around the cottage now, procuring meat wasn't one of them.

Her mind and heart were following the entourage south toward Oxford as her feet flitted through the trees in search of the perfect place. On the other side of the Sceadu, a small stream jutted off from the river into a little pool where fish swam. It was just deep enough to wade in—nearly covering her knees—but Dove wanted one deeper. She dreamed of enough water to cover her neck, and if she worked hard enough, she was sure she could dig her own.

Her high melodic songs drifted through the trees as she sought the perfect inlet to create her pool. Children fishing on the other side of the river heard her and shivered, choosing to move downstream closer to the bridge, but Dove didn't notice. Her attention was fixed firmly on finding somewhere to begin her project.

At last, she found it. Close to where the Wyrm and

Heolstor forests reached the river, the land dipped more sharply, allowing the water to cascade over a few rocks. A large tree grew a dozen or so yards away from the edge of the river with a sturdy branch that would hang low over where she intended to dig her pool.

Excited over her find, Dove turned to fly home to tell Philip and stopped short. Tears fell onto the ground unchecked. After several silent minutes of fast-falling tears, her shoulders shook; Dove crumpled to the earth, drawing herself into a ball, and wept. Her friend was gone—for years. They hadn't known if he would be allowed to return home to visit. Such an expense was too much to ask, and yet so many years without seeing friends or family was too hard to imagine, so they chose to wait—and hope.

The village boys gathered around the great tree in the middle of the village and shuffled their feet. No one had considered what would happen on Thursdays while Broðor Clarke was gone. Their masters had all sent them off, and even the older boys who now worked in their respective trades occasionally joined the group. Liam usually chose Thursday afternoons to have more flour ground for his father. He could leave the bag at the mill, go listen to the stories from the Bible, and then pick up the sack of flour on the way home. Aubrey and Angus often waited to eat their midday meal until the afternoon so they could join their friends. The younger boys, still apprentices, looked up to the young men and imitated their attempts to come—particularly when personal sacrifice was evident. It had been good for all involved.

However, on that sunny Thursday afternoon, Aubrey munched on a cold baked potato and watched Angus and

Liam, taking his cues from them. The younger boys were eager to take the opportunity to spend the afternoon in games on the sward near the Point. Their glances—attempts to be covert—were almost comical in their obviousness.

"I think we should go over the last story that Broðor Clarke told," Angus said as he sat on Broðor Clarke's stump and bit into a chunk of bread.

"Aw, we can't do that. The minister isn't here to make sure we're telling it correctly," a young boy of about eight protested.

"Sure we can." Liam instinctively looked to Angus for support. "We can listen to each other and fill in gaps and correct. It would be a good exercise." As the others digested these words, Liam added another thought. "Afterwards, I think you should all take advantage of the afternoon. We'll not be able to fill up the time like Broðor Clarke can, but we should keep what we've learned fresh."

What the others didn't hear was the eagerness in Liam's voice. He ached to continue any lessons he could. Angus agreed to the proposal and encouraged Liam to begin. From beneath a large shrub near the door of the chapel, Dove listened to the story of Uzzah and his attempt to save the Ark of the Covenant from falling.

As responsible of an idea as the retelling was, it quickly dissolved into debate over whether Uzzah's actions were understandable and what they would have done. Angus argued for protecting the ark, but Liam insisted that God's rules must be followed. The younger boys all gathered round as the debate raged. To everyone's surprise, Liam held his own.

The words flew back and forth. As much as the other lads wanted to support Angus, as much as they agreed with his stand, they had to respect the way Liam held fast to the law of God as told them by Broðor Clarke. "I AM cannot say, 'you shall not' and then ignore it when you do. It would make Him unrespectable—not trustworthy."

Angus shook his head. "The ark was already on the cart. The rule had been broken already. Uzzah just saved it from falling. The blood is on King David's head for breaking that rule."

"But that is not what the Book says. It says that I AM became angry at Uzzah. They weren't allowed to touch the ark. It was forbidden, and he did it anyway."

"For good cause," argued Aubrey.

"According to I AM, the only good cause is to obey Him."

The group watched as Angus' eyes narrowed. The muscles in his arms twitched. Slowly, his head shook. "I do not remember that in the story. I don't remember Broðor Clarke ever saying that."

Owen shook his head. "That wasn't in the story, but remember the one with Samuel and Saul? Samuel told him that obedience was better than sacrifice. It's basically the same thing."

"But it isn't what the Bible says," another boy countered. "Broðor Clarke says we aren't allowed to decide what is just or isn't just. I AM said don't, so we don't."

Once more, Angus shook his head. "I don't understand why it would be a problem with I AM, but I do understand that He can make whatever rules He wants."

Discussion fizzled to nothing as the group stood around shuffling their feet. Owen glanced around the village and frowned. In a deep whisper, he said, "Some of the masters are staring. If we want our time off, we'd better hurry and get out of sight."

Aubrey grinned. "Race?"

For all their claims of manliness and responsibility, the young men were still boys at heart. They missed the days when they could run and play games after a

Thursday Bible session. It took less time for everyone to nod than it did for them to take off down the road and into the grasses at the headland of the Point.

The games began. Several of the fishermen's sons proved themselves to be swift runners, but those who worked at the castle seemed to have the most endurance. Angus couldn't run, but held his own against all of the younger boys in a game of tug o' war. Once Aubrey and Liam joined the lads, Angus couldn't hold out any longer and let go of the rope, sending the others stumbling backwards until they collapsed on top of one another. Liam was nearly flattened in the process.

"Well, we won, but Angus is probably the strongest fellow in Wynnewood."

Despite the bolster to his pride, Angus shook his head. "Not yet. Hugh is stronger, but he's getting older. Someday..." A small smile hovered near the corners of Angus' mouth. They respected him. After years of a fearful kind of awe, now the lads had real respect for him. He liked it. For once, the entire group looked up to him instead of raving over the perfect Philip.

Liam's next words jabbed Angus' spirit. "Do you think Philip has made it to Oxford yet?" Liam sighed. "I wish I could go."

Oxford

CHAPTR 5

The bustle of commerce in Oxford excited Philip as he wandered through the streets just after breakfast. Shops opened, carts rolled into the marketplace, and girls of ten and even younger carried heavy baskets, calling out to passersby to purchase their wares. To Philip, it was all an exciting adventure.

Several students, identifiable by their scholar's robes, strolled out of an inn, laughing about something the innkeeper had said. He'd be one of those students soon. His mind filled with images of the admiration of the locals as they saw him pass, and his eyes followed the young men and then roamed to the townspeople, hoping for a glimpse of it. Instead, he saw antagonism—even hatred— for them.

Feigning ignorance, he stopped a passing boy wheeling a barrow and pointed to the students. "Who are they and why are they dressed like that? The shopkeepers don't seem to like them much."

"Them's university students," the lad answered. "Troublemakers, the lot of them. The church protects them so we have to put up with their shenanigans. My master threatens to move away from Oxford at least once a week."

"What does he do?"

"He's a brewer—finest one in Oxford. You'll not find

better mead or ale anywhere in the county—maybe not even England." With those words, the boy hurried down the street wheeling two small barrels in a barrow.

For the briefest of moments, Philip entertained the fantasy of being the student who finally won over the town and brought peace between the students and citizens. Reality struck when he saw a man jerk his daughter out of sight of yet another robed man—this one much older. "I'm not likely to have any effect at all," he muttered to himself. "The idea is ridiculous. I'll need to focus on my studies anyway."

"Did you ask for something?" A woman with very few teeth and a bent back eyed him curiously. Offering him an apple, she snarled when Philip shook his head and hurried on his way.

Lord Morgan smiled as Philip entered the dining hall of the inn. "He's been out exploring already. You can make a boy into a man, but you'll never eradicate the boy from him."

"I'm sorry, m'lord. Everyone was still sleeping—"

"I wasn't complaining, Philip. Did you find Oxford everything you'd imagined?"

"I learned that the townspeople don't much like the students."

"There've been a few skirmishes, but you should be quite safe. The church has much influence here and protects students."

A frown formed on Broðor Clarke's face, but he said nothing. Several knights, looking quite bored, picked at their food. The minister noticed and commented. "I think your men need much more active employment than a tediously slow ride here and lounging around for us to finish our tasks."

"Perhaps we should send them to Portsmouth to see if my ships have arrived. It wouldn't be as stimulating as drilling at home on the fields, but..."

The little group snickered, earning them suspicious looks from the knights, but a serving girl arrived in time to divert their collective interest. Lord Morgan took that opportunity to suggest the day's plans. "As much as I'd like to rest, I think I'll make inquiries about possible lodging for Philip. While I do that, perhaps you'd be interested in seeking out his instructors?" Charles Morgan watched as Broðor Clarke nodded.

"I'll see what I can learn."

Philip watched, his eyes darting back and forth as the men spoke, curious as to who would mention taking him first. He was eager to see where he'd live, of course. Lord Morgan might choose some place that was unnecessarily fine. He didn't need extravagant accommodations, but would Lord Morgan forget how simply he was accustomed to living?

Even as interested as Philip was about his future home, he was much more concerned with the coursework that Broðor Clarke would arrange for him. What if it was too much? What if he couldn't handle it? Would he have to work extra-long hours or take on more courses for him to catch up to the others? Is that how it worked?

Broðor Clarke turned to speak to the innkeeper about where to find the best masters, and Lord Morgan stopped to speak to his knights. As patiently as he could manage, Philip waited to see who would take him, but to his surprise, each man hurried out of the inn without a word to him. His eyes roamed the room, studiously avoiding the table where the knights sat, presumably watching him, amused.

The streets were even more crowded as midday neared. Tanners scraped leather, pulling the pieces out of vats of vile-smelling solutions. Fullers pounded woven wool in water and clay to clean and thicken it for market. Saddlers and cobblers worked hard at their craft; Philip found it all fascinating. He stopped to speak to several men, curious about how long they'd been a part of the guild, how many boys they'd apprenticed, and what kind of aptitude was necessary.

One weaver did what none of the others had done. He asked about Philip—his life, skills, and where he'd lived before coming to Oxford. Upon hearing that Philip was there as a student, the man shook his head. "What are you asking about this work? You have opportunities few young men ever hope to have."

"I don't want to be a cleric. There is no use for law where I live, and even medicine has certain drawbacks. I want to be useful. Active."

"But you don't have to go back to your village, do you? You could go to London or even stay here or go to Cambridge."

Philip shook his head. "I want to go home."

"Why weren't you apprenticed? A smart young man like you should have been in demand."

With a sigh, Philip turned to walk away, but the man caught his arm, urging him to explain. At last, Philip answered the question. "I was. I wasn't able to become the fletcher I was supposed to be."

Sharp eyes bored into his as Philip tried to keep his answer truthful but evasive. "I assume there is more to this tale than your personal ineptitude? You seem eager enough, willing to work. You're obviously intelligent. I've seen masters who used their apprentices for cheap labor taken before the guild. They were required to make restitution for failing to fulfill their end of the contract. It's a protection for later apprentices."

"I believe my master has chosen not to take on any other apprentices."

"There's that, anyway." The weaver shook his head. "You'd be wasted as a weaver or a tanner. With your ability to keep quiet, you should be a priest or a lawyer."

Philip shook his head sadly and continued on his

way, speaking to every tradesman, craftsman, and townsman he could. A few men hinted that they'd take him on as an unofficial apprentice, but Philip was too astute to agree to impressive-sounding promises without a contract.

Once again, he turned back in the direction of the inn—or so he thought—his errand wasted. The streets seemed to run together in a maze that confounded him. Several times he passed the same church, proving that he had lost his bearing. Just as he was sure he'd have to ask directions, an idea particularly repugnant to him for inexplicable reasons, he saw something familiar and turned down the correct street, amazed at how far he'd wandered.

You'd think after all Dove taught me about paying close attention to every branch and root, I would have thought to do as much in a strange place like this, he mused to himself as he climbed the stairs to see if Aurelia was in her rooms.

"And what of meals?" The question seemed unnecessary, but Lord Morgan asked it as a matter of course. The rooms seemed perfect. Two of them—one for sleeping and one to have friends in to visit. Several innkeepers had insisted it was the common thing among all but the poorest of students. Coming from so many different sources, he was sure it must be so.

"He'll eat in the dining hall, of course. Every meal that we serve. He can order other things as well—for an additional charge of course."

"Of course." The terms seemed reasonable, the rooms well-equipped but not too elaborate, and there were other students living there. The temptation to accept the rooms without looking any further was acute, but Lord Morgan forced himself to appear nonchalant as he turned to leave. "I'll bring Philip to examine the arrangement and see if it suits him. Would tomorrow be inconvenient?"

Warned that he risked losing the rooms to another patron, the Earl of Wynnewood left, chuckling in his sleeve at the idea that there'd be nothing else in all of Oxford that could possibly suit Philip's needs. The next establishment was only one street away and while smaller, was closer to the center of town and a little less expensive. He would inspect those rooms as well.

A familiar cloak caught his eye as he neared the next place. "Dennis Clarke!"

The minister paused as though uncertain the call was for him, but when he saw Lord Morgan striding toward him, the man turned to greet him. "Have you been looking for accommodations?"

"I have. I'm going to the next just now. I think it's that building there. Will you come with me?" Lord Morgan glanced around them curiously. "Where's the boy?"

"Better not call him that here. It'll frustrate him." Amused with his own joke, Broðor Clarke hardly noticed the question. "Wait, isn't Philip with you?

Charles Morgan shook his head. "I thought you took him to plan his courses."

"This is not good," the minister sighed. "I thought he was with you looking for a room."

Standing in front of the next house, the men nodded. "It's clean—not that a boy usually cares about that."

Broðor Clarke grinned. "They don't until they're forced to live in filth. Then they notice."

The innkeeper met them at the door, eager to show the rooms he had available, and as the others had mentioned, he recommended a double apartment of rooms. Upstairs, Lord Morgan turned to his companion and sought his opinion. "What do you think?"

"Quite a lot of space for one young man, don't you think?"

"It seems to be the custom here. Every establishment has acted as though they assumed I wanted two adjoining rooms. See how they even have doors between them?"

"Have you spoken to any of the students staying at these places? Perhaps they could give advice on one or two rooms. You might discover that some wish they had three."

The innkeeper fidgeted as Broðor Clarke spoke. Relief washed over him as a feminine voice called out for him, cajoling at first and then sounding a bit too much like a fishwife for the men's taste. Lord Morgan waited until the room was empty and then said, "How often do you think the b—Philip would be subjected to that kind of display?"

"More than I'd like."

"And yet," Lord Morgan teased, "you claim that you would marry..."

"Do I understand you to imply that your own wife was in the habit of screeching like that over your absence?"

"I yield. Evaline would be horrified that anyone imagined she could raise her voice to speaking level, much less produce that kind of volume." As they turned to leave the room, Lord Morgan added, "Did you have much success finding the right masters for Philip?"

"Well, I think so..." The minister seemed to hesitate. "He's much more prepared in some areas than I thought. I wasn't aware how much they expected in preparations, but it isn't as extensive as I'd assumed. His Latin is above the necessary, and he is well acquainted with the *Liber Abaci*. His Italian is weak and his French nonexistent, but I think he can hold his own theologically."

"That will be good for him. He expects to be so far behind. It'll encourage him to see he isn't as ignorant as he thinks."

"I am concerned with one thing…"

Lord Morgan stepped closer, listening intently. "Yes…"

"I overheard a few of the students speaking. They have heard of Philip already—probably from some of the masters I interviewed. They already think of him as a pampered moneygrubber."

"Philip has the strength of character to prove otherwise."

Adjustments

CHA
PTR
6

Aurelia and Lord Morgan were out discussing the merits and failings of several lodging houses, while Broðor Clarke made final arrangements for Philip's studies. The knights—most of them anyway—had chosen to make the journey south to Portsmouth to see if they could learn news of Lord Morgan's ships. This left Philip alone in his room—again.

He'd heard of a saddler in need of an apprentice. Surely, it was an honorable trade, and Wynnewood didn't have one. No, most of the village didn't have a need for saddles, but Lord Morgan must provide them for his knights at the least. Making up his mind with that thought, Philip dashed downstairs.

For several long minutes, the saddler worked in silence, ignoring Philip, but the lad was patient. At last, the man laid down his hammer and awl and allowed his eyes to meet Philip's. "Are you in need of a saddle, boy?"

The word stung, but Philip ignored it. He was a man regardless of someone's lack of confidence. "Not today, but I was curious about the process."

"Plan to make your own someday?"

"Not without some excellent training. Seems like a perfect way to ruin good leather otherwise," the young man admitted.

The saddler's eyes narrowed as he observed Philip for

a few long seconds. "You've been an apprentice."

"Yes—not that it did me any good."

Again, the saddler turned a sharp expression on Philip before he shook his head. "The man was a fool."

"Or I was."

"I'd wager this saddle it was the master unless they put a b—man of your size into milling or smithing."

Philip reddened as he shook his head. "Fletching."

"You've the right build for it. You're light, but I can see you're strong and agile."

"Too light for saddling?" It seemed pushy, but Philip was determined to find something. Perhaps with his allowance he could pay a man to teach him a craft.

"Not especially, no." The saddler paused as he picked up a long length of leather "string." "That fletcher wouldn't be Henry?"

As tempting as it was to play a joke on the man, Philip didn't want to risk anything that would have him say no. "No. I'm not from here."

"I thought you sounded funny—like those students from up nor—"

"I am a student, and I am from up north," Philip admitted. "Is it so terrible that I would prefer active employment to learning languages that my village doesn't speak?"

"How are you paying for school then?"

"The Earl of Wynnewood is sponsoring me." It sounded less like an honor and more like charity as Philip explained it. "I think he and our minister hope I will become a priest."

"That would be enough to make any reasonable man choose to learn a trade." The saddler thought for several long moments, giving Philip hope that he hadn't dared risk and then shook his head. "I have a boy I've agreed to apprentice, the right age too, or I'd risk angering man who lives that far away, but I don't have enough work for two,

52

and I've a family to support."

"I didn't expect you to take me as an apprentice," Philip rushed to explain. "I thought I could pay for lessons—like I do with my studies. Even if I just watched for a while before you let me touch the leather. I learned to repair arrows that way."

The man's eyes grew stern and his voice lowered. Glancing around him, he growled, "Don't ever make that offer again. People aren't always honest. Do you know how tempted I was to agree—just for the money? I could let you think I was going to teach you all while collecting your money each day or each week. I could have given you verbal instructions that would mean nothing until you had a chance to use them—but if I was smart, I'd never give you that chance."

"Why?"

"The more you invest in the 'lessons' the more likely you'll keep going, hoping for a return. Never offer money freely like that, boy. At the least, you'll be robbed. Get off with you. Go learn to torture honest people with tithes and guilt."

One of Lord Morgan's knights, Harold, strolled through the streets, grateful for another chance to stretch his legs after such a long ride. Several of the others had gone in search of news from the south, but he enjoyed the energy of the town. It was a much less lazy place than Wynnewood.

Something familiar caught his eye as he passed another street, and he stopped short as he saw Philip watching a saddler. *What could the fool want with a saddle? He doesn't have a horse.* Hiding behind the corner of the building, Harold listened to the ensuing conversation.

The impatience that he'd sometimes felt—as if minding a child—evaporated as he heard the man address Philip as boy. The lad stiffened, but kept his tongue, listening and speaking respectfully. He watched as Philip relaxed as the man stopped mid-word and used man instead of boy. *Was I so eager to be considered a man at that age?* he wondered.

The saddler's respect grew as he spoke to Philip. The next time the man addressed the lad, he didn't hesitate at all—man. To Harold's surprise, Philip didn't become puffed up at it. Lord Morgan said the young man was one in a thousand; Harold thought perhaps one in ten thousand.

At the offer of money, Harold's hand clenched at his side. If the man took advantage... It seemed as though hours crawled by in the space of seconds. It was impossible to see the man's face, but his entire body went rigid. There it was—boy. The words were low and quieter, but their meaning was unmistakable—don't offer money and go home.

Philip's dejection draped over him like his strange little friend's cloak. He turned and walked toward Harold, unaware that he was under observation. Just as he passed, Harold draped a friendly arm around his shoulder. At the startled look on the young man's face, Harold asked, "Would you like to explain that?"

"I guess I'll have to."

They traveled halfway down the street, Harold certain that his young charge would find a way to dodge the subject, before Philip finally spoke. In a jumbled, tumbling mess, the words seemed to spill forth in no semblance of order. Harold heard words such as occupation, active, and useless studies, but they made little sense to him.

"Are you saying you don't want to be here, Philip?"

"Oh, no! I do. I mean—no. Well, not that, but—"

"Come on. Let's go outside this noisy place and try again. Lord Morgan would never want you to feel obligated to stay where you did not want to be."

As they strolled toward the North Gate, Harold tried to reassure Philip of his worth as a guard, an assistant to Peter, or even in the stables. "There's much a man your size can do. If you don't care to be an academic—"

"It's not that—really. I don't like to admit it," Philip blushed, making him look more like a little boy than he had in years, "but I like learning. It's just that…"

They found a path that wandered away from the city and toward the river. Almost immediately, Philip relaxed and began to make more sense. "I don't know how to explain it, but I was apprenticed to learn a skill—a trade. I want to be able to wake up when I'm an old man and know that my arrows helped his lordship in battle, or my stonework will stand for a thousand years in the castle, or—"

"Or your saddles were valued by the knights of Wynnewood?"

"I know it is immature and ungrateful, but yes. I could be a guard; Lord Morgan promised me that, and I probably will. My grandfæder was a guard. It just isn't the same as being a part of a guild. I want to be skilled at something." He turned a miserable looking face toward Harold. "Do you think Lord Morgan will understand?"

"If you explain it to him like you did me, yes." Harold's heart remembered the days when he had to behave and think like a man but felt like such a child. "He won't make you stay, Philip. This is about helping you—not hurting you."

"You're going to make me tell him?" The despair would have been comical had it not been so genuine.

"No." The older knight shook his head slowly. "It's not my decision to make for you."

"What would happen if I don't tell him?"

"He'll leave you here to be educated—probably for the church."

"They know I don't want to be a cleric."

Harold turned and gazed at the city behind them. "Then maybe there is something you can learn that would help at the castle."

"But about the saddler—will you tell him?"

"Do you want me to?"

Philip's head shook before Harold could quit asking. "No!"

"Then I won't."

After weeks of effort, the amount of work left to do felt daunting. Dove wiped her forehead on her sleeve, and grabbed the shovel once more. An area the size of their cottage showed evidence of her work, but only just over a foot was missing from it. She'd have to work harder and faster if she hoped to make much progress before the ground became hard and frozen.

Digging was fun, relatively easy, and productive, but slow. She loved seeing pile after pile of dirt leave her hole. However, removing that dirt without creating a large mound somewhere was tedious and exhausting. She piled dirt on an old skin she'd found left behind in the woods near the Sceadu. It took a few tries, but she quickly learned exactly how much dirt she had the strength to drag away from the edge of her pool. She'd tried the garden cart one day, but that required digging the dirt back out of the cart each time. Using the old animal skin, the dirt slowly slid off the pile as she dragged it deeper into the forest. Repeatedly dragging it over the same route as previous trips ensured that the loose dirt was packed down firmly.

Birds sang overhead, but Dove was too focused on her task to pay them much attention. She ignored the rabbits, the vixen, and even the snakes and frogs that seemed to be ever-present in her new area. Never had she been so single-minded in her focus.

The shovel struck a rock, bouncing the handle back and striking her in the cheek. "It's a good thing I'm not vain about my appearance," she muttered to herself as she rubbed the smarting flesh.

It seemed as if the rocks slowed her progress twice as quickly as anything else. Every time she managed to gain momentum, another rock surfaced, taunting her with its appearance. Her shovel bit the dirt all around the edges of the stone, but it refused to budge. Undaunted, Dove dug at the damp earth with her gloved fingers, inching bits away from it until she thought she'd gone deep enough. Using the shovel as a lever, she slowly pried it from its resting place.

After such exhausting work, Dove could think of nothing but a cool drink of water. She leaned the shovel against the great tree and made her way around it and toward the river. Her reflection in the water brought a smile to her lips. The usual white cloak of summer was nearly black with dirt and her face was coated with it as well. A quick glance around her told her that she was alone, so Dove pulled off her gloves, tucking them in her cloak pocket, and cupped her hands to catch the cool clear water.

As she strolled back to her work site, she pulled on her gloves once more, ready to work again. Her muscles protested; her mind and body warred against one another, but her mind won. With each fresh shovelful of dirt, her muscles seemed to relax as they warmed up again. Dove started to sing, her high clear voice ringing through the trees, but abruptly the song ended with a strangled cry.

As Dove enjoyed the beauty of one of God's "natural cathedrals," Philip stood in the Church of St. Mary the Virgin, listening to the Mass and wondering how people worshipping the same God could have such differing experiences. The chants, the vestments, even the architecture were foreign to him; illogically, he hated them all simply for their difference.

His eyes slid sideways, curious to see Broðor Clarke's reaction to all that seemed so stilted and formal. Alas, it was impossible to read the minister's face. He was stiff, but many things could account for that. Just as Philip was certain that Broðor Clarke was just as miserable as he was, he remembered that the minister had studied with the Irish priests. This was probably all very familiar to someone like him.

The church was very different from the little chapel in Wynnewood. Where Wynnewood was just a large open room with a fireplace and altar, this church was large and imposing. The walls were decorated with icons—many of which he understood, but some made no sense to him. The congregants all stood in the nave, some sitting, some kneeling, but most standing. A partial wall and screen divided the room from the sanctuary where the priest stood to celebrate the Mass.

Above all, the Latin bothered him most. How would people learn of I AM if they did not understand what was taught? His eyes roamed around the room, trying to see who understood the words spoken. With so many academics there, it seemed as if many, if not most, did. A wave of pride washed over him as he mentally translated a significant portion of what the priest said. He had been a good scholar, and it now was of benefit.

Broðor Clarke was somber as they strolled from the building, but since most of the other parishioners seemed equally subdued, Philip imagined that it was the custom. It seemed as if a reflective spirit was expected rather than the joyful talkative manner of the villagers at home. Discouraged, he followed the Morgan party back to their lodgings and excused himself to his room.

A knock appeared at the door minutes later. At his call, Broðor Clarke stepped into the room. "Are you well, Philip?"

"I've just been thinking."

"And how did you like today's Mass."

Suddenly, criticizing the church didn't seem like an appropriate thing—particularly from an undereducated and young person such as he. Instead, he latched onto the one positive thing he'd enjoyed that morning. "I appreciated my lessons more than I ever have. I felt sorry for those who did not know what was said."

"And are you that confident in your translation abilities?" The minister sank to a bench and draped his cloak over the end.

"Not at all," Philip assured him. "I doubt I got more than every other word at times, but—"

"You didn't find that dangerous? How can you know if what the priest taught was correct if you do not know all he said? How do you learn the Bible if you cannot sufficiently translate it. Will you recognize error?"

The questions were fired at him, one after another, until Broðor Clarke shook his head and stood. "I'm sorry, Philip. I shouldn't take out my frustration on you. Be careful. Until you are fluent in Latin—confident in your translation abilities—do not assume anything you hear is truth. It may be when it leaves the priest's lips, but by the time it reaches your ears..." The minister grabbed his cloak and opened the door again. "And how much worse would it be if your translation was correct but the words were not truth? How would you know which it was?"

The door closed behind Philip's mentor, and the young man's heart sank. Broðor Clarke's words were true. How many things had he already heard that he wanted to question? He had arrogantly assumed he'd found mistakes in what the priest taught when it was likely his own ignorance and ineptitude.

That thought teased a tiny smile from one corner of Philip's mouth. *Dove would say that. She would tell me I am arrogant, ignorant, and inept.* He sighed and then the smile grew wider. *Then she'd tell me to learn more so that I was less ignorant and less inept. I can hear her now. "Let's hope that would also make you a little less arrogant."*

Alone

CHAPTER 7

"It's not around the midwife's cottage much anymore."

Matill' Wood shook her head as she shifted the baby on her hip. "My Letty says she doesn't even sleep there now."

"The children," Una Fletcher continued, "say that they don't hear it singing anymore. That's almost eerier than the strange songs she always sang."

"But she's still here." Matill's eyes slid sideways, watching her daughter. "I don't think she's gone."

"That's too much to hope for, I suppose." Una stuck her knuckle in baby Adam's mouth to give his little sore gums something to gnaw on.

Letty, home for her Sunday visit, stiffened but kept her tongue. Angus noticed and rose. "Come, Letty. Let's go see if anyone's at the Point yet. Maybe we can lead races for the children."

"It bothers her, doesn't it?" Una frowned at the angry glances Letty threw back at them.

"That the creature is gone? I think so."

"Why? She was never friendly to it before. Don't you worry about it bewitching her?"

Matill' shook her head. "Letty says it's nice to her—helps when she makes a mistake."

"If she were bewitched, she'd say something like that."

"Do you think Philip was bewitched? Lord Morgan? Broðor Clarke?"

"I—" Una sighed. "I don't know about Lord Morgan or Broðor Clarke, but sometimes I did think maybe she'd bewitched Philip. Tom says it's just Philip's way. He's always been kind to everyone—even when Angus tried to bully him, Philip was still friendly."

"Angus has changed too. I think that childish need to prove himself is gone. Working for Hugh brought out an ugly side of him that I didn't know he possessed, but that seems gone now."

"Well, Angus is bright enough to stay out of the thing's path. For all his intelligence, Philip chose an odd sort of friend."

"I think that's the problem," Matill' suggested. "I think the ge-sceaft misses Philip."

"Misses her control over him is more like it."

"I know you don't like it," Letty's mother began cautiously, "but don't you think it's possible that it didn't harm Philip in any way? The minister and the earl both did not seem to think he was touched by it."

"Well, surely it can't keep control over someone that isn't there. Perhaps we'll hear if there was a change in Philip when he got to Oxford. It might have spared Philip, but I don't trust it. I keep begging Tom to move us from here, but he says Lord Morgan needs a good fletcher—the siege three years ago proved it."

"Where would you go?"

"Cockermouth." The answer didn't take a second to come. "Tom's arrows are in great demand there."

"Cockermouth doesn't have fletchers?"

The skepticism in Matill's voice seemed to anger her friend. Una stood, pulling her knuckle from the baby's mouth as she did, and the baby wailed in frustration.

With a disdainful glance at Matill' Wood, Una tried soothing baby Adam as she said, "Several—and the people still flock to buy Tom's anytime he arrives in town. He's the best of the best."

The moment Una's back was turned, Matill' muttered, "Except at being an honest master. He can make an arrow, but he can't teach anyone else to. He'd rather break a contract than have his mark be less than perfect."

The fletcher's wife froze mid-step, and then continued walking, her shoulders slumped. For a moment, Matill' felt ashamed of her verbal barb, but remembering that Tom's failure was what had sent Philip so far away from his family and friends, she shook off the shame. Her words were true, and Una needed to know exactly what the village thought of their fletcher.

Her head whipped toward the tree line where it seemed as if she'd seen something. Scanning the trees, she looked for anything out of place—an animal, a child, the ge-sceaft. Matill's ears strained to hear a twig crunch or wings flapping as a bird took flight, but still silence was the only reply.

The mists slowly rolled in from the sea, thicker than usual. The children should come in from the Point. Her heart pounded at the idea of any of the children getting turned about in the thickness of the fog and tumbling off the cliff, but just as she began striding down the road, she heard Letty and Angus herding the younger ones back into the village, singing of the ships that sail to faraway places.

Symon Wood watched his wife for a moment and then went to stand beside her. "Is something wrong?"

"No. Something is very right. Our daughter has a good place with the midwife and is becoming so responsible. Our son is a man already. Look how they brought in the children from the Point when the mists

63

came in."

"John's waiting for direction. I just thought I'd see what was wrong. Whenever Una comes, you are usually upset by the time she leaves."

"I think," Matill' murmured as she thought about her husband's words, "I have outgrown her influence. She's a good woman, but she's very suspicious. It makes for a very unhappy life, I think."

Before Symon could reply, a child stumbled in the road and fell. Angus scooped the boy up, settling the child on his shoulders and jogged toward the fishermen's cottages. The jostling turned tears to giggles as the procession passed the Wood home. "We'll be home soon, Modor."

As the group continued up the road, Matill' sighed. Her children were indeed grown. "Blessed be the Lord for His mercies," she whispered to the baby as she returned to her house.

Shivering under her blanket, Dove considered making a fire. After five more minutes and the onset of chattering teeth, she capitulated and crawled from her pallet in what would be the swimming hole. She worked quickly, dragging dry fallen twigs and a few branches to the center of her pool. The earth was damp—too damp to make a good fire. Frustrated, she went in search of the last stones she'd thrown from the hole as she worked.

It took some time to make a fire pit safe enough to start a blaze, but at last, she was ready—and had no flint. Warm now from her exertions, Dove almost rolled herself back in her blanket and tried to sleep, but she knew the cold would return—worse than ever since it was later. There was nothing to do but return to the cottage for flints and maybe a little tinder.

Trudging through the trees in the middle of the night was an excellent way to wake up, but not so helpful for providing sleep. She crept into the cabin, glanced at Bertha's empty bed, and then went to work filling her pockets with tinder, flints, bread, cheese, apples, and turnips. A caldron of stew sat nestled in the coals, tantalizing her with the scent. She had time for hot food. After killing the rabbit now simmering in the pot, it seemed silly not to enjoy the subsequent meal.

Within the hour, she was back working on the small fire. From the castle walls, a guard saw the flicker of fire in the trees, but it never grew any larger. Two other guards were wakened and sent to investigate. Fire was a terrible danger to a castle that still had some wooden sections.

Voices woke Dove as they splashed through the river nearby. She hesitated—terrified. Who was coming and why? The crackle of the fire near her answered the question. Fire. She hadn't considered that they could see it from the castle. The voices grew closer, terrifying her.

She only had seconds to think. Grabbing her blanket, she threw dirt over the fire and dashed into the trees, watching to see what the men would do. They came, large men in dripping tunics, inspecting the site.

"See that hole? What is that all about?"

"Too big for an animal," the second man mused. "Unless maybe the dragon..."

"They've said that the dragons have lived in here for centuries." The first man seemed skeptical, but latched onto the idea anyway.

"Think the fire could be from the dragon?"

The two shadows shifted into a shaft of moonlight as they tried to inspect the hole more closely. Dove's heart sank. They'd see the fire pit and know it wasn't the dragon. One guard turned away quickly, but just as her

65

hopes soared again, they crashed at the words of the other. "This is still warm; feel it. There's rocks under that dirt. Someone covered it—probably just as we arrived."

She now had no choice. They'd come looking to see who was there, return to find more evidence of a vagabond endangering the forest, or even refuse to leave. Gathering her courage, she draped the blanket over a tree branch, pulled her hood further over her head, and spread the cloak wide.

The men startled as the familiar, terrifying high-pitched voice came floating through the trees directly toward them. The flapping of the fabric of her cloak made ominous sounds in the night air, and her shadow flitted about them, always at a distance, but growing increasingly closer—much too close for any villager's comfort.

As if called forth by her song, the mists rolled in from the sea at just the right moment. She couldn't have wished for anything more opportune if she'd asked Philip's god for it. Terrified, the men stumbled through the underbrush, one falling into the pit. Twice, Dove halted her singing when they grew too close, and once she was forced to flatten herself against a tree, holding her breath so that they couldn't sense her presence.

At last the men found the bank of the river and half waded, half swam across. However, not until they reached the other side did Dove relax and return to her place in the "dragon's hole." The idea made her giggle in spite of her exhaustion and loneliness. With the fog blanketing everything, she relit her fire, warming her hands before lying down to sleep.

Though Dove no longer felt the cold air nipping at her, the crackle of the new fire did make her curious. Was it cold in Oxford too? Had autumn descended early there as it seemed to have in Wynnewood? It had been many weeks since the horses and carts had rolled out of

Wynnewood toward the south. Had they found him a good place to live? Good masters? Were they already on their way to Scarborough, or were they still there with Philip as he adjusted to life in a large town? Her eyes drooped and Dove fell asleep imagining Philip conversing freely in Latin with another student, oblivious to the friends and family missing him at home.

Dove awakened just after dawn. Thirsty, she strolled to the stream, stretching after a good but cool night's sleep. After digging her apple from the inner pocket of her cloak, Dove rinsed it in the cold water of the Ciele and bit into the crisp flesh.

Her eyes scanned the surrounding trees, the field that separated the river from the castle, and the road that led from the higher castle grounds down into the village of Wynnewood. As early as it was, no one traveled the road, but it seemed as if there were extra guards walking the castle walls and the surrounding fields. Dove twice convinced herself that she imagined them watching her, but at last, was forced to admit that she must be correct. To test her idea, she crept back into the forest and shimmied up a tree. Within the half hour, four men swam the river and crawled up into the Wyrm Forest.

"It came this way."

A younger man glanced around nervously. "I don't want to be in here."

"Then let's find what the men found last night and get out of here."

"That thing is in here; I know it. They say it can burn you with its eyes."

"Lord Morgan has spent enough time with it to prove that if it can, it doesn't always," a third man said, sounding less confident than his words should have.

Again, the younger man protested. "But he's the Earl of Wynnewood. We're just guards!"

"In training." The older men exchanged amused

glances. "What about Philip? He managed to survive the deadly glare."

"Everyone knows he's been bewitched by it—it's a sorceress after all."

On and on they argued, the youngest growing more adamant and refusing to go any farther. At the pool, they speculated as to the purpose. "It's too close to the water for a house."

"Rain would pool in it all dug out like that."

With a terror-filled voice, the young man once more backed away, adamant that the calf-deep hole was part of an evil ritual designed to wreak havoc on an unsuspecting village. "The Ge-sceaft waited until they took away its puppet, and now it's angry. I'm leaving. I don't care what you do to me, but I won't be at its mercy!"

From her perch in the tree not five yards away, Dove stifled a giggle. The young man was not much older than Philip, but his superstitious ideas were so childish they were funny. An idea formed in her mind, and the moment the men crossed the river again, she flew through the forest, into the clearing, alongside the cottage, and into the trees on the other side of the road. Down into the village she crept, dodging behind houses and animal pens until she reached the tavern. There, under the only window, she crawled behind barrels to listen as she often did.

The rumors flew fast and freely. "The creature" was invoking ancient rituals that would destroy the prosperity of the village in the absence of the earl. Some insisted that she'd worked her evil against the entire caravan south, and none would return. The ideas were so ridiculous that Dove found it nearly impossible not to laugh. Her stifled chuckles and giggles were so odd-sounding that a small boy tried to crawl in with her to root out the piglet he was sure hid there.

Screams of terror followed as the child raced

homeward, screaming for his mother. "The Ge-sceaft touched me, Modor! Will I die?"

She had to move. She couldn't stay and listen now. The villagers would come throw rocks again if she did. After peeking around the barrels to be certain it was safe, Dove scrambled from her hiding place and dashed between trees and houses to the forest, the child's words still ringing in her ears. *How strange,* she thought as she lay back on the grass, her hood flung back so the sun could shine on her face. *How strange that this boy would assume he'd die if I touched him, when the woman in Philip's story about I AM cared only that she touched him to live.*

The sun felt extra warm on her skin. Dove sat up abruptly, pulling the hood into place. Had she fallen asleep? Already the heat seemed to leave her, much to her relief. Burned skin was very bad. She couldn't risk that. A glance around her soothed her spirit. The trees were all in their familiar places. Philip had once told her that if she listened—listened to the trees rustling their leaves in the wind or the cry of the animals nearby—she'd hear the truth of I AM in her heart. However, despite hours and days of careful attention in his absence, no matter how hard she listened, no proof of Philip's god burrowed its way into her soul.

Ministers

CHAPTER 8

Autumn

One afternoon early in autumn, after working diligently for hours to master his French lesson, Philip gathered his things, shut them in his room, and hurried down the stairs of his lodging house. He wandered through the streets of Oxford, avoiding the shopkeepers where possible. The stench of the tannery vats pierced his nostrils and pushed him onward. He needed out of the city and into the fresh air.

Once outside the city walls, he stood looking out over the countryside. It wasn't nearly as beautiful as Wynnewood, but the air was sweet, the grasses green, and the press of the town behind him. "Lord, I hate it here," he confessed under his breath as he strolled toward a nearby tree. His lungs missed the salt air. His ears ached for the cry of a seagull or the wistful sound of Dove singing in the mists. He longed to hold a bow and shoot at targets. Even carrying wood and water for Una sounded better than enduring five more seconds of trying to infuse yet another language into his mind.

It wasn't his first escape from the crowded streets of Oxford, but it was the first time he hadn't had to fight back tears. He was a man now—a student. He had responsibilities to the minister and the Earl of Wynnewood as well as his family. He couldn't allow himself to give in to weakness no matter how deep the pain.

He laughed as a rabbit stopped, stared at him, and then dashed through the grasses and disappeared into its hole. The curiosity combined with fear was so like Dove that he'd nearly felt at home for just that moment. His voice sounded loud and out of place apart from the bustle of the town. It was strange to think of it and even stranger to live it.

Thoughts of Dove were common. He missed their conversations, telling her the stories that he hoped would finally yield her heart to the Lord of All. Sometimes he wished he had accepted Lord Morgan's offer to find her and apologize—say goodbye once more, but her farewell in the clearing the previous evening had been her last.

He often thought of the other lads. While he filled his mind with words until his body screamed for activity, his friends were all making lives for themselves. Angus would someday be the village blacksmith. He was strong, hardworking, and skillful already at repairing armor. When the castle blacksmith had more to do than time, he sent some of the pieces to Angus.

Philip frowned at the thought of Liam kneading bread in the hot kitchen of the castle. Liam was reminder enough of what a tremendous opportunity his education truly was. Not every boy had a great patron like Charles Morgan of Wynnewood. He shook his head. He was a man now. Thinking of himself as a boy only made things worse when he became lonely.

Frustrated, Philip kicked a stone. If Tom Fletcher had been even half a decent master, he could be working for the castle even now. Lord Morgan would have hired him to make and repair all the castle arrows if he could have done it. What was he supposed to do with an education, anyway? He didn't want to be a tutor, and he certainly did not want to be a priest. "Lord, we talked about this. I want to stay in Wynnewood, get married, have children, get old, and die in Wynnewood just like my family has done for ages and like all my friends will do. Is that so bad? I don't want to be a cleric or an academic. I like learning—" he blushed as he realized his words were almost a lie. "Well, sometimes I do. I am grateful that I have this chance, but what's the point?"

He could go to sea. It would be hard, but he could do it. His father encouraged him to do anything but go to sea, but Philip thought that life away from his family for half the year would be better than no family at all. He'd spoken with several of the townsmen in Oxford—tanners, coopers, cobblers, and even the bailiff—but none seemed to think he was a good fit for their trade. His only other thought was a hælan. Biggs could train him. It wouldn't be as exciting as an archer or as productive as a fletcher, but it would be meaningful. Even a guard, as boring as that job seemed sometimes, had purpose and merit.

The moment those thoughts came to him, Philip flushed, ashamed. Broðor Clarke had merit. Teaching people about I AM wasn't a wasted life. Wasn't his life the Lord's to do with as He pleased? Weren't his desires supposed to be laid at Jesus' feet?

Philip shook his head. "I want to be willing to offer my life as a sacrifice even if it means I gain nothing that I've hoped to have, but I'm not. Sorry, Lord. I'm not. I'm not even willing to say I am open to having my heart changed." Dejected, he turned back toward town. "I think Lord Morgan wasted his time and money on me. I'm too selfish."

Never had Wynnewood seemed so beautiful to Dennis Clarke. As he neared Bertha's cottage, he watched the swirls of smoke from the chimney and listened for the sound of Dove working, singing, or Letty snapping clothes before she laid them over the stone wall to dry. Instead, the birds sang, the squirrels scurried to gather nuts for their nests, and a pile of freshly chopped wood littered the ground outside the door.

One sound, however, prompted a smirk on the man's face. Just as he neared the corner of the yard, Bertha burst through the door, muttering about not having enough wood, Letty being a lazy chit, and Dove having probably been eaten by wild animals. Those last words wiped the grin from his face.

"Afternoon, Bertha Newcombe. What is wrong at the midwife's cottage today?"

"You're back."

"You thought I wouldn't return?"

If he hadn't seen Bertha's eyes, he might have believed the venom in her tongue. "That would imply I thought of you at all. I didn't. If I had, however, it would have been a hope rather than a thought."

"How could I leave such a perfect place? I have everything I want here—a good home, friends, the patronage of a good noble, and you. Where else would I find someone to keep me as humble and free from conceit as you do?"

She tossed him a scathing look that seemed to say, "If that were only true." Broðor Clarke dropped his pack and jumped the low wall—much more lithely than anyone would have expected—and he knew it. He gathered the pieces of wood that Bertha seemed so intent on gleaning and carried them into the little house, stacking them against the wall.

"I should thank you," the woman muttered from the door.

"Why would you do something so utterly out of character?"

"Why indeed. I won't. Did I see you drop a pack?"

He nodded, willing his stomach to rumble. It didn't. "Why?"

"Just walked in from Oxford today then."

"Yes. It took a lot of effort, but I managed it in just under four hours."

"From Cockermouth maybe," the woman spat, scooping stew into a bowl and nearly slamming it on the table. She shoved a spoon into it and gestured for him to sit. "Eat. If you don't, you'll likely drop from hunger on my doorstep and then what'll I do? I'm too old to try to drag your carcass down that road."

"You make yourself sound like an ancient woman." He frowned as she began arranging the wood in order to make room for more. "Why so much wood in the house?" The minister gulped down a few bites of food, discovering that he was hungrier than he'd expected.

"It's going to get cold tonight—very cold. Winter is coming much too soon."

"And you know this how?"

Much too harshly, Bertha slammed a plate of bread down on the table. "I don't have butter."

Something bothered the woman—much more than she was ready or willing to admit. He grabbed her arm, stopping her before she could turn away again, and asked, "What is wrong, Bertha? You are bothered about something."

At first, she didn't answer, just wrenched her arm from his grasp and went to bring in more wood. When she heard the bench creak as he rose to help her, the woman's voice called back, "Sit there and finish that or I'll dump it on you."

She would, too, Broðor Clarke thought to himself. "Ah, it's good to be home where people are so pleasant and eager to please."

"You can leave now."

Broðor Clarke used his bread to sop up the last of his

stew's gravy, stood, and relieved Bertha of her load of sticks. "You sit now and tell me what is bothering you." Before she could protest, he continued. "And don't argue with me. I know something is wrong."

"Nothing is wrong, you pompous fool. I'm angry with that ungrateful little chit—"

"She's not a child anymore. She's a young lady."

"When you mope around the forests like a baby deprived of its plaything, you deserve to be called a child and treated like one."

He poured some mead and set it before her, pushing her gently into the chair. "How long has she been gone this time?"

When Bertha didn't reply, Broðor Clarke went outside and filled his arms with more wood. Already the air was cooler, hours before the sun should set. The midwife, as usual, was correct regarding anything related to nature. It was almost uncanny. Had he not been taught better, the superstitions he'd grown up with would have reared their ugly heads to torment him.

Even after he stacked the pile as high as he could without it falling into the room, Bertha did not speak. The minister prayed for wisdom, understanding, and above all, patience. He sat beside her, staring at his hands as he waited for the words he needed to come to him. "You pretend—"

"I pretend nothing. I am as I am, nothing more or less."

"Ok, then I'll restate it, but you cannot convince me I am wrong. You believe that you do not care about Dove. You are firmly convinced that duty drives any concern you exhibit. I don't know why you believe these things, but you do."

"If it pleases you to think so, then so be it. I know better."

Anger welled up in Broðor Clarke's heart, but he

stamped it down again. He didn't have time to break down another wall that she'd throw up if she knew she'd affected him. "You are the most stubborn woman alive. Listen. What happened to Dove?"

"She's gone."

"I surmised as much. Why? What happened?"

"The boy, I suppose."

"He's a man now, Bertha. He'd be annoyed never to be allowed to mature in people's eyes."

The woman tore a crumb of bread into bits. "Dennis, I'll consider him a man when he has a full growth of beard on his face."

Laughter filled the little cottage. "I see. That explains much."

"What?"

Broðor Clarke winked at the woman and stroked his smooth chin. "You still think me a child! No wonder you have no respect for me." He sensed her stiffening again and continued hastily. "So what about Philip has upset our girl?"

"I imagine the fact that he's gone. He ruined her. She was accustomed to a solitary life, but now someone important has been stripped from her. She hurts. Had she never made a friend, she couldn't suffer the loss that comes when the friend leaves or dies."

Wisely, the minister ignored her words and focused on Dove. "Where does she go? How long is she gone? Are you sure she is well?"

"She's in the forest. I occasionally see her—"

"Hear her too, I imagine."

"She does not sing anymore. I cannot decide if that is a relief or a loss."

Something in Bertha's tone when she said relief bothered him. "Why a relief?"

"She'd taken to singing your myths. That boy—" She rolled her eyes and spat, "Man, if you must, has

77

indoctrinated her with your ridiculous tales."

Those words both encouraged and frightened the man. Why should she start singing of I AM and then stop? Was she truly so affected? "And she doesn't sing anymore? How do you know she's alive?"

"She comes, does some work when no one is around the place, and takes food." The midwife sighed and added grudgingly, "She also brings it—rabbit, fish, dove."

"I'll find her and talk to her."

"You don't know the girl well if you think she'll let you anywhere close."

"I can try," Broðor Clarke said as he stood. "Let me know if you see her. Just stick your head in the door and tell me. I won't keep you unless you want to stay. She'll adjust."

At the door, he turned again. "You're wrong, you know. It is hard to lose someone close to you, but it is harder not to have anyone to lose." Then, as if unable to resist himself, he added, "I'll be sure not to shave my face in the future."

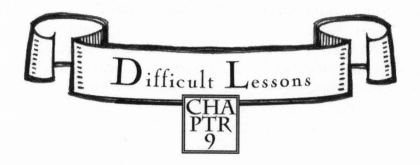

Difficult Lessons

CHAPTER 9

Winter was closing in fast on the heels of autumn. The days grew colder and colder, but Philip hardly noticed. His days were long and full of lessons, reading, and trying to keep up with the expectations on him. Six months had passed since the morning he left Wynnewood. It seemed like six years.

Frustrated, he shoved his book across the table and stood, stretching his legs. He had to get some air—even if it wasn't exactly fresh. The hustle and bustle of the town pressed on him from the moment he stepped out the door, but it was less stifling than the last time. Every day he acclimated more but never enough. Despite the advantages of town, he was a village boy through and through.

Down Catte Street he strolled, trying to avoid the carts that obstructed his path at regular intervals. A sound from behind distracted him, causing Philip to bump into a man "Pardon me! I—"

The man was about Philip's height, pot-bellied, and bald on the top of his head with little tufts of hair encircling it like a crown. "Watch your step there!"

"Are you—"

"I'm fine," the man assured him. "I was just startled. Had to get out of the house."

Philip grinned. "I had to leave my rooms too. For as

cold as it is, I felt stifled."

"First year?"

"Yes. You aren't an academic... are you?" Philip's eyes took in the man's garb and the man's head again. His tonsure marked him as some kind of cleric.

"Not the kind you speak of, no. I'm an illustrator—William is my name. William de Brailes."

The name didn't mean anything to him, but Philip recognized the man's tone. He was someone of import. "Well, again, I am sorry."

The man stared at him for a few seconds and then beckoned him to follow. "I'm going for a walk. Join me. What is your name?"

"Philip."

"And where are you going, Philip?"

They wove through the streets, laughing at children, dodging runners, and pausing as William bought them both apples. "You don't like Oxford, do you lad?"

"Not particularly. The air is foul, there are people everywhere, and most of them hate me simply because of my robes."

"Where are you from?"

"Up north—near the border—Wynnewood."

William jumped out of the way of a galloping horse, frowning as it passed. "Crazy fools. Does your father have plans for your education?"

Philip shook his head. "I think he'd be happy with me being a castle guard, but Lord Morgan and Broðor Clarke want me to go into the church. They don't say it, but that's what they want."

"And you don't like the church?"

He shrugged. The man was a stranger, and Philip didn't feel like explaining himself to just anyone. "I don't know. I'd like to learn it, but I'd rather learn at home from Broðor Clarke." He flushed. "That sounds so ungrateful. I don't mean to. I've been gone half a year already. My little brother will be apprenticed out and done with his time before I even get home. My friends will be married..."

"You make good arguments. I would have expected you to say that the work was hard, your allowance too small—something more selfish. Students often are."

"So what do you illustrate?" Philip asked, hoping to change the subject.

"The Bible, prayer book, book of hours..."

"You might have illustrated books I've seen at the University!"

"I should think so, yes."

They'd reached the gate, and though Philip wanted to follow the man out into the countryside, he knew there was work waiting for him. "I'm pleased to have met you. I'm sorry for running into you."

"That happens in town. It's one of the downsides of town living." Philip began to agree, but William said one more thing. "Lad, I want to remind you of something. When you leave here, you will miss parts of this town. You'll miss the variety of entertainment, the people, and the various foods. You'll miss the architecture, the energy, and the opportunities to learn things that you otherwise couldn't. One man can't teach you everything."

"That's true, I suppose. Home, though..."

"I'm not trying to downplay your love of your home, Philip, but I am trying to say that when you leave, you will miss this place too. Make your time here worth missing if you have to be here anyway."

With those words, the man turned and blended into the crowd that flowed through the gate. Philip stood— hesitating. What the man said made sense. He had to be there. He could mentally resist all he wanted, but it wouldn't change anything. Since he had to stay, why not learn to find the things he liked and appreciated about it? The stories he'd have to tell Dove, Angus, Liam, Letty—

His throat swelled at the thought of his friends and

family. They'd all be married by the time he returned— likely with children. Guilt flooded his heart as the next thought burst into his mind. All except for Dove. Dove would have time for him. No one would marry her. He'd have one friend left to talk with and walk with in the old way. Maybe by then she'd belong to I AM. Just maybe.

"I want you to translate this passage. It's a little beyond your skills, but I have two others to correct, so I thought I'd give you a chance to stretch your mind and ease mine a bit."

Philip glanced up and smiled at Master Adrian. "You flatter me."

"You will make many mistakes, but I think you're up to the challenge." The middle-aged tutor passed him the Bible, opened to the passage at hand, and returned to his own bench to listen as Philip read the passage, translating from Latin to English as he did.

The words were simple enough, but placing them in proper order, in correct tense—those things gave Philip trouble at times. He would have done much better had he not become engrossed in what he read. The passage was one he'd never heard Broðor Clarke read. Because his goal was to interest the boys of the village in the Bible itself, he'd kept his readings to the stories of the Book of Books. This was a letter from the Apostle Paul and he warned of doctrines that were demonic.

"Does this mean what it seems?"

"What do you think it means?" Master Adrian rarely answered a question directly. He usually asked questions until Philip was able to answer it himself.

"Well, it seems to imply that it is wrong to forbid people to eat certain foods or not to marry."

"That is exactly what it says…"

Philip stifled the urge to become impatient. From his instructor's tone, he knew that Master Adrian expected more from him. Unwilling to share his true question, he focused on the question of meat. "Then why do the Jews forbid the eating of pork still?"

"Do the Jews accept Jesus as their Messiah?"

"No."

"Then," the tutor questioned again, "why would they accept anything Jesus' followers said?"

"True…" Philip felt forced to agree, but he hesitated to ask the real question. For a moment, he pretended to go back to his reading and then stopped. "But then why does the church forbid nuns and priests to marry if it is a 'demonic doctrine?'"

"Does it?"

Ready to throw the book out the narrow window, Philip sighed. "Well, they cannot, can they?"

Master Adrian's voice echoed through the room. "You'll become a Socrates yet! No, you are correct. Nuns and priests cannot marry, but not because the church forbids it. Why can they not marry?"

The answer seemed an obvious one, but Philip took some time before he could answer. "I would guess that the priests and nuns would say that they volunteered to take a vow of celibacy—not that it was forced upon them."

"Exactly."

Several verses later, Philip stopped. "But I overheard your lesson with Aldred and Edward. They read that a shepherd must be a man with a wife and children."

More questions followed, each deeper than the last until Philip felt quite confused. Frustrated, he turned his attention back to the book and began the translation process again. *Broðor Clarke would have answered*, his mind argued within him. *He would have shown me from the Bible what is true and what is tradition. If they conflicted, he'd admit it. Here I don't know if I'm just a dunce or if the masters are avoiding my questions. I don't know anything but what they want me to know.*

He glanced at the student next to him—a tall, thin, weak fellow from Essex. Henry of Chelmsford was the son of a noble and had expressed his opinions of students with benefactors such as Lord Morgan freely. The University was intended to educate those worthy of such an education—common village boys didn't fit that image.

Asking Henry would do no good. On the other side of the table, John worked on his Latin translation as if unaffected by the discussion around him. Philip caught the man's eyes and the decided but slight shake of his head. The message was clear. "Don't ask any more questions."

The usual temptation to compare Oxford to Wynnewood with the town coming up short was just as great as usual, but the memory of his discussion with William de Brailes still reverberated in his mind. He could be thankful that he was able to be challenged this way—to know exactly what the Bible taught and how to defend it.

A sigh escaped. *It's not the consolation that it should be,* he thought to himself.

The forest creaked with bare branches that rubbed against each other in the wind. Strange moaning and crackling noises gave it an eerie sound, but Dove loved it. There was something beautifully wild about the forest in late autumn and winter. Once the first snow fell, the ground would be blanketed in white and the branches would glisten with snow and ice.

Philip wouldn't be there to explore it with her. The

thought sent a new wave of melancholy over her, but Dove didn't care about that anymore. She'd resigned herself to a lonely life again. A glance at the sun told her nightfall was coming. It wouldn't be daylight much longer. She raced along the edge of the river, hating being so thoroughly exposed, and hurried over the bridge, dodging stones and ugly accusations.

However, once in Wynne Holt, she felt safe again. Oh, there was still the odd chance that she'd meet someone, but people didn't listen carefully as they crashed through the underbrush. That gave her a large advantage—one she used frequently.

Out of breath, she reached the edge of the Point, her hands on her knees as she gasped for air. As her breathing resumed a more normal rhythm, she sank to the ground, her feet almost close enough to the edge to point over it, and pulled her hood back to allow the last rays of the sun to shine on her.

Philip would say that I should let the Son shine on me—that only I AM's light can truly warm me and make me happy. If that were only true.

The problem was that she didn't believe it. No matter how hard she tried—how much she desired it—Dove couldn't accept the wonderful stories that Philip told. They were just that—stories—nothing more.

Troubles

CHAPTER 10

Winter

Oxford students were split between two main groups, the Australes and the Borales. Being from the north, Philip was part of the Borales. Unfortunately, being part of a group from a certain part of the country did not immediately endear the other students toward him.

As he strolled into a tavern near his lodging house, Philip's heart dropped into his stomach. There at the table he preferred sat four young men from the Australes who delighted in making his life miserable. The temptation to flee was strong, but one of the fellows saw him before he could turn.

"Look, it's the beggar from the north!"

"I hear his benefactor was glad to get the stink from the area."

As usual, Philip refused to allow himself to show any reaction. And, as usual, he also struggled with miserable feelings of rejection. He was used to being accepted—well-liked even. In Wynnewood, only Angus had ever been unkind, and he was unkind to everyone. Just then, Philip would have enjoyed hearing Angus' taunting and threats. Then again, after the adventure with the "pirate caves," the lad hadn't been such a bully anymore.

He nodded, having learned long before that the other students would be even more vicious if he didn't at least acknowledge their presence. Unfortunately, that only increased their taunting. "Oh, he nods. At least he knows what a pathetic thing he is."

The tavern keeper brought Philip a plate of mutton and vegetables. "Mead or ale?"

"Mead, thank you."

"Don't let it bother you, Philip. They're not worth your concern."

When the man returned with the tankard, Philip thanked him. "I just don't know what I did to make them so hostile."

"You're a threat."

Philip glanced around the man as he made a pretense of scrubbing something off Philip's table. "A threat to what?"

"Their supposition of superiority. If a village boy from some obscure area up *north*," the man said north the way most people say dung, "can handle the rigors of academia, then how can they still feel as though they're better than others?"

With those words, the man hurried to serve a new group of students. It made some sense to Philip, but he wasn't sure what good it would do him. They'd still hate him, annoy him, and generally do everything they could to make his life miserable. It seemed to be their greatest talent. That thought amused him. At least there was that.

A shove from behind sent Philip's plate flying across the table onto the floor. "Look, the peasant prefers to eat off the floor."

Philip was still unwilling to engage. His brother's words returned to him as he tried to scoop the mess back onto the plate. *Bullies give up if you ignore them. If you have to, stand up to them. Most don't know how act when someone isn't afraid of them.*

A foot on his back sent him sprawling. "Now that's where a fellow like him belongs—groveling on the floor."

"Get off him," the tavern keeper demanded. "You can't just come in here and attack my customers. I'll call the constable if you don't leave him alone."

It was an empty threat and the young men knew it. However, they backed away, tossing more insults at Philip as they did. He picked himself off the floor, dusted off his robes, and at the insistence of the tavern keeper, sat back down at the table. As he waited for a replacement plate of food, he wondered how long would he live there before they simply ignored him?

"I heard his father is a fisherman. Can you imagine the stink in their house every night?"

"If you can call it a house. People like him live in hovels that our servants would refuse to enter."

Philip's knuckles grew white as he clenched his fingers together. As each insult flew and pierced his heart, he worked to steady his breathing and ignore the barbs. The tavern keeper placed another heaping plate of food in front of him and promised to return with more mead.

One by one, the boys grew tired of their sport and filed toward the door, each mocking him further as they left. "I heard the Earl of Wynnewood sent him down here to rid the village of a troublemaker."

"Nah, Charles Morgan is a fool. He's hardly a noble. Why I've heard it said that his father was little better than an animal the way he drove his people."

Philip smirked at the irony of these men treating another student so meanly while condemning another noble for doing something similar. For a moment, he almost felt sorry for them. Unfortunately, the feeling was brief.

"Didn't you hear? Charles Morgan doesn't have a son. He's probably using the only thing he could find as a substitute. His daughter is a worthless cripple after all—"

The young man didn't have a chance to finish. With a

guttural roar that he didn't know he possessed, Philip flew across the room, his fist smashing into the speaker's face. "Don't ever speak about Lady Morgan like that again."

As a cheer rose from some of the others in the room, the other young men started toward him, but Philip jumped up and advanced as if ready to take on the lot of them. Just as they might have jumped him, the tavern keeper shouted angrily, "Get out of here. The constable is on his way. Go and don't come back."

The man Philip hit had a gushing nose that refused to be stopped. Grabbing it, he pushed his way past his friends and out the door. The other three followed, each calling threats and insults as they did. Philip sighed.

"I am sorry—"

"Don't be. That was the most satisfying thing I've seen in a long time."

Discouraged, Philip pulled a few coins from his pouch and pressed them into the man's hand. "Thank you for trying. I'd better go."

"Out the side door, then. They might be waiting for you out front."

As the tavern keeper roused his other patrons into singing a loud song, Philip slipped through the side door. He winced as the door creaked, but no faces appeared on the side of the building. At the corner of the tavern, he peeked and saw the four men waiting outside the front, the one still holding his nose and complaining.

A horse stopped in front, blocking their view of him. Philip dashed to its side, hurried around another, and then strolled leisurely up the street. Once safe and alone again, he relived the satisfying crack of Richard Melton's nose as his fist slammed into it. For just a moment he felt ashamed, but the man's words, "just a worthless cripple," mocked his guilt.

Philip smiled. He'd defended a lady's honor—in a

manner of speaking. He'd defended his benefactor. They would never know it, of course, but he could know—maybe even Dove. She'd understand why it was so important to him.

He climbed the stairs to his room and closed the door behind him. It took only minutes to undress, wash his hands, face, and feet, and crawl under the covers. To his surprise, for the first time since he'd come to Oxford, Philip looked forward to the next morning.

The snow fell hard in Wynnewood for a week straight. Babies decided this was a perfect time to be born, and three arrived at night, within days of each other. Exhausted from her long nights with laboring mothers, Bertha didn't notice the absence of Dove until the first day without snow.

"Letty, when was the last time you saw the girl?"

"She was here before the snow, and there has been food missing at times, but I haven't seen her."

Bertha swept snow from the inside of the cottage as she opened the door. "Did you chop all the wood or did she?"

"I didn't chop much of it at all."

A new thought occurred to the midwife. "Wait, didn't you sleep here on Thursday?"

"Yes. You said the drifts weren't safe."

"Did she come home that night?"

Letty shook her head. "Not that I saw. Maybe she's at the castle."

"I doubt it."

"She stayed gone all that time last winter, and it was much colder then. We have more snow now, but it isn't as bitterly cold."

The girl's words were true. The blizzard the previous year had been horrible. It was impossible for the girl to have survived that, and yet she did. Perhaps she was concerned for nothing.

"How much food would you say is missing? What have you noticed?"

"Well, sometimes the stew pot seems as if there isn't as much in it. There were a couple of roasted potatoes gone. Porridge some mornings. I don't know how she does it though. I'm here most of the time."

"I imagine she comes in when you bring me things or run other errands," Bertha mused aloud.

"Why did she go? I wasn't mean to her; I promise. I thought she liked me—a little."

"The girl doesn't like people. She just doesn't dislike you like she does most others."

Bertha stifled a snicker as she saw Letty screw up her courage and say, "She likes Philip. No matter what anyone says, she's a true friend to him and he to her."

"Possibly."

Bertha stood near the door undecided. While it wasn't as cold as it had been, it was cold. She could find the girl. After all, she'd taught the child—young woman—everything she knew. However, it wasn't wise to go traipsing across the countryside in search of a forlorn creature like hers. She had new babies to watch over—mothers who needed her services.

A new thought occurred to her. "I'll be in the village if you need me. Just call for me. I'll hear you."

"Where are you goin'?"

"Are you deaf, girl? I said the village."

Another smile formed on her lips as the door closed and she heard, "I meant *where* in the village, which you knew, of course."

The roads were nearly impassable. Bertha grabbed two sheets of birch bark from the side of the cottage, and tied them to the bottom of her feet with leather lacings. With a long stick to test the ground ahead of her, Bertha followed the tree line into the village, panting heavily by the time she arrived. Snow was up to the knees in some places, making Bertha grateful for the wind that seemed to come in each night and blow away some of the snow.

At the chapel, she glanced up at the chimney, saw no smoke, and moved on to the minister's cottage. It galled to think of having to ask Dennis Clarke's help, but her pride wouldn't let her resist any longer. The girl was playing with her life and it was Bertha's responsibility to preserve life.

"Bertha?" Broðor Clarke's face frowned as he saw the midwife standing at the door.

"Are you going to make me stand out here and freeze?"

"Oh, sorry. Come in. I was so startled to see you."

"I know that I am a frightful thing, Dennis, but you do not have to remind me of it."

"That's absurd," Broðor Clarke said, shutting the door behind her. "Have a seat. Would you like some hot cider?"

Bertha moved near the fire as she nodded. "Yes, thank you."

"That must annoy you to say to me."

Since his back was turned to her, Bertha permitted herself a smile. "I suppose it does. Then again, so does my errand."

"So, this is not a social visit? You haven't come to confess Jesus Christ as your Lord?"

"Lord Morgan is enough lord for me. Two would be too confusing. Who do you obey when they disagree?"

"The Lord of All, of course. Are you sure you do not know the scriptures? After all, Jesus himself said that you cannot serve two masters. Either you will hate the one and love the other or the reverse."

"Then that," Bertha insisted, "is proof enough that I should not consider adding another one into my life. Much too confusing."

The pained look on Broðor Clarke's face annoyed her. Why must he always turn everything into a contest of faith? "That is not why I came here."

"Then why did you come?"

"It's the girl. She's gone again. I haven't seen her since the snow started falling. Actually, I haven't seen much of her since the boy left, but not at all in a week. She needs to come home."

"And why are you telling me this?"

"I want you to find her—talk to her. I want you to make her come home more often. This is too solitary even for her, and at this time of year, too dangerous."

"She did survive last winter, but that was unlikely."

"Exactly. I want you to talk to her. Tell her that Philip would want her to come home. He will be very sorry to come home and have his friend dead because she was too foolish to take care of herself."

"Why me?"

"She'll listen to you. You're Philip's mentor. You make up all those silly stories she loves so much. She'll listen."

"I'll try to find her—talk to her."

"Look along the Ciele directly across from the east tower. I think you'll find her there."

Bertha rose and set the tankard on the table. She pulled her cloak tighter around her neck and pulled her shawl up over her hair. At the door, she glanced back over her shoulder. "Thank you, Dennis."

"Bertha, I—"

She closed the door firmly behind herself, shutting out the minister's words. She really didn't want to hear him urge her to embrace his faith—again. It was tiresome of course, but there was a certain bit of fun in their repartee. She enjoyed it even.

Christmas

CHAPTR 11

Up and down the river, the minister tramped, fighting the snow and the drifts, but he saw nothing that indicated Dove had ever been there. After several hours of calling and listening for her songs, he marched until he was in direct line of the east tower, turned, and then headed into the trees of Wyrm Forest. He just hoped none of the villagers or people at the castle saw him. Then again, from this distance, they'd probably assume he was Dove.

Despite knowing that the forest was safe, old superstitions died hard. Each creak of the branches, each bough rubbing against a branch, and each crunch of his feet in the snow-covered underbrush made him jittery. He forced himself onward anyway. It didn't take him long to find Dove's pool, but he didn't know what it was. He just saw a depression in the landscape and wondered at it as he skirted the edge.

"What do you want?"

Broðor Clarke jumped at the sound of Dove's voice. He turned toward her and fear pulsed in his veins for a few seconds as he adjusted to her sudden presence. There she stood, not ten yards away, next to a tree. She'd arrived noiselessly.

Her cloak was the familiar gray of winter, but this one was larger than the previous years. The hem nearly reached the ground, would touch it if she bent too far, and the hood was deeper than ever. For the first time, he saw in her what the villagers saw. Instead of an impish little girl with a quick intelligence and ready wit, she appeared to be a banshee, floating in the forest. Where her face should have been, he saw only a black hole. It was unnerving, even to him.

"Bertha is worried about you."

"Bertha?" The girl didn't step closer as he'd expected.

"She came to me. You know how concerned she must be if she'd ask *me* for help."

He thought he heard her snicker, but the distance was enough for him to know it was unlikely that he could hear something so indistinct. She crossed her arms, the familiar brown gloves resting atop the cloak. "Why is she worried?"

"It's cold. You're so very alone. It isn't how things should be. She wants you home more." Before the girl could answer, he added. "Philip would not like it, Dove. He'd want you to visit the castle, to befriend Letty. You know how hard it is to live with someone like Bertha and you are used to her. How much harder would it be for a girl like Letty?"

"I'm happier out here."

"Will you go in until spring? At least until there is no more snow?"

The girl started to turn and then paused. He saw her shoulders slump and her hand grasp the tree as if for support. "I will go home. I may be gone during the day, but I will sleep there at night."

"Thank you, Dove." As he saw her disappear behind the tree, Broðor Clarke called out to her once more. "There will be the Christmas festivities at the castle next week. I know Lady Aurelia misses you. Will you come to those? She'll be watching the contests from the balcony. You could help her."

The cloak reappeared once more. "I don't think so, but thank you. Tell Lady Aurelia that I hope she enjoys her day."

With those words, the girl vanished. It seemed as if she simply dissolved into the trees. Had the mists been present, it would have looked as if they'd swallowed her. No wonder people considered her eerie. He'd only seen her in the castle on occasion—never in her natural environment unless it was to see her running from those trying to drive her from the village. Yes, it was most certainly nerve wracking.

"Do you see her?" Aurelia peered down into the crowds below, frustrated. "I never thought I'd be so annoyed to see cloaks. Half of them are gray!"

"I don't think she's coming. I'd hoped she'd change her mind, but..."

"Has she been going home at night?" Lord Morgan asked.

"Bertha says she sleeps there every night. Oh, look. They will begin the rope contest now. I think Angus will begin it this year."

The minister was right. Aurelia watched excited as the burly young man stepped into the middle of the bailey and picked up the end of a rope lying on the ground. "When did that get there?"

"They've been stepping over it all this time. Now that everyone has moved, you can see it," her father explained.

Three smaller lads, two of whom she recognized as Philip's friends, stepped forward opposite Angus. "Where are the men to help Angus?"

"He is going to go against them by himself at first."

Aurelia's eyes widened. "Can he hold out against

three other boys?"

"Well, he must think so."

One of the guards counted backwards from five. "Four—three—two—go!"

Angus hardly seemed to notice the three young men on the other side of the rope. At one point, he even let go of the rope with one hand to scratch his head. The crowd roared and cheered.

To Aurelia's astonishment, two more young men joined the opposite side. Now Angus planted his feet firmly and used both arms to hold on. Even from her perch above, she could see the strain on his face. Another young man joined. Angus faltered.

The guard noticed and pointed to Hugh. The blacksmith stepped in front of Angus and held the rope. Angus relaxed some. Three more men joined the other side, but Angus and Hugh held it well.

"How can two men hold out against all those others?"

"They aren't fighting it yet. They're strong," her father explained, "but they didn't start off using the bulk of their strength. The younger boys are fatigued already."

"I think they'll have to add the miller after the next one goes to the other side."

"What a shame."

Curious, Aurelia turned her face to her father. "Why a shame?"

"If there were fewer men here, those two would take on everyone else. There are just too many. It's always more impressive with just them on the one side of the rope."

It seemed impossible, but her father must have seen it happen. She tried to read the men's expressions, but couldn't. Were they already spent? The younger, smaller lads seemed ready to drop.

The crowd cheered gleefully at each addition. There were so many men on the left of the rope, and just the three men on the right, but those men were slowly inching to the other side. "Father, it's not fair!"

"They'll add Symon Wood to—see, there he is. They'll keep adding men until they run out of rope."

"Why do the men on the left file onto the end of the rope, but the right side steps in front of the others?"

"They're spelling the other men's arms. It's hard to be the lead," Lord Morgan explained.

To her astonishment, the four men on the right held out against what seemed like nearly two dozen on the left. There were only four men left, but it didn't seem the right could hold out against four *more* men. Then the unbelievable happened. The man calling the players sent the baker to the left.

"Why did he send the baker to the left?"

"Tobias is strong, isn't he," her father agreed.

"He lifts those big bags of flour and works with his arms every day. He should go to the right!" Her eyes widened until she looked unnatural. "Why is the fletcher going to the right? He's too scrawny."

Before Lord Morgan could answer, the five men on the right gave a great jerk and then jumped out of the way, as the line of men on the left stumbled forward. Aurelia watched, fascinated, as the men erupted in a great roar of excitement, slapping one another on their backs and cheering. Children raced to greet their fathers and wives kissed their husbands. She saw a young woman throw her arms around Angus.

"Who is that? Is he married already? Just last year—"

"That is Letty Wood. The midwife's apprentice."

"Oh, he's her brother. I always thought it would be nice to have an older brother."

"Perhaps you can adopt Angus?" Lord Morgan teased.

"Is it foolish to admit that I've pretended that Philip was my older brother?"

Broðor Clarke's voice, quiet but sincere said, "Philip

would remind you, Lady Aurelia, that you have the perfect Elder Brother in Jesus."

"I had not considered that, but it's true, isn't it?"

Lord Morgan stepped away calling, "I'll send for the winners. You can distribute the prizes."

It took some time for the five men to appear on the balcony. Each one knelt at her side for her to place a laurel wreath on their heads, one after the other. As they rose, she nodded to a servant who handed each a cage with a goose inside. "Happy Christmas."

As Angus knelt, she gaped at his massive shoulders and arms. "You did so well. I couldn't believe that you were able to hold your own against so many!"

Angus blushed like a girl, ducking his head to hide his flushed face. "Thank you."

An awkward silence filled the balcony until the servant whispered into Angus' ear. He rose hastily, apologizing. Aurelia managed to stifle her amusement and pointed to the servant. "A goose for your family's dinner. Congratulations again."

Somehow, the balcony felt empty without the enormous young man even before he reached the door. Feeling foolish, she called after him, "Father is going to send a letter to Philip when he sends Jerome to London in the spring. Is there any message you would like to send?"

At the doorway, the young man halted. He hesitated for a moment, and then turned back again. "I doubt there is much room for personal messages in the note, but he might like to know we all miss him."

"I will do that. Have a happy Christmas."

"What is troubling you, dear heart?"

Aurelia glanced around the room, looking anywhere

but into her father's eyes. She felt ridiculous, but an idea had formed and blossomed in her heart that was becoming quite important to her. "I—"

"I don't know what to think. You've been unsettled for days."

"Restless, I guess." Her conscience pricked her. The words were untrue, but he wouldn't know it. Overlooking the unease in her spirit, she continued. "It's winter; no one thinks it wise for me to go out on the cliffs... I don't have Philip and Dove to visit me..."

She sounded listless and melancholy, even to herself. Lord Morgan crossed the room and seated himself beside her. "Would you like to go outdoors? The knights could carry you out there. It's cold, but with a few furs and blankets..."

"I was thinking..." Her mind swirled as she spoke. "Perhaps if I had a project. Do you remember what that young man said at Christmas? How Philip's friends missed him but it was too much for a letter? I thought perhaps..."

Her father's hand brushed a stray hair from her cheek. "I am not accustomed to you being unwilling to ask anything of me. This is very strange of you."

"It would be asking a lot of his friends, but if they would come and give me personal messages, I could make a long letter full of them for him. It would be something he could have to read often when he felt lonely for home."

Lord Morgan beamed. "That is a wonderful idea, Aurelia! Even if it took several sheets of paper, it would not take up much room and would bring him great joy. I am proud of you." He was silent for another half a minute before asking, "But why did you not want to ask this of me?"

The young lady's cheeks turned rosy as she confessed, "Philip's friends are all young men. I thought it might be awkward..."

"I can stay in the room if you prefer, or I can write the notes for you."

Aurelia took a moment to answer and then shook her head. "No, Father. I know it's selfish, but I wanted this to be my gift for him. Perhaps we can start with Minerva or Letty. Surely, Dove would come for this, won't she?"

"We'll be sure of it. Why don't I call for Liam and Minerva now?"

As her father left the room, John carried Aurelia to a table, placing a cushion on the bench before lowering her to it. "Are you comfortable?"

"Quite, thank you."

"The lad will be thankful—as will his friends. It will be important to the people of Wynnewood that you thought of them."

"May I confess something, John?" At the servant's nod, she continued, "I think this is more for my sake than Philip's. It'll be something to look forward to every day. I'll get to see hi—his friends."

Lord Morgan entered the room again just in time to hear his daughter's words falter. A knowing smile played about his lips as he realized that his little girl hadn't gotten over her fascination with the village lads and how very different they were from the ladies who attended her. This would be a much more interesting project than he'd envisioned—much more interesting indeed.

News

CHA
PTR
12

Spring

Throughout most of the winter, Philip managed to avoid private confrontation with the Australes who enjoyed tormenting him. Each night that he ate away from his lodging, he left the tavern by the side door in case the young men were there. Alas, one evening in early spring, they split themselves between the two doors, and as Philip stepped outside, two young men jumped him.

His rib cracked as a foot slammed into it; his nose bled profusely. At first, he'd thought it best not to retaliate, but when the beating seemed unlikely to stop, Philip gathered all his strength and fought his way out of the group and back into the tavern. Hob, the tavern keeper, helped him into a room at the back and sent for a physician

Philip felt the swollen lip, winced as he tried to stop the flow of blood from his nose, and struggled to breathe without gasping with pain. The strange little physician hurried into the room just a short while later, whispering prayers for healing, and working quickly to make poultices to ease Philip's suffering. Each "cure" hurt worse than the last.

He begged them to hire men to carry him back to his rooms, but Hob wouldn't hear of it. The physician backed him with assurances that being moved would be the worst thing possible. "You won't be able to withstand the pain."

For three days, he lay on the pallet they made for him in the storeroom of the tavern. Serving girls brought him brought, mead, and visitors. Hob visited him often—too often in Philip's opinion—giving him the news of the town and the other students.

"I heard that the chancellor has fined the four young men who jumped you. Apparently he will do something about it if the students mistreat another student, but steal or destroy property of an honest tradesman, and he looks the other way."

"I'm sorry, Hob. You know I don't think it's right."

"You're a gentleman, Philip—much more than any of those nobles' sons."

"I think they'd disagree with you. They don't think much of my lack of property or family." He smiled and then winced as his lip cracked open again. "Then again, I do own my own cottage. I do have *some* property."

"And a great benefactor. James said he overheard the knights from Wynnewood talking. They speak well of Lord Morgan."

"He is a great man. The men spoke truly of Lord Morgan's father. Galbert Morgan was hard by all accounts."

Hob was called away to settle a dispute in the tavern, leaving Philip to lay alone at last. He was tired. His head ached from spending so much time in bed, each breath felt like a fresh stab to his chest, and his heart was heavy. The young men would never pay the fine. Their fathers would protest, and who would enforce the word of one village lad over the sons of four prominent nobles? They'd be even angrier now.

I could leave, he mused to himself. *Why stay where I'm not wanted? Why put up with this year after year? It won't get any better; in fact, it will only get worse now.*

His own thoughts galled him. How could he consider quitting after less than a year? How could he face Lord Morgan? It would be mortifying. *Sorry, m'lord. The other students didn't like me, and that made me feel bad, so I came home.* He couldn't quit.

If he were honest with himself, he'd admit that he'd learned to like the studies. He was learning much more than he'd ever imagined possible. Why, the maps he had seen of the world alone had astounded him. There had never been any doubt in his mind that Wynnewood was a tiny corner of England. He'd heard of the days' journey to places like Scarborough or London. England was a large place in his mind. Then he'd reviewed Ptolemy's map of the world. England was nearly insignificant in size compared to the rest of the earth.

He woke some time later and realized that he had fallen asleep while weighing his options. Philip forced himself up off the pallet. It was time to go home—back to the rooms Lord Morgan provided for him—and get back to work.

"What are you doing?" Hob stared at him in horror as he emerged from the storeroom.

"I need to get back to work. I am getting behind in my studies." Hob looked ready to protest, but Philip continued. "I'll send someone over with money to pay you for your trouble and for the hælan. Will you be sure to pay him for me?"

"Yes, but—"

"When I can walk without pain, I'll be back. I do enjoy your mutton." Philip tried to push the side door open, and gasped at the pain.

"I don't think you should leave yet," Hob insisted as he pushed open the door.

"Lord Morgan didn't pay for me to come and lay abed. He brought me here to be educated. I need to get back to the business of learning."

Philip's confidence rode high for the next week. His lessons went well and his face and chest alternated between blue, purple, red, green, and finally yellow. Though still tender, his ribs no longer felt as though they pierced his lungs with each breath. As if to compensate for his body's broken and bruised state, he flew through lessons as though it was review work.

Spring was in full bloom. Trees budded and blossomed. Green appeared everywhere—even inside the stone walls of the city. After months of being cooped up indoors, he was anxious for a ramble across the countryside. At last he could resist no longer. He closed his books, put away his papers, and removed the scholar's robes that identified him. He tried to put on the clothes that he'd worn to Oxford the previous year, but the legs and arms were much too short, and his tunic was snug.

"Who knew you could grow in such a place?" he muttered as he pulled on his regular clothing. It too was a bit small. He'd have to have new things made soon.

People jostled him as he hurried through the gates, each jar more painful than the last. However, he eventually found himself able to stroll across green grasses and fill his lungs with clean air again. There weren't as many trees as there were in the forests of Wynnewood, but he thought the countryside beautiful with the stone walls separating properties and trees clustering along the river. Sheep grazed in pastures, lambs gamboling nearby. That reminded him of home and the lost animals that everyone attributed to Dove.

Did Sir Dragon still bring fresh meat to his lady? Did she roast them with her breath with a little rosemary, or did she eat them in one gulp?

His gaze turned south. Down there, somewhere, was the sea. His father often spoke of the town of Portsmouth and the trading Lord Morgan's captain did there. In fact, his father could be sailing there even now.

North of him, caravans rolled toward Oxford, laden with wares from the countryside. Wagons, piled high with hay or straw seemed most prevalent. The local animals would be happy for fresh bedding and fodder. From there, the hustle and bustle of commerce in the city was exciting to watch. Perhaps he'd grow used to it over time and learn to love it even when in the center of it all.

Unbidden, his eyes slid southward. An ache formed around his heart as he imagined his father sailing past Wales, around the bottom of England, and into Portsmouth harbor. He'd have a week—maybe two—there. In his mind, he could imagine the town. As often as his father described it, Philip was sure he could have walked through it without hesitating.

Suddenly, the desire to run away to Portsmouth was nearly overwhelming. He could get rides most of the way to spare his lungs. It was warm enough now that he wouldn't freeze at night if he slept out in the open. His father would understand—as would Lord Morgan. Broðor Clarke could teach him all he needed to know. He could even promise to become the minister. Or, he could prove to his father that being a seafaring man would be a good decision for him.

Feeling reckless but excited, Philip turned back toward the city. He'd pay his bills, pack his things, and head out first thing in the morning. There'd be no more worry over persecution by the others or not passing muster in his studies.

As eager as he was to get started, he hardly noticed the pain as he half-ran back to his lodgings. The stairs were hard to climb, but he burst into his room, ready to sort his belongings and decide what to take. The room was occupied.

"Felix?"

"Philip! I've been wondering when you'd get home! You look out of breath—are you—"

"I'm fine. What brings you here? Is Lord Morgan with you? W—"

"One question at a time, lad! Lord Morgan sent me on errand to London and then Portsmouth. He and Lady Aurelia have letters for you."

Letters. Philip swallowed hard. Even as he'd been planning his escape, I AM had provided exactly the kind of encouragement he needed. In his eagerness to take the packet from Felix, Philip knocked it from the man's fingers. He bent to retrieve it, wincing.

"What's wrong, Philip? You are truly in pain."

"Just—"

Felix bent closer and reached to tilt his face to see it better, but Philip flinched, jerking back instinctively. "You've been injured. Come over to the window. Let me—" The sight of yellow around Philip's eyes and mouth and the ginger way the young man moved brought shock to Felix's face. "Who did this to you?"

"It doesn't matter."

"It does to me! Lord Morgan—"

"Oh, don't tell him," Philip pleaded, hating how much like a small child he sounded. "It's fine now, really."

"Were you at fault?"

"No."

Felix eyed him, looking for some sign of dishonesty, Philip assumed, and then nodded. "You have to tell me, Philip. If you don't, I'll drag your father back here and let him beat it out of you. I want to know what happened."

Having no choice made it easier on Philip to explain himself. He told about the general dislike for him as Lord Morgan's protégé, about the mockery and teasing, and finally about the day he'd broken Richard Melton's nose for speaking ill of Lady Aurelia. "I ignored the lies about my family, the lies about me, but when he called her a worthless cripple..."

"You did well, lad. Lord Morgan will be proud."

"Oh, please don't tell him!" Again, Philip begged, too desperate to extricate a promise of silence from Felix to care about his pride. "I don't want any more trouble or Lord Morgan to take action. You know he would if he knew. Please. They'll grow tired of their sport and leave me alone."

Felix hesitated, and then patted Philip on the back. "It'll be ok. You read your letters. I'll go get something to eat." With a reassuring smile, he left the room, his feet clattering down the stairs noisily.

Something in the man's voice made him nervous, but Philip shook it off and opened the packet of letters. Torn between the larger one from Aurelia and the duty owed Lord Morgan, he hesitated. It only took a second to decide. He unfolded Lord Morgan's letter and read it carefully.

Greetings, Philip!

I pray that this letter finds you well and enjoying your studies. Broðor Clarke prays for you every Sunday. Aurelia and I pray as well.

Work on the castle is progressing nicely. The chapel, you will be pleased to know, has commenced. They have enclosed all towers and the keep completely in stone. Several more of the older places have begun to be reinforced with stone as well. By the time the works are finished, this will be the most well-fortified castle in northern England.

Aurelia has hatched a scheme to send news from all your friends. Enclosed are messages from them as well. Inspired by her idea, I went to visit your mother and asked her to send her love as well. She says to tell you that Will is marrying on the summer solstice. Your little brother, his name escapes me at the moment, is growing rapidly and now does many chores around the house to help her. Your father is on the Nicor headed to Portsmouth and then Spain.

Her garden is already green with sprouting plants, but there were holes near the bottom of the walls of the cottage where the snow ate away the daub and rotted some of the wattle. I have some of my men there now making repairs. From all accounts, your young brother enjoys "helping" where he can.

Broðor Clarke says you will be starting studying French this year. Je suis sûr que vous parlerez bientôt du français très bien. If nothing else, you'll soon speak it well enough to prove me a poor scholar of the language.

It is probably poor writing form, but I will tell you how I have missed you. When I think of you growing up in the village and never knowing you, it astounds me how important you have become to my family. Evaline loved you for what we said of you, Aurelia misses her study partner, and I miss hearing your unique perspective on life. Study well, but do not endear your heart to Oxford. As much as I want you to feel at home while you are there, I would not like to think of you staying indefinitely. The years will pass much faster than you can imagine.
Charles Morgan, Earl of Wynnewood

Philip fought back tears as he read the letter. Men didn't cry over missing home. Hastily, he fumbled with Aurelia's letter, unfolding the pages and scanning them quickly before sinking onto his bed to re-read them, savoring each word. Aurelia's writing style suited her. It was friendly, but elegant. Most of the entries were one line or two of well wishes and assurances that he was missed, but when Aurelia enjoyed the visit of one of the contributors, she wrote long paragraphs, interjecting her own impressions and opinions into them. Certain passages burned themselves into his memory as he re-read them time and again.

Liam sits beside me, asking questions much more rapidly than I can write them. He is curious about the languages you are learning, if translating is more difficult than you expected, and if there are other students from our area of the country. He seems fascinated with astronomy and mathematics and wishes to know which you've studied and if you have a preference.

It sounded just like Liam— the Liam he had grown to know in the months before he'd left Wynnewood. Words from Letty made him shake his head. There was much about herbs and helping a mother after birth, but nothing that would interest him—just that which made up her world.

We have seen very little of Dove. She spends most of her time alone in the forest now—much as she did before she knew you. She wishes me to tell you that I AM does not speak to her heart through the trees, but she does miss the stories of Him. She also says that the pool is completed, but she has not yet dug the final few feet to break into the river to fill it. She expects to finish this week and take her first swim. I think she would say, if she was not quite so unwilling to sound too melancholy without you, that she wishes you could swim with her there. I suppose she wouldn't do that though—she'll likely have to remove her cloak, won't she? I should also tell you that she has grown. I imagine that she is taller than I would be if I stood. She also seems, if you can believe it possible, even more graceful than ever. I note a maturity in her voice that wasn't there before. It is a little deeper, but still clear and high for a woman. Yes, I do believe we can call her a woman soon. After all, she is probably in her thirteenth year.

Thirteen. That would be true. She was twelve when he'd left for Oxford—he was now sixteen, so it fit. How hard to imagine Dove as anything but the waif of Wynnewood. His eye spied another entry, one that made him laugh.

Angus sits near me, trying not to look as if he will shatter the bench if he moves. I have never seen someone so large who was not fat. He won, with four other men, the Christmas rope game. There were five men against thirty it seemed. Angus tells me there weren't quite that many. I think there were more. He works all day for the blacksmith, but Father is considering putting him to work on the hinges and latches in the castle. He has developed a fine hand for that sort of ironwork. Angus asks me to remind you that he will keep watch over that which must be watched. I think he suspects that I know what he means. Should I tell him? I don't think I will. It is much more interesting to keep him guessing. I have a terrible feeling that I am becoming quite an obnoxious young lady.

At last he finished reading each letter—twice—and folded them carefully. His former plans were all but forgotten. His friends were proud of him and his benefactor had much faith in him. He needed to be a success and not quit when things were difficult.

"That's your problem, Philip Ward; everything has always come so easy for you. Why, even archery was reasonably easy once you knew the problem. This may be work, but it is worthy work. Make them proud of you," he whispered under his breath. He stashed the letters in a safe place and pulled out his books once more. There would be an examination tomorrow. It was time to quit dilly-dallying.

Lost & Found

CHAPTR 13

Dove watched as every horse from the castle—it seemed, anyway—raced about the countryside, the dogs barking and baying as they pushed on ahead of the riders, seeking, searching. She grew even more curious as she observed them riding across the meadow and into the Heolstor, the sounds growing more and more muffled with each passing second. They were deep within the woods looking for something.

Curiosity drove her to seek the path they were most likely to take when they left the forest. She wandered, trying to look for something amiss until she heard the sounds of the horses returning. Quickly she climbed a tree, tearing her cloak on its branches, and waited for them to ride past.

It was a long wait. The riders seemed to be canvassing every inch of the forest, zigzagging in and out between the trees. At last they came to a halt, just ten feet away from her.

"I don't see a hint of it anywhere. The dogs didn't seem to find anything either."

Dove recognized the voice; it was Lord Morgan's head groom. Before anyone else could speak, a horse galloped up quickly and its rider called, "I think it's back near the lair. I saw hooves."

"If there are more than one, of course there'd be

hooves there!"

"Hooves with shoes?"

It was hard to differentiate between voices as the men argued about where to go next, but she learned what she needed to know. Goldhord was missing; somehow, he'd escaped.

She waited until the men rode back toward the bridge and then scrambled down from the tree. Her light cloak billowed out behind her as she raced across the fields, waded through the swollen river, and hurried through the Wyrm forest.

"What—"

Dove ignored Letty and her dozens of questions as she burst into the house, and filled her pockets with apples. She grabbed a hunk of cheese, spread honey on bread, and stopped at the door where Letty stood, hands on hips. "Out of my way."

"No. You put on your other cloak. That one is torn. I'll fix it."

A snicker escaped as Dove pushed past. "I'll leave it on the peg tonight, but we both know that I will not change right now."

"I'll step outside. You can bar the door. That's exactly the kind of tear that will get bigger just from the weight of those apples. Go!"

To Dove's surprise, she obeyed Letty's orders. She stepped inside the house, shed the cloak, and transferred the fruit. Once she unbarred the door, Dove left. She felt Letty's eyes following her into the forest, but she didn't look back.

The trek back took longer, but she ate her bread and considered what to do. Goldhord knew her. Would he follow her to the castle without the laurel to subdue him? It was worth the attempt; if he refused to come, she could try again the next day.

Near the unicorn's lair, Dove began her plan. She

placed an apple about ten feet away from her and then one in her lap. She then waited.

The afternoon dragged into evening. Other than the occasional twitter of birds, or the rustling of a hare in the underbrush, the forest was eerily silent. She considered singing, but instead, she waited.

There was no moon, which made the forest even darker than usual. Something in the air told her it was time. After months of silence, Dove sang. Her voice echoed through the trees as she sang of a unicorn that had lost its way and the ge-sceaft that brought it home again.

A rustle in the bushes startled her, but she kept singing. Without the moon as her light, she didn't see the animal appear, but the crunch of teeth into an apple told her that the animal was near. She didn't move—not a muscle twitched—but she sang. The unicorn's lips tickled her hand as it nibbled the apple, but still she sang.

At last, the moment arrived. The animal knelt and laid its large head in her lap. "Shh, boy. What is wrong? Why have you left Lord Morgan's stables? How did you get away?"

On and on, she talked to him, smoothing his mane and her fingers tracing the length of the horn. They must still be harvesting the tip for the Mæte. How did they bring it to the little people? She shook herself. It wasn't the time for useless questions.

"Come, Goldhord. Take me home."

She had no rope, but she followed the animal through the forest. At the edge of the Heolstor, Dove fed him another apple before they began the descent toward the castle. Occasionally she stumbled in the darkness, but Dove continued, leading the horse to one of the side gates where a guard slept through the noise of Goldhord's hooves on stone.

At the stables, she led him to his stall, whispering

encouragement as he balked. She smelled laurel and patted the walls until she found it, throwing it outside. "Come inside. It's safe now. I have more apples."

The unicorn whinnied and turned around as if to leave. Dove started to cajole him again, but a shadow darkened the stable door. "You've caught my pet, have you? Well done, Dove."

"Lord Morgan?"

"I wondered if you'd discover he was missing and find him. He likes you."

Goldhord allowed Lord Morgan to lead him back to his stall and stepped inside willingly. Dove passed him another apple as she smoothed his muzzle. "Good boy."

"I haven't seen you since your visit with Aurelia. We miss you. She says you aren't practicing your embroidery."

"I'm sorry, my lord."

"You miss Philip."

She turned to leave, but he stopped her. "He wouldn't want you to be so unhappy. He would want you to have friends. We'll be your friends, little one." Lord Morgan laughed. "You aren't quite so little anymore. I might have to rename you."

Time passed as she stood considering his words. She didn't want to come to the castle and visit with Philip's friends. She liked being alone where she could do as she pleased. However, Lord Morgan spoke truth. Philip would be happier in Oxford if he knew that she was still visiting Aurelia in his absence.

"I am sorry. I will come. Next week maybe."

"Tomorrow."

She sighed, realizing he knew how hard it would be for her to keep her word if it was such a long time. "Yes, tomorrow then."

Dove worked slowly and tediously to perfect her stitches as she sat with Aurelia in the girl's sitting room. Now that Aurelia was older, she spent less time in the great hall and more in a room designed for her comfort and privacy. "I see an advantage to your gloves, Dove," the young lady said as she sucked on a pricked finger.

"They do protect, but I doubt I'll ever be as precise as you with them."

"Do you practice without sometimes?"

"When I am alone, yes. I have a pool where I like to go and sit."

"The one you dug?" Aurelia giggled. "You forget that the whole of Wynnewood reports anything they see or hear to me. I reward them well."

"Yes. It is a beautiful pool. I lined the bottom with rocks so the water won't be muddy at all— just very clear and beautiful."

Before Aurelia could reply, Lord Morgan knocked, peeking his head around the door. "May I come in? Felix has returned with replies to our letters to Philip."

Eagerly, the young women set aside their stitching and waited to hear what Philip had to say. "Is he well? Does he enjoy his studies? Does he miss us?"

Lord Morgan laughed as he handed Aurelia a letter. "So many questions, dear heart. Read for yourself and I will read my letter from him as well."

The letters were unfolded, each reading the words carefully, smiles appearing at random spots, and a few concerned frowns as well. Dove thought she'd go crazy waiting to hear of her friend. The time passed so slowly and took so long that she began to grow suspicious. Then, just as she was about to ask a question, her laughter rang out through the room.

"I nearly asked! I wondered what could take so long to read!"

"She has discovered our secret, Aurelia. We almost managed to fool her, though. I'll read mine aloud first."

To the Earl of Wynnewood, Lord Morgan,

Your letter arrives to find me well and enjoying my studies at Oxford. I do confess that it was a difficult adjustment at first, but I have grown to appreciate my masters and am doing well in my examinations. Felix arrived at a most inopportune time, and I fear my appearance may have startled him. He seems to be bothered more than is necessary. I assure you that I am well and he is concerned unnecessarily.

The townspeople and students do not get along well. I think I have the benefit of understanding both sides of the issue being both a student and a commoner. Many of the students abuse their position, thinking their rank or family gives them the privilege to be destructive or not to pay their bills.

On the other hand, the townspeople do try to take advantage of the wealth of their student patrons. They pad bills where possible and try to accuse the students of destruction that occurred as a part of general use rather than abuse by a single patron.

I was happy to hear of your visit to Modor, and I admit to having a reckless fancy to run off to Portsmouth to see Fæder. However, I am still here, still studying, still working hard so that I may come home well educated and able to assure you that I have done my best. My goal is to learn all I can, make you, Broðor Clarke, my parents, and most of all, my Lord proud.

Do tell Dove to continue her visits to Lady Aurelia. Perhaps they can spend some of their time teaching her to read and write. Maybe when Felix comes south next year, she can send a letter with him written of her own hand. Perhaps also, Lady Aurelia can show her the truth of I AM where I failed to do so.

Please tell Broðor Clarke that I met the illustrator William de Brailes and his wife. I have seen them a few times now, and he is always an encouragement to me at exactly the time I would need him. I do wonder if the Lord doesn't prompt both of us to go out during those times. It seems too improbable for such consistent coincidence.

I send you all my love, my honor, my respect, and my gratitude. I do know what a great privilege it is to be here and I am determined not to waste any of it.

Philip Ward, Oxford.

Dove cocked her head, the hood flopping to one side like a rabbit's ear. "How can he seem so happy and unhappy at the same time?"

"I think you might feel the same. You are happy that he is learning and enjoying this experience, but unhappy that he is gone. I think that's reasonable."

The roles felt reversed to Dove. She was usually the one being sensible while Aurelia allowed emotion to cloud her judgment. Dove just couldn't stand the idea of her friend being all alone in a strange town and unhappy.

"That was my thought," Lord Morgan agreed. "I do wish he had explained himself more. I think while you read your letter, I will go inquire of Felix what Philip meant in the beginning of his letter."

"You do not want to hear the other letter, Father?"

"I'll read it with you later. You enjoy it with Dove."

Aurelia shifted to get more comfortable and then beckoned Dove to "read" with her. "You will learn how to read much more quickly if you see and hear reading at the same time. I'll put my finger under each word."

"I doubt I could remember them all."

The young mistress laughed. "Of course you cannot! That doesn't mean it won't help. Listen."

To the Lady Aurelia of Wynnewood,

Your unusual letter is received with much gratitude. I was astounded to see so many messages in one long letter. It did bring a desperate longing to see you all again, but I have made it my goal to channel that longing into my studies. If I do well, perhaps I can finish earlier than expected. How much will have changed by the time I return! Why, you will likely be married!

I was overjoyed to hear of Angus' success. I have always wondered if he would flourish after he was given a chance to prove himself as something other than just a brawny boy. Liam shamed me with his questions. His eagerness to learn comes to mind every time I think I have more to do than I can bear.

As to your questions, I have not made good friends of the students yet, but I have met an interesting man who encourages me in my studies, and a friendly tavern keeper keeps me mindful of who I am beneath these academic robes. I think my fellow students do not know how to interact with an equal who is not an equal.

Regarding my studies, I am now beginning French in addition to improving my Latin and Italian. The mathematics classes are still my least favorite, and astronomy has been added. At least I now have a use for some of the mathematics I have studied.

Lady Aurelia, your kindness to me is more appreciated than you can ever know. Please share my gratitude to all and assure them of my affection. You are all in my prayers daily.

Philip Ward, Oxford

"How many more years will he be gone?" Dove whispered.

Aurelia's voice was choked with emotion when she answered, "Too many."

Unrest

CHAPTR 14

Summer

Oxford felt oppressed by the second week of June. At first, Philip thought it might be the heat, but there was more—much more. Several of the students had fathers visiting for reasons that seemed strange. Had it been one or two, he would not have thought much of it, but nearly a dozen of the most prominent students had some family—father, uncle, brother—in attendance.

Rumors abounded—whispers about sedition and treason. Philip actually heard of a new government that severely weakened the monarchy. One man even said the crown would be unnecessary.

Of all the men in town, Simon de Montfort, Earl of Leicester, was the most prominent. Why, even Philip had heard of him! Knights dressed in full armor seemed ever-present, and there was talk of battle.

The temptation to creep into the streets to see what he could learn was strong and twice nearly overpowered him. The first time he made it to the street before turning back, mentally quoting the third chapter of John in Latin as a diversion. The second time he made it almost to his favorite tavern before he turned back, unwilling to risk being caught and dishonoring Lord Morgan's name.

He made it nearly to his lodgings when it occurred to him that he could eat dinner and possibly hear something. Once more, Philip did an about-face and hurried to the tavern. The building was nearly bursting at the seams with travelers and students, but Hob beckoned for him to follow. There, at a table shoved into the corner, was a place just perfect for him.

"I'll bring you mutton. Ale or mead?"

"I'd appreciate ale tonight. Thank you."

"There's a lot of talk in here tonight," Hob warned. "A lot of beer and ale flowing. Loose tongues might be interesting, but it's dangerous too. You be careful what people think you hear."

To his dismay, a group of knights shoved back a bench, knocking it over, and pushed through the door. Their chain mail looked heavy and uncomfortable in the heat, but they wore it regardless. What could it mean? Hob picked up the bench, frowning at something, and then set it aright.

Another group of students, some of them the most respected of the Australes, burst through the door, singing and laughing at some trick they'd played on someone. Philip just hoped they wouldn't notice him. They called for food and ale, laughing at a ditty sung by a minstrel about a fool who thought he could control the world without work or inclination—a thinly veiled reference to the king it seemed.

"Not for long," one called out.

They sat at the table in front of him with several knights and talked loudly and eagerly of all they knew. Angry barons were banding together to draw up a new charter. One of young men joked that this time the barons took care to look to the future. "We won't be caught without a plan this time."

To Philip's horror, the words fight, battle, war, and army were mentioned in the same breath as London and the king. One lad mentioned that the Scots were involved. Those words struck new fear in Philip's heart. All he knew of the Scots was the attempt of some to gain control of Wynnewood Castle—using Lady Aurelia as leverage to do it. How could this Simon de Montfort support such an idea?

He chewed his mutton, nearly swallowed his potato without bothering to chew, and gulped his ale when pieces of meat or potato stuck in his throat. This Montfort was a cousin of the king. What would happen if this overthrow—or whatever it was—actually succeeded?

The more he heard, the more alarmed he grew. With each new fear, his caution weakened until he heard the name of one of the barons and gasped. The man closest to him turned and stared at him, but Philip managed to cover his gaffe by pretending to have a mouth full of overly hot food. His relief didn't last. The men grew quiet, serious glances tossed his way at irregular intervals.

He was afraid to leave, but staying seemed foolish. A slip through a side door wouldn't be sufficient to escape men such as these. One call to any of the knights roaming the streets would earn him a beating at the least. The words he'd heard were seditious at best.

Just as he was certain there was no hope for escape, an argument between the Australes at the next table and Hob began. Philip saw the signal to call for the constable and sighed. It would be an ugly night. The students would rally together against Hob, and the tavern keeper would try to prove whatever he thought had occurred. It would be bad for everyone in the end.

The constable arrived in record time, likely expecting some sort of altercation with the unrest in the town. Hob pointed at the broken bench and tried to insist that the students had broken it. Philip frowned. Hob knew it was damaged before they even entered the door. Why was he trying to put blame on the students that they didn't deserve?

"He can verify my words," the man cried, pointing at

Philip. "He saw it all. They broke the bench, made a mess, and refused to pay the bill. It isn't the first time they've been trouble in here."

The constable seemed to want to appease the tavern keeper. He had no jurisdiction over the students, but he asked Philip to attest to the veracity of Hob's statements. Philip felt sick.

"I think Hob is mistaken. The men who broke the bench were the knights who left before these students came in. Remember, Hob? You inspected it carefully. These knights weren't on that side of the table and those men weren't even in here."

"What about the bill?" the constable queried before Hob could protest.

"I didn't hear anything. If they refused to pay, they did it quietly."

"The boy lies to protect himself," Hob insisted. "Several from that group gave him a severe beating outside this tavern some weeks back. He probably fears worse if he speaks."

This angered Philip. Hob knew the men who had jumped him weren't there. "It is true that some of the students did attack me last month, but none of these men were involved." His face turned and met Hob's eyes squarely. "I know that Hob has endured much at the hands of some of the students, but I have never seen these men give him any trouble at all."

"He lies!" Hob cried again.

The constable pulled Philip aside. "If you speak against your fellow students, I can take it to the chancellor. The man will get justice instead of a blind eye—if he speaks truth."

"Constable, if these men were guilty of the accusations against them, I would tell you. I have been taught to speak the truth even when it is difficult, but just as I will not lie to ease my own life, neither will I lie for revenge."

A fight broke out as Hob threw insults at Philip. He had clearly expected Philip to back up his story in revenge against the other students, but Philip would have none of it. He waited until Hob's and the constable's attentions were distracted and slipped through the crowd and out the door.

The streets were crowded for a summer evening, but Philip did not mind. It would be harder to find him in such a crowd. As he reached his lodgings, unmolested, Philip sighed in relief. "Now to survive until these people leave," he whispered under his breath as he raced up the stairs two at a time.

Shovel in hand, Dove glanced at the last several feet of earth that blocked the inlet to her pool. It wouldn't take long once she started digging. A pile of smooth stones lay beside her, waiting for their place in the inlet, but she doubted many would be laid before the water broke through the weak dam of earth.

Her foot stomped on the edge and another shovelful flew in the air behind her. All caution was gone. She'd be happy with piles of dirt if it could only be done now!

The day was hot—hotter than she'd ever remembered. The cold water of the Ciele was exactly what her body craved. She was hot, sweaty, and sticky. Dirt clung to her hands, arms, and legs. Her cloak hung over a tree branch and her sleeves and breeches legs were rolled up to help her stay cool.

Always, she listened. Every twig that cracked, every bird that tittered, and every leaf that rustled in the wind sorted itself in her mind as safe or threat. She was ready to spring for covering at any moment, but she wanted nothing more than to rid herself of her shoes, gloves, and breeches in order to wade in her new pool.

The next shovelful saw a trickle push through the dirt. The crack widened until the force of the water pushed the dirt out of the way. Eagerly, as the water rushed down the inlet to the pool, she jerked her gloves from her hands, pulled her shoes from her feet, and pulled the string that held up her breeches. Her tunic nearly reached her knees, making it the perfect cover to swim in while giving her free range of movement.

It took much longer to fill the pool than she'd imagined. Stones fell out of their place in the sidewalls, but she worked hard to shove them back. It was hard work, constant movement, and as the water rose, pushing through it to the next repair became more difficult than she'd imagined.

At her knees, the water seemed perfect. It was cold, but refreshing on her hot, tired feet. Once it rose above her knees, she began to feel half-frozen. By the time it reached her waist, she walked nearly on tiptoe, trying to keep the coldness off her belly. The torture was so great that she nearly crawled from the pool several times, but pride drove her back to the center.

Dove was surprised to discover that once her stomach was fully submerged, she didn't feel nearly as cold. Her hands floated atop the water beside her and her tunic billowed under her arms. Delighted with her buoyancy, she found herself dancing in the water, her feet hardly touching bottom much of the time.

At last, the pool was full, and to stand with her head out of water, Dove had to stand near the edge of the inlet. Nightfall was coming. For a moment, Dove dreamed of floating in the water under the moonlight, but she then remembered there would be no moon that night.

Disappointed, she crawled from the water. It was harder to climb out of the pool than she'd imagined. Her muscles were weak and sore as if she'd been active for the first time in months. It made no sense! She'd been working on that pool for most of a year.

By the tree, she pulled a spare tunic from her cloak and allowed it to slip over her head. Her teeth chattered as she pulled on her breeches, cinching them at the waist, and then her gloves. Item by item she redressed and then grabbed the shovel for the last time. From now on, she would come to the pool to think, to reflect, sleep sometimes, and of course, swim.

As the sun set, plunging the forest into a much dimmer light, Dove glanced back at her handiwork. Philip would love it. She'd transplant the violas and the ferns that grew near the clearing to her new sanctuary. It would be beautiful and serene. She smiled and thought, *If I cannot find I AM here, can he even be found?*

A loud shout sounded outside. Feet pounded up the stairs and Edward burst into the room. "They have ten students—" he gasped. "There is a mob ready to lynch them."

"Why?" Adrian paused in his Socratic questioning and rose to look out the window into the street.

"Something about not paying rents and damaging property. They've sent for the Chancellor, but students are rioting and I think Aldred is among them."

The words were hardly out of Edward's mouth before Master Adrian rushed from the room, down the steps and into the street. Philip watched from the window as the man fought his way through the growing mob toward the center of town. Concerned, he turned to Edward. "Do you really think Aldred—"

"I saw him head that way with a club. He was with a

large group of the Borales..."

"Are they fighting with the town or the Australes?"

"Don't know." Edward eyed him curiously. "Aren't you even interested in what is happening?"

"Of course."

"Then why do you sit there watching from the window?"

"Why are you standing there questioning me when you could be down there with them?"

Edward shook his head. "Not me. If I get into trouble, I'll lose the patronage of Baron de Percy. My father is already in trouble with the family. It's not likely I'd get another chance."

"Well, for similar reasons, I'm not going down there. I won't risk bringing reproach on Lord Morgan's name after all he's done for me."

"From what I heard, you've done him great service though—saved his daughter twice, didn't you?"

"No. Helped twice, but just helped." For the first time, it felt good to admit that Dove had been the brave one. He'd wanted to do great things, but Philip was slowly learning that doing right things was one way of doing great ones.

"Well, that's not how the story goes around town. Saved from kidnappers and beaten in a siege because you wouldn't tell where the girl was." The admiration in Edward's voice was unmistakable.

"Well, as I said..." His father had always insisted that the only thing worse than no modesty was false modesty. Philip shrugged. "I just did what I could. Dove did more, but she needed me to help, and I couldn't have done what she did at all. We were just fortunate, I guess."

"I suppose," the young man agreed reluctantly. "Stories do get embellished, don't they? I mean, to listen to the minstrels, some strange creature saved you from a dragon by mesmerizing it with flaming eyes."

"It's a lie!"

"Well, of course it is! Dragons don't let dinner just prance out of reach!"

When he realized he was shaking, Philip forced himself to breathe steadily and calm himself. "Dove is just a little girl—or was—but she did save me from a dragon. She does not have flaming eyes, and she isn't a creature."

His attempt at calm didn't last. Before Edward could reply, Philip stormed out the door, down the hall, and into his own room, shutting it a little more forcefully than necessary. The moment he sat on his bed, remorse flooded his heart. No matter what any fool said, it wasn't right to lash out at people like that. The sound of footsteps on the stairs prompted him to look out the window, and he saw Edward burst out into the street.

He started to call out to apologize when two men grabbed the young man and dragged him out of sight. Amazed and dismayed, Philip ran downstairs to see if his fellow student needed help. There was no sign of Edward anywhere. A cry of pain seemed to come from everywhere at once, making him nervous and even more determined to do something. The riots needed to stop before other innocent people got hurt.

Sent Away

CHAPTER 15

Oeep within the forests of Wynnewood, animals hushed their nighttime chatter as shadows darted between the trees as if racing toward the village. Occasionally a twig snapped or a branch brushed against something. Crouched low, two eyes watched the cottage, but all was quiet inside. Several yards away, another pair eyes glanced across the distance and then the head nodded. The man took a deep breath and bolted across the yard, pounding on the door. "Lord Morgan demands your services immediately!" Then, without another word, the man disappeared into the trees and waited. The door opened a crack, and a woman's voice answered, but there was no reply.

Just minutes later, the door creaked slightly as the midwife crept outside into the night. Her shawl covered her head and arms. It was warm, but not oppressively so. She carried a basket and a large drawstring sack, and made her way down the road toward the village of Wynnewood.

Two pairs of eyes waited. Seconds slowly passed into minutes until an hour had passed. The second man stepped from the protection of the trees and strode toward the cottage. He opened the door quietly, just enough to let him inside the house, and then disappeared inside. The other man kept watch.

The little light that shone from the coals of the fireplace showed two pallets on each side of one end of the large room. The one nearest the front of the house was clearly empty—the blankets folded back over the end. In the other, he saw a small mound. The Ge-sceaft.

A hand clamped over her mouth as she slept. Terrified, the girl's eyes opened wide as she tried to scream, but one look into the man's eyes relaxed her. He put one finger over his lips and slowly moved his hand. "Shh."

"Jakys!" Her whisper was hardly quieter than a shout.

"Gather what things you can. You need all your clothing, both cloaks, your sling, and—"

"Why?"

"Get them. We must go. Now." The command in Jakys tone was unmistakable.

For years to come, Dove would wonder what made her follow Jayk's orders so implicitly. Not until she was outside in the moonlight did she see his knife tied to his belt and realize that had she not obeyed, he would have compelled her to go with him. She'd woken up terrified, became curious, and then grew afraid again, as he led her into the woods where Grifon stood waiting.

"Grifon!"

"Shh!"

The silence nearly stifled her as she tramped between Jakys and Grifon, ducking under low branches and stepping over fallen logs. Once again, the animals didn't move and even the usual breezes that rustled the leaves in the night air seemed still as if the world was holding its breath for a moment. However, the mists rolled in from the sea and made the journey through Wyrm Forest, across the Ciele River, and into the Sceadu almost treacherous as the moon slipped behind the clouds.

She'd grown since her last trek into the Sceadu. The

small opening from the cave into the tunnels was even harder to slip through, but Dove managed. Once inside the familiar cavern, Jakys pulled his hood off his head and took a deep breath. "We made it."

"What—"

"Waleron will explain. We must hurry."

As if reliving a dream, Dove followed the little man who had found her in the caves of the Sceadu so many months ago. He'd saved her more than once, and that knowledge was all that kept her from shaking in fear. Grifon behind her laid his hand on her shoulder when she stumbled once, and the familiar gesture made her smile inside her hood. These little people—the Mæte—there must be some reason they spirited her away in the middle of the night.

Merewyn sat embroidering outside her grandfather's chambers. Much braver now that Dove had risked so much to help her mother, the king's granddaughter threw her arms around Dove. "I've been waiting ever since I heard they went to fetch you. Modor is so much better now. You probably saved her life." The young woman ducked her head before whispering, "I had to thank you."

"Send Dove in. We have no time for tears and hugs. This is important."

Grifon pulled aside the tapestry that functioned as a door to the king's quarters, and Dove saw that the room nearly glowed with light. Every lamp was lit and the little fire pit in the center of the room sent dancing shadows all around her. "You needed me Waleron?"

"I've received word about young Philip."

"Oh, that's not possible, your—Waleron. He's not here. He's at Oxford."

"Yes, I know. There were riots there some weeks back."

"How did—"

"We have our ways!" The king's voice thundered,

reverberating through the room. "Be quiet, girl, and listen to me." Then, as if an afterthought, he pointed to her. "And take off that hood. Show respect."

Miserably, Dove lowered her hood feeling quite vulnerable. "I'm sorry. I forget..."

"I was sharp. I'm sorry. The news was so distressing. Now listen to me. You have to get to Oxford. A ransom note is on its way to Lord Morgan, but it might not arrive in time. I have a map of where the boy is being held. If you're fast enough, you can help him escape."

"Held? Ransom? Philip? That doesn't make sense. Philip is just a seaman's son. His family has no money. Why—"

"Because he's under the patronage of Charles Morgan, the Earl of Wynnewood. There are unscrupulous people in this world who will do anything for a little silver."

"But how can *I* help him? Once Lord Morgan gets a ransom note, he'll send payment to redeem Philip and it'll be over. Why—"

"You're so naïve for such a bright little one. If the lord does pay the ransom, it'll never make it back to Oxford. The kind of men who do this will not go back and share with their comrades. They'll disappear with the money."

"Surely Lord Morgan knows this. He'll go deliver the money himself."

"If he gets the note in time. Criminals are desperate. We've seen this happen many times and rarely does it come out well."

Dove's eyes narrowed suspiciously. "How did you hear of this? How do you know this is true?"

"We have our ways."

"Waleron..." Jakys voice held a warning tone.

"We cannot divulge all of our secrets—"

"After all this girl and her friend have done for us, after they kept our secrets, we have no right—"

With eyes darting back and forth between the men, Dove waited anxiously. The men argued, sometimes in their own language. It was hard to pay attention when her own mind whirled with questions and plans. What if she could get to the south in time? Could she possibly help Philip escape? Perhaps the people of Oxford wouldn't fear her like those in Wynnewood. Would that help her or hinder her? It was warm; people would not expect a cloak without cooler temperatures.

"All right. You tell her, but she must leave tonight. Immediately. She must travel by night and sleep hidden in the day."

For a moment, Dove started to protest. Traveling in the dark was dangerous. Wild animals might find her and sleeping during the day meant she could be seen. However, before she could speak, the wisdom of Waleron's words hit her. During the day, someone might see her. She must hide herself well if she slept, but in no way could she risk meeting anyone at any time. In Wynnewood, though the villagers feared her and tried to drive her away at times, she did enjoy a measure of protection from Bertha, the minister, and Lord Morgan. Once away from there, she'd be alone and vulnerable.

"What can I take? How much can I carry? How—"

"We'll provide you with money and food. Minna will pack it and show you how to tie it onto your back."

"You didn't tell me how—"

Dove listened in amazement as Waleron described the tunnels and caverns that traversed across the whole of England, Scotland, and Wales. By his account, the world she knew hovered over another one, entirely underground. He told of messengers that raced between communities, sharing news, and sending warnings.

"Rabbit holes and fox dens are not always what they seem, Dove. Sometimes, often times, they are vents to allow an exchange of our smoky air for fresh air."

"But you don't use fires that often—not here. I noticed that the dragon—"

"Yes, most of our communities are close to a dragon. Their heat is most beneficial to us, and they are great protection."

"Will I be traveling in the tunnels then?"

Waleron's head shook and his eyes looked sorrowful. "We would gladly offer the use of them, but we cannot." He gestured to Jakys, some sort command that she couldn't understand, and then reached for her cloak hood. Pulling it over her head, Waleron hugged her briefly. "Save our young friend. You can do this. We know this. Call on your friend's god. Call on any god, but save the life of the lad that has done so much for us. We cannot help him, but you can."

Without another word, Waleron nudged her through the doorway and closed the tapestry behind her. She listened from the anteroom as Jakys and the king of the Mæte discussed something of great import, her own questions growing in her mind. The moment Jakys stepped from the chamber she fired them at him in rapid succession.

"Why is Philip's life in danger? Lord Morgan can travel much faster than I can. He'll ride horses— and what if Bertha refused to let me go? I—"

"Come with me." Jakys led her through the tunnels to the common room. No one was there, not even faithful Baldric, but seconds after they arrived, Minna came in, arms laden, and began assembling her pack.

"Jakys—"

"Listen; you can't go back to the village. You must leave tonight. Philip was taken about a week ago. If you walk fast, you can make it in less than a fortnight, but you must hurry. Our runners can get here faster because of the tunnels. Most of the messengers ran to get this news to the next post, so we have it faster. Any day now, the news should arrive at Wynnewood Castle. You need to be gone before they get it. You can get in there where Lord Morgan cannot."

"But—"

"These men will become more afraid every day. Every minute that they have him will make them more paranoid. He's dispensable. If he was an heir or a relative, he'd have a chance. Criminals would fear the repercussions of killing a nobleman's kinsman, but the son of a seaman?"

Before Dove could counter with another question, Jakys pulled out the map. "Here is where he's being held—for now. They could move him, of course, but this is what we learned."

"Why would your friends tell you about Philip?"

"If we heard of something happening to a man from Oxford, we'd get word to our Oxford friends. It's a courtesy." Jakys voice grew impatient. "Now listen. This is important."

For the next several minutes, Jakys explained how to get to Oxford. She was to follow the sea to Liverpool and then follow the River Mersey, walk south to the Thames, and over to Oxford.

Dove bit her lip as she thought about the trip she must make. Would it work? Would she get there in time? What if she failed? What if— Disgusted with herself, she shook off the doubts that plagued her and focused on how Philip had gone out in the deep snow, freezing, to search for her and didn't give up despite the unlikelihood that he'd find her

"I must leave."

"Minna will show you how to tie on your pack. There are coins in there—enough silver to pay for any food you must take."

"Take?"

"You won't be able to carry enough food with you.

You'll have some, but don't use it until you think it'll go bad. Then replace it. Keep some food at all times in case you're trapped somewhere. Find food in gardens, empty houses, eggs from chickens, whatever you must."

"Steal." Dove didn't like the sound of that. Immediately, her mind went to the story Philip had told her of the rich man who stole the poor man's only lamb.

"It is not stealing if you leave money behind."

"Will I have enough?"

Jakys laughed. "You'll have plenty." With a wink to Baldric, he added, "And we'll expect Lord Morgan to replace them. We've given you quite a store of pennies."

"Jakys, you can't delay any longer. She needs to leave now. She won't be able to travel for more than a few hours as it is."

The dread in Baldric's voice told her that he knew the trip was dangerous. One glance at Jakys confirmed that he'd already stalled too long. "Baldric is right. I should go. Thank you—" she choked, trying not to cry, "for helping us. I'll do my best."

Dove thanked Minna and then turned to leave. Through the caverns, she followed Griffon, climbing slowly as they neared the opening in the cliffs. Once outside, Grifon patted her arm awkwardly. "Follow the Ciele to the sea and then to Liverpool. Be careful, Dove. Be very careful."

With that, the little man disappeared into the rocks and left Dove all alone in the night. She took a deep breath, glanced heavenward, and tried to will that the clouds would roll away from the moon, but to no avail. Determined to get as far as humanly possible before sunrise, Dove hurried through the forest, forcing herself not to run in the smoother places. She reached the Nicor Cliffs in record time. With one backward glance at the dark village behind her, Dove began the long journey, approximately four hundred miles, to Oxford.

Hidden & Alone

CHAPTR 16

Philip fought against the crowds as he tried to find Edward. Fear shot through his veins and muscles as he realized the danger in trying to take on four men alone, but what could he do? If he took the time to call for help, they'd be gone. At the least, he could see where they took the young man and then lead the constable there. Yes, that was what he'd do. He was too old to expect to fight off so many. *Maybe I'm not such the child after all*, he mused to himself as he darted down another alley. *I am learning my limitations.*

No sooner had that thought appeared, than a hand clamped over his mouth. "Got 'im," a gruff voice shouted. The triumph in that voice made Philip ill with fear.

Edward tried to help, but one of the men had slugged him, sending the young scholar spinning into the corner of a building. As they dragged Philip away, he saw Edward lying on the ground, unconscious. Bile rose in his throat as he remembered the menacing looks on the men's faces. The first punch slammed into his nose almost the minute they arrived at the cottage. "That will teach the fool."

"Let's just get this job done and get out of here," another man complained.

"We were hired to teach him a lesson before we disposed of him."

Philip's stomach churned. "I don't know why I'm here," he stammered, his mind racing in many directions, "but I—" A kick to the gut cut him off short. The moment he could breathe, Philip said, "I have money. Quite a lot of it. You can have it if you let me go."

One of the men allowed Philip's money pouch to swing from one of his fingers. "This money?"

He swallowed hard and nodded. "There is more. I don't keep it all together."

"Hey Gipp, did you find more?"

The suspicious tone in the man's voice heartened Philip. If they began squabbling amongst themselves, maybe they'd forget about him long enough to leave. The man, Gipp, shook his head. "I didn't expect him to be quite that resourceful. Send James back. Tear the place apart if you have to."

"You don't have to tear it apart. I'll—"

Another blow felt like an explosion inside his head. Philip stumbled and then crumpled to the ground. Panic rose up within him. "I—" He didn't want to say it. The one thing that might save him galled him to speak. However, as another of the men advanced, the muscles in his forearms twitching, Philip's reticence vanished. "I enjoy the benevolence of Lord Charles Morgan, Earl of Wynnewood. He will pay a ransom for my safe return."

"I doubt he'll consider you worth anything by the time we're done with you," one of the men growled as he unsheathed a knife.

"I—" Terror filled Philip's heart. They'd torture him before he died. Why, he didn't know, but they would. "There is no reason not to get the most money you can for me, is there? Lord Morgan will pay. He owes his daughter's life to me. Have you not heard the stories?" The words burst forth from him in a desperate jumble.

The tip of the knife pierced Philip's chin as the man spoke to him, threatening him with malevolent glee. "But that's all they are, aren't they? Stories."

"Why else would a man like him send someone like me to the University?"

Gipp frowned. "Back down, David. He has a point. We can have him write a note and I'll take it up north. We can just as easily kill him after a ransom has been paid as before."

"With the kind of money a ransom would give, why kill him at all? Take the money and leave. Who cares about teaching the other students a lesson? They can rob the tradesmen all they like. We take the money and run."

Philip had a strong preference for the fourth man's suggestion but thought it best to keep his opinion to himself. His heart sank further as Gipp said, "Hob won't like it. He wants this fellow's carcass strung up outside the lodging house."

"Who cares what Hob wants?"

I certainly don't, Philip thought to himself. *So, Hob did this. Why?* He couldn't risk asking, but he did hope they'd keep talking.

"Do you want the students to get away with breaking property and not paying the bills? Those men think they're above the law."

"This is about that bench? He wants me killed because I wouldn't lie and say students broke a bench that knights broke? Killed?"

Philip's question earned him another kick and a box to his ear. Gipp stared at him as he tried to shake the darkness that threatened to overtake him. "What knights? He said you lied to protect fellow students."

"Why should I protect the people who torment me every day?" Philip couldn't understand Hob's reasoning. "Hob always seemed friendly toward me. I can't believe he would hire my death!"

Gipp laughed, the other men snickering as well. "You can't believe that Mad Hob wants any student dead? Are you really that much of a fool?"

"Mad Hob?"

The one they called David nodded. "He's a strange one. Always making a pet of someone until they cross him. Many of his 'friends' go missing either by escape or worse. Who knows which?"

"Stop the chattering and let's decide. Do we kill him, hang him at the lodging house and get to Portsmouth, or do we hide him until we can extract a ransom?"

Gipp's voice turned greedy as he offered the option of the ransom. All Philip could do was pray that they took it. The men squabbled amongst themselves for several minutes as Philip faded in and out of consciousness, but at last, David hurried from the cottage in search of paper, quill, and ink.

Cold and angry, Bertha allowed the cottage door to slam shut as she hurried indoors just before daybreak. Of all the foolish, inconsiderate things for someone to do, calling her out unneeded in the middle of the night was just about the worst. Her eyes glanced at Dove's pallet out of habit, and then she shivered out of her clothes and into dry ones. The cottage felt cooler than usual, so Bertha added a couple of logs to the fire and laid her skirt out to dry.

Once under the covers, the woman lay as still as she could, waiting for warmth to radiate around her. The glow of the blaze sent odd shadows across the walls. Bertha hated those shadows. Her old pagan superstitions sometimes overrode her good judgment—particularly when suffering from prankster-induced sleep deprivation.

She frowned. The covers on Dove's pallet didn't seem to resemble any human shape she'd ever seen. Was the child growing humpbacked too? Another malady was the last thing she wanted to endure. Curious, she grabbed her shawl from the peg near her bed and wrapped it around her shoulders as she crept to Dove's bed to see why the child looked so oddly shaped.

The empty bed infuriated her. She jerked the covers back to air out the linens and huffed her way back to her own bed. Where had the chit gone this time and at this hour of the night? They'd caught the ridiculous unicorn. The mists were too thick now to see the dragon, and it was much too dark to enjoy a leisurely stroll through the trees. She seemed to have gotten over her need for solitude. She'd slept at home every night for weeks.

If the boy had been home, Bertha would have assumed some strange new adventure. Philip Ward seemed to thrive on excitement. At fifteen—or was he sixteen now?—it was time to settle down and become a responsible man, but he'd still rambled through the woods playing her silly little games as if he had a lifetime to show some semblance of maturity.

It had occurred to Bertha that this friendship might be the best thing for her. Young boys grew into young men and those men eventually married. With a little careful manipulation, she could easily make him think it was his duty to marry the girl and protect her from the villagers.

She drifted to sleep with those thoughts in her mind, and was still dreaming of a life alone when the fire grew brighter and warmer, waking her up. "Letty?"

"I'm just getting started. Were you out late last night? Was it Phoebe?"

"Pranksters." She glanced at the empty bed across the room. "Was the girl gone when you got here?"

Letty's eyes slid toward where Dove usually slept. By the confusion on the young woman's face, Bertha knew that Letty hadn't noticed anyone missing at all. Shaking her head, Letty stepped closer. "She's gone and so is her blanket." The girl's forehead furrowed. "I was sure she had two pairs of breeches and tunics hanging on those pegs—winter cloak is gone too."

Bertha had intended to roll over and go back to sleep, but Letty's observations were astounding on two levels. First, she'd noticed something missing, and then the fact that anything was missing at all was quite unusual. After a quick glance over the cottage, Bertha found several things that were gone.

"Her sling shot is gone too. Maybe she's hunting, but the extra clothes don't make sense. It's still quite warm yet."

"You'll have to ask her when she comes back." Letty stared at the sack of oats. "Do I make enough porridge for her or not?"

"No. It'll just go to waste."

As Letty went to carry out the slop bucket, she froze. "It's almost empty."

"She probably emptied it before she left."

Bertha's surly tone worked. Letty quit asking questions and making suggestions and went back to work. All seemed to go back to normal until she tried to cut the bread. "Um, Bertha?"

The midwife, almost back to sleep now, nearly screamed with frustration. "What is it now?"

"The knife is gone."

Three days later, Bertha trudged up the hill to the castle. As much as she hated to do it, a messenger had arrived saying that Aurelia wanted Dove's company, and the woman felt obligated to explain the girl's absence. She ignored the grumbles of the guard, strolled through the walled corridor around the perimeter of the castle, and knocked on the kitchen door.

Tobias Baker flung open the door, ready to send Dove away from his kitchens, and started at the sight of Bertha there. "Is someone sick?"

"I don't know, Tobias, have you been making sour bread again?"

"Ha, ha. You're such a wit. What do you need?" He shooed her inside and shut the door.

"To stand by your oven for a minute. It's unseasonably cold out there this morning. Someone can go tell Lord Morgan that I have news for him."

"Listen to you all high and mighty. Don't request, just let him know that you deign to speak to him."

"He'll want me to talk to him. Tell him I have news of Dove."

The baker's eyes flew to little Minerva who scrubbed pots in the corner. The child dried her hands and slipped out the door, nearly unnoticed. Bertha nodded appreciatively. "You have fine help here, Tobias. If that girl was a little older, I might have tried to steal her from you."

The repartee between baker and midwife continued until Minerva returned and beckoned for Bertha to follow. "Lord Morgan is anxious to see you."

Just as they reached the great hall, Minerva curtseyed. "You're to go in and wait. He'll be there in a moment. I think he's received some distressing news."

Before Bertha could reach the large fireplace, Lord Morgan strode into the room, fire in his eyes and his face resolute. "Bertha Newcombe. I was hoping you had Dove with you."

"That's why I came. The messenger said Lady Aurelia wanted her, but the girl is gone."

"Gone?"

"Three nights ago, someone pounded on my door and

said I was wanted here at the castle. When I returned, Dove and most of her things were gone." At the alarm on Charles Morgan's face, Bertha had the grace to temper her words slightly. "She hasn't yet returned, m'lord."

The Earl of Wynnewood's face went pale. He sat down suddenly and called for some wine. "Some for the woman too, John."

Lord Morgan's personal servant, John, brought two goblets of wine and passed one to each of them. "Anything else m'lord?"

"Would you like some cheese and bread, Bertha?"

"I'm not hungry, but thank you." She was growing impatient and knew it probably showed in her tone.

"This is quite distressing, Bertha. I just received news about Philip Ward."

"I thought he was at Oxford, sir."

"He is—or was. I've just received a ransom note."

Her shock was too great to hide. Why would anyone kidnap the son of no one? "And the note came to you and not his father?"

"Clearly, they assume that if I'll educate the boy, I'll pay for his release as well."

"And will you?" Bertha asked curiously. Immediately she realized how inappropriate her question was. "I'm sorry. I'm a little stunned."

"It's no matter. Of course, I'll pay the ransom if I must, but I'll have to travel south immediately."

An idea, one so fantastical that Bertha nearly pushed it out of her mind as quickly as it came, grew as Lord Morgan spoke. "Is it possible that Dove somehow heard of this scheme and tried to go south to help him?"

"I'd believe she would do it, but I don't believe it's possible that she heard anything. The man came alone. He wouldn't have anyone to talk to, so how could she overhear?"

"Then she has disappeared too. The first time she

was gone for days, I knew she went out in a storm. I wasn't concerned for her. She was likely dead." Bertha saw the lord's eyes narrow at her coldness, but she continued. "Then when the boy left, she disappeared for months without showing herself at home. This time is different. She disappeared without reason, into the night, and with her spare clothes, her slingshot, and my knife. She was probably going hunting. I fear she could be hurt."

"Why are you concerned with the possibility of injury but you weren't concerned with the likelihood of death?"

"Lord Morgan, my duty is in preserving life. If she's hurt, it's my duty to try to help her. Once she was dead, and who expected her to live through such a blizzard?— my responsibility toward her had ended."

As she spoke, Lord Morgan nodded. "I see." He rubbed the beard thoughtfully. "I'll send out what knights I don't need to ride with me. We were planning a trip to the south anyway—Kent—away from the snow that will be here all too soon..."

Though he didn't say it, Bertha knew exactly what he planned for that trip. It was time for the Earl of Wynnewood to take a wife—produce a viable heir. Aurelia couldn't possibly manage the title with her affliction even if she did live long enough.

The woman nodded and stood to leave. "I suppose it is a good thing that the girl is gone. If she knew Philip was in trouble, she'd go down there herself, but as you said, she couldn't possibly have known that—not three days before you learned it." At the door, she remembered her earlier thoughts of Philip and Dove and turned back once more. "M'lord, please bring him home. He's good for her."

"I think Philip would say that Dove is good for him."

Lonely Trek

CHAPTR 17

Finding a safe place to sleep unnoticed was more difficult than Dove had imagined. Each night when the sun went down and the world slowly grew cooler, she rose, rolled her pack into her blanket and cloaks, strapped it on, and continued her journey south. Finding her way to Liverpool was as simple as walking along the edge of the sea, but from there, things would be harder. She'd have to follow the river as much as possible, but people lived near rivers for a reason and she had to find a way to avoid people.

Twice she'd found caves to sleep in, but one had the unmistakable stench of dragon around it, and Dove was too sensible to risk her life for a dry bed. As she walked, often using the stout stick she'd found to help pull her over a rough patch, she wondered about Bertha and Lord Morgan. Had a ransom note arrived? And of course, she worried about Philip. Her scruples about praying for Philip were gone. After months of feeling awkward about praying to a god she didn't know if she believed existed, Dove had decided it couldn't hurt. If I AM was the god that Philip claimed he was, then he'd understand her concern. If he wasn't, well, Dove didn't really care what he thought of her prayers. Furthermore, if he didn't exist, her concerns were wasted anyway.

The one thing she prayed for most was that they

wouldn't move Philip. If he wasn't where she expected to find him, she didn't know what she'd do. If he was, she had several plans in mind.

Her favorite idea was simply to watch to see how many there were, wait for them to leave, and help Philip escape—simple but effective. Her second plan was to lure them out in some way. She thought of fire, cries of knights, anything, but all ideas along that vein were risky. There was one idea—almost foolproof—that she knew she'd do if she must, but Dove dreaded it.

As she trudged over the rocky terrain, listening to the waves crash against the rocks below, Dove shivered. It would save Philip; she knew it. It would also be the likely death of their friendship. If the men were ready with arrows, it could cost her her life, but Dove didn't think that was likely. Anyone they expected, they'd meet with knives or swords. That was something else to pray about, but then, if she did, she'd be praying for herself. That felt uncomfortable.

Occasionally, she heard wolves howl as they hunted in the night. Lord Morgan had been vigilant in his attempts to eradicate the vermin from his lands, but the further she got from Wynnewood, the more she saw and heard evidence of them. There were rocks in all of her inner pockets and she kept her sling handy as she tramped over the ground on her way to Liverpool.

The pennies that the Mæte provided were heavy, but because there were so many, it was easy to leave one at every place she took food. People would have balked at the "prices" she paid—three eggs for a penny—but Dove had no way to barter or carry more. Each meal was a penny and that was just how it would have to be.

One afternoon, the scent of baking bread nearly drove her crazy. She hid behind a tree, wondering if there was enough bread to take a little and not leave a family without their dinner. The problem was how to get the house emptied long enough to dash inside and take a piece. She pulled one of the pennies from her pocket. She kept some in her shoes, some in her pack, and a few in her pockets. Dove was determined not to risk losing them. Forcing someone to "sell" their food bothered her greatly. Stealing would almost kill her.

At last, she devised a plan. Ready to run away from her hiding place, she screamed as loudly as she could and then ran. A woman and a little boy dashed from the cottage, the woman dragging him straight toward where Dove had been standing. They crashed through the bushes, while she crept into the house, glancing around the room for supplies. A large bag of flour still sat on the table and three loaves were cooling. She wrapped one in her gray cloak, and laid the penny down. Feeling terribly guilty, although it was an enormous price, she put a second penny next to it and hurried out the door.

When she'd taken her second step from the door, the woman rounded the corner of her house and screamed at the sight of a stranger leaving her cottage. "What are you doing?"

Dove ran. Her feet flew across the ground as if blown by the wind. She glanced behind her and saw the woman pursuing her, swifter than she would have expected. "I'm sorry!" she called back and then darted into the trees, weaving back and forth until she no longer heard the crash of feet behind her.

Her hood hung down her back, but her feet still propelled her away from the cottage, but now in a straight path toward the sea. The timberline separating the forests from the sea loomed ahead of her, and she collapsed at the base of a tree, gasping for air. The view across the sward to the cliffs looked just like the one near the point at the Nicor Cliffs.

Habit forced her to pull her hood back over her head, and then her hands enjoyed the warmth of the bread through her cloak. "I AM? If Philip wasn't in danger, if Jakys and Waleron weren't certain I could help him, this wouldn't be worth it. I'm used to people looking at me in fear or suspicion. I'm not used to people seeing me as a thief." She hung her head, the scent of the bread taunting her. "There was more, and they had enough for another meal later. I did *pay* for it."

Talking to Philip's god had become quite a habit with her. There was comfort in having *someone* listening, even if that someone was just imaginary. As much as she was inclined to believe that, Dove couldn't help but suspect that maybe Philip, Lord Morgan, and their minister were all correct. Philip's logical arguments made as much sense to her as the stories did.

Her gloved hand picked up a pinecone and turned it over with her fingers. *Everything was made and is still made after its kind.* Philip's voice echoed in her memory. If that book that Broðor Clarke read from when he taught the boys really said that, and it really was written so many thousands of years ago, then at least that much was true. People gave birth to people. Chickens laid eggs that hatched chickens. Sheep did not give birth to cows or vice versa. These things were simple common sense, but some of Bertha's stories told of great sea monsters giving birth to grown men and vomiting them onto the shore to conquer rebellious lands.

That thought made her pause. It was almost like Philip's story of the prophet who didn't want to go to that evil place—Jonah—it was like Jonah. The people were evil, and Philip's god decided to destroy the whole city, but Jonah didn't want to go. She remembered the disgust she'd felt when the man tried to run away from I AM. That was just ridiculous. Any god who could destroy an entire city like that would be able to stop one little man from hiding. But the stories were so similar. She wondered if maybe Broðor Clarke was retelling the old tales with I AM as the great god rather than the sea gods or one of Bertha's other gods.

Disappointment washed over her. It was the first time that Dove truly felt she wanted to believe in Philip's god. Perhaps it was the other way around. If the stories in Broðor Clarke's Bible were so very old, maybe they had just been retold for so long that they weren't quite the same anymore. People valued a tale that twisted and changed over time. If a minister wasn't as diligent as Broðor Clarke and didn't ensure that his people always recount the tales exactly as he told them...

Her stomach growled. Putting aside all thoughts of stories and the gods, Dove unwrapped the loaf from her winter cloak and tore a piece from it. The inside was still warm and soft. The woman was a good baker. She knew how to make a loaf of bread. According to Bertha, some of the villagers' wives were terrible bakers. In some homes, Bertha refused to eat the bread because she knew she couldn't digest it.

Thoughts of Bertha brought back dreams of home, and the similarity of the place she was in caused her to pull back her hood to expose a little of her face. The weight of the responsibility on Dove's shoulders grew heavier as she sat munching her bread and allowing the evening sun to shine on her. With the salty air, the scent of damp pine, and the mists that rolled in from the sea, she could almost imagine that she was home again.

After a hearty meal of bread and a little cheese leftover from the previous day's "purchase," Dove pulled a few pieces of bread from the loaf, stuffed them in her pockets, and then put the rest in her pack. She strapped the pack back on her back, grabbed the walking stick, and began her nightly tramp through the woods, along the sea, and possibly into Liverpool.

She didn't know how far it was to her first destination, but Jakys had suggested it might take a full week to get there. Of course, walking along the sea that far made her journey longer, but she was strong, a fast walker, and had the stamina that a journey such as this required. Tomorrow would be seven days. Seven long, exhausting days—would it all be for nothing? Would Lord Morgan hear of it and ride his horse as swiftly as possible to Philip's rescue? Would he send a knight?

It was hard to imagine that such a generous man would not, but what if he was waylaid on the trip? What if this was all some kind of trick to call Lord Morgan from Wynnewood so that he might be kidnapped himself? That thought sent chills through her as Dove paused to consider. For a moment, she was so certain that her fears were accurate that she nearly turned back. Memories of his well-trained knights reassured her. Lord Morgan was safe as long as he took his knights, and of course, he would do that.

Her hand felt for the map in her deepest pocket. Jakys wouldn't have given her a map to Philip's location had he not been kidnapped. Doubts began to gnaw at her again as she started walking. If the Mæte wanted something, something that Dove would find objectionable, they could have lied— no. Waleron's concern, the look in Jakys eyes as he told her to be careful and to rescue Philip—it was all genuine.

Dove stumbled, her hands flying out to catch her as she fell, but they hit nothing. Her chest slammed into the ground, knocking the wind from her. She struggled to regain normal breathing as she crawled backwards from the edge of a cliff. She had to be more careful. Her hands felt around for her walking stick, but even as she groped, she realized that it was gone. She must find another one, but Dove didn't think she'd find one as good.

The darkness, the thickness of the mists, and no stick to feel her way in the night brought a new level of fear to Dove's heart. She'd been afraid of the dragon, afraid for Philip, and even afraid of harm at the hands of the villagers, but never had she been afraid of being alone. She was now. Terror slammed into her chest and with it, took her breath away once more. She gasped for air, crying, wailing, begging I AM for help without realizing she'd done so.

All alone along England's rocky coast, covered in a thick blanket of fog, Dove curled into a ball, whimpered for help, and then sobbed out her fears until she fell fast asleep.

Discouraged

CHAPTER 18

Broðor Clarke sat across from Lord Morgan in silent prayer as the two men waited for preparations for the journey south to be completed. As much as the idea of setting off for Oxford immediately was appealing to both men, they each knew that such foolishness was an excellent way to ruin animals and a poor way to treat faithful servants and knights.

Aurelia was beside herself with worry for her friends, causing Lord Morgan to regret telling her of the situations. It had seemed best to let her know how she could pray and why Dove wouldn't arrive as bidden. Yes, logic sometimes seemed the best course, but at others, especially when dealing with his daughter, Lord Morgan found that remembering the effect on emotions was vital. As it was, the girl slept under the influence of a few herbs that Malcolm Biggs had administered to calm the girl's hysterics.

Those hysterics were eating at Charles Morgann's conscience. His daughter wasn't prone to excess in any area of her life. Oh yes, at times she felt the limitations of her infirmity keenly, but she rarely complained and never flew into fits of self-pity or despair.

"I do believe I envy you, Lord Morgan."

"For?"

"I feel the overwhelming desire to follow you to

Oxford. The closer it comes to time for you to go, the deeper my unease grows. He's intelligent, brave, and I know he's now a man, but he seems such a boy to me."

"You could come, Dennis. I know—"

"That someone should be here to help if Dove needs anything. I'm the only person the villagers might possibly listen to aside from you. I can't leave here until I know she's safe or..." He didn't seem to want to finish his thought.

Since the subject had been broached, Lord Morgan asked the question that both of them had avoided. "What do you think are the chances that she will return home safe?"

"It's been a week. Good weather, no reason for her to be gone... I just—"

The Earl of Wynnewood drained the last of the ale from his tankard. "That's what I thought. This is going to break Aurelia's heart. I don't know how to tell her."

"Maybe..." Dennis Clarke's voice dropped into the low, earnest, gentle tones he used when encouraging his congregation to put their whole faith in the one true God—I AM. "Time will tell her what would be hard to hear spoken."

A sound in the corridor outside the great hall brought Lord Morgan to his feet. "They are ready. Pray, Broðor Clarke. I beg of you to pray."

"I will, but your prayers are just as effectual, Lord Morgan. Mine are no more special than yours. You pray too."

The eyes of the two men met from across the room. Neither held much hope for Dove, but for Philip... "We'll do everything in our power. You'll tell his mother?"

"If necessary, I will. I'll wait three weeks, and if there's no news..."

Broðor Clarke heard whispers of Philip's abduction three days later. Though he'd hoped to wait until he had news of the young man's release, he knew it was his duty to tell Magge Ward of her son's troubles. With a heavy heart, he strolled through the village and down toward the fisherman's cottages along the shore. Children played in the streets, chasing each other with happy squeals in the afternoon glow.

One look in the dear minister's eyes, and Philip's mother knew that the rumors she'd heard were true. Her lips trembled, her hands shook, and tears filled her eyes. "It's true?"

"I'm sorry, Magge. I was waiting for word that they'd found him before I came. I didn't expect that people would find out so quickly."

"He's just a seaman's son. Why—"

"He's a seaman's son under the patronage of the Earl of Wynnewood. Someone saw him as worth the risk."

She stepped backward, beckoning Broðor Clark into the house. "Come sit. I just made cakes. Una brought me a basket—" Her head ducked. "She does that sometimes. I think she feels the loss of Philip."

"Has Tom found another apprentice yet?"

Magge was known for her discretion, and she didn't fail even when provoked with a reminder of how Tom Fletcher had failed her son. He hadn't filled the terms of the contract, and had they been so inclined, the Wards could have brought Tom Fletcher before Lord Morgan for breach of contract. John had been ready, but Philip had protested.

"I think Tom has decided to put off apprentices for a while."

"Well spoken, Magge. I will say," Broðor Clarke

added, "I appreciate that Una and Tom haven't forgotten you; it's the least that they could do, considering..."

Magge handed Broðor Clarke a small tankard of ale and a little cake. "Can I ask—" She swallowed. "I—I overheard some men talking down by the shore. They said that finding Philip alive..."

"Don't borrow trouble, Magge. After all, the point is to get money. If they want the money, they'll have to produce him. Lord Morgan will do everything he can."

"But if they're afraid of getting caught—they'd be hanged. What if—"

"And that is where prayer comforts us. No one loves Philip more than our Lord."

The distraught woman wiped her eyes on her sleeve. "That is exactly what terrifies me. The Lord loved Ellie so much that He took her from us... I can't lose Philip too." Grabbing little Adam as he dashed past, the woman buried her face in the little boy's hair. "Adam and Will would be all I have left—unless Will has children, I suppose."

Though he tried, Broðor Clarke saw that he couldn't comfort Magge Ward, so he prayed with her and after a romp with Adam, left the cottage, shutting the door behind him. Dejection threatened, but years of practice in turning over his cares to the Lord came to his rescue. He wandered up the road that left Wynnewood and headed for Bertha's cottage. Perhaps the woman had news of Dove. Even if she didn't, sparring with the midwife always brightened a gray day.

Letty was scrubbing and hanging clothes and linens when he arrived. He grabbed one side of the sheet and helped the girl twist the water from the fabric, laughing as she told about a dog that had been chased from the yard by a vulture. "I would have loved to see that."

The girl's face drooped. "So would Dove." With a quaver in her voice, Letty asked, "Why haven't they found

her? What could have happened? Do you think the M—"
Her mouth clamped shut.

"I think that Dove had good reason to do whatever made her leave. What I don't know is why she hasn't returned."

"It's been so long..."

He nodded. As much as Broðor Clarke wanted to assure Letty that Dove was likely alive and doing well, he couldn't lie. It had been over a week since the child vanished from Wynnewood—almost as if the mists had rolled in and swept her away again. "And yet, I continue to hope."

"It'll be terrible for Philip when he returns. He lost Ellie. To lose another—almost like a sister—would be hard for anyone, but it is almost like Philip discovered her."

"Because Bertha just happened to wake up and find her living in the cottage one morning—is that it?" The midwife's voice interrupted them.

"Good evening, Bertha. Any births to announce?" Broðor Clarke couldn't help the twitch around the corner of his lips.

"Not today. I'm afraid you won't be able to perform any magic spells on any babies this week."

"No spells, Bertha Newcombe. We certainly wouldn't want that. Just the nice cleansing that comes with the Lord's baptism."

"Foist it on an unsuspecting child, don't you? Load them up with all your rites and rituals when they can't protest and then spend their childhoods telling them how they are trapped by those things. It's shameful!"

"It is beautiful to see parents raising up children in the nurture and admonition of the Lord," Broðor Clarke countered.

Letty watched, fascinated as the two adults bantered in the old familiar way. She knew instinctively that Dove would be amused at the way the faithful minister returned barb for barb, and yet he was gentle and kindly about it. Only Broðor Clarke could intimate that you were a fool, damned without the salvation of the Lord, and make it sound like a compliment.

"At least I have the wits to only believe that which I see."

"While I," the minister added, hardly bothering to stifle his chuckle, "choose to believe and worship the One who created that which you see." Before she could counter he added, "So, as you see, we are not so very different at the core. We both respect intelligent creation and beauty in the world. I simply give credit where it is due. Who would ever praise a garment for its existence when the tailor is nearby?"

"Because a seamstress could not be responsible for something worthy of praise, I assume?" Bertha's scorn seemed almost palpable.

"Ok, I can concede that. Who would ever praise a garment for its existence when the *seamstress* is nearby?"

"So you admit your god could be feminine?"

"Not unless fathers and sons are now women. Our Lord does call Himself the Son, and refers to His Father. He did not tell us to pray, 'Our Mother who art in heaven.'"

"Just like a man too, isn't it? Take credit for everything. Did not your Jesus have a mother? It seems I've heard the boy tell stories of her."

"That He did, but—"

"But I suppose she is of little consequence." Bertha's hands were now on her hips, eyes flashing.

Broðor Clarke winked at Letty and shook his head. "The scriptures say that she found favor with the Lord. I would say that means she was of great consequence. What Father would choose just any woman to be the mother of the greatest man who ever lived—of God in the flesh among us?"

To their surprise, Bertha whirled and stormed into the cottage, slamming the door behind her. Letty's eyes sought those of the stunned man with her and shook her head. "She hates men so much. I don't understand it. I guess that is why she hasn't married."

"I think it is likely that she has known only unkindness from men. That would make it hard for any person to trust a Heavenly Father. We will keep praying for her; won't we, Letty?"

They finished the laundry in silence. Letty had dozens of questions she wanted to ask the minister, but the sad look on the man's face made it impossible to try. Though he tried to focus on his task, Broðor Clarke found his prayers shifting from a little cloaked girl to a strong, stout, middle-aged woman.

To the surprise of both man and girl, just a short while later, Bertha's voice called out the front door, "The stew is getting cold. You both better come eat it before it's inedible."

Outlaws

CHAPTER 19

Fatigue had become Dove's constant companion. Ever since she'd crept around the outskirts of Liverpool and headed across the fields and along the Mersey River, she'd known that her stride was shorter, and she was taking much longer to travel. Though she knew it was illogical, Dove blamed the lack of the salt air for her lethargy, but the truth was that she was simply tired and afraid. She hadn't slept well since leaving Wynnewood; her meals were irregular and unbalanced, and her feet ached miserably. Had her fear for Philip not been greater than her discomfort and fear for herself, she'd have holed up near a village somewhere and rested until she felt well enough to return home.

It had been surprisingly easy to avoid most people. Staying off the road, listening carefully for the sounds of men and women working in fields or near villages ensured that she didn't suddenly come upon someone and frighten them. As the days were unseasonably cool, she didn't worry about people questioning her cloak, and her talent for dodging those who would chase her away kept her from persistent pursuit.

The third night after leaving Liverpool was bitterly cold. Even with both cloaks and the thick woolen blanket she used to hold her things, Dove found it impossible to stay warm even while walking. Near midnight, she was forced to stop and build a fire. This was dangerous and she knew it, but her teeth chattered so loudly that they hurt, and her fingers ached with the cold.

It took time to find enough wood to sustain fire for long. She stumbled through the darkness to find fallen branches and twigs. She kept birch bark for tinder and a little kindling in her pack at all times. After ensuring there were no houses nearby, Dove went to work. She cleared dried leaves beneath a hawthorn tree, and dug a shallow pit. With a few rocks around the outside to help protect against sparks, she laid the wood in the pit, carefully arranged her kindling, and then began to strike her flint to ignite the tinder. It took little time to get a blaze going, but it made her nervous. A fire practically begged for someone to come investigate.

An hour passed comfortably. Her hands were no longer numb with cold, her teeth didn't chatter, and the shivers that had wracked her body until she was exhausted from them had gone. In their place, a cozy warmth spread around her and made Dove drowsy. Several times, she found herself dozing off, but each time, her head snapped up quickly. She couldn't sleep. She needed to stay awake until almost daybreak and then find a place to rest.

The warmth of the blaze, the flames that danced for her, and the comforting crackle of the wood eventually lulled her to sleep. It was not the restful kind of sleep that she needed. No, she sat with her head resting on her knees, her back bent, and her body rigid—unaware that danger grew closer with every passing minute.

A sound—unmistakable but unidentifiable—pierced her consciousness. Dove's hand reached for her sling and wrapped her cloak and blanket more tightly around her as she stood. Voices. Terrified, she tried to kick dirt into her fire, but it was too late. Three men rose up from the hill behind the tree and stopped, staring at the little cloaked figure.

"What have we here? A boy out on a lark? What do you have there, boy?"

Panicked, she backed away from the fire, her hand swinging the sling. They were almost too close to risk it. She started to run, but checked herself. If they were too close to knock out with a stone, they'd be able to catch her. Hands shaking, she backed away slowly and tried to disguise her voice to sound like the boy they expected.

"Go away."

"Aw, he's not very friendly, is he Martin?"

"Might have to teach the lad some manners."

The one called Martin looked at her curiously, and took another step forward— almost menacingly. Dove made up her mind. She had one chance to get away. As untimely as the thought was, her mind immediately thought it would be a good test to see if it might work to help Philip. So, with every ounce of courage she possessed, she stepped forward, closing the gap between the men, and reached up to pull back her hood.

"I said," she growled, trying to sound as fierce and ugly as she could, "go away!"

With that, Dove flung back her hood and met the eyes of the three men. She knew the flames were reflected in her own eyes. Her hair alone, as wild and unkempt as it looked, was terrifying in itself. A flicker of fear in the eyes of one of the men was all the encouragement she needed. With a prayer in her heart that she didn't realize she uttered, she threw back her head and screamed as loudly as she could before rushing toward them again.

The one man, Martin, hesitated, but his companions fled. He didn't move toward her, but she saw something in his face that terrified her more than any response anyone had ever made to her—interest. Unsure what else to do, she kicked as much dirt into the fire as she could, wrapped her blanket and cloak around her, trying to keep the things she'd stowed in her pockets from falling, and ran.

"Wait!" The man took a step forward, but she was already yards away and nothing would have induced her to stop. Her heart raced as she stumbled and then flew over the ground.

What made a man step toward her when she was so exposed? She knew the flames added to the terror of her own features. She knew that this combined with her wild hair made her look like the Scynscaþa that the Mæte had called her. In her terror, she'd been unable to identify what had so unnerved her, but once she was a mile or two away, she knew. Recognition. He'd seen someone like her before and was not afraid. Nothing had ever petrified her more.

Daybreak had never been more welcome for Dove. She'd hardly traveled twelve miles throughout the night. It was nearly wasted, and she knew it, but it was time to sleep. Finding a safe place seemed impossible now. How could she rest comfortably, knowing that those men were out there? Of course, they weren't likely to come near her again. Dove couldn't resist a slight smile at the sight of two grown men fleeing like little girls running from a boy with a snake.

The rumbling in her stomach warned her that she needed to find more food. Dove's hand wrapped around the last apple in her pocket. As much as she wanted to eat it, she knew it was foolish to risk it. She was hungry, but she'd need the sustenance once she was ready to start out again at night. A small stream provided enough water to make her feel full, and a dense thicket was exactly what she thought she needed. She dug out a small area, crawled inside, and curled up into the dip she'd hollowed out of the earth. With her blanket and cloaks giving her a soft pallet, and her summer cloak wrapped around her, Dove was not too cool or too warm— much more comfortable than the previous night.

Doves cooed, rabbits hopped before scampering away again, and dogs from nearby farms roamed in search of those rabbits, but Dove slept through it all. Her dreams were odd things that made no sense the next morning. She dreamed of three men who roamed the countryside, trying to find Philip and sell him to the Mæte. Each time they got close to her friend, she'd jump out of a hiding place, throw back her hood, and sing the songs she sang to the dragons, and the men would fall asleep.

As the night descended, hunger forced her awake, and Dove decided to try to find food once more before she ate her apple. She crawled from her place in the thicket and brushed the dirt from her blanket and shook out her hair. It had been days since she'd allowed herself to bathe in a stream, but she needed it again. She could feel the grit and grime of travel between her toes and under her fingers. Her hair felt itchy and miserable. She'd make it another night, maybe, but she couldn't risk getting sick, and Bertha said disease lingered in unwashed bodies.

Just a mile away, she found an empty farm. Why no one was there, she couldn't imagine, but the house was eerily silent. Nervous, she crept indoors, glancing around her, expecting at any moment for someone to jump out and grab her arm. Inside, apples, pears, and turnips hung in baskets from the ceiling. She filled her pockets and then smelled stew simmering in a cauldron over the fireplace. As crazy as it was to risk it, she filled a bowl and ate hungrily.

Bertha's training didn't allow her to leave an unwashed bowl. She hurried to clean it, took three pennies from her dwindling stash, and laid them in plain sight on the table. Just as her hand reached for the door latch, voices reached her from the yard. Panicked, she glanced around the room for some place to hide. Instinctively, she moved toward the darker corners near the beds and curled in a ball behind a curtain that separated the spaces. With her pack on her back, she hoped it looked like a bundle of nothingness if someone looked closely enough.

Her heart froze as she heard the voices of the men who stumbled through the door. Instinctively, she began praying, begging Philip's God for help and protection. She'd frightened two of the men; one had frightened her. If they saw her again, she felt sure they'd kill her.

"Look, there's stew on. I'm famished!"

From her corner, Dove listened as they filled bowls and nearly inhaled the food. At first, she wondered if the men lived there, but when they started rifling through the food and filling a bag full, she knew they were just thieves. "Why d'you suppose someone just left three pennies sitting on the table like that?" one asked.

"Don't know, but take 'em. I found a few more coins in that box on the shelf." The second voice came from near the fireplace where he rifled through something. "Got me a knife over here. Martin, check over by the beds. Maybe there'll be something else of value in there.

Beads of perspiration formed on Dove's forehead and upper lip. Nervous and afraid, she tried to hold as still as possible as the curtain parted and the man who hadn't run in fear began a thorough search and then stopped short. An irritated voice came closer. "What'd you find, Martin? Hurry."

"Nothing, James. I just thought I heard something."

"Well hurry up then."

Martin made more noise than ever, whispering just above Dove's head, "I'll not give you away. Travel the north side of the road."

With those words, Martin grabbed a hatchet from the wall and carried it to the other side of the curtain. "All I found was a hatchet. Think it would bring anything?"

"Bring it along. Can't hurt," James agreed. "Let's get out of here before someone comes back."

As the door shut behind them, Dove exhaled loudly, or so it seemed to her ears. Why had the man helped her? Why wasn't he afraid? She trembled slightly, but forced herself to pull out three more pennies and leave them on the table. She had no intention of paying for whatever the thieves had stolen—until she remembered the hatchet. Dove was certain that Martin had only taken it to appease the other men. She didn't know how much a hatchet would cost, but she added a few more pennies to the little pile. She could justify that.

As she slunk away, keeping north of the road, Dove grew thankful for all of the pennies Jakys had given her. She'd paid too much for things, but her conscience wouldn't let her take the full amount from people who might need it before they could replace it. Money was a wonderful thing when you found it hard to come by, but you couldn't chew a coin like you could a loaf of bread. Pennies didn't fill your belly like eggs or apples.

She also couldn't get Martin out of her mind. Why had the man protected her, and why wasn't he afraid? Sure, the firelight wasn't very bright, but he'd seen—he'd recognized her for what she was. He wasn't the only one— Lord Morgan knew. Even Broðor Clarke seemed to know. Bertha wasn't afraid, but the Mæte had nearly killed her.

Alongside the road, about twenty yards north of it, she tramped, listening for the men, occasionally hearing Martin's laughter off in the distance. They weren't walking quite as quickly as she was, but their longer strides and the torch they carried made the trek along the road easier, but it also gave her something to follow. Her cloak helped keep her movements stealthy and it almost seemed as if Martin was trying to make a lot of noise.

It didn't take long to discover where the family from the farmhouse had been. A large festival was winding down as they reached the next town. People spilled onto the road, sending the men away from sight. It was difficult to hide from so many people, but once she'd traveled five miles on the other side of the town, she felt confident again. For a while, trees grew very close to the road, almost as they did near Wynnewood, and Dove chanced a walk along the road. She hadn't seen the three men in hours, and it was easy enough to jump behind a tree and climb it quickly. On the road, she made very quick time, walking faster than she had since she'd started for Oxford just eleven days earlier.

According to Jakys, she had just four or five more days' journey at the most. She could do it. She had to— no matter how much she wanted to turn around and run home. Her throat tightened and her heart ached as dawn crept over the morning sky and sent Dove looking for yet another place to sleep.

As she lay down to sleep in a partially dugout abandoned haymow, her exhaustion, fear, and loneliness encroached on her until she felt truly despairing. Tears splashed down her cheeks and deep sobs overtook her. Her shoulders shook, her throat ached, and her heart squeezed as she gave full vent to her grief.

Dove planned her approach into Oxford. It had worked with two of the men. Surely it would work with kidnappers. Her last thought before she drifted off into another strange world of dreams was to question why someone like her would have such experience with kidnapping. It seemed a bit preposterous.

Delays

CHAPTR 20

lord Morgan's bones ached from the long ride. As swiftly as he tried to go, the horses could not be ridden hard without being refreshed. They were strong, powerful battle animals, and he wasn't ready to give up the fine steeds he had for the horses in the stables along their route. He made discreet inquiries to see if anyone had seen Dove, but no one had seen a child wandering anywhere. While Dove followed the sea to Liverpool, the Mersey River across England, and then down to Oxford, Lord Morgan took the most direct route, taking the roads that left northern England and led to places such as Oxford, Cambridge, London, and south to Portsmouth.

The knights showed all proper respectful deference, but he sensed their desire to charge onward and slay the dragon, otherwise known as kidnappers. They trained for battle—to fight for the crown. Going on a hunt for a common boy held for ransom was beneath their station and training, but still, it was active employment and held a sense of danger and the unknown that drills and improvised tournaments never could.

Lord Morgan's knights did more than protect Wynnewood and the castle from siege. They were ready to be called by King Henry of Winchester at any time, and over the years, some had gone with other knights from all over England and France to fight in the Crusades.

Contrary to stereotype, not all knights loved a joust or a swordfight. They didn't all ache to go on quests to prove themselves. Lord Morgan's knights were all as different and varied as the nobles, villagers, and farmers. Some knights loved travel, others not so much. There were natural scholars, those who loved riding, and others who hated both. However, there was one thing that they all had in common—loyalty to Lord Morgan.

Philip had been something of a pet of most of the knights, his bravery and loyalty something they admired. He'd orchestrated the capture of the elusive unicorn, and yet he hadn't grown vain or arrogant. They'd missed him around the castle over the past year. Of course, there were a few who were annoyed by him, and those men found themselves left behind to protect the castle in the absence of the Earl.

It was a dry time in England, making travel much easier than usual. Each morning they searched the skies for signs of rain, but it didn't come. This should have gotten them to Oxford at a reasonably swift pace, but they couldn't ride at much more than a walk without exhausting the animals.

The town of Strafford was a market town, very important in the area. The men were tired, sore, and ready for a good meal and a good night's rest. There were three inns available to them, but since one didn't have enough room for all nine men, they chose to seek another. The second inn was directly in the middle of town, and several of the knights suggested that they might not sleep well if the town was noisy late. After a moment's thought, Charles Morgan agreed. "We'll also have the advantage of being on the other side of the town when we ride on tomorrow."

Dinner smelled delicious. Long tables in a dining hall were soon laden with roasted goose, vegetables, and large tankards of refreshing ale. Having worked up excellent appetites on their thirty-mile ride that day, the men attacked their meal with gusto, laughing and joking about some of the sights they'd seen. Lost in his own thoughts and exhausted from the ride, the Earl of Wynnewood hardly joined their banter, preferring to relax and enjoy his meal.

Several of the knights strolled through the town after they ate, but Charles Morgan wanted nothing more than a long night's rest. He waved those who hesitated to leave him off to join their comrades and climbed the stairs to his room. The moment his boots were off and his surcoat draped over a chair, he crawled into bed and fell sound asleep.

Lord Morgan woke in the middle of the night, vomiting violently and shaking. Two others were equally sick, and within hours, the entire inn succumbed to the illness, which they attributed to bad meat. After long, miserable hours of purging, the men all lay collapsed on their pallets and beds, exhausted. They sipped water, often expelling it as swiftly as they drank, and tried to rest.

One younger knight, Jerome, had been ill before they left Wynnewood and could not rally. Despite the ministrations of a physician, the man was too weak to rise with the others on the third day. Lord Morgan, unwilling to leave the man alone but anxious to hurry to Philip's aid, conferred with his men.

"We cannot stay any longer. I know we'll likely not be able to go far, but we must try. Is anyone willing to volunteer to stay, or should we draw straws?"

The knights exchanged glances, none wanting to stay in the inn where they'd been so miserable, until Lord Morgan suggested moving Jerome to new lodgings. "I do think it would be best if we found another inn. I'm not sure he'll be ready to trust the cook here, and he needs nourishment."

Upon hearing those words, the oldest of the knights stepped forward. "I'll stay."

Lord Morgan was not comfortable with that idea. Edward was an expert horseman and an excellent conversationalist. He'd be able to get anyone to open up about whatever they'd seen. "I—"

Another man, Harold, stepped forward. "I'll stay, m'lord. I've had training in healing, and I'm not as hardy as some of the others. Do we go home when he's well or wait for your return?"

Lord Morgan thought for a moment, and then decided. "Stay until we return. It is possible that we'll need you for something. Being closer would help."

The men gathered their things and tried to hurry to their horses, but all were still somewhat weak from their ordeal. Jerome looked pitiful lying on his bed, his face gaunt and gray. "Harold will take good care of you. Rest and try to eat. I'll send men to carry you to another inn."

At the door, Jerome's weak voice called him back again. "I pray you find the boy. I've not been very patient with him—jealous, I expect. He's a good lad."

"That he is. He's going to be a fine man."

Without another word, Lord Morgan shut the door behind him and forced himself downstairs. The innkeeper, apologetic and effusive, refused payment and promised to take excellent care of the remnants of the Wynnewood party, but Lord Morgan shook his head. "We'll be moving him. He needs to eat, but he's nervous."

Apologetic, the man tried to change his mind, but Lord Morgan stood firm. "Someone will be along to carry Jerome into town. Good day."

It took more strength than any of the men wanted to admit to climb up into their saddles and ride away from town. They were weak, weary, and a little disheartened with having to leave Jerome and Harold behind.

Ten minutes down the trail, the clouds that had

seemed to hint of rain in the next day or two darkened, the wind picked up and pushed more gray clouds their way. Less than an hour outside of Stafford, rain—steady and cold—poured down on them.

In the wee hours, ten days after the party had left for Oxford, the steady beat of rain on the roof woke Dennis Clarke from a troubled sleep. Wynnewood had enjoyed the dry spell. Broðor Clarke had spent many hours in prayer, begging the Lord for favorable weather both for the villagers and for the travelers. He couldn't help but include Dove in those prayers, although he had little hope that prayers could help the child now.

Instinctively he began praying that the rain would hold for the travelers—that they were far enough south that they could hope to arrive before the rain reached them and that the rain had not traveled north from their direction. A glance out the window saw a shadow moving past his cottage, and his heart leapt with hope until he realized the shadow was too large to be Dove. He watched the figure make its way toward the fishermen's cottages and smiled. Another baby—it was Bertha. He'd seen Wilmetta waddle home from the baker's the previous afternoon, and the way the woman had clutched at her abdomen every dozen or so steps had made him nervous.

Without dry wood in the house, he'd be cold inside a few hours, so the minister hurried outside and carried in enough wood to last a few days. He laid two logs in front of the fire and put his last dry log on, stirring up a good blaze. It occurred to him that he'd been blessed by Philip's diligence in ways he'd never given much notice. His water bucket had been filled, his wood box replenished, and even the emptying of his slop bucket had often been done by Philip as he passed on some errand or another.

An hour later, the cottage was quite warm and Broðor Clarke had nearly prayed himself to sleep when a knock jerked him into full consciousness again. He flung the covers from him, and wrapped a blanket around his shoulders before hurrying to the door, immediately praying for the Lord's mercies. Knocks before daybreak usually meant bad news.

Isaac West stood there, rain soaking him as he shivered. "Broðor Clarke. The midwife said you're to come to Wilmetta. She won't live long and she's calling for you."

Before Dennis could answer, the young man raced down the street, obviously anxious to get out of the rain. He hurried into his shoes, pulled on a fresh tunic, and wrapped his mantle around him. With a prayer on his lips and a heavy heart, he stepped out into the rain and hurried toward the row of cottages at the end of the center street in Wynnewood. A dim light flickered in the tiny window of Wilmetta's cottage, and the door opened the moment his knuckles rapped softly on the door. "Come in, myth monger. She's calling for you," Bertha spat.

So it was true. Wilmetta would die. Bertha always took her irascibility to a stronger level when she couldn't save a life. Before he could ask, the faint cry of a newborn startled him. "The baby survived?" That didn't happen often. If Bertha couldn't save the mother, she usually lost the baby as well.

"Don't know how. I've done everything I can for Wilmetta, but I can't stop the bleeding. She's almost gone. Hurry."

He sat holding one of the young woman's hands, stroking her hair away from her face, and whispering the shepherd's psalm. His voice choked as he reached the sad words, "yea, though I walk through the valley of the shadow of death..."

One glance at Bertha showed her hands covering her face. Anyone who didn't know her as well as Broðor Clarke did would assume she wept, but she didn't. From the rigidity of her shoulders, the balled fists that hid her eyes, and the occasional shake of her head, he knew she restrained her wrath at him and his God only to give Wilmetta a peaceful passing.

"Broðor Clarke?" Wilmetta's voice was a ragged whisper.

"Yes?"

"Will you tell David— so sorry. I couldn't—" she swallowed the water he offered. "The baby—"

"Your baby will be fine. We'll take good care of it until he returns. The men should be home any day as it is— especially with the good weather we've had until now." He saw Wilmetta's face grow paler and shook his head when she tried to speak again. "Shh. Rest. Rest in the arms of Jesus. The Everlasting Arms. Sleep."

She slept. Her last breath exhaled in one weak whoosh, and Broðor Clarke gently closed her eyes. "She is gone."

"What good is her death? She was terrified and you speak of fearing no evil. Death is evil, you fool!"

Bertha wouldn't cry—not when he could see anyway. Nothing he said or did would comfort her, and that was not a familiar experience for him. People usually found him sympathetic, encouraging, and a shoulder to lean on during difficult times, but not Bertha. She blamed him, the Lord, and everything and everyone else she could when death took another life from her hands.

"Bertha..."

"Don't. What good is your god? What good were all those silly words? That baby," she glanced at the infant that lay sleeping next to its dead mother, "that little boy has no mother. How can that be good? How can you say your god was with her and comforts her when you know that her husband is coming home to an empty home and a child who needs him—if we can keep the child alive?"

He didn't defend himself when her hands pounded his arms and chest at random intervals as she bustled around the room. Wynnewood's minister took these rare occasions when she was willing to discuss anything related to his faith and prayed for the words that would pierce the armor that she wore to protect her from his "myths."

"I can say that because those who have endured so much worse have reminded us that 'the Lord gives and He takes away. Blessed be—'"

"Stop! There is no blessing in death. Death is my enemy. I fight it every day. I refuse to listen to you talk about it as if it were nothing."

"Bertha..."

"Just take your stories home. I don't want them."

"The baby..."

"I'll take him home. Perhaps Letty's mother can nurse him for a while. I'll ask."

As he opened the door, Broðor Clarke had a thought and shut it again. "Philip—did you know how much he loved his sister?"

"Another absolutely wasted life. That child should have lived, but the fool Biggs—"

"He lost what was most precious to him when Ellie left us."

"What's your point, Dennis?"

He stifled a smirk. If she thought she'd insult him by using his Christian name rather than the title of "Broðor," she was sadly mistaken. "Philip has personally suffered the snatch of death, and likely will feel it again when he returns to find Dove gone."

"Then we'll see just how much comfort your myths are to him," Bertha sneered.

The minister crossed the room to stand before the hurting woman he longed so much to see yield to the Lord. He waited, seconds passing without any hope for her to relent, until at last she looked up at him. "What?"

Dennis Clarke tried to use his eyes to comfort where his words could not. "The lad will not deny the Lord God. He will remain faithful to I AM. His heart will hurt for the loss of a friend, and ache that his friend may never have developed faith in Jesus, but he will be comforted to know the Lord loves her more than he ever could." The man swallowed hard.

"You have no heart if you can speak of loss so glibly. He's a strong boy—a man in so many ways—but he will deny his faith. It has failed him. You'll see."

Broðor Clarke turned to leave again, shoulders squared as if facing a hard task instead of leaving one. "He won't. Our pain isn't in the loss—it's just a temporary separation when the one who goes before us belongs to the Lord—our pain comes when death creates a permanent one. When we know we'll never see the ones we love again; and yet, even then the Lord comforts us."

"Be comforted in your myths if you like. You've ruined this village with them. I loved this place as untouched as it was by the superstitious nonsense of the church, but you've ruined it."

"Good day, Bertha. Bring the infant to me any time you need sleep. I know babies. I can help."

With that, Broðor Clarke opened the door and stepped out into the rain again. He strode to the house of Peter the carpenter, told of the need for a casket, and walked home, Bertha's last words echoing in his mind. "Lord, is it not strange that she would choose old superstitions that she rejected rather than embrace Your Word? How long will she reject You?" He sighed as he opened the door to his cottage. "How long?"

Progress

CHAPTER 21

Ⅽ sneeze broke the steady drone of rain on the roof of the hovel where Philip shivered through the days. It hadn't been horribly uncomfortable at first, but when the rain began, everything became damp and miserable. A cold settled into Philip's chest, causing wracking coughs that shook his body and made his head feel as if it would explode.

His captors feared catching the illness so they came less often and gave him nervous glances. It bothered him greatly. Philip knew that their interest in him ended the moment they thought he became a liability.

Until he'd arrived at Oxford and become more acquainted with news from around the country, he'd considered the attempted kidnapping of Aurelia to be something highly unusual and irregular. When pressed, he hadn't been able to resist mentioning the part he'd played in foiling the attempt and was surprised to learn that many people tried to abduct those of high rank for various purposes and that most of them did fail.

"People become desperate and do crazy things when they need money," Master Adrian had insisted.

Based upon what he'd overheard, Philip thought he had less than a week before his captors changed their plans. There had been some argument as to which alternate plan would prevail. One man, James, seemed to be the ringleader. The others didn't like what he had to say, but they eventually acquiesced. James wanted to sell him if the ransom didn't arrive in time. "Might as well get something for him," he'd insisted.

Where they planned to take him to sell him, Philip wasn't sure, but it would have to be England unless they found a boat... Philip swallowed hard at that thought. Once sold, the chances of escape were slim, and he knew it. Even if he did manage, he'd never find his way back home. He had to escape now, but how?

Another fit of coughing sent more fevered chills over him. That was another strike against keeping him alive. No one would buy a sick boy for any kind of work. Without a buyer, they wouldn't bother to keep him alive. That thought unnerved him. He shuddered.

As much as he tried to reason out a plan, his brain refused to cooperate. He was cold, muddleheaded from his fever, and the rain that had often been such a comforting sound in Wynnewood seemed to antagonize him in the tiny shed.

"I tell you, Gipp should have been back by now. They've caught 'im! We have to leave."

"Gipp said three weeks, so we wait three weeks," James insisted. "Just how sick is he?"

"He's coughing pretty bad."

"He's seen us all anyway. Bring him inside. Let's get some broth in him and maybe onions for his chest." The other man argued for a moment, but James yelled, "Just do it! I'm getting inside before I catch my death as well."

Hugo, a scrawny man with beady black eyes and terrible teeth dragged Philip out of the hovel and into the house. A roaring blaze radiated heat all over the room, making Philip warmer simply by stepping into it. "Th-thank you."

"We're not doing this for you. Just get warm and dry. I'll make a poultice. My modor was a fine herbal woman.

She could cure anything."

Philip didn't like thinking about his own mother. His father would arrive any day now, and it was likely that she'd have to tell them about his abduction. That rankled. He'd tried for the past three years to show his maturity, but this would just make him look like the child he no longer was. As it was, Dove was going to tease him until he was fifty—if he lived that long.

That thought made him smile. If he lived that long, he and Dove would be like Broðor Clarke and Bertha— always sparring in some manner. Oh, they tried to hide it, but Dove missed little and she'd pointed it out several times. Several times, Philip had been tempted to ask if Broðor Clarke had been friends with Bertha at some point, but he'd never gathered the courage. It seemed such a silly thing now. Why not ask? The minister wouldn't have minded.

As his tunic dried, his shivers lessened. The fever still caused his teeth to rattle, but the broth that Hugo brought him helped warm him a little as well. Philip watched curiously as the man chopped onions, fried them in a pan, added a bit of flour and oil, and folded them in a piece of fabric. "C'mere, you. Let's get this tied on you."

With the onion poultice strapped to his chest, Philip curled up on the floor in front of the hearth and fell asleep. For the first time in nearly two weeks, he slept soundly, only stirring when a fit of coughing shook him awake for a moment. He slept so deeply that he didn't hear the men talking when Gipp stepped inside with news that Lord Morgan was on his way to Oxford to pay the ransom.

"I thought you were going to try to get the money there," Hugo protested.

"He wouldn't do it. The man I sent in said that Lord Morgan thought we'd just take off with the money and not return to the rest of you."

"Smart man." James sounded impressed.

"He is that. He's mad too. I followed them until they got to Strafford. They didn't ride on the next morning as usual, but I did. I thought I could beat them back here."

"Well, if he's coming," James insisted, "we've got to get that young man well. No lord is going to pay a good ransom for a corpse."

After two days of eating little and drinking much, not to mention the mental comfort in knowing his food came from a different kitchen, Jerome began to feel better. In fact, he was feeling a bit restless. When Harold left to visit the horses and ensure their proper care, Jerome pulled on his clothes and slipped outside.

Stafford was a busy place, full of people, animals, and commerce. Goods exchanged hands, usually without benefit of money. Chickens were exchanged for flour and cobblers fixed shoes in exchange for tools. A tavern beckoned him. A fresh glass of ale accompanied by a local storyteller sounded like the perfect way to pass the time.

Sometime during his second glass, Jerome saw a man come into the tavern. Something about the man seemed familiar, but he couldn't place what. Despite the temptation to engage, Jerome dropped his head and wrapped his hands around his tankard, trying to appear standoffish. Maybe if he could observe for a minute, he'd know where he'd seen the newcomer. It didn't take long. The moment the man spoke, Jerome knew who he was.

"H-have you seen a man come in here? H-he's about my height. S-southern accent? H-hook nose?"

"I see all kinds in here. Can't say I haven't, but I wouldn't know when."

"I-it would have been in the last week. C-can you try?

H-his name is Gipp. G-gipp Doggett. H-he's going to Oxford." The man sounded desperate.

"Yeah, we've had a couple of men come through to Oxford recently. One might have had a hook nose, but I didn't hear a name."

"W-when?"

"Maybe three days ago? Four? No more than four, because I was home sick for two days before that." The tavern keeper held up a tankard. "So, do you want a drink or not?"

Jerome stood and slid a coin across the counter, keeping his back to the man. "Thanks."

He wanted to run through the town, but he also knew he was still too weak to do it. Instead, he forced himself to keep to a steady stride. He wove easily in and out of crowds, nodded greetings to friendly hawkers, and finally reached the stables—spent.

"Jerome, what are you doing out here? You're supposed to be resting." Harold eyed him closer. "You're sweating again. Get back inside—"

"I went for a walk," Jerome gasped, hating how winded he sounded from a simple walk. "Found a tavern and waited for someone to start telling stories."

"Well, you obviously weren't ready for that kind of exertion. I guess the room must get tiresome, but—"

"No, really. I was fine. I felt great. I just sat there, drank my ale, and watched as people came and went. Then a man came in. Remember the one who brought the news of Philip?"

"The stutterer?"

"That's the one! He came in looking for a man with a hooked nose and with a southern accent—said the man's name was Gipp Doggett and he'd be on his way to Oxford."

"Gipp Doggett?" Harold crossed his arms across his chest like he always did when he was thinking. "And the man specifically said Oxford?"

"Yep."

"Would you recognize him again?"

Jerome nodded without hesitation. "Definitely."

Harold's eyes slid toward the horses. "Do you think you could ride?"

"After a short rest, yes. I need some water. I tried to walk here, but I practically ran."

"That wasn't very bright."

"Do you think," Jerome asked, ignoring the jab from the older man, "we should find the man and insist he tell us everything?"

The elder knight didn't eve hesitate. "No. If we follow, we find. We may have to split up so that one of us can hurry ahead to inform Lord Morgan, but if we try to confront him now, he'll likely refuse to speak."

"So we follow..." Jerome echoed.

A satisfied expression settled over Harold's face. "We follow—and we catch these criminals. They'll be at the gallows inside a fortnight." He nodded affably at his younger comrade. "You did well, Jerome."

As he built the fire in the chapel, Broðor Clarke sang the familiar chants that stirred his soul. They were all in Latin, a familiar language to him but not to the villagers. Local mothers felt a swell of pride when their small children sang the songs they heard from the little pulpit each week, their semi-monotonic melodies occasionally interrupted by a rise or fall in tone before returning to one or two closely related notes. It sounded educated to them, but to Broðor Clarke, it felt unnatural. He often wished he had a talent for music. When he sat in the corner of the tavern and heard the minstrels and the troubadours, he sometimes wished he could combine their musical storytelling abilities with the psalms and Bible stories.

"Dove could do it, Lord. If she were here, she could do it. Philip has often said she make any conversation lyrical."

Bertha's prediction pricked his heart. Deep down, he had an unshakeable faith that Philip would never deny his Lord, but at times, particularly when things looked so bleak, he had trouble remembering that the Lord who was powerful enough to save man from their sins also knew what He was doing when disaster struck. Dove being gone—indefinitely it seemed—was most certainly a disaster.

To ease his mind, Broðor Clarke tried to imagine what song he'd choose first if he had a chance to speak to Dove. He'd only truly conversed once with the girl; she always ran from him. The impossibility of one thing seemed to spawn another, but the minister didn't mind. He finally settled on the faith of Noah. One righteous man—in a world full of people, God found just one righteous man. He liked the way it naturally segued into the church. It could be a marvelous teaching tool if a song was written in a tune that people knew. People loved music. They'd learn faster and the words would strike deeper into their hearts and much more quickly if sung in their own language and to tunes that they enjoyed.

The first boy burst through the door. "Good afternoon, Liam. You seem in a hurry."

"I thought you might have news of Philip, Broðor Clarke—or Dove."

"Neither, I'm afraid."

Liam nodded and grabbed the broom from the corner. As he swept, he glanced curiously at the minister, but didn't ask the questions that clearly plagued him. Just as Broðor Clarke decided to open the conversation, the boy finally took a deep breath and asked in one long, breathless word, "Why-doesn't-God-speak-to-you-like-He-did-to-Moses-and-tell-us-about-Philip?"

The question was a valid one, but the minister was disappointed to hear it. He'd hoped that the boys would see God as the Great Communicator—the loving Father who speaks to His children, teaching and loving them through His words. If Liam were any indication, he'd managed to make the Lord seem like a mystical being that operated more like a genie in a magical lamp.

He smiled at Liam, trying to hide his frustration. "And when did the great I AM tell Moses where to find a missing child? When did I AM reveal a wish rather than His will?"

"You mean..." Liam sounded confused. "Oh. You're saying that what seems important to us may not be the Lord's will because He sees all and knows the future."

"You're a bright young man, Liam. That's exactly what I'm saying. I don't know why this has happened to Philip or where Dove has gone, but if the Lord wants both of them to return home, we can trust that He can make it happen."

End in Sight

CHAPTR 22

Dawn approached; the hint of light that hovered near the horizon taunted her with its arrival. She'd hoped to reach Oxford before daybreak, but the moon, hidden by clouds and intermittent showers, had made the road muddy and she'd spent most of her time slogging through puddles. Twice the rain had fallen so hard that she'd crawled under a bridge to wait out the storm.

To keep herself going, even when she was so tired and wet that she wanted to quit, Dove sang. Unaware that four hundred miles away, Broðor Clarke dreamed of having his people sing songs of praise and the stories of the Bible, she sang of those very things. Her songs were of Esther, Jonah, and even Peter as he cut off the ear of Malchus. Her high sweet voice that once sounded eerie amid the mists of Wynnewood sang of Jesus' prayer in the Garden of Gethsemane.

Had she known that each word, each memory, each word of the Lord that she sang impressed itself into her heart, she might have resisted the tug of those now familiar stories. One song became almost her constant companion—comforting her when nothing else could. She sang of Miriam watching over Moses in the Nile and then rejoicing as they reached the other side of the Red Sea and watched the destruction of Pharaoh's army.

Her stomach rumbled as she neared the village of

Somerton. Travel made eating difficult. It was hard work to stumble over roads and along fields next to them. The harder her journey, the more food she needed, but she was often too exhausted to put forth the effort to find any. Her conscience also made it difficult to take the food she truly needed. No amount of self-admonishment could convince her that her pennies made taking what wasn't hers an acceptable thing to do.

Knowing the light would overtake the sky soon, Dove scrambled over a low wall and hurried toward a group of trees to think. She felt safer among the trees, even though few people wandered the roads in the dark. Unlike the forests of Wynnewood, she didn't know instinctively where tree roots or branches were. When it rained, the trees acted as ineffective umbrellas—better than nothing, although she still tended to become soaked. However, sometimes she needed the speed that she could only find on the open road. Philip would laugh to see her trip so often after all her teasing when they'd met. Her forehead was bruised and scraped from so many whacks against low hanging branches.

Farms on the outskirts of the little town meant food. She had to find something and soon. Although the rain had finally stopped, her blanket and cloak wouldn't dry for hours. She really needed a new blanket. The temptation to trade hers for a dry one at some house was huge, but Bertha's opinions on disease lurking in bedding squelched it. Even Bertha didn't know if her ideas were mere superstition or fact, but it was true that they got sick much less often than the rest of the villagers did.

She followed the little grove of trees, watching to see where the road went and looking for some kind of house. "Well, I AM, I'm very tempted to ask for meat. I need meat, I think—or eggs. If I could find a way to boil an egg..." Her prayer dissolved into new plans for finding food.

The morning was cool and the threat of rain hovered in the sky. Even as the sun rose, the light it brought was pale and gray. It seemed more like nightfall than sunrise. Dove's mind whirled in a dozen directions. She could go into town and buy from a baker. No one would question a cloak on a child on a chilly morning when rain threatened. She could act shy and mention her father. It would be hard to start a fire to cook anything, but maybe she could find cheese and some fruit. It seemed likely—dangerous, but likely.

Dove had one serious concern, however. Exhaustion. She was truly more tired than she'd ever been in her life. If someone questioned—insisted even—and wanted to see her, she'd have to run. Did she have the strength to get away with the pack on her back and the extra weight of the sodden blanket?

One final idea clinched her decision. She could ask the distance to Oxford. It was risky; oh, how it was risky, but Dove couldn't stand the suspense any longer. It could be only a few miles or it could be fifty. She just didn't know. She'd do it. If there were only a few miles left, she'd continue onward after her breakfast.

"Bread, please." Dove tried to lower her voice a little, hoping to sound a little older.

"What'dya say? Can't hear you."

"Bread, please," she repeated, louder.

"You're not from around here. Where are you from?"

Without thinking, she answered, "Oxford." Realizing she'd switched destination with home, Dove started to correct herself, and then clamped her mouth shut. "How much for the bread?"

"Two pennies."

Dove started to pass the coins to the baker, but a hand clamped over hers, startling her. "One. He's lying to you."

Shaking, she dropped the coins in the baker's hands and grabbed the proffered loaf. "Thank you anyway. Good day."

The moment the hand had touched her, she'd planned to run from the town and be satisfied with the loaf, but a cheese monger rolled a cart into the street only a few yards ahead of her. Fighting back tears, she forced herself to stop and purchase a small wedge. Another cart, just at the edge of town, offered apples and a few vegetables. Dove bought enough to fill her pockets, asked the distance to Oxford, and then hurried from the town, beaming.

"There are only twenty miles left," she murmured to herself. "I could make it before nightfall if I hurry."

A large barn adjacent to an abbey was all Dove needed to see. Barns weren't plentiful on her journey, but when she came across them, she found that they were dry places, much more comfortable than being outside, and often she could dry her clothes. She dashed over a wall and across a field, praying no one saw her. That was the worst part of any attempt to hide during the day. Anyone looking could see anything. Unlike Wynnewood, the southern areas weren't smothered in trees.

After a few glances around her to be sure no one noticed her arrival, she dragged open the door and crept inside. As dreary and dark as the day was, the inside of the barn was much darker. Two small, narrow windows at each end of the barn let in the only light the massive structure provided. She allowed her eyes to adjust, and then went looking for a safe place to hide.

A ladder gave her the hideaway she sought. Though her muscles protested, she climbed up to a loft high above the rest of the barn where light and air came through the windows. There were bags of grain stored up there, and just a little straw. It would be less comfortable than she'd hoped, but Dove decided that some straw was better than the wet ground.

First, she laid out her blanket over the bags of grain. Her cloaks followed, the white one placed directly in the path of the window in case sunlight had half a chance to shine on it. She opened her pack and carefully laid out everything she owned around her. One tunic was hardly damp at all, so Dove stripped her clothes, laying them out to dry too, and pulled on the tunic. It was much more comfortable than the damp things she'd been enduring.

Once everything was spread out to dry, Dove examined her food, trying to decide how much she could eat. With only twenty miles to Oxford, she would only need two more meals until she could find Philip. He could buy her more food. She counted her pennies. There were only twenty-three left. That was a lot of money, but not the way she'd been spending it. She had a long journey home, and couldn't expect to make it without more. She hoped that Philip would have money he could spare. With more pennies, she'd get home just fine.

Hunger overrode prudence. Dove ate the cheese and two carrots. Still hungry, she tore off a chunk of bread and drank an entire flask of water. She'd need more before she could continue her journey, but there was a well in Somerton. If necessary, she'd walk back there and fill it, assuming she couldn't find one at the abbey. That seemed unlikely.

That familiar sleepy contentedness that comes after a filling meal washed over her just as the sun broke through the clouds. She turned every piece of clothing and her blanket over to the other side, laid down on a small pile of straw in the sunlight, and fell asleep.

Despite her best intentions, Dove awoke many hours later, darkness surrounding her. The barn was pitch black and no moon shone to give any light. Her hands felt for her clothing and thankfully, it was all mostly dry. The woolen blanket was still damp, but her cloaks were fine. She layered all of her clothes on, barely pulling her breeches over the other pair, and then folded the blanket into the pack. Her hands fumbled to find her flint, the coins, and the knife. It took what seemed like an enormous amount of time, but at last, she found the empty flask and hooked the strings over her neck.

Dove was halfway down the ladder when she remembered her walking stick. Though tempted to leave it, she knew it was a bad decision. That stick had saved her from running into rock walls, stumbling over large roots or falling into holes and twisting an ankle. She needed it. Back up the ladder she climbed, amazed at how much energy she had after such a good sleep.

She usually sought food, rested until closer to midnight, and then walked until the wee hours of the morning when she'd start a new hunt for food, but this last night on the road was different. She had the food, and if she walked quickly, she might be able to release Philip while his abductors were asleep. That seemed to be the best option—assuming it would work.

Near a kitchen garden at one corner of the abbey, Dove found a well. She filled her flask, drank thirstily, and then filled it again. She washed her hands and face, and replaced her gloves. Within minutes, she walked along the stone wall that separated abbey lands from the road. A low wall wasn't as comforting as trees were, but if she heard someone, she could always jump over it and hide.

The chances of actually seeing anyone wandering the countryside in the dark were so slim, Dove should have felt silly for even thinking of it, but she didn't. A lifetime of fears overrode her common sense at times like that. So she created her escape plans as she walked, comforting herself that she hadn't expected to meet anyone, and the three men had shown up seemingly out of nowhere. Bertha would be proud of her forethought.

The thought of Bertha sent an odd pang to her heart. She didn't have deep affection for the woman—certainly not the kind she imagined people felt for their mothers, but even so, the woman had been the only mother-like person in her life, and she did feel somewhat guilty for leaving so abruptly. Did Bertha think she was dead? Would the midwife's life be easier now that her little charge was gone? Dove instinctively knew it would.

Yes, Dove felt a certain sort of gratitude to the woman who had saved her life and kept her fed, clothed, and housed for so many years. Bertha had taught her how to keep house, hunt, cook, and the rudiments of healing. With as many stories as she'd heard, Dove was certain that she could assist a woman in a normal delivery. However, Dove also had a certain matter-of-fact acceptance of Bertha's "sacrifice." After all, it was a midwife's job to preserve life. Bertha had said as much over the years. She'd simply done what her calling required of her.

As usual, stumbling over the road was awkward, and twice she fell, but after two weeks of using her walking stick to feel her way along the road, she made good time regardless. She drank half her flask in the first two hours, and then paused to refill it in another town.

Owls swooped overhead, hunting their prey. Sheep bleated in fields, and dogs howled over odd sounds in the night. The occasional rustling of creatures in the grass would have terrified a child unaccustomed to late night rambles in the forests, but for Dove, they were a challenge. Was that a fox or a rabbit? Was the whoosh overhead that of an owl, or were there dragons here as well?

As she passed the church at Woolvercote, Dove nearly screeched to see a cloaked woman nearly running through the street. "Get home, boy," the woman called without a glance back to see if she'd been obeyed, "I'll tell your mother you were out again."

Another half mile down the road, and Dove understood. It was a midwife. The shrieks coming from a ramshackle hut near the edge of the town told Dove everything she needed to know and much more than she wanted. As she hurried along the final stretch to Oxford, Dove smiled to herself. Some poor child was going to get in trouble for doing something he hadn't done. If Dove knew anything about children, she knew that he'd not been caught more often than he had, so the punishment he got would be earned, albeit a bit delayed.

She needed light. To read the map once she arrived, she'd need light to see. It seemed to her that the easiest thing to do was find the North Gate and then follow the map from there. If she ensured a specific point of reference, surely she couldn't misread the crudely scrawled directions.

At last she arrived. In the distance, she saw the tiny flicker of the gatekeeper's torch, and grew excited. If she could get close enough to that torch, she could read the map and find Philip. Although she was a bit discouraged, Dove forced herself to stay back and wait. Perhaps if she observed the guards for a while, she'd find a way to get close to the torches.

Bad to Worse

CHAPTER 23

Several days after Lord Morgan left for Oxford, Jakys watched as his daughter played with her dolls in the corner of their sitting room. His face looked stern and grim, but the child, absorbed in an imaginary world of her own making, didn't notice. He was thinking of Dove. *She shouldn't be making that journey alone*, he thought to himself. *She's too young.*

Young or not, the girl was gone. Several of the young men had tried to sneak around Wynnewood for news of the girl, but it had been useless. Either the village hadn't noticed her absence, or they were afraid that mentioning it would hasten her return. Jakys was furious at the thought.

"I should have gone with her," he muttered aloud, unaware that he'd spoken.

"What, Fæder?" Durilda smiled at him from the corner, but the sight of his tense features concerned her. "What is wrong?"

"Nothing to worry about."

"You're worried though, aren't you? Is it Dove? Meryld said that she was sent south to help Philip."

He shook his head as his daughter recounted the gossip she'd heard in the kitchens. "Nothing is private in this place, is it? Yes, Dove has gone to Oxford."

"Isn't that very far away? I thought you said when

Philip went that we might never see him again because he'd be so far away and gone for so long."

"That's right."

Durilda left her dolls on the little beds she'd devised and went to sit on her father's knee. "Why did she go there?"

"He's in trouble, little one. We heard of it and told Dove so she could help. We couldn't go to Lord Morgan and still protect ourselves, but we could tell Dove."

"Did she tell Lord Morgan?"

That thought hadn't occurred to him. Had the child waited long enough to inform the Earl of Wynnewood? He doubted it. The chances of being forbidden to go were too great, and Dove wanted to help her friend herself. Being so little—just a child really—would help when she arrived. Kidnappers wouldn't expect a child to free the lad, and it might save Lord Morgan a very large sum of money.

"I doubt it."

"What kind of trouble is it, Fæder?"

"Someone wants money from Lord Morgan, so they took Philip and are holding him. They'll trade him for the money when Lord Morgan arrives—unless Dove arrives first."

The little girl's forehead furrowed as she stroked her father's beard and thought. "Did you give her money for the men?"

"No, but we gave her money so she'd be able to buy food along the way."

Those words contorted the child's face in fear. "They'll hurt her! They'll scream, 'Scynscaþa' and try to kill her like Maulore did. She shouldn't have gone!"

"She'll be fine. She'll have to buy food without asking, but she'll be fine."

"Buy without asking?"

Jakys nodded. "She'll find the food she needs, take it when the owner isn't looking, and leave pennies for payment. We gave her a large number of pennies to use for payment."

"But isn't that stealing?"

The little man shook his head, his beard tickling her face as he did. "No, it's not stealing to pay for what you take. It's probably wrong; I'm sure that minister in the village won't approve, but it isn't stealing. Coersion of some kind is a better word."

"I suppose..."

Before Durilda could ask another question, footfalls, running swiftly, grew closer and shouts calling for him echoed through the tunnels and into the room. Jakys jumped from his seat, setting his daughter down clumsily. He hurried to the tapestry that closed off the room and peeked out.

"What is it?"

"A runner has more news from Oxford. Waleron is calling for you."

"More news?" Jakys motioned for Durilda to grab her dolls. "Come."

The three little people hurried from the little sitting room and to Waleron's quarters. Merewyn caught Durilda's hand and sent a warning look to Jakys before asking the child if she'd like to go get some of the fresh cakes the women were baking for the evening meal. Jakys nodded. "Go with her. I'll be along shortly."

The runner was panting hard in his chair. He took occasional sips of water and wine both, but tired from his run, he found it difficult to talk. At last, he found his voice. "They've moved him. Engelard sent runners immediately with this new map." The young man dug in his pocket for the paper. "It is likely too late, but he insisted you know."

"That is very good of him. We'll send back gifts for all of you for your trouble," Waleron promised.

Jakys sent a tortured look to his king, begging

silently for the man to ask the unthinkable. Waleron demurred, shaking his head sadly, but Jakys persisted. "Waleron, your daughter! What they did for Reynilda!"

The runner glanced from man to man, curious about the nearly silent argument, taking place before him. "What is the problem?"

"Jakys..." Waleron warned, his eyes flashing.

"Waleron! They're children! We have an obligation—"

"Enough!"

The king's terrible tone would have quelled a less desperate man, but Jakys couldn't stand the idea of a terrified Dove searching all of Oxford with no idea of how to find her friend. "Do you know what they'll do to her if they expose her? Can you live with that knowledge? The child who saved Reynilda's life? Can you not ask? Engelard can say no, and I will respect that, but please, Waleron. Ask for her sake."

"What is it? What do you need?"

A brief nod was all the permission Jakys needed. "We'll send back a message with one of our runners. You rest for a day or two. I must go find Owyne and tell him to get ready."

"What message? What is going on?" The runner demanded information, but Jakys was already gone. Waleron, unhappy with the turn of events, sank back onto his throne-like chair. "He's going to ask the brothers near Oxford to find Dove and tell her where Philip has been hidden."

"This is bad?"

"If they see her, yes. She's perfectly harmless—just a child—but she terrifies men and Mæte alike."

"How can a child terrify anyone?"

Waleron studied his hands for a moment until he lifted his eyes and met the curious gaze of their visitor. "She has the appearance of a Scynscaþa."

Letty's heart leapt when a small, gray-hooded child crept into the village one afternoon. She'd been sent for meat from the butcher and had relished the job in anticipation of a good dinner, but nothing was as exciting as seeing Dove return. She hurried across the street to greet the girl, when a flock of children burst around a corner and began chasing the cloaked creature.

At first, Letty stepped back with a sigh, allowing the group of tormenting children to pass, but when several picked up stones and began throwing them in their chase toward the bridge, she grew angry. What a homecoming for Dove! It was terrible. Furious, she abandoned her quest for mutton and raced behind the group, shouting, no, demanding, that they stop.

At the smithy, Angus heard the familiar shriek of his sister and stepped out to see what was happening. He was confused at first as he saw Letty pick up a few stones and start hurling them with abandon. A grin split his face when he realized she was throwing them at the children who refused to stop at her command. He rushed out into the street, grabbing Dove and pulling her behind him. "Just stay there until I get them settled down," he muttered under his breath.

The girl wriggled, but his grip was like the iron he forged— nearly immovable. Letty caught up to them, gasping for breath, and threw her arms around Dove. "I'm so glad you're here! I was so worried." Then, as if she hadn't just shown absolute joy, she whirled, face furious, and began berating the children who all stood with stones in hand, stunned.

"How can you be so cruel? She's just a girl who has risked so much for Lord Morgan and—others. You need to leave her alone. Go home and stop being so horrible!"

A smirk twisted the corners of Angus' lips. Letty had been almost sedate of late, trying to put on airs of maturity, but in her defense of Dove she was magnificent. For the first time in many years, he was quite proud to have her as a sister.

"Aw, go on, Letty. Leave us alone. That thing had no business coming back. You're just bewitched by her after spending so much time in that sorceress' cottage."

"Bertha is a midwife, not a sorceress. You're crazy!"

"Is too," a girl agreed. "My modor won't have her near the house after spending so many years with the Gesceaft in her house! She's sure it'll bring demons into our home."

"Broðor Clarke would be ashamed of you," Letty screeched.

He'd planned to let her handle her own battles, but when a boy drew back and hurled a rock at his sister, Angus roared. He dropped Dove's hand and pulled Letty against him, sheltering her from the impact. Once the rock struck his shoulder, Angus let his sister go and leapt for the boy.

"Timothy Cooper, don't you ever try anything like that again." He backhanded Timothy's face.

The others backed away slowly, eager to watch the fight but not so eager to be caught in the backlash. As long as Timothy fought, Angus pounded him. At last, Hugo stepped out of the smithy to see what the ruckus was. At the sight of his assistant pummeling the cooper's son, he took several long strides and jerked Angus off the other boy as if it required no effort at all.

"What's this? What's gotten into you, boy?"

"He threw a rock at my sister."

Broðor Clarke arrived and stood behind the children, watching the altercation with interest. A couple of the children grinned up at him, expecting him to agree with Hugh and give Angus a dressing down for his misdeeds, but they found his eyes trained on the little cloaked child that stood behind Letty.

While Angus explained the situation, Broðor Clarke skirted the edge of the group and gripped the cloaked child's shoulder. His face wrinkled in confusion and then he frowned. A collective gasp went up as the minister jerked the hood off the village pariah.

"Elmer Buck." His tone implied he should have guessed.

"How'd you know it wasn't Dove?"

"Aside from the fact that they caught you? When have they ever caught Dove?"

"Well..." the boy kicked a stone in the dirt. "All right, aside from that."

"You're too tall and you don't have Dove's grace. She's grown, but not that much!" The minister turned to the group of incensed children. "You all go home. I'd better never hear," the usually gentle man growled, his voice growing more stern and imposing with each word he spoke, "of this kind of cruelty again. Dove is gone. Instead of being concerned for her safety or her soul, *you*," Broðor Clarke jabbed his finger into Elmer's chest, "mock her and incite the others to do wrong, and *you*," his hand swept the semi-circle of chagrined children, "torment an innocent girl."

A few chuckles prompted the minister to roll his eyes. "Well, an idiot posing as an innocent girl anyway. Go home and stop this nonsense. I'm ashamed of all of you."

Hugo pushed Angus back to the forge. Once Broðor Clarke turned to drag Elmer and Timothy home, the blacksmith stepped forward menacingly. "Do what the Broðor says, or you'll wish you had. He might not tan your backsides but I will."

The group dispersed, each child shuffling toward home, all anxious to avoid the dressing down they'd receive if their parents got wind of their scolding by the minister. Timothy and Elmer glanced at each other and then at Broðor Clarke. To their surprise, he was smiling—nearly grinning.

Dove Sings

CHAPTER 24

Jerome and Harold exchanged glances. They'd been riding at that slow, steady walk that was good for the horses but not for overtaking men who were many miles ahead of them. At last, Harold shook his head. "How attached are you to that mare?"

"I'm more attached to Lord Morgan. If he knew we had the chance to capture those men and didn't to keep our horses..." Jerome let the rest of his thought drift into Harold's mind, unspoken.

"We'll alternate trotting and cantering to the next town or village and then switch horses. If we do that, we can overtake them before they reach Oxford."

The younger man nodded. He was disappointed to lose his horse, but Jerome knew it was the best thing to do. Just as he urged his horse into a trot, a new idea occurred to him. "Perhaps we can pay someone in the town to keep them for us. It couldn't hurt to try."

Harold agreed. For the next couple of miles, the horses trotted before the men spurred them into a canter. Over several miles, they alternated a mile or two of trotting followed by a mile or two of cantering. As much as they both wanted to break out into a full gallop, the horses wouldn't hold out if the distance between towns were much farther.

At last, evidence of a village appeared around a bend

in the road. Jerome agreed to go find food while Harold made arrangements for care of the horses and hired new ones. The blacksmith insisted that a farmer on the outskirts of town was the best choice for the care of horses. "I wouldn't trust Jacob with a dead rat," he insisted. "That man, when sober, is the best horseman around, but he's on a drunk right now."

"I wouldn't want to leave these horses in such dubious care," Harold agreed. "We're hoping to return for them in a week or two."

"You with that group that rode through a few days back?"

Harold nodded. "You saw them?"

"Hard to miss a group of knights riding with someone obviously a lord or something."

"I suppose that's true."

"Where're you going?"

"Oxford."

The blacksmith shook his head. "Heard a lot of stories about that place—students rioting and causing trouble. Did the king call for help?"

"Worse than that, I'm afraid. Lord Morgan's protégé is being held for ransom. We're on our way to redeem him— if we must."

"Going to try to rescue him first?" The smithy grinned, one bad tooth showing at the side of his mouth.

"That was the idea. We won't risk the boy, of course, but if we can prevent criminals from getting away with his crimes..." Harold thought for a moment and then added. "We could use some help, though— if you're keen to make a little money."

"Always happy to improve the coffers. What do you have in mind?"

"There's a man riding behind us. Seems he was used by the kidnappers to deliver the ransom note to Lord Morgan. If you could find a way to detain him... get him talking... tell stories... anything. We'd be appreciative." The knight passed several coins to the man. "If you learn anything that'd help us catch these men, we'd be happy to hear it when we return."

"I'll do it, and be glad to. Times are tough, but there's no call for extorting money from honest folk."

Although Harold nodded in agreement, he didn't agree with the assessment. *It's easy to be smug when you have a skill that people always need. If you lost your hands, you might be singing a different tune.* "I see Jerome has found us some food. It's time to get back on the road. First farm on the left after the copse of hawthorn?"

"Yessir. That's the one. Will'll take good care of you."

"Um, Harold?" Jerome stared pointedly at the horses they'd ridden from Wynnewood. "We can't take those horses any farther."

"I know. The smithy here suggested a farmer outside of the village." He eyed the food in Jerome's hands. "Did you find what we need?"

"The baker's wife sold us some ham and cheese to go with our bread and I found apples and dried fruit."

"Ale?"

The smithy pointed to the edge of the town. "The tavern's there. Joseph makes the best ale there is."

Despite the desire to spur their horses onward, Jerome and Harold allowed them to walk the short distance to the tavern and then the half-mile to the farm. There, the farmer agreed to take care of the horses for a reasonable price and the men were trotting back down the road within the hour. Their new horses weren't quite as dashing as their battle horses, but they were fresh, smaller, and gave the men the speed they needed.

"He's still sick," David groused as he watched Philip stir restlessly in his sleep.

After the first night of good sleep, Philip had taken a sudden turn for the worse. Nearly delirious at times, the men took turns watching him while the others wandered through the town, listening, waiting. While Philip shivered and talked wildly of a ge-sceaft and scynscaþa, whoever was in charge would slice more onions to strap to his chest to stop the wracking coughs that seemed to grow worse, not better, with their ministrations.

David knew that Gipp was nearly ready to abandon the plan. Even if Lord Morgan did arrive, and it didn't look like he would, the chances of him paying a ransom for a young man who might not even live seemed unlikely. There had also been plenty of time for Lord Morgan to arrive, but there was no sign of him yet. That didn't bode well for their scheme.

He glanced at the fitful boy shivering under the blankets near the fire. It wasn't looking good at all. If it took too much longer, he'd run. It wasn't worth risking his neck, even for the hundred pounds they'd each receive. That'd set him up for life—no living in fear of being an outlaw.

"If he doesn't arrive by day after tomorrow," the frustrated man muttered. "I'll go work with the fishermen at Liverpool or something."

A fresh bought of coughing shook Philip from his sleep. David shoved a flask of water into his hands. "Drink."

After a few more choking gasps, struggling for air, Philip took a large swig. "Hungry," he whimpered.

The strong brave young man was gone. At first, Philip hadn't asked for anything, regardless of how much he may have wanted or needed it. His illness had reduced him to a pleading boy, begging for basic needs. David winced at how pathetic it sounded and then at the breakdown of such a healthy lad.

Gipp had brought home a chicken and had boiled it into a good rich broth. Too weak to feed himself, Philip lay miserably on his side, swallowing dutifully each sip of broth from the bowl David held for him. It felt hopeless. Stealing chickens to keep the boy in broth only to have him die seemed like an unnecessary risk, but without the broth, he'd die sooner.

A noise outside sent David to the door. He'd grown jittery with the delays and Philip's illness, but he couldn't help it. If they were caught, they'd be hanged. He'd been nervous from the start; so many things could go wrong. That promise of a hundred pounds had been too tempting to resist, but in retrospect, he regretted agreeing to the scheme.

The night was inky black. Without a moon to illuminate the churchyard across the way or even the church, it looked like a vast void. "James?"

At first, he saw nothing. It seemed as if the sounds had been a figment of his nervous imagination. However, just as he started to close the door once more, the noise came again. He shivered, a bead of sweat forming on his upper lip. It sounded eerie, but he couldn't pinpoint what it was. Nervous, he shut the door and latched it.

Noises became torments for him. The cracking of a log in the fireplace made him jump; a dog howled outside sending fresh shivers down his spine. From the scurrying of a mouse in the corner to the imaginary sounds that his mind conjured from the fear in his heart.

A rattle outside the window nearly made him jump out of his skin. He swallowed, choking on his dry mouth. Was that a shadow? How could there be a shadow when there was no moon? There it was again. David stood and shook himself. "It's just the wind. Calm down. You're acting like a little girl," he muttered to himself.

Eager to focus on something, anything to keep his

mind from wandering to greater fearsome heights, he rose and began chopping vegetables. They might as well make a soup with the meat from the chicken. To keep the silence at bay, he sang. *Sumer Is Icumen In* was a new song to him and perfectly in season; it was sprightly, comforting, and drowned out the strange sounds that persisted on invading the cottage.

Philip stirred again, this time blinking. "Wha—"

"Need another drink?" David would do nearly anything to ensure the young man got better.

"Where is she?"

Now the lad is crying for his modor. Can this get any worse? David gave a sad glance at the door as if hoping the others would return and decide what to do. "Where is who, Philip? Want some water?"

"I hear her singing." The boy forced himself to a sitting position. He blinked slowly as he glanced around, trying to orient himself.

"That was me," David admitted. His irritation had to have been evident in his voice. Since when did he sound like a woman?

"Not you. Can't you hear that? Listen."

David did hear it. A high-pitched song seemed to float as if on the wind. After a few seconds, he realized it was probably just that—the wind whistling through tree branches or humming over a jug outside.

Philip seemed to have new life in him, though. He watched the door eagerly as if waiting for something. David couldn't help but fear that "something" was an angel of death.

"Look outside! Open the door, please!"

Anxious to quiet Philip, David dropped the carrots he'd been breaking into the pot and wiped his hands on his tunic. "All right, all right. There's nothing out there unless maybe the others are home. Can't see how you'd hear them before me, though."

With the bar shoved out of the way, David opened the door, allowing the cold, damp air of the night to enter the cottage. He glanced over his shoulder to ensure that Philip saw the empty doorway. "See, there's nothing there." However, when he turned back to shut and bar the door, something stepped into the tiny shaft of light that emanated from the cottage.

Beneath Dove's Cloak

CHAPTR 25

The last mile of tunnels before Dolfin reached Oxford seemed to take forever. His calves ached, his lungs burned, and his heart pounded so loudly he could hear it in his ears. He wanted to stop, to rest. What could an extra half hour matter? No one would know. He'd run faster than ever in the past few hours.

The Mæte were deceptively swift runners. With endurance that any man would envy and a quickness that compensated for the shortness of their legs, the runners in the tunnels beneath England covered ground in a fraction of the time it would take their counterparts above ground to traverse.

At last, he began to see familiar faces. He was his king's favorite runner, often trusted with important and sensitive messages—like this one. Just seeing the looks of admiration in the faces of some of Oxford's runners made continuing much easier. A young lady, one he'd seen often on his trips, smiled at him as he passed, inspiring him to kick up his speed a little just when he wanted most to stop.

The entrance to King Engelard's chambers was guarded as usual. While he gasped and panted, guzzling the water the motherly women of Oxford brought him, Dolfin waited for entrance to Engelard's room. It was much richer and finer than the king's room of his community, but then it was an older settlement and had a rich mine to work from without the hindrance of an irritable dragon.

The large tapestry parted and a fierce-looking guard held it aside for him. "Engelard is pleased to welcome you."

"Thank you." He never really knew what to say to the guards. He knew his messages were often an interruption, but they weren't *his* idea!

"Dolfin, you've brought news?"

Engelard was the oldest man he'd ever seen. According to legend, he was the oldest of all the Mæte save a great, great, grandmother near the border of Scotland. The dwarf had the large flat nose that defined the look of his people—the men anyway. His beard reached his feet and was stark white. He wore robes of rich hues and fabrics that made him seem even more imposing.

"I have— from Waleron. He asks that I give you this." Dolfin passed the letter from the leader of the Wynnewood Mæte.

The silence seemed to echo around him as he waited for Engelard to read the letter. His breathing, the shuffle of his feet, and even the shifting of the guard's hand all sounded unreasonably loud to him. After what seemed an age, Engelard folded the paper and slipped it in an unseen pocket. "You know the contents of the letter?"

He nodded. "Yes. We were told to memorize it in case something happened to it."

"Do you know what Ganelon thought of this—this—request?"

"He feared it was too dangerous, but he said he would not refuse Waleron. He said Waleron would never make a request such as that without extreme provocation." Dolfin swallowed hard. "He told me I was to volunteer to go if my strength was with me."

"And will you?"

"How long before we would leave?"

The king glanced at his guard before answering. "Some hours yet. It's still full day out there."

"With some food and a little rest, I'll be ready to go."

"Tonight isn't necessary. Tonight you rest." Engelard pointed to the guard. "Gobin will escort you to the gathering room. Sleep tonight. If we don't find this child tonight, we'll need you tomorrow. You need to be fresh, though. Trying to go tonight will just ensure that mistakes happen."

Though the words stung a little, Dolfin was grateful. He followed Gobin through the familiar tunnels to the wide circular gathering room that was the hub of all Mæte communities. There he found himself almost instantly surrounded with good food, plenty of ale, and children clamoring for stories of his run. As he ate, he told of running through tunnels with his little torch, dashing over ruts in the floors. He explained how the dirt-packed ones were easier on the legs than the hard, stone-inlaid ones, and how fast his time had been.

From the corner of the room where an archway led to the various family chambers, that same young woman watched him. An unconscious swagger entered both his voice and his step as he demonstrated for the children. A giggle reached him in time to make him flush. He was being ridiculous. The Grand Fete was coming soon, and that was soon enough to get to know the pretty girl with laughing eyes.

"Well, I need to rest. I've been running for hours. I'm tired."

Just outside the North Gate of Oxford, Dove waited.

She listened to every rustle, every bark, every cry in the night. The previous night she'd wandered through the streets of Oxford listening, waiting, but hearing nothing. The map had done her no good. She'd found an abandoned hut at the edge of the city within the city gates. So, with nothing else to do, she'd wandered the streets, listening, occasionally asking questions and then dashing off into crowds before someone could ask who she was and what she wanted.

Late that second night, she'd been stunned to find a Mæte at her elbow, beckoning her to follow. In a secluded corner, hidden from the watchful eyes of the guardsmen, the man told her to meet them outside the North Gate the following evening. No matter how she'd pleaded, the little man had been adamant. "You cannot get out of the city without being seen. Tomorrow, be out before the gates are shut. We will come to you. We know where the boy is, and Waleron asked us to show you."

So she waited, anxious to hear again from the little people who could help her find her friend. Nervousness made her jittery, and despite stern self-admonitions, Dove picked at her cloak, kicked at rocks, and jerked her head at the slightest sound.

A tap on her arm nearly caused her to scream. Heart racing, she glanced sideways and saw the familiar outline of a Mæte. "Come with me. I will show you where he is." He took a few steps and hesitated. "We think he is ill."

"Where," she whispered, "should I take him once we get out of there?"

"You will take him to the other side of the church. Several of our men wait for you there. Tomorrow they'll help you sneak into the town with him, but you must get him out alone. We cannot be seen."

"I fear I may have to be."

"Dolfin's note says you are perfectly harmless to us." The doubt in his voice was hard to miss.

"I cannot harm you even if I wanted to. I'm no different than any child you see on the streets except that I look frightful."

"Come with me then. Hold onto my cloak so you don't stumble. Without a moon, it'll be hard to see anything tonight."

With one hand full of his cloak, Dove stumbled after him, nervous at the idea of leading Philip away from pursuing captors without light. He led her along a road, over a stone fence, and across a field and then lit a torch. "It's over there—that house by the church. He's in there, and if his captors are to be believed, he's sick." The man pointed to the other side of the church. "Get your friend to that side and I'll be there with the others to help you get him to a safe place for the night. It won't be comfortable, but it'll be warm enough."

She nodded. "I should put out the light before I get within sight of any windows, right? Are there any on this side?"

"No, there's only one window on the opposite side from this one next to the door."

It took a couple of minutes to decide what to do. At last, she straightened her hood, grabbed the torch, and set off toward the little house, thanking the little man for his help. Everything could go wrong after this. Everything.

Hacking coughs greeted her as she reached the back of the house. Philip sounded terrible. With the torch driven firmly in the ground, Dove crept around the sides of the house and listened near the door. As hard as she tried to listen, she heard little but Philip's coughs and a whimper. The window would not show the light, covered as it was with some kind of curtain. Eagerly, she rushed back for the torch; it would help.

Her heart sank as the door opened. She wasn't ready. Not yet. A man stepped outside and glanced around before he closed the door and barred it. Dove's eyes rose heavenward. "Oh, I AM. We need You now. I can't do this alone. I am so scared."

Singing from inside the cottage gave her an idea. If the man could sing, so could she. Once he was distracted with helping Philip, she'd sing. Philip would recognize her voice, surely. Somehow, they'd get that door open, and this time, Dove would be ready.

The moment came. Immediately, she began singing in the high, eerie voice she used when charming the dragons. With each line, her voice grew stronger and richer, but it did no good. The door stayed barred. If she had to, she'd knock and try to sound like a man, but she knew the chances were slim that such a crazy plan would succeed.

Then suddenly, as if her prayer was answered, the creak of the door bar sent a discordant note into her song. This was it. She stepped directly into the path of the door and waited. The door opened and she took a deep breath, raising her hands to pull back her hood.

Philip couldn't believe it when he heard the familiar sounds of Dove's melody. At first, David ignored his attempts to hear more, but at last, his pleas sent the man to the door. What happened next seemed as if part of a dream. David opened the door, and there stood Dove as if coming to make a call. Before he could call out, she threw back her hood and screamed.

In all the different ideas he'd ever considered, the vision before him was as far from anything he could have imagined. She looked wild, crazy. White hair stuck out on all sides of her head, matted and with some of the ends curled. In the light of the fire, her eyes seemed to flicker and glow red. Her skin, ghastly pale, was nearly translucent.

Before he could warn her, she screamed and rushed at David, brandishing a torch. The man, panicked and horrified at the sight of what seemed to be a ghost in a dark cloak, backed away until he tripped over a bench and struck his head on the corner of the table. Blood spurted from the wound, but the man's eyes went glassy before he slipped into unconsciousness.

The next few minutes were a blur. Philip tried to scramble to his feet, but they refused to hold him. Dove was at his side in an instant. "Come on, Philip. Hold onto me. We have to get out of here before he wakes again. Come on!"

As she spoke, Dove dragged him up from the floor, draped his arm around her shoulder, and half-hung the blanket he'd been using over his shoulder. "Hold onto that." His fingers clutched the fabric desperately. Then, as each second turned into minutes, he stumbled along with her, surprised when she shut the door behind her.

"Why—"

"You don't want it to look suspicious if the others return, do you?"

"I can't walk all the way back to town, Dove. I just can't."

"Stop whining. We'll have help once we get to the other side of that church."

Philip's answer was drowned by a fresh wave of coughs. Despite his weight on her, Dove dragged him across the yard and around the back of the church. There, four Mæte waited with a stretcher. "He does sound quite ill," the little man who had guided her to the house admitted.

"He is, but he'll be better with some fresh air and good food. That cottage was the stuffiest thing I've ever been in."

"Get on the stretcher. We have to go." Once Philip was stretched out, the little man pointed to Dove. "Now, cover him as if he were dead. If he coughs, pretend it's you."

"I suppose I'm supposed to cough without moving," Philip added dryly.

"It would help, but we'll try to cover it. Just go! We don't have much time."

The trek would have been easier in the moonlight, but the advantage to having the darkness on their side couldn't be denied. Their little party interested the guards, but not enough to leave their posts for what must have appeared to be removing a highly infectious body from somewhere. It was nearly a mile from the church before the little men stopped and pointed. "See that hovel? Stay there until morning, and then get him to town. He needs a physician."

Dove nearly dragged Philip into the small hut, extinguishing the light as they entered. She made a pallet on the floor with her blanket and then tucked his around him. Her flask, full of ale from a street vendor, helped quench the raging thirst of her fevered friend. "I wasn't sure I'd find you. You weren't where Jakys said you'd be."

"Jakys sent you here? How'd you manage to—"

"Shh. I'll tell you all about it. You listen. There are tunnels that connect our Mæte to other colonies of them. They have runners that send messages back and forth, and the Oxford people heard of someone connected to Wynnewood being kidnapped, so they sent news to Waleron."

"I had no idea."

"I don't think we were supposed to know, but Waleron is still grateful. He sent Jakys and Baldric to my cottage one night..."

All through the night, Dove told of her adventures, how she'd left the village without a word, traveled along the coast, essentially stealing to keep herself fed, and then about the three men who had frightened her after she'd turned east from Liverpool. "Philip, I don't understand why he didn't run. You saw me! You saw how that man that had you reacted. That's how everyone reacts, but this man almost seemed as if I looked familiar. I think he knows someone like me."

Between coughs, Philip asked questions and finally said, "I think, Dove, you have seen an angel. I think he protected you."

"Why me? That makes no sense. Why would an angel ever consider—"

"Think about it, Dove. The verse says that 'many have entertained angels unawares.' I think the angel was helping you to get to me. Why, I'm not sure, but it seems to make sense. He found you twice. The first time, he didn't attack you or run which helped you trust him when the next time came. You knew he wasn't afraid. Fear is what makes people lash out at you."

She didn't speak. A good half hour passed with Dove lost in thought as she tried to take in Philip's words. It seemed too fantastical to be true, but her only other idea was even more preposterous. "That makes more sense than my idea."

"What was your idea?"

"That I look like my mother and he knew her. I thought maybe he recognized me because of her, but it was so dark and there was only the light of the fire to see by. That is crazy."

"Well, it's possible," Philip mused. "I mean, why couldn't it be that?"

"Because I think your idea, as odd as it is, is much more logical."

"I never thought I'd see the day when you considered the interference of angels in your life to be logical."

Again, several minutes passed before she spoke. "I've

been talking a lot with I AM—praying, really. Do you think He listens to me?"

"I do."

"I think He answered my prayer. I was so scared, Philip. I knew I'd have to throw back my hood and—"

"And what?"

Dove shrugged with a deliberate air of nonchalance. "And I thought you might refuse to come with me, but you didn't."

"That's just silly. Why wouldn't I go with my friend who traveled hundreds of miles to rescue me?"

"You saw me, Philip. You know why."

It was Philip's turn not to answer. At last, he shrugged. "I can't remember what is real and what isn't. I'm not sure this is real. It *seems* like you're here and talking to me. I think I remember you giving me a drink, but then everything blurs and I'm not certain anymore."

"You saw me, Philip. I saw the look of horror in your eyes."

Philip shook his head. "Amazement—that you were there—certainly, but not horror. I think you were littler than I imagined and your hair is all wild. I know that. I just can't remember any more."

Resolved, she tucked his blankets in more firmly. "Good. Sleep, Philip. We still have to get you inside the city without someone blaming me for your abduction."

D ovely

CHA
PTR
26

horses at full gallop, pounded the road behind Lord Morgan's retinue. "Two riders behind us, Lord Morgan—gaining fast."

"Can you see them?"

"No, but I suppose I will be able to once they round that curve. We just moved out of sight."

"Turn, dismount, and draw your swords," the frustrated leader called.

Charles Morgan's frustration mounted with every thundering hoof beat. He didn't have time to deal with outlaws. With just a couple of hours left on their journey, he wanted to go, not fight someone for a few coins or a horse. Why would two men think they could overpower a lord and his knights?

"Here they come," William called.

The knights stood at the ready, swords drawn, and in an arc blocking the road. The two riders barreled around the corner and then reigned in their horses, one rearing in fear. Edwin dropped his sword. "It's Jerome and Harold!"

The two exhausted knights swung down from their horses, patting the animals' heaving sides, and praising the speed with which they'd traveled. "We made it! These are the best horses yet."

"What are you doing here? We thought we were going

to be waylaid by outlaws."

Jerome stepped forward. "I was in a tavern in Strafford and overheard the man that brought news of Philip's capture—you know the one with the stutter. He was looking for a man named Gipp Doggett. He said the man had a southern accent and a hooked nose and was heading to Oxford. We thought you should know."

This was excellent news indeed! "So you rode here at full gallop?"

"Of course not!" Harold protested. "We alternated between a trot and a canter and changed horses at every town. When we saw you ahead, we kicked up speed. We'll reverse it on the way home and try to get our horses back, but if not..."

"Philip is worth the loss of good horseflesh. I'll reimburse you."

The men had been stepping along at a slightly faster walk, but they slowed to allow Harold and Jerome to lead their horses behind them. As they walked, they listened to funny stories that had occurred along the route and told a few of their own. The entire group was relieved when they reached the next village and managed to change the horses for fresh ones.

"Let's go!"

Unfortunately, Jerome had grown accustomed to swifter travel. Mile after mile, he shifted in the saddle, anxious to arrive. Harold smirked behind his beard. "I think Jerome has developed a taste for speed. He seems fidgety."

The other men laughed, teasing Jerome as they rode onward, watching eagerly themselves for the sight of the city walls. At last, just a few hours before sundown, they spied the city. With just a little more than a mile to go, the men urged their horses into a trot.

The town bustled with commerce. Lord Morgan led his men to where he'd found lodgings for Philip and went to speak to the proprietor. "Wakeley, is it? I've come to help my protégé. Have you heard anything of him these past weeks?"

The man look confused. "He was gone for a couple of weeks, yes, but he came home two days ago, ill. He's in his room with the physician's assistant."

"Physician's assistant? Do you know this man?"

"Oh, yes. Joseph is one of the best in the town," the proprietor assured him.

"And the assistant? What do you know of him?"

An odd look entered Wakeley's eyes. "I've never seen him before. Short boy—quiet. I'm thinking he's an apprentice."

"You don't seem to like him." A fleeting thought entered Lord Morgan's mind, but he shoved it out again. Impossible!

"He's just so queer. Always skulking around the room in that gray cloak. He won't take it off, and Philip gets agitated if anyone even hints that he should."

Impossible or not, it seemed as if Lord Morgan's suspicions were correct. He waved for his men to find shelter for their horses and hurried up the stairs. Despite the knowledge that Dove must be there, Charles Morgan's eyes lit up in surprise when he saw Dove peek through a crack in the door. "Dove!"

The door flung open and a gray bundle flew at him, burying her head in his chest. "Oh, you're here and so soon! I was so scared."

"How did you get here, child?"

Dove tried to extract herself from the lord's arms, but found herself nearly trapped in them. From the other side of the room, Philip called out, his voice sounding quite odd and thick, "Isn't she dovely? I couldn't believe it when she showed up and rescued me. She's a rescuer—a tiny little rescuer—a dovely girl."

The child's hood rose to Lord Morgan's face and a

giggle escaped. "He keeps saying the silliest things. Joseph, the hælan, said the herbs and medicines are doing it." She giggled again. "Last night he acted so strangely, I thought he was drunk!"

"Well, I'd agree with him that you are a 'dovely' girl, but yes, I see what you mean."

Lord Morgan reluctantly released Dove and crossed the room to Philip's side. A hand on the boy's forehead and temples seemed to show only a slight fever, but the occasional coughs were worrisome. Cool air blew into the room from the window, making him wonder if it was a bad idea. "Does the physician recommend the open window?"

"No, m'lord," Dove whispered. "Bertha would insist, so when Joseph comes, I close the window. He thinks this room is just abnormally cool."

"Are you warm enough, Philip?" Though he knew the child had learned much from the midwife, he didn't like the idea of risking Philip's health on the advice of an young girl.

"Fine and toasty. When the window is shut, it's stifling in here. Dove keeps the room just dovely. It's a wonderful thing, isn't it?"

"I think," he murmured to Dove, "we should find out what herbs and medicines he's giving Philip. The boy does sound quite drunk."

"At least he's a funny drunk." Dove giggled. "He was singing last night between coughs. I couldn't make him stop. He sang the song that the minstrels sang about the night Lady Aurelia was supposed to be kidnapped, but he got it all mixed up. It was so funny!"

"Funny, funny, funny. All she thinks of is funny. She's a smart one, that Dovely. She scared David with a flick of her hood. Yessir, just a flick of her hood and the guy dropped dead."

Philip's words alarmed Lord Morgan. He turned to

Dove to see how she reacted, but nothing changed in the child's stance. Until his acquaintance with Dove, Charles Morgan had not realized how much he relied on people's eyes and expressions to judge what they were thinking.

"Is that right? You showed yourself to someone?"

"It's the only thing I could think of."

"And the man just dropped? He's surely not dead— fainted perhaps?"

The little hood shook. "No, he's not dead—I don't think. I frightened him, and he backed away. He tripped and hit his head on the table. There was a lot of blood, but there always is from a head wound, isn't there? I didn't stay and nurse him; I had to remove Philip."

A new thought occurred to Lord Morgan. "How did you know he was here?"

"Um…" Her hands fidgeted as she tried to think of a truthful answer that wouldn't betray her little friends. "Someone heard of Philip's abduction and came to tell me. I left right away."

"We couldn't have been far behind. How did we not overtake you?"

The child settled herself on a low stool next to Philip's bed and began helping him drink a glass of medicine-laced water. "I think you must have taken the road, and I followed the sea to Liverpool."

"You must have walked all day every day—"

"Night, m'lord. I walked at night."

"How did you see?" The idea was unfathomable, and yet, it was just the sort of faithful thing the girl would do. Dove was nothing if not loyal and true to her only friend.

"I used a stick mostly. It was silly, but I tended to walk off the road so no one would see me. Sometimes when I knew nothing was around I used a torch, but that wasn't often. The moon helped, though."

"Wynnewood thinks you are dead," Lord Morgan reproved gently.

"I couldn't wait. I had to go immediately if I hoped to be successful."

"Why did you not come to me?

The little hood ducked as she whispered, "I didn't think. I was told to go, and I went."

As he listened to her describe her journey and what they'd done for Philip since she'd dragged the boy from the cottage, Lord Morgan watched her. To his surprise, she hovered near him as if unwilling to be too far away from a source of strength. It seemed out of character, but nonetheless, she didn't shrink from him when he squeezed her arm or hugged her after describing something particularly frightening.

She's just a child. We forget that. She's so old for her years that we don't realize how frightening life is for her. People fear her—how terrifying that must be at times. She doesn't have the love and affection of a mother or father. How does a child live without that?

The questions filled his mind as he watched her care for Philip. To his surprise, he realized that her hands were bare, the small, slim, white fingers working almost effortlessly and with a grace that elegant ladies worked hard to achieve and often without success. "Dove, why are your hands exposed?"

Instantly, she withdrew them into her cloak. "I— I can't feel his fever through the gloves."

"I wasn't reproving you, child. I was just surprised."

"Dovely hands," Philip murmured stupidly.

Lord Morgan stood again and crossed the room, grabbing the bottle of medicine. "Is this what you're giving him?"

"Yes."

One sniff and Lord Morgan's head jerked back from the bottle. "And the physician said that this is what he needed?"

"He assured me it was essential. I've smelled similar

things from Bertha, so I didn't question it. You seem uncertain."

"He's had too much. Maybe a small amount a few times a day, but the boy is drunk—or nearly so."

"Drunk! I'm not drunk! I'm getting well! How could I be drunk. I feel just d—"

"Dovely, I know," the man agreed. "However, I think you should drink ale instead. This is too strong and you aren't used to it."

"Oh, ale sounds delicious. That stuff does taste nasty. I like ale." Philip rambled on for several minutes about his favorite foods, drinks, and a snowball fight he had in his dream. "I got him right in the backside. Right in the backside, it was."

Lord Morgan pulled Dove aside and murmured, "I'm going to go tell the men what I've found and get him some ale. Try to get some food—porridge would be good—into him."

"He's been talking funny ever since I found him. He can't even remember what I look like—keeps saying I was an angel. It's funny."

"Well, it could be fever delirium. Either way, let's stop the medicine for a bit and see if it helps." He stepped out the door and then returned immediately. "By the way, Dove. Thank you. You may have saved his life, but even if not, you certainly made my job of finding him easier. He is very blessed to have such a loyal friend."

Dove watched the door close behind him, sank to the floor, her back leaning against the wall next to the door, and wept. Weeks of long nights of walking as quickly as her legs would travel left her sore and exhausted. Her shoes were worthless. She'd "appropriated" rags from most houses and tied them over the shoes to help protect them from wear, but it only helped a little. Her feet had sores on several places, and she limped after standing for too long.

However, aside from the physical aches and the weariness, she was emotionally spent. Nights of wandering through strange forests, stumbling along lonely roads, and meeting up with the trio of outlaws—twice—took a toll on her that she hadn't anticipated. Simply speaking, she was weary—emotionally, physically, and if she'd admit it to herself, spiritually. For two weeks, she'd had no one but Philip's God to talk to and to trust. It was unfamiliar territory.

Now that Lord Morgan had arrived, the weight of the responsibility for finding Philip, for taking care of him, and for keeping free of the kidnappers was gone. Her tears were more than just pent up exhaustion and pain; they were also tears of relief. He would help her find new shoes and decent food. The Earl of Wynnewood was a powerful man. He'd bring Philip's captors to justice, and perhaps he'd loan her a horse for the journey back to Wynnewood.

Life could go back to normal. Dove's heart felt soothed with that thought—normal. There'd be no more late night prayers to a god she wasn't sure she wanted to trust. She wouldn't feel the desperate need to create songs of the stories about I AM and His people. She could put Philip's God back where He belonged—in the corner of her mind reserved for good stories and fun legends.

For just a moment, that idea sounded more wonderful than anything. She ached for that feeling of normalcy where myths of Jesus walking on water were fanciful tales to amuse her on a lazy summer afternoon. Just as she was sure life would be comfortable again, the thought of no more prayers hit her heart and nearly left her breathless. Her quiet weeping erupted into deep, sobs that made no sense to her. That lack of understanding grew into a fear she couldn't comprehend.

Dove didn't hear the door open. She didn't hear the alarm in the voice of the man who gathered her up from the floor, holding her in his arms in a way that fathers have since God created fathers. The broken little girl didn't even hear her friend's cry of alarm as she woke him from his brief nap. However, she did hear the gentle murmur of a kind man who promised her that he was there for her; he would protect her. He loved her. And in the quiet that followed the last strangled sob, Dove wondered if the words had been whispered into her ear by Lord Morgan or into her heart by the Great I AM.

Reluctant Confession

CHAPTER 27

Joseph, the physician, ranted at Dove when he discovered Philip sitting up in bed chatting animatedly with her and the bottle of medicine not empty as he'd expected. The girl sat, head bowed, silently accepting the verbal beating without a murmur. Philip tried to intervene, but trying to shout over Joseph sent him into fits of coughing.

"Get that hood off, you insolent little—" The enraged little man lunged for Dove, but she dashed out of reach, and Philip flung himself at the man, his weakened body ineffective.

"Stop! Leave her alone."

"Her? Who?" The physician frowned and glared at Dove. "Come here."

The gray hood shook and she backed toward the door. As she retreated, Joseph advanced, growing angrier with each step. "Stop! What is the matter with you? I will not put up with this. You were told—"

The door opened and Lord Morgan stepped into the room. His hand immediately reached for Dove, pulling her behind him protectively. "Who are you and what are you doing in this room?

"Get out of my way. That little—"

Lord Morgan's voice dropped low and stern. "Get out. I don't know who you are, but get out."

"It's Joseph, *Lord Morgan*—the hælan." Dove couldn't resist the emphasis on the lord's name.

"That little—who?"

Without a word, Lord Morgan opened the door and gestured for Joseph to leave. When the man hesitated, he grabbed the physician's sleeve, jerking him out the door. "Your services are no longer required. I'll have the innkeeper send you payment."

"But—"

The door slammed in Joseph's face. Dove's eyes grew wide as Lord Morgan hunkered down on his heels, his face nearly close enough to see into her cloak. "Are you all right, Dove?"

"Yes. He frightened me, but he did not harm me."

The man's eyes traveled to where Philip sipped some water at the end of a coughing fit. "Are you not feeling better?"

"I was until he came in." There was no doubt who the *he* Philip spoke of was. "Dove told me I was a little intoxicated last night."

"Or delirious. It could have been the fever," Dove insisted. "But you did talk foolishly."

"Has she told you your new pet name for her?"

Philip's head whipped to see what Dove would do and found her examining a crack in the floor with her toe. "No, what is it?"

"You kept referring to her as—"

"Lord Morgan, *please!*" Dove pleaded. "He never would have if he wasn't sick."

"What is it? I'm curious now."

The girl sank onto a bench in the corner, drooping. Lord Morgan glanced at the interested eyes of his protégé and back at the upset girl in the corner. He moved to her side and sank onto his knee. "Philip wants to know, but if it bothers you..."

"It'll bother *him.*"

"People always say foolish things when they're sick. My father gets high fevers that make him silly. It's ok, Dove," Philip assured her.

"It's his decision. He should know that he won't like it, though." The stubbornness in Dove's tone seemed to say more than the words.

"I want to know."

"Dove? Do you want to tell him?" The teasing was gone from Lord Morgan's voice, and in its place resignation held. The fun was gone.

"No."

"Oh, come now, just tell me. I can't imagine I said anything terribly cruel." Sounding a little panicked, Philip added, "Did I?"

Dove's head shot up instantly. "No!" More quietly, she repeated, "No."

"You kept calling her Dovely. It was funny more because of when and how you said it rather than *that* you said it."

Philip's laughter filled the room and prompted a fit of coughing. Dove hurried to his side, pounding his back with her little hands and encouraging him to take slow deep breaths as the coughing subsided. "I—" he gasped, "—have to remember not—" Philip gulped for air again, "—to laugh so much."

"I think he needs more medicine. He's obviously still quite delirious."

"I am not," the lad protested. "I'll have you know, I've often thought that Dovely would be a fun nickname for you."

"I thought," Dove countered as she tried to stifle a snicker, "that Dove was the nickname. You told me that I was probably the first person to be given a nickname before I was named."

"Regardless, I am glad to see you feeling so much better, Philip. I'll send one of the men to pay the physician and find us a new one."

"I don't think we'll need one, Lord Morgan. I think he just needs good food, plenty of sleep, and a lot of laughter to break up the stuff in his lungs." The high childish voice seemed out of place with the maturity of Dove's words.

"As long as he continues to improve, we'll leave him in your hands. What do you need?"

"Shoes."

"Philip!"

"Well, she does. She has holes in hers. She limps when she thinks no one is looking."

"Let me see your feet, Dove."

Ignoring the command in Lord Morgan's tone, Dove shook her head, pulling her feet under her. "They'll be fine."

"Dove..."

"I can't," she choked.

"You've shown yourself to several people, and we both know that I know what you are. Now, don't be foolish. Show me your feet."

"Bertha—"

"Won't ever know. The shoes, Dove."

Hands shaking, Dove unlaced her shoe and pulled off her sock. Tears splashed onto her hands but she continued to pull off shoes and socks and handed them to Lord Morgan. She tucked her feet back under her and brushed the fresh tears from her eyes.

"Oh, Dove..." Lord Morgan gathered the child into his arms and held her close. "You can trust me—us. We are here to be your friends, and friends help when one of them is injured."

As he spoke, Lord Morgan gently lifted Dove's foot and turned it so he could see. The angry sores on the ball and heel of the foot turned his stomach. From across the room, Philip sat upright, horror on his face, but Lord Morgan shook his head before the boy could speak.

"Well, that needs some cleaning, and I don't think you should wear your shoes until it has healed. We'll get a cobbler in here—"

"No!" She tried to wrestle free of Lord Morgan's arms, but he held her fast.

"How does Bertha have shoes made for you?"

"She measures a strip of rag and takes it to him."

"Then we'll take a measurement as well." He turned to Philip. "Where are your papers?"

In minutes, an outline of Dove's foot, as well as a straight-line measurement were drawn onto the paper. They sent these with an errand boy to the cobbler with an order for a pair of low boots. Without thinking, Lord Morgan called for a housemaid to come wash Dove's feet, but when the girl flung herself on the other side of Philip's bed, cowering like a whipped animal, he sent the servant away again. It seemed as if her skittishness was worse than ever.

"I am sorry, Dove. I didn't think. I'll call for a bowl of warm water and arnica."

"Comfrey?" The request was barely whispered.

"You want comfrey?"

"It'll heal and help with the pain."

"Well then," Lord Morgan agreed, "I'll certainly ask for comfrey."

"Will they capture all the men, do you think?" Philip asked the question with great trepidation. He had a secret—one he'd rather keep to himself. However, there'd be no hope of it if they captured the men who abducted him.

"We have the man they hired to bring me the news and one of the other men, David. We've heard that James and Gipp went south, so some of the knights are after them."

They had David. The man was a coward. He'd do anything to avoid a hanging, but it would do no good. They'd all hang if caught, but a desperate man will try anything—even confession. He had to tell his story.

"Lord Morgan?"

"Hmm?" The Earl of Wynnewood was at the window, watching as a child dashed away from his mother only to be dragged back to her side by an older sister.

"I need to tell you something. I did something wrong when they took me."

"That doesn't sound like you."

Philip squirmed. "It's just that they were going to kill me—that's why they took me."

Stunned, Lord Morgan whirled to face Philip. "Kill you! Why?"

"The men were hired by a tavern keeper that I know. He had befriended me. I think he liked that I was not noble like the other students. He thought I sympathized with him—and I did."

"Then I don't understand," Lord Morgan said. Why would he want you dead?"

"I didn't understand that either." He coughed, his chest screaming with pain. "The men, they called him 'Mad Hob.' It seems he plays up to people and expects their loyalty in return." Philip hesitated, not wanting to admit the trouble with the other students.

"There is more." It wasn't a question; it was an order to continue.

"Some of the students, mostly Australes, objected to my presence. Hob helped me avoid their schemes. He thought I was so against the students that I'd lie about them. He accused several of damaging property and refusing to pay a bill. The constable was called, but then he asked me to give proof of his statements."

"And you wouldn't lie about it."

"It seemed cowardly," Philip admitted, "to get revenge with a lie. I wouldn't have protected the students had it been true but..."

"I see." The amusement on Lord Morgan's face told Philip that he really did see.

"I wanted to. It was tempting. One of the students has tried to torment me since the day you all left. He thinks I'm too unlearned, not aristocratic enough— everything. It was so tempting to agree with the townsmen, but I couldn't lie. I started to, but I couldn't."

"They were going to kill you over a bench? I think you're being a little paranoid."

"I thought it was crazy too!" he protested. "When they started talking about how to kill me without them getting caught, I thought it was kind of a 'teach the young pup a lesson' kind of thing. I thought they were just trying to scare me." Again, Philip's voice grew quieter. "Then I realized that they weren't joking. Hob wanted to make an example of me to the other students. Don't cross the townspeople. By the time I realized how serious they were, I did start to panic. Then I did something—I'm so ashamed of myself."

"What did you do, Philip?" Dove asked the question before Lord Morgan had a chance to open his mouth.

"I was a coward. I talk a great deal about how wonderful heaven is with Jesus, but I was terrified. Death itself wasn't so bad, but the dying part..."

A strangled sound came from Lord Morgan. Dove laid a sympathetic hand on the man's arm, but Philip knew that sound. It was the sound of a man desperately trying not to laugh.

"It's all right. What did you do?" This was all Charles Morgan could say without dissolving into laughter.

"I told them who my benefactor was." Choking, Philip's voice rushed on quickly, trying to stop the roar of protest that he expected. "I'm sorry, Lord Morgan, but the man had a knife out and was coming toward me. I've never been so terrified. The beating I got during the siege was nothing. Gipp wasn't going to stab me and walk away. He was going to torture me just for the fun of it. So—" a choked sob stopped him. Philip couldn't continue.

Lord Morgan sat his tankard of ale on the table and moved to Philip's side. "I don't care what you said, what you promised, what you suggested. It kept you safe long enough for us to get to you."

"I suggested that if you were willing to put so much money out for my education, maybe you'd be willing to put some out to spare my life."

"That was intelligent." Dove sounded impressed.

"It was wrong. I had no business using someone as generous as Lord Morgan to save me from my own fears."

"You had every right to do whatever you could to keep yourself alive when in the hands of criminals. I would have been angry if you had not. If we had lost our friend for something so preventable—"

"I felt as if I was taking advantage of you, but—" Philip dropped his head and whispered, "I was so scared."

"Well, it worked. That's what matters."

"It was wasted. If you paid the ransom, they were going to kill me afterward. If you didn't pay it quickly enough, they were going to kill me. The only reason I'm alive is because Dove found me and terrified David into knocking himself out."

"Well, I think she played up her situation. I doubt the average man would have been that bothered by her—not down here. People aren't as superstitious down here as they are in the north." Lord Morgan smiled at Dove.

"I don't care," the child protested. "It helps sometimes. If I'd have been just any girl, the man wouldn't have been startled at all." She glanced at Philip. "For the first time I am glad I was born as I am. When I

AM says that I am fearfully and wonderfully made, I can agree now. I frightened the man and there was a wonderful result."

As if he hadn't heard Dove, Lord Morgan leaned closer and said, "I think you have proven yourself to be resourceful. I'm proud of you."

Relief washed over Philip. "I'm just glad you aren't ready to thrash me for my impertinence."

"Well, I didn't say I wasn't..."

Laughter erupted in the room, accompanied by a few coughs. The chambermaid cleaning the room next door shook her head. "Those northerners are so odd."

Recognition

CHAPTER 28

Justice was swift. Philip watched with Lord Morgan as his captors were led to the gallows. The crowds cheered as the noose slipped over Gipp's head. Students and townspeople alike applauded as the hangman kicked the bench out from beneath Gipp's feet. "I'm glad Dove didn't come," Philip murmured to himself.

"I am too. She's such a sensitive soul."

"As soon as her shoes are done, she'll leave. I'm worried about her. I don't know how much money she has left, and Dove won't take what she needs without paying for it. She'll starve first."

"Leave? Lord Morgan frowned. "She can ride back with us. Why would she leave?"

Philip shook his head. "She doesn't think like we do. She protects herself, and part of that protection is how she hides from sight." He sighed. "She won't ride out in the open during the day."

"But we'd be there to protect her."

"Lord Morgan, she traveled at night and still stayed off the road on the off chance she'd actually meet someone. Who wanders the roads at midnight?"

The next man must have been hung as they were talking, because a cheer erupted from around them. Lord Morgan glanced at the gallows and then turned back to Philip. "How would she react if I asserted my authority? I don't want to make her more fearful, but she cannot walk home alone again. She's just a child."

"She's thirteen, m'lord—at least."

"She seems too small to be thirteen. Surely, she's a little younger."

"My modor says that she thinks Dove didn't have enough to eat when she was tiny—that it stunted her growth." Philip shrugged. "Then again, she's almost taller than the baker's wife."

"You have a point. I always see her as so young, but it would explain part of her maturity. She is unusually mature for such a little thing."

"I think part of that is living with Bertha," Philip mused. "I think that woman would strip the child from anyone's heart."

The moment he spoke, Philip's eyes grew wide. "I'm sorry, m'lord. That was inappropriate."

His words were nearly drowned out by Lord Morgan's laughter. "I think you just spoke what most people in Wynnewood think."

"Not all?" The question bordered on the impertinent, but Lord Morgan's amusement gave Philip the courage to try.

"I suspect that at least one of our friends thinks very highly of her."

Oblivious to the idea that it could be anyone but Dove, Philip shrugged. "I don't know. I know Dove is appreciative, and she respects Bertha's knowledge, but I don't think Dove is as immune to Bertha's lack of care and consideration for her as a person as it seems she is. I can't imagine anyone thinking it is acceptable to be so unkind to a child as Bertha was—still is!"

"I didn't say acceptable, Philip. I just mentioned that I think there is one who thinks very highly of Bertha— despite her deficiencies as a mother figure."

When the fourth man was hung, the students began

dancing in the street, almost taunting the townsfolk with their success. Someone pointed to Philip and called out, "He's the one that started all this!"

Before Lord Morgan could speak, several of his knights burst through the crowd and surrounded them protectively. Harold's voice rang out over the din of the protestors. "Stand back. Let the Earl of Wynnewood pass."

As if the name were magical, the people made a path for Lord Morgan and Philip to pass. With swords drawn, the knights led them from the streets, still blocking the onlookers from getting too close until they all reached the inn. Philip glanced at Lord Morgan as they climbed the stairs. "I can't imagine what Dove would have done if she'd have been there."

"Probably tossed her hood off and screamed like a banshee to make them run screaming."

Laughing, Philip opened the door to his room. "It sounds like she has made somewhat of a habit of that, doesn't it?"

"Who has made a habit of what?" A shadow at the window moved and stepped into the light. "I saw the crowds and the knights with their swords drawn. What happened?"

"Someone recognized Philip and the students got a little rowdy. Harold was just preventing a problem before it became one." Lord Morgan pulled up a chair. "What have you been doing?"

"Breaking in my new shoe. One is done. The innkeeper brought it up a while ago and left it." She laughed. "He came up a bit later to bring fresh water and was so confused when it wasn't on the bed."

Lord Morgan glanced at the floor, but her stocking feet showed no shoes. "How are you breaking them in if you aren't wearing them?"

Her hands appeared from within her cloak, the shoe

in one of them. She worked the leather back and forth, side to side, rolling, twisting, folding. Each movement made the next easier. "I'll put them both on and wear them around the room to help my feet grow accustomed to them before I start home."

"About that—"

Dove set the shoe on the table and spoke as she turned to face him. "I'm not going back with you, m'lord. I cannot. Don't ask it of me. I won't."

"You—"

"No!" Without another word, Dove hugged Philip, pulled on her old shoes, filled her pack, and strapped it onto her back. As she worked, Lord Morgan explained his plan, trying to keep his voice as patient as possible, but she ignored him. She pulled the little pouch of pennies from behind a cupboard, and slipped it into one of the inside pockets of her cloak.

"I'm glad you are safe, Philip. Come home soon."

At the door, Lord Morgan stepped in front of the door to block her way as he dug into his own money pouch for more coins. "Here then. Be sure you have enough."

At the pile of coins, Dove shook her head. "It's too much. I need a little for each place, not this much."

"Ask the innkeeper to exchange them for you." Feeling helpless, the man waited until she began to shut the door behind her and then added, "Find the Mæte. They will help you. Tell them I will pay them."

Philip stared, horrified, as the door shut behind his little friend. Anger welled up in his heart as he realized that had Lord Morgan listened, she might have stayed longer. "Why didn't you stop her—convince her to stay until you left at the least?"

"Because we both know that she would have slipped out in the night. This way she might possibly reconsider. It isn't likely, but it's better for her to go of her own accord, than for me to force it."

"The Mæte. How did you know?"

"It only makes sense. Who else could have learned of it? There are fairytales of little people who live in the earth and have an enormous labyrinth under the whole of England and Wales. If the little people exist, why not the tunnels?" Lord Morgan watched as Dove slipped into the crowd, blending into the throng that still cheered the death of Philip's kidnappers.

Philip stood. "I want to talk to her. I'll be back. She might give me an idea of the route she'll take. Maybe you and your men..." Philip grabbed his own cloak and hurried out of the room.

Standing at the window, Lord Morgan shook his head and prayed for the safety of Philip's little friend. "They call her the ge-sceaft, Lord. She's more like an angel." He snickered. "I suspect that Dennis Clarke would chastise me for my faulty theology."

As he jogged down the stairs, the innkeeper beckoned. "The other shoe is here. Would—"

"Thank you!" Philip took the shoe from the man. "I need this."

"Where are you going?"

Dove jumped at the hand on her shoulder. "Philip! What are you doing here? If Lord Morgan—"

"I just wanted to walk with you for a while." He passed her the other shoe. "And the cobbler sent this. I thought you'd need it."

Through the streets of Oxford, they spoke little, but once outside the North Gate, Dove paused. "I have to go." She gave him a brief hug and then stepped back again. "Study diligently. Come home. Wynnewood isn't the same without you."

"Did you finish your swimming hole?" Philip felt the grin on her face even though he couldn't see it. It amazed him how often he could "read" her face without ever having seen it—well, not that he could remember.

"Yes. I enjoyed my first swim the day before I was called away."

"Do you know how to find the Mæte?"

The little hooded cloak shook with her head. "They found me. I saw which way they went, and I'll try to look, but I don't expect to find them. I don't know if I'd risk their help anyway. It would be best to go home the way I came."

"Along the coast? Isn't that a much longer route?"

"It is, but I don't have to worry about missing the village. At night it's hard to follow road signs and things. From Liverpool to here was very hard, traveling at night."

Philip kicked a stone, frustrated. "It isn't safe, Dove. You shouldn't go alone. What if I came with you? I could walk with you and then take the regular road home. Lord Morgan would loan me a horse, I'm sure."

"You're here to study, Philip. You need the education. How else will you be able to convince other children that I AM is the one true God?"

"I didn't quite succeed with you on that; why should I be able to convince anyone else?"

"You haven't failed with me—not yet. Sometimes I think..." Dove's voice trailed off as she remembered the long nights of prayer and song. "I sang most of your stories. You need your education to tell me more stories. Even your children—they will want you to tell them about Solomon and Daniel."

"I never got to tell you the story of Daniel, did I?" He felt it. That quickening of excitement in her when Dove was eager for something. She wanted to hear Daniel's story. "Let's go find a quiet place and introduce you to Daniel the young Hebrew in Babylon."

To his surprise, Dove didn't object. However, as they walked, a new idea formed in Philip's mind. They settled under a sprawling oak, and she slipped her pack off to be more comfortable during the story. "Ok, tell me about Daniel."

"I was thinking..." He swallowed hard, praying she'd agree. "You know, Daniel lived hundreds, maybe thousands of years before Jesus."

"He did?" Dove relaxed against the trunk of the tree, pulled her knees up to her chest, and wrapped her arms around them. "How do we know it?"

Philip started to explain about how they learned the dates, but he didn't want to become sidetracked. "Well, that's another story, even more amazing than Daniel's and happened a little earlier—I think you'd like it."

Silence was his answer. He waited, trying not to encourage or pressure her to accept the suggestion, but each second that passed made him anxious. Had he put her on guard? At last, she nodded. "That is a wonderful idea. You can tell me the other story now and I will have Daniel's story to look forward to when you return."

A sigh of relief escaped before he could prevent it. "Well, when Nebuchadnezzar was king of Babylon, he built an enormous statue of gold."

"How big? The size of a child, a man, a tree?"

"The Bible says it was sixty cubits high."

Dove's head jerked up, her hood slipping back enough that he felt as if he'd seen her. He whipped away while she reached up to adjust her hood. "You're good to me, Philip."

"You don't know how tempting it was to look. I mean, you showed yourself to a stranger—and me I guess—but now you hide again. I don't understand."

"But that is why you are so good to me. If you didn't care to see, turning away would mean nothing. You are curious and yet you give me my privacy. You *are* good to me, Philip." Her voice told him her eyes were twinkling—or would have if the sun shone on them. "Now, tell me about the king and his gold statue. That must have taken a lot of gold."

"Well," he continued, "I don't know if it was pure gold or gold poured over some other metal or wood, but it did take a great quantity for either, I imagine. When it was complete, they put it up on a plain in..." Philip hesitated. "Well, anyway, they put it up and the King called for all his counselors and advisors for a dedication. Then an announcement came. When all the musical instruments began playing, everyone was to bow down to the statue and worship it."

"Oh!"

"I see that you know what happened. Yes, the instruments played and everyone bowed to worship—except for three men. Their names were Shadrach, Meshach, and Abednego."

Dove's giggle made his heart ache for home. Even with her here, listening to stories in the old way, it wasn't the same. He wanted to be in the middle of the clearing, the sun smiling down on them and the birds in the trees unbothered by their presence. He wanted to practice his skill with a bow, chase her through the trees, across the sward, and around the point. He wanted to wave at the fishermen, and listen for the shouts telling that the men were home from sea. He ached to hear Broðor Clarke tell the stories that he now shared with his friend.

"Philip?" Dove sounded concerned.

"Sorry, I was just missing home. Where was I?"

"You just told me those funny names. Shackrack and the one that sounds like 'to bed he go.'"

Laughing, Philip nodded. "I suppose it does sound odd to us. I've grown used to the Hebrew names, I suppose—except for Mephibosheth. That still makes me laugh."

"You'll have to tell me about her sometime, but I want to hear about the three men who didn't bow." Dove's voice grew quieter. "I don't think you would have bowed, Philip. You are too loyal to I AM."

"Well, I hope I wouldn't, but I might have. You see, anyone who did not bow was supposed to be thrown into a fiery furnace."

A gasp from within Dove's hood made Philip smile. She always became so involved in his stories. "That is strange, isn't it?"

"What is strange?"

"Well, I AM says that those who do not believe and obey Him will be thrown into a lake of fire—even bigger than a furnace. These men had a choice between a furnace that would kill them quickly or denying their God and a lake that would burn them forever."

Now Philip was frustrated. How could Dove grasp something so vividly and yet still not believe? With more self-restraint than he knew he possessed, Philip nodded and continued. "That was the problem. The king gave them another chance, really. He didn't just toss them in the moment they were brought to him, he told them once more to bow, but the men told him they would not."

"How brave they were!"

Philip's lips twitched. She sounded like a besotted maiden mooning over a knight. It was one of those rare times when Dove was every bit the normal girl that she usually disdained. "They were. They stood before that king and said that they would not bow and worship a false god—that I AM would deliver them from the furnace and the king's hand."

"Oh, like Elisha?"

"Elijah," he corrected. Philip thought for a moment. "I suppose they could have meant like that, but the Bible doesn't say. It just says delivered from the king's hand which could mean a lot of things."

"Go on. What happened?" Dove nearly quivered with excitement.

"Furious, King Nebuchadnezzar ordered that the men be bound and thrown into the furnace."

"Oh no!"

Without waiting to hear her next observations, Philip continued. "The furnace was so hot that the guards who threw the three men into it were consumed by it."

A sniffle caught Philip off guard. "What's wrong?"

"I thought I AM would save them. I thought they'd avoid both hells. I thought you said that Jesus paid the penalty for—well, He hadn't done that yet, had He? I suppose that's why they had to die. I understand now."

"But they didn't die, Dove. The king was watching the furnace and stood, astonished. He said, 'Did we not put three men, bound, into the furnace?' And the counselors and advisors all agreed that three men were bound and tossed into it. Then the king said, 'But I see four men in there, just walking around.'" Philip couldn't help the excitement in his voice as he added the king's next words. "'...and the fourth one looks like the Son of God!'"

"The Son of God? Jesus?"

He nodded. "Yep. Jesus was in there with them."

Neither of them spoke for a long while. At last, Dove's quiet voice whispered, "What happened next?"

"The king called and told them to come out of the furnace. When they did, their hair was not singed, they had no burns, and they didn't even smell like smoke."

"I bet that king figured out who the true God is."

Philip's anger nearly boiled over and scalded Dove. He sat fuming as his mind threw accusation after accusation at her. *Why can you see that the king would see that, but you can't see it? Why can't you open your eyes and your heart to the God who gave you the intellect that makes you doubt? Why must you always reject what you are commanded to accept?* The words remained unspoken, but his heart hardened a little against his friend.

"Why are you angry?"

"I'm not."

The hood shook slowly. "That's a lie, Philip. You are very angry—with me."

He began to deny it. His pride welled up larger and more stifling than he'd ever felt it until he thought he'd choke with the intensity of it. He couldn't see it for the ugly pride that it was; he saw it as righteous anger. Philip was certain that Dove was deliberately hardhearted toward the Lord for reasons he couldn't understand.

Just as he began to protest, the truth of his heart hit him. His pride had overtaken him once again. He wasn't angry that his friend was rejecting the one true God. He wasn't hurt to think of his friend lost for eternity. He was frustrated and a little embarrassed that he hadn't been able to convince her to believe. It had been three years— three and a half nearly. How long would it be? Would she ever have faith? *Not if you keep pushing her away with your arrogance, Philip Ward*, he scolded himself.

"You're right. I am angry. It's wrong of me; please forgive me."

"But why, Philip. What did I say?" Before Philip could answer, Dove pulled his tunic, jerking him close and whispered, "Look behind you. See that man?"

Philip turned, staring over his shoulder at a man walking toward them. "Yes..."

She rose quickly, dragging him across the field. "That's him—the one that I saw. He's the one who acted as if he recognized me and hid me from the other men in that house."

"Maybe I should go ask—"

"Let's just go, Philip. He scares me. No one should see me and not run. He didn't run!"

The crazed, panicked sound in her voice confused

him, but Philip raced behind her, across the fields, over a stone wall, and then toward the river where they could hide amongst the trees. Had they bothered to glance back, they would have seen the man stop, turn, and with shoulders slumped, make his way back toward the city gate. As it was, it took Philip some time to calm his terrified little friend.

Through the Tunnels

CHAPTER 29

Darkness surrounded her, but Dove still waited near the low bridge just east of Oxford where the Mæte had disappeared the night they rescued Philip. She sang in her high, clear voice of little people—miners—who lived out of sight. After a while, she created a chorus to sing after each verse, hoping that it would bring them to her.

The night air was cool, but her cloak was warm and the blanket she'd carried for such a long distance covered her lap as she waited. Philip had tried to convince her to let him wait with her, but it wouldn't work. The Oxford Mæte barely trusted her as it was. If they saw him when they heard her voice, they'd never come.

The hours crawled past so slowly that it seemed as if time stood still. The noises of the night were familiar— even comforting—but nothing sounded out of place. She was tired; her body ached to sleep, but still she sang in that almost ethereal tone. She sang of a long journey, through tunnels under the earth, skirting little communities and finally reaching Wynnewood. Dove's song promised money from Lord Morgan and that King Waleron trusted her—they could too.

A hand on her shoulder broke the song. Before she could turn to see who was there, a voice rasped close to her ear, "No more singing. We'll take you to Engelard. He will decide."

As Dove stood to follow, her heart sank. She'd grown. Would the Mæte see her as harmless if she stood so much taller than them? Would she arrive home with her head intact?

"Lord Morgan promised to pay—"

"Tell Engelard."

A familiar dread filled her as the man and his companion handed her a blindfold. They led her, stumbling over unfamiliar ground, to a small building, and from there, Dove couldn't tell what happened. She followed the men, holding onto one of their tunics, the other hand held overhead to try to prevent her forehead from slamming into low places in the ceiling of the tunnels.

Unlike in Wynnewood, the distance was short, but she did feel like she was spinning in circles. They passed others who whispered, but Dove couldn't hear or understand what they said. She stood near a doorway, her hand resting on a tapestry, and waited as her guide went to speak to his king.

"Come with me." One of the escorts led her into the grand rooms of the king and disappeared behind the tapestry again.

Once in the king's chambers, Dove grew nervous. He would expect her to remove her hood and that would likely mean he would refuse her request—or worse. A prayer formed in her mind before she realized she'd done it.

"You may remove your blindfold." Engelard's voice was much higher than any man's she'd ever heard—he almost sounded like a woman.

She pulled it off and held it out to her escort, but the king shook his head. "Remove the hood. It is rude to hide from me."

"I am frightful. I'm harmless, but I don't look harmless. Waleron trusts me."

"This I know." Engelard was quiet for a moment and then ordered the others from his room. As she stood alone before the man who might make her journey home less terrifying and much shorter, Dove trembled. "There. I cannot risk my people to someone whom I do not understand. I have given you more leeway than I usually would. Remove your hood."

Shaking, her hands rose to push back her hood, and as she did, Dove smoothed down her hair as much as possible. The little man's eyes widened. Pulling her hood back over her head, Dove turned. "I will go."

"Stop." Engelard stepped closer and pushed back the hood again. "Bianca."

"What?"

"You look like her—Bianca."

"Who is Bianca?" Dove whispered.

"A legend I heard in the town when I was a little boy." His eyes twinkled in the firelight. "They say that a woman named Bianca, all white from head to toe, had eyes of fire when angered against injustice. The town called her Scynscaþa, but to those she helped, she was like an angel." Engelard stroked his beard as he watched the fire glow in her eyes. "Are you angel or demon?"

She dropped her head. "I'm neither. I'm just a girl who has no color to her hair, eyes, and skin. Otherwise, I'm no different from any other girl in Oxford or my village of Wynnewood."

"And you want to get home using our tunnels."

"Lord Morgan said he has heard legends. He said if they were real and your people helped me home that way, he would pay whatever you asked."

She held her breath, anxious to hear his answer. He went to a table near the fireplace and poured her a glass of something. "Drink. You will sleep here and Gildon will lead you to the next settlement after breakfast."

"Thank you. How much—"

"We can help a friend of Waleron's. I've heard what you did for Reynilda. You risked your life to capture that unicorn. We can escort you home. Gildon will show you to where to sleep."

Relieved, Dove curtseyed. She crept into the other room and presented herself to the men who had escorted her there. "Engelard says that Gildon is to show me where I sleep."

"You're staying?"

"Until tomorrow. Then someone will lead me home."

Home. That word wrapped itself around her heart like a warm blanket. She was going home.

Three days later, Dove followed Dolfin through the tunnels past the second community. Her first escort, Jevan, had not been friendly. Accustomed to running through the caverns that connected the communities, he'd walked faster than she'd ever imagined possible. By the time they'd reached Worcester, she'd been exhausted.

Dolfin, unlike the others, was chatty. He wanted to know about Wynnewood, how she'd gotten from there to Oxford, if she'd seen a pretty, young miss with laughing eyes and red hair, and if she'd attended the hanging. From the minute they stepped out of the gathering room, the questions flew.

"So you found Philip?"

"Yes. He was very ill, but he's fine now. He was to resume his lessons today."

Dolfin pointed to the archway ahead. "That one is low; be careful. So, how long ago did Lord Morgan send his son to school?"

"Oh, Philip is just a seaman's son. Lord Morgan decided to educate him when he showed aptitude for learning."

"How old is he?"

Dove ducked as she reached the archway. "He's sixteen."

"They didn't apprentice him to someone? I thought that boys were sent to be apprentices."

"He was," she agreed, "but his master taught him nothing. He should have been brought before the guild, but Philip didn't want them to do that."

"I don't understand."

As they walked, at a pace faster than she'd managed on her trek to Oxford but slower than with Jevan, Dove explained what had happened and how Philip had felt sorry for the perfectionist fletcher. "It was nice for me. Philip had much free time from his duties so he would come and help me hunt, work in the garden, and tell me stories."

"What kind of stories?"

"He tells me about I AM and the stories in I AM's book." The torch flickered on Dolfin's face as he turned to look at her. He was visibly confused. "You don't know I AM? I didn't either."

"Who is I AM?

"He is Philip's God. You know, the God of the churches where people go to worship." Her patient explanation would have insulted a less curious young man. It was nearly patronizing.

"But he isn't your god." Dolfin turned again, walking as swiftly as ever.

"No. I sometimes want to believe, but it is hard..."

"Tell me one of the stories."

Still enamored with the tale of Shadrach, Meshach, and Abednego, Dove retold it, careful to remain faithful to the exact facts that Philip shared. "I think he said that they were bound before they were thrown in, but I am not sure."

"It doesn't matter. It makes a better story if they were and then the King sees them walking around."

"Oh no," Dove protested. "Broðor Clarke requires us to tell the stories exactly as they are in the Bible."

"Why? A story should be told as interestingly—"

"But these stories are true—they really happened; I AM values truth. He doesn't want His book changed because then it isn't true."

Dolfin stopped mid-stride and turned to look at her again. "I thought you said you didn't believe in this god of Philip's."

"I don't." Confusion flooded her voice. "I told you that."

"You sound as though you do. You say the stories are true, you defend what this I AM says, how can you not believe?" He hesitated, remembering. "The son of god. This god has a son?"

"Yes, Jesus. That is the best part of that story. He walked in the furnace with those men hundreds or even thousands of years before He was even born!"

"How is that possible?" Dolfin was audibly skeptical.

"I think that is what Philip meant when he said that Jesus is 'the same yesterday, today, and forever.' He always has been God, but He came to live on earth as a baby.'"

"You know a lot about a god in whom you do not believe. You speak with great confidence. Why don't you believe?"

The next mile or two passed in silence as Dove pondered the question. Dolfin seemed to know she needed quiet to consider his question. However, the silence seemed to oppress him and he asked another question. "Do you pray to this god?"

"I have..."

"But you don't believe."

"Well..." Dove didn't know how to respond. "I—"

Anger welled up in her. "I don't see how it is any of your concern. You asked for a story and I told it."

"What does I AM require of His followers?"

"Everything," she whispered.

"Everything? Your money? Your family? What?"

Dove stopped, leaning against the wall, panting. She hung her head, unwilling to look up at Dolfin who waited for an answer. "He wants everything—you, your whole heart and life."

"And you don't want to give it up?"

"I don't know if I can." Admitting it aloud took more out of her than she expected. She slid to the floor, hung her arms on her knees, and dropped her head onto them.

"Why not?"

"I don't trust Him. I want to, but I don't." The words sounded wrung from her, even to her own ears. She glanced up at him and saw Dolfin nod. "I really want to."

Dolfin pulled out a flask and passed it to her. "What would he have to do for you to trust him?"

Her mind whirled. It was a question she hadn't considered. What else could I AM do to gain her trust? He had created her, sent His Son to die for her. He had possibly used Bertha to protect her even from death. Philip was convinced that I AM had led her to the cave in the blizzard. Why else would she have chosen to go up a steep cliff rather than to a familiar tunnel—into a cave where a dragon would keep her from freezing.

"He can't. He's done everything. It's me. I *can't* trust."

With his arms crossed, Dolfin stared into the depths of her hood, seeing nothing but understanding much. "Most gods must be taken on faith. What makes this one any different?"

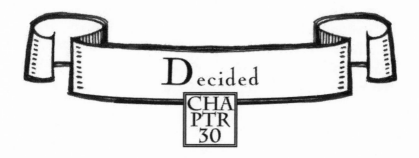

Decided

CHAPTER 30

Not two days after Lord Morgan and his knights rode out of Oxford toward home, Philip sat listening to his Theology master expound on the story of Elijah and the ravens. He'd heard strange things in Mass, but had attributed it to his weak translating abilities. This was unbelievable.

He was confused. After all, Master Adrian had insisted on perfect translations from the Latin, but now Master Francis took that translation and made it a mystical jumble of ideas that added much symbolism to the original story. Broðor Clarke would be appalled.

His questions were not answered satisfactorily. Confused and a little disillusioned, he strolled through the streets, trying to get his mind wrapped around the strange new ideas that his masters were teaching him. The sight of the church gave him a new idea. Eager to discover what he was being taught, he went inside in search of the priest.

A voice nearly made him jump out of his skin. "Can I help you?"

Philip turned and met the kindly eyes of the priest. "I—I have questions. I'm a student..." He sighed. "I guess that is obvious."

"Somewhat."

Halting at every third word, Philip tried to explain his

265

dilemma. After retelling the story he'd heard, he shook his head. "Broðor Clarke has always been adamant that we only retell things exactly as the Bible says."

"And who is Broðor Clarke?"

"Our minister. He teaches us what the Bible says. He prepared me for Oxford."

"Any man who does not teach the doctrines and traditions of the church has no right to teach anyone. Only a priest—"

"Oh, Broðor Clarke was taught by the priests in Ireland. I think he is a priest, but he just goes by Broðor Clarke."

"Heretical Irish priests. They've finally been brought under the authority of the church, but he was likely taught by men who resisted the pope." The man's kind eyes grew cold and hard. "Do not listen to the teachings of such a man. The church should try him for heresy."

A fearful dread washed over Philip as he listened. What had he done? If this priest pressed things, he could make trouble for the minister who had taught Wynnewood faithfully for many years now. "I see," he said, trying to sound agreeable. Well, thank you for explaining it. I'll have to study harder I suppose."

"Do you plan to study theology?"

He hadn't allowed himself to decide, but now Philip was certain. "Yes. I think I will."

"Good. We need devout men like you in the church."

Before the man could ask the name of his village, Philip made excuses to leave and hurried out of the building. He wandered the streets aimlessly for quite some time and then found himself outside the gates and strolling toward the tree where he'd told Dove the story of Shadrach, Meshach, and Abednego.

He dropped to the ground beneath it, his arms spread out beside him, lying up looking at the sky. Swallows flew overhead on their flight to places unknown for the winter. Where did the birds go? How did they know when to leave and when to return if the Lord did not somehow whisper it to them? Perhaps it was on the fifth day of creation. When the Lord spoke birds into existence, did He whisper directions to them then, or did it happen every year? Who knew?

What could he do? If the Bible was the Word of God, and even the priests and masters said that it was, then how could it be right to create doctrines from within it rather than teach those that *are* within it? Broðor Clarke had to be right. You must keep faithful to what it says rather than what it could mean in a mystical sense. The masters at the university seemed to have corrupted the teachings of the Bible—even reaching to the priest!

His spirit checked him. Did he have proof of his assertions? Was he certain of his suspicions? It would be a terrible thing to accuse godly men of spiritual corruption. Then again, was it not better to avoid the possibility of it if he was correct?

It hardly seemed possible, but the evidence was there. Did he want to put himself under the instruction of such men? Was he willing to risk his faith being altered by those who might not hold the same loyalty to the strict truth of scripture?

The moment the thought came to him, Philip knew he was not. Resolved, he jumped to his feet and strode back to town. The closer he drew to his lodgings, the more convinced he was that he must leave. He entered his room and immediately found his money, counting the coins carefully. He had a generous allowance that Lord Morgan had just replenished before leaving. There'd be plenty of money to pay for food and lodging along the way. Perhaps he'd be able to ride with wagons traveling between towns. Regardless, it was time to go.

It took him much longer to pack everything he needed to take than he expected. The moment he hefted the pack, he knew he'd not be able to travel far with something so heavy. After three or four repacks, more things coming out each time, he found a weight he was sure he could carry long distances.

He was late for his French tutoring, but Philip didn't care. He knocked on the door, opened it, and asked to speak to the master. "I'm going home. I just wanted someone to know that I'm fine, but I'm leaving Oxford. You've been an excellent instructor. Thank you."

"Philip, you have great promise as an academic. Are you—"

"I should have gone home with Lord Morgan. I didn't, but I'm going now. Thank you for your patience with me. Bye."

Unwilling to risk anymore questions, Philip turned and hurried out of the building and toward the gate. He couldn't get too far in one day, but out of the town seemed imperative. A farm wagon rattled past, offering him a ride less than a mile from the town, much to Philip's relief.

"Where're you going?"

"North— home."

Dove tramped ahead of the runner, Rodney, the light from his torch doing little to help her see the path. The first five runners had been helpful even if all of them weren't as friendly and chatty as Dolfin had been. Rodney was cold and suspicious. He'd demanded she pull back her hood and only the reprimand of another at Whitton kept Dove's secret safe from him. So he forced her along ahead of him, presumably for self-protection.

As they passed an unlit torch in the wall, Dove pulled it from the sconce and turned to light it. Rodney started to protest, but Dove had endured enough. "I'm bleeding from where my forehead has hit the lower arches. I need light."

"You'd see better if you took off that ridiculous hood."

"Well, I'm not going to, so let me light this torch and let's go. The sooner we reach Croxden, the sooner you can get rid of me."

"Not soon enough," the young man muttered as he extended the torch."

To Dove's surprise, her heart softened as she pressed onward through the tunnels, turning where he said to turn. She prayed that Rodney would not fear her and that they would pass quickly through the tunnels to Croxden. A new thought occurred to her as they passed tunnel after tunnel. If her songs could mesmerize a dragon, perhaps they would soothe an irritated Mæte.

All through the long trek, Dove had been creating a new song about the three men tossed into the furnace for their faith. If she was going to sing, the song of the trees whispering to the birds of the coming of spring didn't seem as meaningful as sharing the amazing story of Jesus saving men from a small form of hell.

A groan from behind her nearly squelched the idea of singing, but Dove forced herself to continue. The tunnels reverberated with her high voice, surrounding them with the melody of the song. She had no doubt that, Rodney would demand her silence, but to her surprise, he didn't.

At the end of the song, he asked, "Where did you learn that song? I've never heard it, even in the town."

"It's just one I've been working on ever since I heard the story. I liked it and thought it would make a good song."

"You—" As if realizing he was sounding interested in her as a person, Rodney halted. "How did you hear the story?"

Feeling a little like a minister herself, Dove began

telling the story of the three men. She felt him slow as she told of the guards who threw the men into the furnace being consumed by the fire. "Then the most amazing thing happened. The king looked into the furnace and asked, 'Did we not throw three men into the furnace? I see four in there and one looks like the Son of God!'"

"Which god?"

"He is known as 'I AM.'"

"I do not know that one." Rodney sounded skeptical but interested.

"He is the God of heaven and earth. He created all and sacrificed all."

"And have you seen him?

"No."

"Wait," the little man behind her stopped in his tracks. "Did you say your god, I AM, sacrificed? Do you not mean that you sacrificed to him?"

"No. I AM came to earth as a baby—Jesus. He sacrificed Himself for man instead of the other way around." Unaware that she hadn't corrected Rodney's assertion that she spoke of her God, Dove explained sin, the crucifixion, and the resurrection.

"That is impossible!" Disappointment almost shrouded Rodney as if he believed Dove to be playing a joke on him.

Delighted, Dove agreed. "Isn't it! Isn't it wonderful that God used the impossible to prove that He is greater than all the imaginary gods of this world? Had He done any less, who would believe that He is who He says He is?"

"I've never heard anything so unbelievable. How can you be sure? Did you see it?"

Sadly, Dove shook her head, the flop of her hood looking a little discouraged in the flickering light. "I wasn't there—it happened hundreds of years ago—maybe over a thousand. I don't remember. But there were witnesses.

People wrote the story down for those who did not see. Even people who didn't believe that Jesus was I AM said they saw Him."

"Gods always want something—what does this one want."

"You."

"Me? Why would a man's god want me?"

Shrugging, she explained. "He created you. He wants *you*."

"What does He want of me? My money, my—"

"He owns all—even your money. He wants you." She wasn't sure how to explain it, but of this Dove was certain. I AM didn't need the paltry bits of coin and stones that men valued. He didn't need animals or land. He had everything He could want except the hearts of those who did not believe.

"That seems like so little, and yet it is everything, isn't it?"

"Yes." Her whispered answer seemed to echo in the chamber.

"Do you find yourself trying to take yourself back?"

"Take myself back?"

Rodney nodded. "I think it would be hard to remember, every day, that you are not your own—that a god you have never seen owns you."

"But if that God has given His all, would it not only be right to give yours in return?"

Her words seemed to return to her heart and pierced it with a wonder she couldn't hope to describe. It was true. I AM had created her, loved her enough to come to earth and die for her, was it not her duty to yield her will to His? A prayer, whispered in her heart went out to the Lord who must be the Lord of her life. *Help me to yield. Help me.*

Home Again

CHAPTR 31

Jakys met her and her latest runner at Cockersand. The young girl, weary with travel and a little overwhelmed with the influx of faith in her life, threw herself at the little man, sobbing. Anger flooded the little man's face. With one arm around his little friend, he grabbed the runner's hair with his other hand and growled, "What did you do to her?"

"N-nothing! I don't understand. She was singing just an hour ago— talking about some god called I AM."

"I'm all right, Jakys. I am glad that I'm almost home, and then I saw you..."

With more gentleness and understanding than Jakys had ever exhibited, he whispered instructions to the runner and then led Dove to a small room. "Rest, little friend. We'll leave just as soon as you're rested and have a good meal."

"Jakys?"

The man pointed to the bed. "Lie first, then sleep. And remove that silly cloak. I will guard the door for you."

Obediently, Dove slipped from her cloak, draped it over the foot of the bed, and pulled the covers over her as she curled up on the strange bed. "How many days has it been, do you know? Some days I've gone through three runners. We slept, walked, slept. It's all a blur."

"I'm not sure when you left, but it's about a day's

journey home. I just walked south until you were expected here tonight and then waited until you arrived.."

He told of the stories that passed between communities as Dove hurried home after saving her friend from certain death. Stories of the dragon mingled with the kidnappers of Oxford until she'd become almost a legend among the Mæte. The familiar voice lulled her into a deep sleep—the first true rest she'd had since she left Wynnewood the previous month.

As she slept, Dove dreamt of primrose covered fields, the sounds of the ocean slamming into the rocks nearby, and the scent of salt spray in the air. A cottage with smoke rising from the chimney materialized as the mists faded and an old woman hurried out the door, a bag of herbs and supplies on one arm. She stepped through the open doorway, and the scent of rabbit stew twisted her stomach in hungry knots.

The cottage vanished, leaving her wandering along the Ciele, water splashing over the rocks as it danced toward the shore. A high clear voice seemed to follow it. Dove glanced around her, looking for the source of that voice and then realized it was hers. It filled the air, surrounding her with stories of a babe, lying in a manger, growing to be the Savior of mankind.

Then she felt it again— the touch of someone who loved and cared for her. She heard that gentle murmur of a kind man who promised her that He was there for her; He would protect her. He loved her. And in the quiet that followed, Dove was certain that this time the words were spoken into her heart by the Great I AM. His Word indeed had been hidden in her heart through the sharing of her faithful friend, ready to comfort her even in her sleep.

Dove stepped from the tunnels into the Sceadu. The sunshine felt wonderful, as obscured as it was by clouds every few minutes. Jakys stood at the opening to the tunnels, watching as she left. She turned once more, waving at him, and called, "Thank you again. I'll come to the cave soon and tell you all I've learned."

Never had she been so eager to get home. Her sore, tired feet flew through the trees, across the river, and then across the clearing. Her eyes scanned the yard as she burst through the trees and saw Letty scrubbing another burned pot.

"Have I not taught you to use sand, Letty?"

Letty's eyes grew wide as the hooded creature, the gesceaft of Wynnewood, entered the yard as though she hadn't been gone for a month. "Dove? We—" Then, before Dove knew what happened, Letty flew across the grass and wrapped her arms around the smaller girl.

Dove stood frozen, awkwardly waiting for the hug to end, still unused to responding to impulsive shows of affection. Just as she opened her mouth to tease the girl about being clingy, Letty stepped back and erupted in shocking fury. "Where have you been? Do you know how worried we were? I looked everywhere for you—all of your favorite places. I even tried to find the Mæte to see if they knew—" Something in Dove's posture must have answered the question for her. "They did know, didn't they?"

"Shh. We can't talk about it so openly, but yes. They heard about Philip—"

"You must be joking. You decided to go all the way to Oxford, didn't you? How did you expect to do him—" Again the odd glance at Dove. "You found him? You? How—"

"It doesn't matter. He's safe now and back at his studies."

"Lord Morgan isn't even back yet. How could you

travel so quickly?"

Dove took the pot from where Letty had left it and hopped over the little stone wall that separated the cottage yard from the trees. "I'll be back in a while. Let me clean this for you first, and then we can go into the clearing and I'll tell you everything."

"Promise?"

She shrugged out of her pack and dropped it into the yard. "Will you put that on the floor by my bed? I'll clean it out later."

With a wave, Dove flitted through the trees, making her way to the edge of the village, and skirting the houses and streets, hardly noticed by the villagers. That seemed odd. Why had she not caught the attention of those who liked to chase her? They'd scarcely raised their eyes as she dashed here and there.

At the shore, several fishermen raised their eyes from their nets and then shook their heads before going back to work. One frowned and called, "It's not funny anymore, lad. Get to your work and stop playing games." It all seemed so curious.

The sand felt wonderful on her sore feet, soothing them as she tramped through it to the water. However, as she knelt in the sand some hundreds of yards away, she noticed a change. The men drew closer together as if consulting, and one pointed to her. Still, she added fistfuls of sand to the pot and rubbed them into the metal, swirling the water and rinsing until all the charred remnants of a ruined meal were gone.

As she passed the fishermen again on her way home, they seemed more normal somehow. They ducked their eyes, scowled, or threatened her with sticks. In a strange way, it was a good feeling. She was home.

That good feeling lasted until she jumped the wall once more and carried the pot into the cottage. "I'm back. Remember to keep the pot on the edge of the coals—"

"You!"

Dove raised her eyes to see Bertha's furious face looming over her as she turned. "Wha—"

She choked back her words as Bertha jerked the hood from her head to see if it truly was the little gesceaft of Wynnewood. A stinging slap sent the girl reeling into the stone hearth, her eyes exploding with pain at the force of the blow.

"Where have you been! Do you not know the trouble you have caused me? I've had that horrible myth monger at my door every week, his eyes accusing me of the worst crimes. The village has finally relaxed, happy that their tormenter is gone, and in you walk as if you hadn't been gone an hour!"

"Bertha Newcombe!" The voice at the door stunned both the midwife and her charge. As the terrified girl jerked her hood back over her head, the minister continued, "Dove, I'm happy to see you returned safe, but right now I want you to leave the cottage. Bertha and I have something to discuss."

Bertha's hand grabbed her arm and held fast. "Mind your own business, Dennis Clarke."

Never had either Bertha or Dove ever realized how large and imposing a man the minister of Wynnewood was. He stepped into the cottage, ducking beneath the low door, and grabbed Bertha's wrist. "Let go, Bertha. Now," he growled as if barely containing his fury. As Dove stepped back, the man gave her a brief hug and whispered, "Go!"

"Watch out!"

Dove's cry came just in time. The freshly cleaned pot, swung by Bertha's strong arms, nearly cracked open Broðor Clarke's head, but at her warning, he ducked and then turned, jerking it from Bertha. "Go, Dove."

Eager to avoid being sideswiped by the heavy thing, Dove stepped outside the door, listening on the other side. She wasn't disappointed. Bertha's furious voice required no straining to hear clearly. "Who do you think you are? Get out of my house."

"I believe this is Dove's house, Bertha. Even still, I won't leave until I am certain there'll be no more abuse of that ch—girl."

"What business is it of yours? I'm warning you, I'll take this to Lord Morgan. He doesn't tolerate interference in families."

"Since when are you a family? You've made it quite clear to that girl and everyone in this village that she's a duty and nothing more. Regardless, Charles Morgan will not stand by and watch you manhandle the girl. He's quite fond of her."

"Sometimes I understand this village's superstitions regarding the little chit. It does seem as if she either repels or enchants people."

Second after long second, Dove waited to hear the minister's reply. She knew how he hated the superstitious nonsense surrounding her. At last, he spoke again, barely suppressed anger punctuating each word. "She's just a girl, nearly a young woman. What kind of welcome home was it to have her exposed and humiliated like that?"

"Again, it's none of your business! What mother wouldn't scold, or even beat a child, for disappearing for well over a month without a word?"

Something changed in Broðor Clarke's tone as he replied. "I arrived just as she entered the cottage. You didn't ask where she'd been, didn't let her answer you. You slapped first and then asked. You were angry that she returned, not that she'd left. She's a person, Bertha. She needs concern, understanding, affection, and love just like everyone else does."

As the minister spoke of love and affection, his voice grew thick—as if he was hurting as well. Dove wanted to run into the room and tell the man that she had those things now. She had friendship with Philip and the Morgans at the castle. She had affection from them even, and from the Lord of All—from I AM—she had all the love she needed. She knew that now. Without I AM, Bertha couldn't hope to be understanding in the way Broðor Clarke wanted. However, despite the desire to defend the bitter, angry midwife, Dove couldn't bring herself to move.

"Bertha, you have a calling to save life—I admire and understand that—but you also are blind to the real life of the girl you saved so long ago. Your duty to her didn't end with preserving life. You wouldn't want someone to treat your own child so meanly." The words were quieter, almost impossible to hear as he continued, "But Bertha, you are above this ugliness. You have such a loving heart toward everyone else. Extend just a little of that to a poor motherless girl who could be a comfort to you in your old age—if you'd let her."

"Who says I want comfort from that freakish thing?"

"I don't understand your cruelty. She's not freakish. She's exactly as the Lord chose her to be. That alone makes her beautiful."

"Maybe to your strange god, but—"

"Aah, Bertha. Should not the opinion of the God who made her decide her worth?"

The midwife didn't answer for several frustrating seconds. "This is where we will never agree, Dennis Clarke. I do not believe your god is anything more than a figment of your imagination. If he were real, I might agree, but he is not."

"What can I say or do to show you the truth of Jesus?" The pleading in Broðor Clarke's voice made Dove curious again. Was he always so desperate to teach the villagers about Jesus, or did only such stubborn ones as Bertha see this side of him?

"You can't. You're wasting your time, and you know it."

"Fine." The steel had returned to the minister's tone. "I'll drop it for now, but you will not lay another hand on that girl. If for no other reason than all the work she saves you, you will treat her decently if not kindly. If I hear—and I will, I assure you—of any mistreatment at all, I'll appeal directly to Lord Morgan. You may not respect my position in this village, but you cannot ignore him."

Without waiting for reply, the man stormed from the house, beckoning Dove to follow him, but the girl shook her head and hurried into the cottage. As he watched the door close behind her, Broðor Clarke heard her say, "Did Letty not make something for your supper, Bertha? I'll make some potatoes and onions. Maybe I could go get a fish while the potatoes bake."

A Tale of Dove?

CHAPTER 32

The journey home was quite different from the trip to Oxford. Where he'd traveled with a large entourage accompanying Lord Morgan, he now walked alone or rode on farm wagons. His favorite times were when he reached a village in the late afternoon or early evening. Rather than be left behind to tend the horses or entertain Aurelia, on his way home Philip spent each evening in the local tavern, eating his dinner and listening to the stories of the locals and the minstrels.

His third night outside of Oxford, Philip was dropped half a mile from Ibstock. Hungry and long past thirsty, Philip hurried into town, grateful to have been able to leave his pack off for the past twelve miles. He hurried along the road, smiling at two boys chasing a dog with a chicken in its mouth. It felt so long ago that he had been such a boy, racing through the village of Wynnewood on some errand or game.

The tavern was full for an early evening, but Philip didn't mind. Those were the best nights—when the people were there and almost drunk with good company rather than drink. The storytellers told their tales more freely, and the minstrels usually made up silly verses to add to their repertoires. An audience made the entertainment that much more entertaining.

The tavern keeper's wife was young, not much older

than Philip himself. She teased and flattered him as he seated himself. He'd heard horrible stories of innkeepers hiring men to rob and beat the guests. With swollen eyes, it was hard to identify an attacker. Philip had made precautions. He kept the bulk of his money hidden on high beams or behind furniture, and kept enough coins to appear to be all in a pouch on his person. At each stop, he always hesitated as if the requested amount was too much before sighing and agreeing to the price.

From the corner of the room, Philip watched the pretty young woman exchange glances with her husband. Perhaps he should just move along rather than risk a beating. He felt strong again, but how much could his body take? Even as he thought it, Philip knew it was foolish. He'd never make it stumbling over a dark road until he reached the next town. He could end up taking a fork to the east and then what would he do?

A new idea hatched in his mind as he ate the plate of excellent stew. Prepared to give up his money and save his face from further battery, he ate, drank, and listened to a new man who started telling a tale.

"I met a man while I was down south of Oxford who told of a cloaked creature..." Philip's ears perked up as he listened to the story. "This creature while small, hides itself in a dark gray cloak and blends with the people, but one night, he came upon it suddenly, and its hood was back. White as moonlight, it was, with wild snowy hair, even though it was young—almost childlike. It had fiery red eyes that flickered like candle flames. He said it took one look at him and screamed—such a terrifying horrible screech that seemed to call the demons. Scared him, it did. Rushing at him and then vanished into the mists from which it was born."

"Born from the mists?" Philip couldn't resist asking, although he knew his voice sounded scoffing.

"Aye. They say the mists were so thick one night that

from them, this ge-sceaft was born and now walks among us, tormenting us."

"Tormenting how?"

The man leaned closer, eager to send shivers up and down Philip's spine. A storyteller loves nothing more than an intrigued audience. "They say that the eyes are those of a sorceress who charms dragons and sends people mad with one glance." At Philip's exaggerated horror, the man continued. "I've heard of entire flocks of sheep falling dead at the sound of its voice."

Lost in thought, Philip didn't notice that a new tale began—one of dragons marauding villages, hauling off their maidens to be slaves in the dragons' lairs. How could Dove's story—for it must be about Dove—have made it so far south? Was he with the three men who met Dove on the road from Liverpool? Could he be the one—Martin—who had not run in fear? What did that man know about Dove that made him so willing to help her?

Before his mind could riddle out the question, a musician began playing. Some men danced, and the tavern keeper's wife found it hard to do her work without swaying and spinning to the music. Now was a good time to yawn a few times and go to bed.

He felt rather clever as he yawned, feigned interest in the music, swaying a bit to a slower tune, and then yawned again. Once Philip was certain that the innkeeper's wife had seen him tired, he slipped two fingers into his pocket and tugged on the pouch string. His plan set in motion, he stood, allowing the table to catch the top of his pouch and knock it from his pocket, but he pretended not to notice.

On the second floor, Philip went into his room, removed his shoes, washed his face and hands, and then removed his breeches. Then, as if panicked, he threw his clothes and shoes back on and thundered down the steps. A quick survey of the room told him he'd do better to tell the husband and let the wife overhear him.

Speaking a little louder than necessary, Philip brushed through the dancers and shook the man's sleeve. "Have you seen my pouch? For my money—it's gone. I know I had it when I paid you, but when I got upstairs…"

There it was—just what Philip had hoped to see. The innkeeper sent a glance toward his wife, and from the corner of Philip's eye, he observed the wife hurrying to where he'd been seated. Certain that they were roped into his plan, Philip added the final touch. "I must find it. I don't have much money as it is, and I've still got a good way to go before I get home. I'll be sleeping out in fields and begging food if I don't find that!"

"We'll look for it. You probably dropped it on your way to the table. It'll surely turn up when everyone is gone. Shall we keep it for you until morning, or would you like me to bring it up to your room?"

"I'll get it in the morning. I'm going to look around the room first, though. Just in case. I need that money."

The balance between sounding desperate to find his "only" money and not sounding like a bad actor was so delicate that Philip feared crushing it. Would the man believe him? Would it work? It had to work.

"Suit yourself. I don't see how you expect to find anything with all those feet stomping around."

The utter confidence in the man's tone told Philip that his wife had likely already retrieved the pouch. He stumbled between people, apologizing profusely, and then made a great show of searching all around the benches and table. He asked everyone around him if they'd seen it and started making noises about pickpockets.

When enough time had passed—as much as anyone would spend looking for their money—Philip shuffled dejectedly from the room and climbed the stairs. There, that should do it. If they tried to search him now, it wouldn't be for lack of trying. All they'd find was a pack of three books, a change of clothes, and an apple that was probably a little too mushy to be any good—and he'd probably find a couple of black eyes and a cracked rib.

Weary, Philip turned toward Wynnewood off the main road that led north. As familiar landmarks passed, the scent of the salt in the air grew stronger until he felt as if around the next bend, he'd see the village stretch out below him. Of course, it was a ridiculous thought. The trees kept the village hidden until well past Bertha's—now Dove's—cottage. He knew it was a fanciful thought, but the closer he came to home, the less he cared.

For days, he'd struggled within himself. Would it be wrong to go straight home to see his mother? What about Broðor Clarke—should he go there first and explain? Or, would it be best to walk straight to the castle and confess to Lord Morgan why he'd returned home so soon after they'd left Oxford? If what he'd heard was true, he was only a few days behind the Wynnewood party.

He passed the tree where Dove had collapsed after their escape from the Mæte. Just remembering that horrible time made his heart ache for home. Dove had been so strange—so melancholy. Only Broðor Clarke had known what to say to assure Philip that his friend would return to her old self. Broðor Clarke...

With longer and sprightlier strides, Philip hurried toward town. He'd talk to Broðor Clarke first. Maybe the minister would go with him to speak to Lord Morgan. It would be better to get his explanations out of the way before he went home. If he did that, he wouldn't have to leave again once he arrived home.

Philip saw the smoke from the cottage long before he reached the yard where Letty chopped wood, stacking it carefully as she went. Bertha's tidy ways were becoming second nature to the girl. Somehow, Philip knew that there was more to it than a spotless home. Keeping things clean probably made births safer for mothers or something. It seemed reasonable.

"Letty!"

"Philip? What—" The girl flew across the yard, flinging the ax behind her.

"Did Dove make it home safely?"

"Yes, she got here about a week ago. I—"

"And Lord Morgan?"

Exasperated, Letty threw up her hands. "It's good to see you too, Philip. Yes, the weather has been nice. There are two new babies at the castle, and—"

"Sorry. I'm in a bit of a hurry. I'm glad to see you, Letty. I know Dove probably felt better about leaving knowing you were here to help Bertha."

Mollified, Letty nodded. "Lord Morgan got home three days ago." Her cheeks flushed and her head ducked as Letty asked, "Is it true? Did Dove really save you from the kidnappers? How did she do it?"

"It's true. She threw back her hood and screamed. Scared the man, he stumbled and hit his head. Then somehow, she dragged me from the cottage—I was sick."

"She showed herself!" Letty's eyes grew wide, surprised. "I didn't think *anything* would—"

"I think Bertha's concern with preserving life overrode her own self-preservation." He pointed down the road. "I have to go, but if you see Dove, will you tell her I'm back and I'll meet her in the clearing tonight?"

"If I see her. She's been avoiding the cottage as much as possible. She comes when she knows Bertha is gone."

As much as he wanted to ask, Philip was eager to get to Wynnewood and get his confession out of the way. He nodded, thanked Letty, and walked away, waving. "I'll talk to you in a day or two."

Philip Returns

CHAPTER 33

Each step closer to the little cottage beside the church seemed harder than the last. Cheerful villagers waved, children swarmed asking questions, but Philip pointed to where Broðor Clarke lived and said he had to go there first, promising he'd tell everyone about his journey soon. A small group of children followed him to the door of the cottage, but the moment he knocked, they scattered like leaves in the wind.

The minister opened the door looking weary, but when he saw Philip standing there, his eyes brightened. "Philip! What are—"

"Can I come in? I've come home, and—"

"Yes, yes, come in, lad! I was never more surprised." Dennis Clarke led Philip into his cottage and dragged a bench from beneath the table. "Have a seat. Lord Morgan said he'd left you healthy again and ready for your studies. What brings you back?"

It took several long minutes for Philip to gather the courage to explain his concerns. "There was a session in which the master was talking about Elijah and the ravens. He had all kinds of explanations for what the story really meant. Elijah represented Christians and the ravens were priests who feed their people, Elijah, through the sacraments. The river Cherith was really baptism and where he hid himself was the church. There was more, I can't remember all the symbolism, but in the end, the lesson was that that the Church is the resting-place of the soul, and provides everything the soul needs."

"Take a breath, Philip. What is this? The lesson was not God's provision for His servant?"

Sadly, Philip shook his head. "No, Broðor Clarke, I asked him after class to be sure. Master Adrian said that everything in the Bible had deeper meaning than the simple story it seemed. It is all a metaphor or a picture of a more mystical meaning. I didn't recognize any of the stories you taught us once everything had been defined by the symbolism."

"You could have found another master. It wasn't necessary to leave, Philip."

The young man's shoulders slumped. "I didn't just run away from the first things I didn't like. When he verified what he'd taught, I went to the priest and spoke to him. I explained how you'd taught us to stick strictly to the scriptures." He swallowed hard, fighting back the inexplicable and embarrassing urge to cry. "He called you a heretic and insisted that I not listen to your nonsense— that it was wrong to take the Word of God so literally."

"Oh, I had hoped the things I'd heard weren't true. They seemed too fantastical to be believed."

"I'm scared for you, Broðor Clarke," Philip confessed. "He seemed to want to have you brought up before the church courts and have you tried for heresy. He was so angry. I didn't tell him where I was from or my name; I did tell him your name before I knew he would object, though. If he asked the right questions..."

"Lord Morgan would protect me. I might have to go live in the castle for a while, but he would protect me. He values the truth."

"I was afraid that Lord Morgan would feel obligated to follow the church," he confessed. Philip raised his eyes to meet the kind ones of their minister and sighed. "When I left here, I was so certain that I did not want to be a minister. I wanted a home and a family. I wanted to live a normal life. I don't like to be alone, but when that priest asked me if I was going to study theology and said that the church needed devout men like me..."

"Yes?" Broðor Clarke urged gently.

"I know I have much to learn and am a very prideful person, but I think that priest was right. I think the church does need more devout men like you and me and Lord Morgan. I think the church needs fewer devout men who will twist scripture into something unrecognizable. Even with my faults, I can preach the Word of I AM exactly as He left it."

"Yes, you can. I'm sorry we didn't prepare you for this. I'd heard stories, but they all seemed so unbelievable. I assumed they were exaggerated for interest; you know how the storytellers are."

Philip took several deep breaths and then forced himself to say the words that would probably change his life forever. "I hoped you would teach me yourself—like the Irish priests taught you. I will study, learn everything I can, and I will take over when you are ready to move to the castle to be their chaplain."

"Why do you sound so downcast? Is being a minister so terrible? You can still practice your archery, you know. You won't be a guard at the castle gates, but you can be a guard for the truth. You won't wield a steel sword, but you can fight fallacy with the Sword of Truth."

"I just—"

As if he remembered something, Broðor Clarke nodded. "Ah yes, you wanted a home and family. Tell me, Philip, why do you think you cannot have one?"

"Priests cannot—"

"But you will not be a priest. You will be a minister—like me."

The dejection on Philip's face seemed to grow into

despair. "Exactly—like you." Broðor Clarke laughed heartily, and Philip's eyes widened with alarm. "I don't mean that you're a bad thing! I'm sorry; I didn't say that correctly."

"You mean, I suppose, that I am not married and do not have children. I know how important a family has been to you."

"Not just me. All the lads want families. We may talk about exciting adventures that take us away from here, but we all expect to have similar lives to our parents. It's a good life here in Wynnewood and—"

"And what, Philip?"

"And I like children. I always have." He leaned his elbow on the table and rested his head on his hand. "I'm sorry. Aurelia once said that you have lots of children—all the children of the village—but it doesn't seem the same to me."

"It isn't, Philip. I'm sure of it."

"Did you ever have that longing?" Desperation entered the boy's voice, and he despised himself for it.

"Yes."

"How long—" he choked on the words but forced himself to continue. "How long before it went away?"

"It didn't, Philip. Every time a baby is born and I pray over the mother and child, I pray that the stab to my heart will heal as well. Whenever a father comes to me about a wayward son, I want to shake him and tell him to thank God that he has a son to go astray—never to give up hope—trust that the prodigal will return and be ready."

"I don't think I can stand it. I don't know how to give that much up. I think I would be forced to leave."

Broðor Clarke pulled his bench a little closer to Philip's and gazed into the lad's eyes. "Philip, you don't have to give it up. Marry and have children. Be an example to the town of how to train up children in the way they should go. You can do for this town what I never can."

"I can marry? Because I'm not a priest, it is allowed? Why have you not married? If you could—"

"Philip, Christians have a duty—a command—only to marry other Christians."

"There are Christian ladies in the village. What about Bea? She's a widow with two small children. She would be a good wife for any man. She's kind and pretty—"

"Would she be a good wife to a man who would always have to fight not to think of another?"

The minister's words seemed odd. Why would he think of someone else? It seemed as if he was expecting the worst. Was it possible that Broðor Clarke was confessing to fickleness of heart? That didn't seem to fit his character.

As their eyes met, understanding dawned. "I feel foolish. I couldn't imagine why you'd expect to be fickle."

"I suspected as much."

"Who—"

"That isn't important, lad. The important part is that you can marry, and you will. You will be a very happy man when the time comes."

"Assuming I'm wise enough to marry a good woman like my mother."

"I have no doubt," the minister added with a twinkle in his eye, "that you will be very happy with your choice. She's a good girl, Philip."

"Who?"

"The one who will be your wife."

"You speak as if you know who that is. How could you know—"

Broðor 'Clarke shook his head. "You're young to be thinking of it now. Just remember when the time comes that I told you this."

"'I told you so' before the fact, is it?"

"Something like that. Now, shall we go explain the new plan to Lord Morgan?"

Leaves rustled in the trees surrounding the clearing, and the occasional whoosh of an owl's wings soared overhead. Philip lay on the ground, his hands behind his head, and one ankle resting on his knee. It felt as though he'd never left.

Of course, that was ridiculous. His time in the south had changed him—dramatically. He felt as though he left as one person and returned as two. Broðor Clarke had laughed when he heard that, but the man had admitted he'd felt something similar when he went away to be taught by the Irish priests. "It seemed as if people expected me to be very different when I returned, but I was still me," he'd said. Philip understood that idea.

He sensed it before he heard anything. It took several seconds before he realized that much if not all of the night sounds were silent. "I know you're there, Dove."

"You've gotten lazy."

Philip sat up abruptly at the sound of Dove's voice just feet away from him. "I have not! I—"

There it was—that familiar stance that showed disapproval and a bit of amusement. "You cannot admit when you're beaten, can you?"

"I suppose I can't."

"The village is all abuzz with speculation as to why you've returned. I've heard stories that range from failure in your studies to an arranged marriage to a baron's daughter."

"Both are ridiculous."

"Of course," she agreed. "I assumed that Broðor Clarke's explanation is correct. Are you really home for good to study with him?"

"Most things, yes. Latin, mathematics, and Bible for sure. I'll continue with French with Lord Morgan. Who knew he and Aurelia were fluent? He intimated that his knowledge was weak."

Her silence was a little unnerving, but Philip sensed his little friend had something to work out in her own mind. "You won't have time to play as you once did," she said at last. "You'll be busy with your lessons and helping your modor?"

"Broðor Clarke says my lessons will end an hour before supper, and of course, there will be no lessons on Sunday. I'll have less time than I did, but I will have some. If I am careful to help Modor before I leave to study, I should have the evening to myself."

"That'll give me more time to work on my pool." She settled herself behind him, leaning against his back for support in the old way, and allowed her hood to slip down over her shoulders. "Were they really changing the Bible stories?"

He nodded, forgetting that she couldn't see him. "You wouldn't recognize them."

"You were wise to come home, Philip."

"I didn't want to admit it to Broðor Clarke, but I had to. They valued cleverness. I know I would have gotten caught up in searching for exciting and mystical new ways to embellish the scriptures and make me look clever. It wasn't a temptation when I left, but had I stayed..."

"'The heart is deceitful above all else,'" she whispered.

"Exactly." Eager to change the subject, Philip asked another question. "I wonder if you'd like to learn French as well."

"What would I do with French? No one around here speaks it."

"But," Philip countered, "You are competitive, are you

not? Come learn with me and prove yourself the better scholar."

"That won't take an effort." Dove retorted. "I'll accept that challenge and win it."

Their laughter filled the little clearing much in the way it had before Philip left for Oxford. Two voices, one low and cracking with odd changes and one as high pitched as it seemed it could be, chattered into the wee hours. As the sun broke over the eastern sky, Dove stood and glanced around her. When Philip had stood and walked home, she did not know, but it was nice to know that her friend was home again.

"To think, Lord I AM, it'll be a little like it was before he left now, won't it? Studying with Aurelia. I'm proud of him for leaving. He did the right thing. But why," she added in a whisper, "could I not tell him how I believe now? That seems so silly."

The Seeker

CHA
PTR
34

Winter

The tavern door opened, and a man entered. Covered in dust, with shoes caked in dried mud, he looked weary and travel worn. His broad shoulders drooped as if carrying the burdens of a lifetime, but he carried only a small pack in his hand.

"Good evening, friend. Can I get you some ale?" Like most tavern keepers, the man at the tap seemed eager to serve anyone who came in the door.

"Have y'got mead?"

"That I do. I'll bring it right over. Would you like something to eat?"

The man, taller than most with pale red hair nodded. "I'd like that, thanks."

A bench was shoved against the wall in the corner of the room, and the traveller sat on it, leaning himself against the wall for support. Bone weary, he kicked off his shoes to allow his feet to cool, pushing the shoes beneath the bench. It had been such a long day.

A long day, Martin thought to himself, *it has been a long few months.* Every day a new village, and in every village, a new tavern or smithy where he could ask the same question he asked at every new place. He'd nearly lost hope, but he'd never give up. Never.

The tavern keeper handed him a tankard of mead

and a plate of bread and cheese. "Here you go. Tough traveling, was it?"

"Yes... will it be busy in here tonight?"

"Sorry. It's busy here almost every night."

Martin nodded. "Good. Know anyone who can use a day laborer?"

"Maybe the farm down the road. Tyne has been shorthanded since we had that sickness last spring. We lost a dozen people or more."

All through the afternoon and into the evening, the stranger watched and listened. The tavern keeper's wife kept a sharp, suspicious eye on him, but at last carried their boy upstairs as if she'd decided he was harmless. A few of the locals asked him questions, trying to draw him out, but Martin waited until the stories began to flow along with the ale.

"Hey, you there," one half-intoxicated young man shouted, "tell us a story. We could all use a good one"

Martin nodded and leaned back against the wall, rubbing his palms on his tunic as if preparing for some distasteful task. "I do; I have one. Wandering the roads of England is a cloaked girl. She has a high voice that sings to ward off animals that might want to attack. She fears people—hides from them. People often misunderstand her and if they see her, some are frightened." A man made a snort of disgust, but Martin forced himself to ignore it and continue. "She has hair, almost as white as an old woman's and eyes that nearly glow red in firelight. Her skin, unless flushed with anger or exertion, is also white, and looks ghostly to those unfamiliar with it."

The room waited. Martin waited. Seconds passed as expectations were left unfulfilled. At last, one of the men closest to Martin said, "So what happened with the freakish looking creature?"

"People drove her from her home. I'm looking for her."

A woman frowned. "You mean it's not a story?"

"Well, it sort of is—after all, she is wandering around out there."

"Well, I'd better not see her; that's all I've got to say," a scrawny young man added. "I'm not putting up with anything from some wandering ghost. That's what a knife is for."

"I'd kill a man for that. I want her found and I want her alive."

Another man gazed at Martin curiously. "The girl steal something from you?"

Martin began to shake his head and then nodded. "In a manner of speaking, yes."

Town after town, village after village, farmhouse after farmhouse passed, but Martin hadn't found the little creature. In the south, it had been easier. He'd describe her and people would apologize, shake their heads, and suggest some other place to go. Once he reached the middle of England, he'd discovered people were less and less likely to be willing to help. They were more closed-mouthed and suspicious of strangers the farther north he traveled.

A fletcher by trade, he'd abandoned it years ago, but in trying to keep himself fed, he found that people in different places needed arrows made and repaired and he could earn a few coins fletching in the evening. Sometimes, he even worked on arrows while sitting in a tavern and listening to the stories that he always hoped might include the girl.

At Durham, he worked for nearly a week, pushing the millstone for the miller. Each night he entered the tavern, drank his ale, and listened to the stories, telling different ones he'd heard all over England when asked, but he didn't mention a cloaked creature or a girl with hair like moonlight.

With more patience than he'd ever had, he waited until the last day the miller had work for him. Once he'd taken advantage of a bath in the miller's kitchen, Martin put on his clean clothes, thanked the miller's wife for good meals, a clean bed, and freshly laundered clothes, and took off toward the tavern. It was time.

He pushed open the door, the darkness of the room contrasting greatly with the glow of the setting sun outside. Candles flickered in sconces along the wall, and the tables held thick round candles, large enough to burn for hours. The great fireplace cast a warm glow over the room, but still, with only one small window, it was dark and that made it seem a bit dingy. But still, it seemed a nice place to gather of an evening.

"Hey, it's Martin! Come give us a song—that one about the maid who gave her life for the knight," the tavern keeper called as Martin entered the door.

"Let me get a tankard of mead in me first! Father Henry is always good for a story. Ask him first. I've been working all day while he sits around here waiting for the rest of us to cease our labors."

The banter flew back and forth between the local priest, Martin, and George the tavern keeper. The locals loved it. When it seemed as though they'd leave off their verbal sparring, someone would insert a comment designed to rouse it again.

"I think Father Henry has won again."

"When you're educated in the art of debate, what can you expect but to win over uneducated peasants?"

"Speak for yourself, George. I happen to have a trade, I can read, and I've traveled all over England."

"Then," another voice called from across the room, "why don't you have the last word if you're so clever?"

The priest's eyes rolled exaggeratedly, but Martin

shook his head. "Some things I don't discuss with those who have no knowledge of them. A priest cannot marry, therefore he cannot comprehend the life of a man with a wife and a family. It isn't fun to beat a man who has no chance at winning."

"Oh, ho, ho!" the room called, laughing at the priest's expense.

"Come on now, Martin. Surely, there is another story or two that you haven't told us yet. I've never heard of someone traveling so much and hearing so many stories—not someone who wasn't a minstrel."

It was time. The question wasn't whether to ask the question but when. Should he ask first and then appease with a story or smooth the way? Instinctively, it seemed, he chose the latter. Had he the talent to form his own stories, he would have woven a tale of such a creature as he sought and then asked if it seemed familiar. Next time. He needed time to plan it. Like many of his comrades, he had a talent for fleshing out a story—drawing out new details until it almost seemed new. Alas, creating one from a few facts was beyond his abilities.

He told again of the maiden who saved the knight and died as a result. Despite his eagerness to ask the question burning in his heart all week, Martin dragged every detail out of the story that he could muster. He told of the way the young girl's arms shook with the weight of the sword, how her first thrust into the giant's heart barely pierced its skin, and smiled as the room erupted in applause as he finished with a bit of gruesome flourish in the detail of the final plunge of sword into the fearsome beast. After a tale such as that, he was sure they'd be eager to help him find that which he sought.

"You know, I've heard of a creature who wanders the forests wearing a cloak at all times—a little thing with a high-pitched voice like a little girl. Does anyone know that story?"

Murmurs of a less than helpful kind filled the room until one older man in the corner turned to someone near him. "Seems like some time back, that woman came through here with a little thing wearing a cloak—remember? Scared the children to death it did. They all said it was a ghost wearing a child's cloak—white it was."

A few others nodded. Martin, eager to hear more, moved closer to the man. "When was this?"

"About ten years ago, wasn't it? Seems like it was the spring before my Sarah died."

"That it was," a woman nearby agreed. "I remember because my little sister got so close the thing touched her. Modor was sure Mary would die of some terrible disease."

"What happened to her?"

The woman shrugged. "I don't know. Everyone chased them out of town—didn't want no ghost-child here!"

"Who was the woman with her?" He was pushing it, he knew, but Martin couldn't help asking.

"Don't know her name. She was a midwife though. Modor was angry that she'd brought a thing like that here. We needed another midwife." She eyed Martin curiously. "Why do you ask?"

"I've heard tales about her, but I never knew they were true. I just thought I'd get the northern version of the story."

Even as he spoke, Martin was making plans to leave. They'd been seen this far north in the last decade. It wasn't much, but it was something. One piece of the puzzle was firmly in place.

Days turned into weeks as Martin traveled across England, searching—always searching. From Durham he traveled to Finchale, Blanchland, Hexham, Lanercost, Carlisle... each town or village brought a little work, enough food to keep him going, and sometimes a longer stay when he needed new shoes or wore through his breeches. Tavern after tavern he sat and listened to the stories of dragons, unicorns, brave soldiers in battle, and knights with their fair ladies.

Occasionally, bits of a story or song sounded nearly like what he sought, but with the tradition of changing stories as they are told, no one could be sure of the origin or even if it was based on truth. It discouraged him, yet he trudged onward, determined to find the girl. Time was against him. As each week passed with more stories but no answers, she seemed to slip further from his grasp.

He'd been working on making his question into a story. As his feet slogged over muddy roads, he recited the words that he hoped would finally spark some kind of memory. Desperation spurred his feet onward as he filled in every detail he'd ever known or imagined about the girl. It had to be perfect.

At last, he entered Cockermouth one Saturday in early spring. As he spent almost the last of his money to buy lunch, Martin realized that it had been most of a year since the meeting where the little thing had flung back her hood. In his mind, he could see the fire reflected in her eyes and the terror on her face even as she screamed to frighten away the men who threatened her.

A boy raced toward him, carrying a live chicken by the neck. A rotund man, huffing and panting, waddled after him, shouting for him to stop. People in the streets paused, laughing at the scene before him. Somehow, Martin had a strong feeling that it was a common occurrence.

Why he did it, Martin didn't know, but he stepped in front of the boy and braced himself for impact. Glancing behind him, the boy didn't notice someone in his path until seconds before he plowed into the larger man, knocking the wind from both of them.

"Whoa, lad. Why is the man chasing you?"

"Let me go!" the boy screamed, trying to wriggle out of Martin's grip. "Let. Me. Go!"

The pursuer lumbered up to Martin, gasping his thanks. "This young scamp has stolen his last chicken. I'm turning him over to the constable this time."

Without another word, the man grabbed the boy's ear and dragged the child up the street. Martin shrugged and stared at the chicken that now pecked the ground at his feet. He scooped it up and tried to follow the others. An old woman pointed to a street a dozen yards away. "Down there to the left. Peter will be along soon."

The directions weren't very helpful, but once Martin turned down the side street, he knew immediately where to go. Peter was a butcher—a nasty job if ever there was one. He'd worked for one down in Dorchester, and though it paid well— and he ate well, of course— the stench of freshly killed animals had lingered in his nostrils for weeks.

Bringing back the chicken might be an excellent way to make a little money, but was it worth it? He didn't want to. The idea was utterly repugnant. However, he needed food, money, and information. This was a means to two-thirds of that.

"You brought it back?"

The voice behind him nearly made Martin jump. "I thought it wouldn't do you much good to catch the culprit and still lose the animal."

The butcher gave him a slow onceover. "Looking for work?"

"For a week or two. I'm looking for someone, but a man has to eat while he travels."

"I'll give you all the work you want for as long as I have it. Honest men are difficult to find around here, it seems."

Martin took a deep breath and met the other man's eyes. "I haven't always been an honest man. You should know that."

"You're honest now and that's what counts. Keep watch over the stall while I get this boy to the constable. He's stolen his last animal from me."

Martin pushed open the door of the liveliest tavern in Cockermouth. He'd spent a week going from business to business to see where he was most likely to hear a good story and better yet, be asked to tell one. After all his practice, it was time to see if anyone in this area had heard of the little cloaked girl.

The mead was terrible. Had he not had an agenda, Martin would have left the tavern and returned to one of the better establishments. Instead, he barely sipped it, waiting for the right opportunity to insert his own story. It didn't take long.

"Hey, you there—the butcher's assistant. What's your name?"

"Martin."

"Got a story for us?"

He wrapped his hands around the tankard as if enjoying the contents. His eyes fixed on the candle on his table and he began telling the story he'd worked so long and hard to improve. "Over the roads of England, a little cloaked girl wanders, singing in a high voice to ward off animals. Afraid of people, the cloaked girl hides any time she encounters them. Some say she's a ghost, terrorizing villages and towns with her white hair and pale skin. It has even been said that her eyes glow like fire at night. One night, three outlaws came upon her and her fire.

Frightened, she threw back her hood and screamed like a banshee—"

"Aw, he's a terrible storyteller," the man nearest him insisted. "I've heard my son tell of the ge-sceaft of Wynnewood better than that."

"Ge-seaft?"

"Sure. You were telling of the cloaked creature of Wynnewood, right? The one that was formed from the mists and charms dragons? The one who saved the Lord's daughter?"

Martin's heart pounded in his chest. At last, someone knew of the girl—actually knew who he sought. It seemed impossibly easy after such a long search. A few others took up the discussion, telling harrowing tales of death by one glance of the uncovered eyes and the creature enchanting unicorns.

"Why I heard that she can control the dragons of Wynnewood with her eyes," someone cried out from near the door.

Other rumors flew throughout the room. Horns, strength of ten oxen, and the ability to fly were just a few of the attributes that people claimed the child possessed. She mesmerized dragons, unicorns, and demons—in fact, people assumed she was a demon, their princess. Scynscaþa.

At last, Martin couldn't wait any longer to ask. "Where is Wynnewood from here?"

"About ten miles maybe?" The man looked to his friends for affirmation.

"Sure—about that," another one agreed.

"North? East? West? I know it isn't south."

"Northwest. Follow the road until it branches and then go west toward the sea. What do you want in Wynnewood?"

"Your ge-sceaft—I hope."

Stranger

CHAPTR 35

The sound of an axe biting into logs rang through the trees as Martin rounded the bend toward Wynnewood. There a girl swung an axe, splitting wood into manageable pieces and then stacked it beside the little cottage. Her golden hair curled around her temples as if evidence of hard work.

"Hello, there. Strong girl for someone so young."

Letty glanced up at the strange man, smiling, her natural cheerfulness and friendliness welcoming him before she spoke a word. "Good day to you. Long travel?"

"Yes."

She hurried to the water bucket and carried a dipper over to the man. "Drink?"

"Thank you. That's very thoughtful of you." After drinking the water, he pointed to the neat yard and solid cottage. "You have a nice house here. I imagine not everyone in Wynnewood has such a pleasant home."

Taking the dipper from him, Letty offered another drink, but the man declined. "This isn't my home. This is Bertha the midwife's house. I'm just her assistant. I'm in training," she added proudly.

Something in what she said interested the man and that made her uncomfortable. She picked up the axe to split another log when he asked an unexpected question. "Is there a girl in this village—one who wears a cloak?"

Letty froze. She glanced over her shoulder, shaking her head. "I don't know what you mean. Lots of people wear cloaks when it's cold."

"This girl wears them all the time."

"I—I think that'd be inconvenient. Excuse me. I'd better get this wood inside and start the stew. Bertha will expect her supper on time. Good day."

Inside the cottage, Letty took a deep breath and glanced around her as if looking for what to do next. She couldn't go find Bertha—not without passing the man on the road and letting him see that she'd lied to him. She couldn't go through Wyrm Forest. No, the dragons didn't live there after all—Dove had proven that—but it was still a frightful place, particularly when the mists were slowly encroaching over all of Wynnewood. They'd be particularly thick in the forest.

Another idea occurred to her. Letty banked the fire and then hurried out the cottage, across the road, through the trees, and into one of the fields. It was a long route, but she'd reach Bertha faster than waiting for the man to reach the village and start asking about Dove there. What could he want with her anyway? She would never have shown herself—not to anyone but a man who was now dead. What did it all mean?

The huts along the shore where the fishermen lived were a crowded, smelly place. Letty hated having to go near it and had even suggested that when *she* became midwife, she wouldn't go there. The fishermen's wives could find someone else to catch their babies. Just the memory of it made Letty's hand cover her cheek as if she could still feel the sting of the slap. Bertha had been furious. If anyone's baby needed a good, healthy start in the world, it was a fisherman's child, the woman had asserted. There was no excuse for being snobbish; their responsibility was to preserve and enhance life.

Were it not for the familiar face of old Sanders, she

wouldn't have found the correct cottage as quickly. "Good evening, Sanders. Is Bertha with your daughter?"

"Aye, she is. Always seems to be here checking before a baby, during a birthin', or after a baby."

"Bertha is a good midwife. Can I go in?"

"Can't stop you."

That was as close to "You're welcome in our home" as Sanders ever came, so Letty nodded and knocked as she entered. "Hello? Bertha? Sanders said I could come in..."

"What do you want? You're supposed to be doing the laundry."

"A man—" Letty gasped, "—came to the cottage. A stranger. He asked about Dove."

"About the girl? That doesn't make sense. Why would anyone ask about her? Go home and do your work, girl, and quit being so ridiculous."

"But he did. I've never seen him before, but he asked about a girl who wears a cloak all the time. If you'd have seen him, you'd know I'm right. What does a stranger want with Dove? I thought—"

"Stop thinking and go finish your chores. You're the most exasperating child at times."

"I'm not a child!" Letty backed away from the angry woman advancing on her. "I was just worried about Dove." She took another step backward and added, "Not that I should be surprised that no one cares. She's just a nobody around here." With those words, Letty flew out the door and toward the church. If Bertha wouldn't listen, Philip would. He was very protective of his friend.

She burst into the chapel, calling for Philip long before she stepped inside. "You've got to come with me, Philip. Someone's looking for Dove—a stranger."

"What?" Philip pushed his bench away from the table where Broðor Clarke glanced up from his book. "Who?"

"I told you, a stranger. He stopped at the cottage on the way into town and asked if a girl lived in town—one who wore a cloak all the time. I think he's headed for the tavern."

The look on Philip's face sent a cold dread over Letty. He was terrified and worse, angry. Before Broðor Clarke could ask a question, Philip raced out of the room calling out behind him, "That man in the tavern on the way here—he said someone told of a girl who looked just like Dove. It has to be him."

Letty stared at Broðor Clarke, confused, and then burst into tears. "I wish they'd never have left Wynnewood. Life was fine before they went away, and now everything is horrible. Philip was nearly killed, Bertha is crabbier than ever, and even Dove doesn't talk to me like she used to—not that it was much."

Broðor Clarke stared at the empty doorway, the blur of Letty's skirt disappearing with her down the road. Confusion grew into concern and that prompted prayers. Somehow, Wynnewood's notorious tattletale had grown into a caring young woman. When had that happened?

Martin wandered down the road toward the village, glancing over his shoulder from time to time and looking for evidence that the girl followed. He had no doubt that she was hiding something if not lying. This was the place. Now the question was whether the tavern was best or if he should go straight to the castle. Some of the stories he'd heard told of the ge-sceaft saving the lord's daughter from kidnappers.

At the sight of the village church, the options became irksome. If anyone knew the happenings around a village, it would be the priest. Why, people told those religious men everything.

Still uncertain, Martin found the tavern and went to

see if the keeper had a spare room to rent. Tiny out-of-the-way villages didn't often have inns, but even a place like Wynnewood might have a room he could use until he knew if he was staying or not. His resolve strengthened. He was staying. The girl was here.

John Brewer showed him to a small chamber off the main room. "I mostly use it for storage, but whenever someone wants a room, I move the stuff into the kitchen. We can work around the barrels for a short while."

"How much?"

The bartering began. Martin didn't have much money and suspected that the brewer had work for him—including moving those heavy barrels. After nearly half an hour of good-natured bickering, the men came to an agreement. Food and shelter for Martin; help around the tavern and the rest of his coins for John.

Of course, it didn't give him much time to relax or even to start making inquiries about the girl. To have some place to sleep, he'd have to begin his work now. That was discouraging. He'd waited so long and now, just as the child was in his grasp, he had to ignore her. Why was survival such a necessary part of life?

The tavern was nearly empty—too early in the day for people to come in and enjoy a tankard with their friends. Martin started to lift the first barrel and then thought better of it. Instead, he laid it on its side, rolled it from the little room to the kitchen, and stood it in the corner. One after another, he repeated the process until six barrels crowded the kitchen.

As he worked, he joked with John, integrating himself into life at the tavern. Just before he finished, Martin tossed out the comment that he hoped would open up looser tongues than that of the midwife's apprentice. "When I was in Cockermouth, the stories of your village ge-sceaft were the favorites of an evening. I imagine your stories of her are even better."

"Stories. Who wants to talk about the creature we all hope to avoid. She was gone for over a month. We thought we were rid of her, but she returned after all. The children are terrorized whenever that obnoxious cloak appears. Again."

"Oh, so it's real. A girl? That's what the story said." It wasn't true. The story hadn't given a gender to the creature—just the terror associated with it. This was perfect news.

"Oh, she's real. The midwife says she's harmless, and Lord Morgan protects her somewhat, but..." John Brewer's voice trailed off ominously.

That was all Martin needed to hear. The question now was whether he would go first to the midwife who had saved the girl or to the Earl of Wynnewood who protected her. The priest didn't sound like someone who could help this time.

"Then again," John added, breaking into Martin's thoughts, "Philip Ward is great friends with her. He says she's just a little girl who looks a little different than most, but I don't know if he's actually seen her."

"He's probably right." It was all Martin could do to keep his opinions to himself. *Ignorant peasants.*

It took some time to extricate himself from John's many stories about the so-called creature. Poisoned oysters indeed. They'd probably not bothered to wash the things properly; that was more like it. Insanity—the village seemed populated with people afflicted with it. Creature, poison, demon—what would they come up with next?

"Does this village have a fletcher?" That should be a safe change of conversation.

"Yep. He's a good one. I recommend him highly."

Frustrated, Martin nodded. "I suppose he has a good assistant."

"Nope. His apprentice spent six years fetching and

carrying like some old woman. It was shameful, but the Wards didn't bring him up before the guild. Lord Morgan's doing, I suspect."

"Lord Morgan is the lord of the castle then? They mentioned him in Cockermouth."

"That he is. Good man, our lord. Not like his fæder and grandfæder. He treats us right."

Martin grew curious. "Why would the Earl of Wynnewood care about a village boy?"

"It's like I told you; the earl isn't like most others. He takes care of his people. Philip is a good lad—smart."

"The same Philip who is friends with the girl?"

"The ge-sceaft?" John poured himself a tankard of mead and took a swig. At Martin's nod, he smiled. "You're like him. You don't like calling her 'the creature.' Why is that?"

"It seems cruel to call a child names. What good does it do?" Before the tavern keeper could answer, Martin answered his own question. "Nothing. It might cause terrible harm, though. I've known normal people who were stoned, hung, or even driven mad to suicide by the cruelty of people who don't understand a little difference."

"'Tain't just a little difference. They say she has horns and a tail."

"Have you ever seen them?"

John took another swig of his drink. "No I haven't, and I don't want to. Freakish thing that one is."

"Then how can you know she's anything but a normal child?"

The other man's eyes narrowed and he leaned forward. "Why should you care? You're a stranger to these parts, aren't you?"

"I am, but as I said," Martin repeated and then stopped. "I'm just curious."

Panic

CHA
PTR
36

Dove wasn't in the clearing. Philip spun in circles, debating whether it was worth the few minutes to dash to the cottage to see if she'd mentioned hunting or working in the forest. She could be at the castle. Why, just yesterday, Aurelia had told him, in French no less, that Dove finally had learned to remove her gloves for their embroidery sessions.

His mind made up, Philip sprinted toward the cottage. If the shovel was missing, it might mean Dove decided to work on the pool. She was constantly transplanting new flowers and plants to enhance the beauty of it. The shovel was not on the pegs at the side of the house. She was planting.

Trying to ignore the rising panic that came with each new mental question about the stranger, Philip walked quickly across the clearing, turning east toward the part of Wyrm Forest where Dove had dug her pool. Who was this man and what did he want with Dove? Was she in danger? It seemed impossible that she was not. Should he go to Lord Morgan first? Half way to the part of the forest where the river flowed deepest, Philip paused. Perhaps he should go first to the castle.

As quickly as he thought it, he dropped that idea. Broðor Clarke would be there long before Philip could make it up that hill. He'd see Dove first. Besides, she might go home and hearing it from Letty would be disastrous. Memories of a terrified girl cringing behind him as Dove advanced told him he should be the one to tell her. Dove wouldn't hurt him; would she?

As he neared the chosen spot for Dove's project, Philip realized that he hadn't even noticed her high voice singing through the trees. He'd been home long enough that such things were familiar—comforting. How he had survived a year in Oxford without the scent of the salt air, the taste of it on his tongue, or the sound of Dove's songs floating on the mists that rolled in from the sea?

This was where he belonged. This village. These people. He'd be a good minister. They'd call him Broðor Philip or Broðor Ward, and he'd teach them to trust the Bible, to protect it from being adulterated. He'd put on Broðor Clarke's mantle until he was too old and weak to wear it and then perhaps another village boy would be ready to take it on—maybe even his own son.

He was amazed at Dove's progress. Ferns grew beneath the great tree, and violets were clustered at the base of the ferns. It was beautiful.

"Dove?"

"I wondered when you'd speak."

"So why didn't you say something?"

The hood turned toward him, and in one of those rare times that the light hit it just right, he was sure he could see the tip of her nose, pure white in the sunlight. Instinctively, his head ducked.

"Thank you, Philip. It means more to me than ever."

"What does?"

The girl turned back to her flower bed and stomped the dirt down more as she talked. "That you try to respect my covering. Now that you've seen me—"

"Which I don't remember."

"—you could just keep looking. It would likely fill in your memory. I'm thankful, though. I wonder how long we'd be friends if you did."

The anger that had welled up in his heart at the news of the stranger returned even stronger. "You don't trust me!"

"You're right, I don't."

Her words stunned him. He stammered at first and then spat, "I've been your friend when I didn't understand, when it nearly cost me my own friends, and when it put my life in danger, but you can't trust me to stick by you because you look a little different than some people do. It's unjust, Dove."

"It is what it is. What brought you here? Your footsteps weren't those of someone looking for a way to pass time."

"You can tell more about someone by their footsteps than most people can by what they actually say." The words were meant to be a compliment, but even to Philip's ears, they sounded peevish.

"What have I done now, Philip?" The sigh in her voice indicated weariness from more than the hard work of the day.

"Nothing—sorry. I didn't mean it how it sounded. I was trying to pay you a compliment, but..."

The hood turned again, and once more, the tip of a nose showed. She was getting careless. "What's wrong, Philip? You're not yourself."

He wandered to the base of the enormous tree that overhung the pool and sank to the ground beneath it. "You always know what I am thinking, don't you?"

"Obviously not, or I wouldn't have asked."

There it was—the impish teasing that characterized his little—Philip glanced at Dove once more—not so little friend. He hated to frighten her. "Remember when I told you about the stories in that tavern? Remember how I said that the man said a man was wandering through the south asking about a girl that sounded just like you?"

"Yes…"

"I think that man is here. Letty says a man wandered past the cottage a while ago asking about a girl who always wears a cloak. She was terrified."

"Letty is afraid of her own shadow. It's probably one of those minstrels who tries to find all he can about something before he writes his song."

"I don't think so, Dove. I have a bad feeling about this."

Dove sat next to him, tossing the shovel aside as she settled against the rough trunk of the tree. "What could he want with me?"

"I don't know. It just seems so—"

She stood. Gathering her flask, shovel, and a bucket for what use he couldn't imagine, Dove began walking back through the forest. He watched as she seemed to float through the trees and over the ground until she was nearly out of sight. He'd have to run to catch up if he didn't hurry.

"Where are you going?" Philip asked the question when he was still ten or fifteen feet behind her. The sound of an animal in the underbrush made him miss the answer. He started to ask again, when her words sank into his mind. "What?"

"You heard me."

"You can't do that. What will Bertha say?"

The hood turned and glanced over Dove's shoulder. There it was again—that white-tipped nose. Why was Dove being so careless? She'd never—He stopped mid-thought. The cloak barely covered her knees. It was too small.

"Dove, you need a new cloak."

"This one has plenty of wear in it."

"I'm sure it does, but look how short it is. I keep seeing your nose. You aren't hiding yourself well in it. I thought you were growing careless, but—"

The hood jerked forward and Philip smiled. The back no longer drooped as it had when he'd first seen her swing up over the edge of the Nicor Cliffs. The impatient flick of her fingers told him that she felt it. "Bertha won't like it."

"Why?"

"She'll have to spend money on the cloth. The weaver hasn't had a baby in seven years.

"True, but she hasn't paid rent in over three years thanks to you. A little fabric for a cloak or two should be nothing."

"You'd think, wouldn't you?" It was clear that Dove hadn't intended for him to hear her, but Philip did.

Not willing to get into that subject, Philip returned to the previous topic. "I still think you're asking for a tongue-lashing if you think taking off to the Mæte is a good idea."

"Jakys will hide me until this man leaves. You can tell Bertha that I'm safe."

"No."

Dove spun to look at him, her hood sliding back in that odd way it seemed to do now. She jerked it in place and stood with hands on her hips. "What. Did. You. Say?"

"I said no. First, we go to Lord Morgan and tell him. Then if you still want to go, I'll tell Bertha that you heard about him and fled, but that I'll be meeting you at night sometimes."

"And if I don't go to Lord Morgan?"

"Then *you* can deal with Bertha when you get back."

Her hands flew up in the air in a gesture of impatience and disgust. "So you'd leave me at the mercy of the woman who attacked me when I returned home after a long journey to try to rescue a friend."

"I would." As hard as it was to say it, Philip was determined to have Lord Morgan's influence over Dove if at all possible. He remembered the last time she'd been a guest of the Mæte—and how it had nearly cost them their lives. Yes, she was under Waleron's protection, but for how long?

She turned, carrying her things back to the site of the pool, and hung them in a tree. Without a word, she strode to the edge of the river and walked downstream until she reached the narrowest, shallowest part. Dove didn't even hesitate—she plunged into the water, the current trying to sweep her with it, but the girl was stronger than she seemed.

Her voice called back to him from halfway across the river. "This was your idea. If you want to tell Lord Morgan, you'll have to do it yourself."

"And if I don't?"

"I'll leave and you *will* tell Bertha that I have gone to hide. I'll have done my part."

Grinning, Philip stepped into the river, working his way across as his father had taught him years before when he was just a young boy. Adam would learn in just a couple of years. The child was headstrong—like Will, Philip's mother said—and autocratic. For a moment, he pictured Dove as a five-year-old, standing at the edge of the Wyrm and glaring at Bertha screaming, "I get hare!"

When he caught up with her, she snorted. "You find something too amusing for me not to be curious."

"I was just picturing you as a child, informing Bertha that you *would* have rabbit stew for dinner if you had to kill the creature yourself."

To his astonishment, she ducked her head. "I didn't know anyone ever saw that. Did you see the beating she gave me after she caught me?"

Fury flooded Philip's heart. "I didn't see any of it," he snapped. "I just had a mental picture of you wanting something and being determined to get it whether she'd help or not." He wrung out the bottom of his tunic as they began the climb toward the castle. "Sometimes I hate her."

"Philip, no. I was saucy—impertinent. I deserved it."

"You were just a child."

"Would your fæder allow Adam to speak so to him?"

"He wouldn't beat—" Philip stopped and considered. "Not excessively anyway. He will teach and—"

"Bertha and your fæder could give the same gift and Bertha's would be a curse in your mind. They could each scold for the same thing and your fæder's would be justified while Bertha's would be excessive. She's not evil, Philip. She's wise and committed to life. I owe her mine."

"You owe Jesus more, but you will not give it." The words spilled from his lips before he could check them.

"It would seem so, wouldn't it?"

His brow furrowed. Something in her words sounded strange, as if she meant more than she said, but he could not imagine what. "What do you mean?"

"I mean—" Dove hesitated and then shook her head. "It isn't important right now."

"I AM is—"

"I meant what I was going to say isn't. I need to get away, quickly. I don't have time to discuss I AM. Let's hurry."

Martin's Tale

CHAPTER 37

Charles Morgan listened to the story of the stranger asking about Dove with great interest. As Philip spoke animatedly about the stories he'd heard on the way home, Lord Morgan watched Dove. She was even more skittish than she'd been in Oxford.

"Dove? What do you think of all this?"

"I just want to hide until he goes away."

"I suppose you plan to hide where you were the winter you were gone for that week?"

Aurelia's head snapped to see what her father meant, but Dove answered before she could ask. "Yes."

"I don't think you should go. You should go home. If this man has been wandering England all this time, he's not going to leave until he is satisfied. I will find and talk to him. I will make sure that he does not approach you without your consent."

"How can—"

"Lord Morgan is the Earl of Wynnewood. People will not cross him, Dove!"

She didn't answer. The cloak didn't even twitch. Lord Morgan and his daughter exchanged glances and then Aurelia asked, "What is it, Dove? Don't you think Father will protect you?"

"I think," Dove began carefully, "that you cannot understand."

"Lord Morgan is right, Dove. This man will not stop just because you disappear for a while. Who knows how long he's been searching?"

Despite their arguments, Dove shifted uncomfortably. She clearly wanted to run. A new idea occurred to Lord Morgan just as he was sure she would refuse to go home. "I can offer a compromise. You will go home. If at any time you feel unsafe, you get to the tunnels and let yourself into the castle. I will give you a key to the door and instruct the guards to leave you alone. You can go to Aurelia's rooms and sleep there until I have dealt with the man."

She seemed disinclined to accept the offer, but Philip held out the winning argument. "Will you truly defy the Earl of Wynnewood? He has given you a home, ensured your protection from the villagers. He shows you friendship at every turn, and yet you do not trust him."

"It isn't that I don't trust you!" the girl protested. "I don't trust this man. It makes me mad with fear to think of what he might do to me."

"I know that, dear one," Lord Morgan began, "but even if I did not care to bother with your protection for my own sake, my daughter would likely have me smothered in my sleep if I did not assure you that you will be protected."

"That's right!" Aurelia's eyes sparkled with mischief. "I am pleased that my father has the appropriate respect for me."

A snicker escaped from deep within Dove's hood. "I will go home, Lord Morgan, but I do not promise not to run. I will try to come to you as you have suggested, but I live on instinct. Sometimes I act before I think. That may take me into—" she checked herself "other places."

"I can agree to that. You should leave now. I imagine this man will present himself to me soon. Even if not, I will have him brought here. I'd rather you be far away before he comes."

As Philip and Dove strolled across the meadows to the narrowest point of the Ciele, Aurelia watched from a high window in the castle. At the sound of her father's voice behind her, she asked, "Do you think Dove is overreacting to this news?"

"I think before her journey south, it might not have been such a fearsome thing for her. That trip changed her. She is both more confident and more jittery than ever."

Martin stood in the great hall, just inside the door where John had left him. Minutes passed and then an hour, but still he stood as bidden. Servants eyed him suspiciously as they passed by, but no one spoke. At last, Lord Morgan strode into the room and seated himself by the fire. By all accounts, the Earl of Wynnewood was a gracious and generous man—friendly even. This man seemed angry and aloof.

"John, I will see him now."

To Martin's surprise, the servant, John, was at his elbow. They strolled across the wide room, and as they stood before the earl, John asked his name. "Martin Bowman, m'lord."

"Bowman. Are you an archer? An artillator?"

"I can shoot, yes, but my training is as a fletcher. My father was an artillator."

He stood, nervous, as the man before him pondered his words. Lord Morgan seemed imposing, almost harsh in his manner of speech. Martin was quite unnerved after such glowing reports of how affable and kind their lord was.

"I understand you are making inquiries about one of

the villagers. Why?"

Martin fidgeted as he tried to explain himself. "I—that is—well, I think I saw her last summer. I was with two other men—"

"Outlaws?"

His head dropped in shame. "Yes."

"Go on."

"We were trying to evade capture. We didn't usually travel at night, but we'd nearly been caught stealing a chicken. It was cold, dark, and we saw the light of a fire near a tree just over a rise." Martin continued to describe how they'd seen the fire from a short distance and decided to investigate. "She was just there, backing away. The others thought she was a boy. When we didn't leave, she threw back her hood to scare us. I couldn't believe it."

"And what," demanded Lord Morgan," could you not believe?"

"It was her—Rosa."

"Who is Rosa?" The earl sounded confused.

"My daughter."

Lord Morgan's laughter rang out freely. "You don't expect me to believe that you recognize a child you couldn't have seen for ten years." He paused, mentally calculating. "Yes, she's been here ten years now I believe."

"I can. She is the image of her mother. Even in the low firelight, I saw her face and then when my friends ran, and I realized why, I was sure. She is pale too, like my Margaret."

The other man stood and paced in front of the fire as he asked more questions in rapid succession. "Where were you when your wife killed herself? Why did you not take your daughter with you? Have you any proof that this girl is your child? Where have you been all of these years?"

"When Rosa was just a little thing—nearly four—I went south for work. We'd been happy in a little village in

Essex but then Margaret began to develop terrible sores. People had been a little suspicious of her, but Margaret was kind and helpful, and in spite of her unusual appearance, she was beautiful. People always trust a pretty face over a plain one."

Lord Morgan nodded. "That is, unfortunately, quite true."

"Well, when the sores appeared, the villagers became uneasy around her. I knew that I needed to find work somewhere—set up a business and make me indispensible to the community. Then, I could bring my wife and child to live with me again. We thought it'd be just a few months."

"It was longer?"

"It has been ten years since I've seen my wife or child. It was much longer. I found a baron in Lincolnshire who needed arrows and was willing to hire me immediately. Once I had produced a thousand arrows, I was free to return to Essex to bring home my family. I took the position and was well paid, but when I returned to Essex, the villagers told me my wife and child were dead."

"Dead? They said Do—your daughter was dead?"

Martin nodded. "I was devastated. One young boy told me that it wasn't true—that a woman had taken Rosa away with her—but I didn't believe him. I never believed him until the night a girl with skin white as chalk and hair paler than a primrose threw back her hood."

"You've told that tale too often," the earl accused. "You've made it into a legend almost."

Though he flushed at the accusation, Martin nodded. "It is true. I used everything in my power to find her." He stepped forward, earnestly pleading with his eyes. "Lord Morgan, I became a man I am ashamed of the day I learned that my wife and daughter were dead. I wandered England, took what I needed to survive, and didn't much care what happened to me. If I was caught and hanged, that really might have been a relief. When she fled from me at Oxford, I left my companions and began a search for her. I've not stolen since then. I've worked hard to make my way, staying longer than I liked in places so that I could at least hold my head up again."

"Is there no mark on her, nothing to prove what you say?"

"As a child, she had my nose. I didn't notice that night, but I suspect she still does. I think I would have noticed if she didn't. Apart from that, she is the very image of her mother. Perhaps the woman who brought her here could tell you if she looks like the woman who killed herself in Essex."

Lord Morgan was silent for a long while. As he waited, Martin shifted his feet, eager to ask another question, but unwilling to irritate the man who held the power to prevent his search from continuing. At last, he could not take it any longer. "My lord, does she truly sing? The one they call the ge-sceaft," he nearly spat at the term. "Margaret had the most beautiful voice—high and clear. I loved to hear her sing. She'd make up a song about making dinner if that was what she was doing."

"Dove sings."

A lump rose in his throat at those words. "Dove," he choked. "Is that what the midwife called her?"

Several seconds passed before Lord Morgan answered. "Dove is a nickname given to her by the young man she was with in Oxford."

"What was she doing in Oxford?"

"She heard of his abduction and went to try to rescue him."

Martin was astounded. "That is what she was doing alone so far south? She was walking all that way to try to rescue a man?" His eyes narrowed. "Is she fond of this man? Do they plan to marry?"

"They're both young yet, don't you think? How old is

Dove? The midwife assumed around three when she found the child. We've all assumed she was in her thirteenth year."

"Fourteen last month," Martin corrected and then stopped himself. "Wait, does that mean you believe me?"

"I think I believe you, yes. Particularly if Bertha confirms that Dove looks like her mother and agrees that she has your nose."

"And Ros—I mean Dove—has no plans for marriage to this man?"

"The man is Philip Ward and is only sixteen. He is under the instruction of our minister for the next few years. There'll be no talk of marriage for either of them for some years."

He knew it was too soon to ask, but Martin couldn't contain himself. "Can I see her?"

"That I cannot allow. Until she is willing to meet you of her own accord, you must not bother her. Stay away from Bertha's cottage and out of the Wyrm Forest."

A throat cleared behind them. Martin turned to see a young man standing there. "Philip? You have something to say?" Lord Morgan's voice made him jump, but Martin forced himself to meet the young man's gaze.

"I do. He needs to stay away from the Point near sundown. I know Dove sometimes likes to go out there for a little sun in the evening."

"I will. You are Philip? The one she was with in Oxford?"

The young man nodded and then glanced past him to exchange glances with Lord Morgan. "May I?"

"Certainly, Philip," the earl agreed.

"She is terrified of you. If you want her to trust you, show respect for the fact that her life has been hard and people unkind. Do not try to force her to accept you or she will run." He stepped closer looking much more menacing than a young man should be able to appear. "I

327

will defend my friend, Martin Bowman."

The Good News

CHAPTER 38

The village buzzed with excitement over the news of the visitor and his summons to Wynnewood Castle. Usually, Bertha ignored the gossip of the area, but when rumors began that Lord Morgan believed the man to be the ge-sceaft's father, she grew ill at the idea. To be sure, she had saved Dove's life as a child, and a man might be grateful for that. However, if he talked to the girl and heard of Bertha's harshness and coldness...

Remorse flooded her heart. She could have been kinder. Why shouldn't she be? She'd taken on the duty of the child's protector; why not protect the girl's spirit as well? Instead, she'd barely tolerated Dove's existence.

"Bertha, have you heard?"

"Heard what?" She winced inwardly at the edge to her tone. Old habits die hard.

"There is a man in town who claims to be the ge-sceaft's father. Do you think he's a sorcerer?"

"Of course not, you fool. Do you think I'd live with the child of a sorcerer?"

"Everyone in town," the woman protested, "knows you do. We've known it for years. How else are you so successful with your births?"

She'd heard it before, and it rankled every time. "Skill and wisdom couldn't possibly have anything to do with it. It must be some mystical thing that makes a woman get up in the middle of the night and sit with a screaming, blubbering idiot when she could just have her personal sorceress drag that baby out of the woman's body with a toss of her head."

"You are out of temper today," the woman complained. "I just asked if you'd heard."

"I have now anyway, haven't I?"

The woman turned to flounce away, but the sight of Martin Bowman walking toward them was too much for her. "Look, there he is."

Something about the man was familiar. Had she ever seen him? She didn't think so. A child raced past, causing the man's head to turn, and Bertha drew in her breath sharply. It had to be Dove's father. It seemed impossible not to be. The profile was nearly identical—the nose. That was Dove's nose without a doubt.

When Bertha didn't respond, the woman strode away from her, straight to Martin's side. To her dismay, the man listened and then looked across the street directly into her eyes. He nodded, and then his long legs crossed the distance in seconds.

"Bertha Newcombe?"

"Yes." The word sounded choked and she knew it.

"I am—"

"I know who you claim to be." Why she was so fractious, Bertha didn't know.

"Do you doubt my name or my reason for being here?"

"Neither. I simply have no proof of either."

"Lord Morgan warned me that you might be a bit resistant to talk to me."

"Not at all. Let's have a large formal dinner and hire musicians and guests so that we can—"

"Are you always this pleasant?"

Something in the man's tone warned her that she'd gone too far. If Lord Morgan believed the man, he could easily have Bertha removed from the cottage, allowing the man to move in with his daughter. It was a logical conclusion, but then where would Bertha live? The idea horrified her. Ten years of making the cottage healthful and comfortable. No Dove to provide fresh meat or ensure Letty properly aired the room or the beds.

"When concerned for my charge, yes."

"So you are concerned for Ros—Dove."

"What were you going to call her?"

The man studied her for a moment and then answered, "Rosa. We hoped she'd get my coloring to save her the heartache her mother sometimes suffered."

"By giving her a name that doesn't fit before she is even born. What if she had been a boy?"

"There were no blanca boys in Margaret's family. Only girls. It usually skipped a generation, but not with Rosa, or Dove. My sister is very pale, not nearly as pale as Margaret was, of course, but we thought maybe it meant something."

"Traits do run in families. Fathers and sons look alike and have similar mannerisms—even if they never see each other. Daughters look like sisters or grandmothers even if they look nothing like mothers. The gods give us ways to know that a child is truly ours if we look and listen."

She hadn't noticed, but a crowd had gathered. Bertha wanted to send them all away, but knew she couldn't make them go. Instead, she glanced at the sun, studying it for a moment, and then moved past him. "I have things to do and a woman ready to give birth any day."

"Bertha Newcombe." Martin's voice held an edge of authority—something she hadn't expected.

She didn't even turn her head. As she continued walking away she asked, "What?"

"Thank you for protecting my daughter. I have a

chance to know her again thanks to you. I owe you her life."

She paused, her feet stirring up the dust as she did. "You owe me nothing. Preserving life is my calling. I did my duty."

"Thank you just the same."

Unsure what else to do, Bertha continued walking again and called back, "Then you are welcome."

Water tumbled over the rocks at the end of the inlet and splashed into the pool. The way Dove had designed the two-foot waterfall was almost ingenious. He'd been sitting on the log that faced the pool for the better part of an hour, but still there was no sign of Dove.

He slid to the ground, using the log as a pillow, and closed his eyes. There it was— a rustle that didn't fit the trees. "I hear you."

"You did well. That was much earlier than usual."

"I met the man." It seemed best to come straight to the subject.

"I know. I heard the rider from the castle call you to the interview." She sat beside him, her gloved hands folded in her lap.

"He's your father, Dove."

Several seconds passed as she digested the news. "I'd heard rumors, but I thought it was just the silly villagers as usual."

"He says you look just like your mother—that was how he recognized you. He also said that you used to have his nose."

"And you believe him."

He nodded. "I do. Even more important, Lord Morgan does. Well, he says he will believe if Bertha confirms the nose or that you look like your mother did."

"It's not possible. I don't know what this man is trying to do, but it isn't possible. My mother had no husband. We were alone. Bertha made sure of it."

"People lie, Dove. The man says that they all told him you'd both died—all but a boy who said a midwife had taken you away with her, but he didn't believe her until the day you threw back your hood." Philip chuckled. "You know, he likes to say that—and often. I think he's proud of how you handled yourself."

"And he says I once had his nose."

She sounded as if ready to yield. The idea was exciting to Philip. Dove having family who wanted her— loved her enough to traipse all over England to find her— that would be an enormous improvement in her life. "Yep."

Slowly, she pulled the gloves from her hands. Instinctively, he averted his eyes, but Dove held her hands out in front of her. "Look at my hands, Philip. What do you see?"

He hated the tremor in her voice. She was afraid again—afraid that he would reject her if he saw her. At one time, he might have steeled himself to ensure he didn't react negatively, but since that day in the cottage, he didn't fear his reaction. He'd seen her. No, he didn't remember, but there was no fear attached to the hazy memory he did have.

"I see five fingers on each hand. The fingers are long and I suspect there are callouses on them."

She pulled back the sleeves of her tunic. "And here?"

Philip swallowed, understanding beginning to dawn. In all the times he'd caught glimpses of her hands or even the tip of her nose, he'd attributed her paleness to the light of the moon or the lack of light. She was truly that white. Blanca, the people would call her if they knew. No wonder the Mæte had cried "Scynscaþa!"

"Arms, pale ones."

"You are so diplomatic, Philip. That man, is he pale?"

"No, but your mother was—this we know. Some parents have dark hair and are married to people with light hair. The children can't have both."

He heard her take a deep breath. Her hands trembled as she raised them to grasp her hood and then slowly pulled it back, allowing it to fall behind her. Seconds passed, but she didn't speak, and he didn't turn his head.

"Look at me, Philip."

"No."

"Why not?"

The words tumbled over themselves on his lips, but at last he managed to stammer out, "Because if I do, you will find an excuse to avoid me too."

"If you want to be my friend after you see me, I will be grateful to I AM forever."

Philip's eyes slid sideways. Unconsciously, he steeled himself against whatever he might see, but it was unnecessary. Her profile though unusual, was nothing so horrifying. "You do have his nose, Dove. It is very distinct. Long and straight, but not too long."

She didn't reply. With her hands clenched together in her lap, Dove sat there, staring at the water that splashed into the pool, waiting. He realized after a few seconds, that she probably waited for him to leave. To test her, he stood, watching closely for any reaction. There it was, a tear splashing on her hand. She truly believed he would reject her for something as simple as pale skin, hair, and eyes. It seemed nearly inconceivable.

"Dove, look at me. I want to know what this man saw that night. What I saw of you was nothing to make people run. Startle because of its unusualness, sure, but not run."

"You won't see it, Philip. There is no fire here. The stories of my eyes being full of fire are true—somewhat.

Everyone's eyes reflect fire, but if I am angry or embarrassed, my eyes become reddish purple. Near fire, the flames reflect in them in a way that is truly terrifying. Combine that with my wild hair—"

"It isn't wild now," he contradicted.

"It usually is. Merewyn taught me to braid it to keep it from matting and looking so frightful." She sighed. "Do you really think I could have frightened away those men, made that man who was there to kill you; do you think I could have terrified those people if I was not frightful?"

"I think you used the element of surprise to disarm people who didn't expect to see something so unusual." He knelt before her with his eyes to the ground. "Will you look at me, Dove? We need to know. I'm sure of it from your profile alone, but don't you want to know if this man is your father?"

"If he is, he left us—"

"To find work, Dove. He left to go find work and returned for you. That is what my father does every spring. Should we not be willing to welcome him home?"

She shuddered, her hands shaking even as she clenched them together. "I can't trust—"

"You can't trust a man who married a woman like you, or a friend like me who saw your profile and was unshaken?"

"Look at me then."

His eyes rose to meet hers, but they were closed. "Why are your eyes closed, Dove? There is no fire here."

"Trust me, Philip. Don't ask that of me."

Determined not to press her too much, he focused on the rest of her face. Her nose was definitely that of the daughter of Martin Bowman. She had a name, a real name. Dove of Wynnewood was Rosa Bowman, daughter of Martin and Margaret Bowman.

He smiled. Her fearful face relaxed a little. One corner of her mouth turned upward before she smiled. "You do that just like your father."

"Do what?" She squeezed her eyes tighter, but she held her head high.

"You give a hint that you're going to smile before you do. The odd thing is I've noticed that since I've known you, but I never saw it. I can hear it in your voice just as easily as I can see it on your face."

"You're not repulsed by me?" Even as she asked, she reached to pull the hood back over her face.

"Not at all. You don't need the hood anymore, Dove."

"But I do. I need it to protect me from the villagers. I need it to protect me from the sun."

"But here in the shade of the trees and with a friend..."

"I cannot become careless, Philip." Her hand brushed away a tear. "Tell me a new story. Surely you learned one in Oxford or have one you've wanted to tell me."

Disappointed, Philip sank back to the earth and leaned his head back on the log. "I could tell you about the man named Philip."

"Oh, I want to hear of him!"

He had been sure Dove would be excited about it. Before he began, Philip prayed that I AM would show Dove how important it is to yield and obey. "An angel of the Lord came to Philip and told him to travel on the road from Jerusalem to Gaza. The Bible says that Gaza is a desert—a place with little water and very sandy."

"How can there be sand if there is no water pushing it up on shore?"

"I haven't seen it, but some of the masters talked about entire places as big as England being nothing but sand, so it can happen."

Dove's voice was full of awe. "I AM likes variety, doesn't He?"

"I think He does. Now a eunuch from Ethiopia had been to Jerusalem, you know, the holy city of the Jews, to worship. He was on his way home, riding in his chariot and reading from the prophet Isaiah."

"He had part of the Bible? Isaiah is part of the Bible, is it not?"

Philip nodded. "Yes. He must have obtained scrolls from the priests in Jerusalem. Or maybe he brought them from home." Philip shifted so that his spine no longer lay on a tree root. "When Philip saw the chariot, the Spirit of I AM told him to join the chariot."

"Philip, this must have been a wealthy man to be able to buy such a scroll. Was he?"

"Yes. He was a court official to Queen Candace and in charge of all her treasure."

Dove pulled apples from her pockets and passed him one. "Queen Candace was from Ethiopian?"

"Ethiopia—yes. So, Philip ran up the chariot and seeing that the man was reading Isaiah, asked him if he understood it."

"An intelligent question."

Without commenting, Philip continued. "The eunuch said, 'How can I unless someone explains it to me?' So the eunuch invited Philip up into the chariot, and starting with the scripture that the eunuch was reading, explained Jesus to him."

"What was the scripture? Does it say?"

"It was the one from Isaiah—"

"Of course."

He felt foolish as the silliness of his words struck him. Chuckling, he agreed, "Naturally. It was the verses that say that He was like a sheep at slaughter, silent before the shearers, who did not open His mouth. He was humiliated and denied justice and His life taken from him."

"Jesus. Did you not say that Jesus refused to give a defense when they tried Him? They humiliated Him and killed Him."

"Very good, Dove. That is exactly what happened, so Philip explained it to him. The passage says that beginning with that scripture, Philip told of Jesus, which seems to imply that he used many more because soon they came to water."

"I thought you said there was no water in the desert."

"I believe they have wells and things, but no lakes and rivers like we have. However, the scripture just says that the road led from Jerusalem to the desert, not that they were in the desert yet."

The discussion of desert and lack of water seemed to make Dove thirsty. She pulled a flask from her cloak, poured the water over the violets, and then laid out across the ground near the edge of the pool, allowing the fresh water to fill it. "Go on."

"So, when they came to the water, the eunuch pointed to it and said, 'Look, here is water! What prevents me from being baptized?'"

"Oh, yes. I see. Philip must have explained more of Jesus than just that scripture. The one word, beginning, is very important there, isn't it? How else would we know that we are not to infer baptism from the words in that passage? I can't think of anything in there that sounds remotely like baptism."

"That's what brought me home, Dove. They were doing that at Oxford—inferring all kinds of things from passages. That alone might have been interesting, but it was adding to scripture the way they did it."

Dove nodded, the hood slipping down further and into its usual place. "You were wise to come home. Now, what happened to the eunuch?"

"Well, both men went down into the water, and Philip baptized them, but when they came out, the Spirit of I AM carried Philip away to preach somewhere else and the eunuch went home, rejoicing."

He waited for her to ask about why Philip was sent

away from a man who needed to learn, but she didn't. Silent, she sat, sipping her water and watching the pool as if transfixed. At last, just as Philip was ready to explain it anyway, Dove pointed to the pool. "Philip, *here* is much water. What hinders *me* from being baptized?"

It was Philip's turn to be speechless. He turned, his arm on the log supporting him, and gazed at the profile of the cloaked waif of Wynnewood. "Dove? You believe?"

"Yes."

He sat upright, peering closer as if able to see the twitch of her lip before she smiled even through the darkness of the cloak. "How long have you believed? I cannot think that the story of a eunuch's baptism prompted instant faith."

"You will be angry, I think."

"Never, Dove! I am trying not to shout for joy!" Her giggle prompted a slight whoop. "I can't contain myself completely. Tell me all!"

"I suppose it began on the trip to Oxford. I prayed, Philip. I prayed all the way there. I was scared—terrified, really—and so alone. I sang and prayed to keep me sane. I was frightened for you and—" The hood dipped lower. "Me."

"Oh, Dove. When I imagined you walking along those cliffs in the dark, across the countryside and meeting outlaws—"

"And my father, if what you say is true," she interjected, the familiar impishness back in her tone.

"And your father... it shames me. I don't deserve such a loyal friend." Before she could contradict him, he urged her to continue. "So prayer produced faith instead of faith producing prayer. Tell me more."

"I fought it, Philip. I didn't want to trust. I thought I had to have a complete trust in I AM or I could not truly believe, but one of the Mæte challenged me. He said that all gods required some faith to believe. I saw then that this was my problem. I was trying to believe without faith. You said once that it is 'not of yourselves' but I was making it of myself. Once I quit trying to control my belief, I no longer struggled."

His joy was a little tarnished by the realization that a dwarf who knew nothing of I AM had accomplished that which he had failed to do. "Why did you not tell me all these months?"

"It was awkward for me." She sighed. "All the stories you told me, all the lessons you shared, they were such a part of me that I sang them constantly, mulled them over in my mind constantly. I couldn't have gotten away from them had I tried. Thank you, Philip. No one else in Wynnewood would have cared enough about me to teach me of I AM. If you hadn't..."

"You really believe..." Philip spoke as if he couldn't quite believe it himself.

"Yes, and since all of your stories of new faith include baptism, I want you to baptize me. The pool is here, what stops you?"

"I can't. We'll bring Broðor Clarke—"

"No!" She turned as if to leave. "I will not have it, Philip. You must baptize me. How can you refuse me? It is wrong."

"It is wrong for me to do that which belongs to a priest. I am not a minister yet, Dove!"

"You will be. That is enough for me. I do not want to wait all those years, but I will. My lack of obedience will be on your head, Philip Ward." She strode through the trees, clearly upset with him.

"Dove, wait!" She halted but didn't turn. "I will ask Broðor Clarke. I can't do something so important without consulting him. He is my mentor. He will be the one who decides when I am ready to be a minister. I cannot ignore his authority in this. Do you understand?"

She returned to him and pulled on his sleeve. "Then

let's go. You will ask him."

Never had he seen her so eager about anything. "I will. And will you meet with your father?"

They traveled nearly a quarter mile before Dove finally answered. "If you will be there, I will meet him. I do not promise to stay," she added hurriedly. "I don't trust him yet. But I will try."

B aptism

CHA
PTR
39

"She wants you to baptize her?" Broðor Clarke's astonishment discouraged Philip. He would say no.

"Yes. I didn't even know she believed until yesterday."

"And why didn't you baptize her?"

His eyes widened. "You—I—what?"

"I said," the minister spoke very slowly, "why did you not baptize her? Is she not worthy of it?"

"You would approve of that?"

"A fellow believer wants to be as Paul. She wants to arise, be baptized, wash away her sins, calling on the name of the Lord. Why would you not help her with that? What if Ananias had refused the Apostle Paul?"

"I thought you—"

"You thought I'd refuse baptism to anyone who wished it?"

"No!" Philip's face flamed. "I just thought that a minister—a priest—must be the one who—"

"And Dove agrees to this plan? She is ready for me to touch her, see her without the hood covering her face? This is something she is ready to endure?"

"No. She says she will not if I do not baptize her."

"Then why would you assume I would deny her baptism? Are my hands holier than yours?"

"No, but you are a priest—"

"As are you, Philip. Peter teaches us of the priesthood

of all believers. You must not deny one of the basic blessings of the Lord. Baptize her—now if you can find her."

"It'll have to be later. Dove and I are meeting with her father at the Point."

"She agreed? Are you certain he is really her father? That seems like a dangerous place to meet a stranger who might want to hurt your friend."

"I am certain." Philip struggled to find the right words. "She has his nose."

"What—how—" Broðor Clarke's eyes widened. "She removed the cloak?"

"The hood, yes. I didn't see her eyes, but her nose..."

"Go! Meet with them. Take her to be baptized later! This is very wonderful news! First, she is united with her Heavenly Father and then her earthly one. I AM is so good!"

Broðor Clarke practically shoved Philip out the door. He stood on his step, watching the young man stride down the street, his head high, nodding to the other villagers. Pride filled his heart. Philip's first convert—it was a beautiful thing.

An odd sight caught his attention. Was that the Fletchers' goat with blankets tied to her back? He hurried to take a better look and saw Tom Fletcher pulling his large cart with all of their belongings and two chickens tied to the top of it.

"Fletcher! Where are you going?"

Tom put down the arms of the cart, the chicken cage shifting precariously. "We're going to Cockermouth. I can do better there. The new man—he is a fletcher. He can take over my business and work for Lord Morgan."

"This seems sudden; are you sure?"

Tom nodded, his eyes refusing to meet Broðor Clarke's. "I am respected in Cockermouth. Here..."

The minister nodded. "I understand. Godspeed to

you, Tom." He turned to Una standing beside the goat, little Adam seated on the animal's back as they stood still. "My prayers are with you both."

"Thank you, Broðor Clarke. You've been a good minister to us. We will not forget you."

"Have you seen Philip?"

Tom picked up the arms of his cart, adjusted the weight, and stepped forward. "He is better off now. The new man can teach him what I could not."

Broðor Clarke stood in the middle of the road, watching as Tom and Una made their way out of the village and up the road, past the midwife's cottage, and out of sight. An indignant sniff behind him wiped the sad expression from his face and replaced it with a smile.

"Bertha, how do you feel about the loss of our fletcher's family?"

"Good riddance, I say. He cheated that boy."

"Philip is a man, Bertha. You will make yourself appear old if you persist in seeing everyone under thirty as a child."

"When the *boy* is over twenty, I'll try to consider him a man."

Broðor Clarke laughed until he saw the midwife's eyes. "What troubles you, Bertha?"

"Nothing. You're a fool."

The words were familiar, but the conviction behind them was gone. He watched as she looked everywhere but toward the cliffs near the Point. "Are you not pleased that you may be free of your charge now that Martin Bowman has come?"

"So that I may be kicked out of my own home to make way for a father who abandons his family?"

"You know better than that, Bertha. He went to find work. Men all over England do it every day." Broðor Clarke frowned. "The cottage is what truly concerns you. Do you think Lord Morgan would allow one of his people

345

to live on the streets? What about the Fletcher's cottage? They have left. You'd be in the village—closer to your mothers. Letty could live with you. It would be better for her, don't you think?"

As he spoke, the anxiety seemed to vanish slowly from the woman's face. She turned toward the empty fletcher's cottage, eying it curiously. "I should speak to Lord Morgan's agent. It's a good cottage—clean. Una was one of the more intelligent women in Wynnewood."

"Because she listened to your notions of cleanliness?"

"Some of them, yes. I never could get her to air beds. She was certain it'd allow in disease rather than keep it out."

Smiling, Broðor Clarke stroked his chin. "I'll be sure to air mine daily from now on. I wouldn't want to incur the wrath of Bertha Newcombe."

"Dennis Clarke!" She sounded appalled at the idea that she could produce such wrath. "You imply that you have never before seen my wrath. I must remedy that— after I speak with the agent. I do not want someone else to convince him to let them have it."

As the woman hurried down the road and over the bridge, Dennis Clarke chuckled and returned to his own cottage. The sight of his rumpled bed brought a fresh smile to his lips. He turned back the covers and opened the door to allow the morning air to flow through the cottage.

"Things are changing in Wynnewood, Lord. Things are definitely changing."

The man was there, talking with Philip, when Dove stepped from the trees. The sward that separated the timberline from the Point seemed both a mile wide and much too short at the same time. He saw her and moved a little closer, but Dove stepped back to allow the trees to hide her.

Philip's voice called to her in the same way he had when she first heard it. "Wait! Dove, please wait!" He ran through the grasses to her side, much faster than he'd been when younger. He held out his hand. "Come. You know I won't let anyone hurt you."

She took his hand, but resisted as he tried to pull her with him. "I don't know, Philip. I—"

"Imagine how he feels, Dove. His family was stripped from him. He can see you. You're within his grasp, but you won't come. It's killing him."

"He was a criminal." Her protest sounded weak even to her own ears.

"He stopped thieving the moment he saw us at Oxford. He lost all desire to be a decent person when he lost you."

"You'll stay? You promise?"

"I promise, Dove."

She followed him, one step behind, ready to bolt if... *If what?* She asked herself. *If he spoke to her? Of course he would. If he reached for her? It would be natural if he was her father. If he asked to see her? That was reasonable, wasn't it?* Her stomach clenched. It may be reasonable, but it didn't feel reasonable.

"Ro—Dove?"

"What were you going to call me?"

"Rosa. Your mother named you Rosa before you were even born. She hoped—"

"I'm sorry."

The man stared at her, trying to see into her hood, but she shrank at his scrutiny. "Sorry? Why are you sorry?"

"That I did not fit the name."

"I wasn't. It was her desire, not mine. I wanted a

daughter who looked just like her and a son who looked just like me. I never had the chance to have the son, and I thought my daughter was dead."

The man stepped closer, but she stepped back again. Despite the pain in his face and the hope in his eyes, she resisted him. Philip was right. She did have his nose.

Screwing up her courage, she stepped forward, offering her gloved hand. Martin, her father, glanced at Philip first before taking it and squeezing it. "Can we walk?" His eyes slid toward the cliff. "Perhaps you'd be more comfortable if we went toward the trees or up the road near your cottage—somewhere not quite so close to a cliff."

She turned to Philip for encouragement. "You'll stay close?"

"I can if you like. I'll just give you a little time to get ahead of me—for privacy."

At first, they didn't speak. Martin held her hand in the same comforting way that Philip did sometimes. She slid her eyes often to see what his face might reveal, but she didn't speak. The man seemed quite comfortable just being there with her, and the more that she thought of it, the more sense it made. After ten years apart from anyone, just knowing they were alive would be a great comfort.

"Tell me about my modor."

Without hesitating, the man began telling of a beautiful girl who lived in his village. She'd grown up there and people accepted her, although as she grew older, they were a bit unnerved by her. "Her beauty helped. People forgive in beautiful people what they will not in the ugly."

"This is true. I have often thought that." She shook her head, the cloak hood flopping with the motion. "I usually have thought of it in the opposite manner. That which people admire in the average person is

348

unforgiveable in a freak."

"From what I have heard, people have been unkind to you. Your cloak adds mystery to you and frightens them."

"Yes, but it also protects my skin. Bertha is sure that is why I have never had any sores."

"Margaret didn't develop sores until her twentieth year."

"Then it may have been for nothing," Dove agreed sadly.

"I don't think so. The sores were worse in summer. I think that rolling back her sleeves and working without a hat made them worse anyway. By the time we figured it out, it was too late. They seemed permanent."

"She wasn't as beautiful then, I suppose."

"No, and the villagers began to fear her. I thought we'd move to a town where no one had known her as the beautiful Margaret. I thought it would help, but..."

A sense of loyalty, one she couldn't quite understand, blossomed in Dove's heart. "It is not your fault that you tried to protect your family."

"You still look like her."

"I don't think I do. Philip says I have your nose, and I do. I can see it, but I am not beautiful. You saw me. I frightened those men away."

"It was your eyes. Your face was hers. I almost lost my mind when I realized who you must be."

"And you hid me from the others in that farmhouse."

Martin nodded. "If they had not been there, I would have tried to detain you—convince you of who I was, who you were. I just couldn't with them there. They might have killed both of us."

"Philip says you searched all of England looking for me."

"Yes. Almost a year, but I found you."

Dove hesitated. It was such a personal thing, but at last she spoke. "Fæder?"

A sob choked the man as he answered, "Yes?"
"I am glad you found me."

"Philip! Are you here?" Dove crashed through the underbrush with an abandon very unusual for her.

"I could hear you coming for a mile."

"I was trying to find you." She glanced around the pool. "What are you doing here?"

He shook his head. "What did you want?"

"Bertha has moved out of my cottage!"

"She has? Why?"

"I went to see her," the girl gasped as she collapsed on her log, "and she wouldn't see me. She told me to go home and leave her alone. Letty followed me though. She says that Bertha expected me to turn her out, so she spoke to Lord Morgan's agent about the fletcher's cottage."

Philip's heart sank. He'd heard about Una and Tom, but didn't know what to think of it. "If I had only learned enough, I could make Lord Morgan's arrows for him. I'm only good for repairing them."

"Fæder says he will teach you if you want to learn. He says that you are intelligent and quick." She nearly bubbled with excitement. "Is not I AM good to bring us a new fletcher before the old one leaves?"

"He is, Dove."

She started to speak, but hesitated. "I wondered..."

"You wondered what?"

"Would I be foolish to offer Fæder a place in my cottage? I don't know him, not really, but he seems—"

"I don't think you would be foolish, but we'll ask Lord Morgan's advice." Philip pulled two bundles from behind the tree and handed one to her.

"What is this?"

"Open it."

Dove untied the string and opened the cloth that covered a pair of breeches and a tunic. As she raised her hood to him, Philip was sure her eyes were questioning. "What—"

His answer was to untie his revealing a larger pair of breeches, with a patch on the knee, and another tunic. She would recognize the patch. "He said yes."

"Who said yes? Why did you bring us clothes? Where are we going? Wha—"

"Broðor Clarke. He said that believers are all priests. That I can baptize you."

Astonished, Philip watched as she flung her cloak from her, jerked off her boots, and dove into the water. Her head came up, facing away from him, her hands splashing as she bobbed up and down in the cold pool. "Come on then! How does it work? We both go down into the water. Philip said so. Then what?"

Philip pulled his own shoes from his feet and eased himself over the side of the pool. "This is really cold, Dove."

"Refreshing, isn't it?" Her voice caught. "I suppose that is appropriate. Refreshing, clean water for baptism."

Epilogue

for
Sensible
Readers

The sun slowly set over the ocean, its fiery beams stretching for miles. Waves crashed against the rocks, sending salt spray into the air. Philip glanced beside him at Dove and smiled at her. "Martin asked me to work with him."

"I know."

"I told him no. I'm ready for the church. I might even be Wynnewood's first married minister."

"I am glad you listened to Broðor Clarke." Dove's voice held an air of satisfaction to it. "When will you be finished?"

"Broðor Clarke says at least four years. I'll be twenty—maybe twenty-one."

They sat and watched as the sun sank lower in the sky, neither saying anything, both happy just to be there. At last, Dove spoke. "I never expected to be so happy—to have family. You never expected to be a minister with a family."

"'God sets the solitary in families.' You were alone even with Bertha, but now you have the Lord's family and your natural family. I have a family that I left and returned to again. I expected to be solitary without a family, but God seems to have given me that opportunity."

Before Dove could respond, a rumble near the caves

sent both young people scrambling to their feet. Slowly, they backed away, eyes wide at the burst of fire from the cliff. "Philip..."

A terrible roar erupted seconds before the dragon burst through the cave, diving down toward the water and then up again, soaring over the ocean, circling, her wings flapping powerfully. Another roar—it sounded triumphant—filled the evening air.

"Why has she left her egg? Is it—"

The dragon swooped down to the water, its great claws grabbing an enormous fish before flying back toward the cliff. "Down in the grass," Philip hissed. "Keep your head down."

They dropped to the ground, flattening themselves and watching in awe as the dragon gave one more terrifying roar as she landed at the tops of the cliff—exactly where Dove had escaped her wrath just four years earlier. She climbed down and returned to her lair, carrying the fish in her ugly mouth.

Philip stood cautiously. "She's gone back—already. Why—" He grinned as he pulled Dove up beside him. "The egg has hatched! She was calling to her mate!"

"Should we be out here if he might be coming?" Dove's question came as she backed away toward the timberline. "I don't really care to be his present to his wife."

Once more, Philip and Dove raced across the sward, into the timberline, over the road, and into Wyrm Forest to escape the wrath of a dragon. The great thundering sweeps of Sir Dragon's wings pounded overhead as he flew over Wynnewood and to the cliffs. Another father reunited with his family—at last.

Five years later...

Weeks had passed since Philip had last spent time with Dove. It seemed like months. Ever since he'd taken over the duties of the chapel, Philip's time seemed to belong to everyone but himself. However, he'd awakened that morning to a sunny day, no pressing needs, confidence in his Sunday lesson, and a little excited at the prospect of seeking out his friend again.

Broðor Clarke's words teased him anew as he pulled on his socks and boots. *Dove needs you now more than ever. Don't let your duties to the village crowd out the duties you have toward your friends.*

He was right. Philip grabbed a chunk of bread and a wedge of cheese, filled a flask with mead, and strolled out of his cottage door. In the early hours of the morning, the tradesmen were beginning their days, but the villagers were still home eating their breakfasts and getting their day started. It was the perfect time to leave.

He waved at Aubrey as he passed the mill and set off for the clearing. If she wasn't there, and he didn't expect that she would be, he'd move onto the pool. She'd said many times that she felt closest to the Lord there. Particularly since her baptism.

As he approached, her voice reached him, tugging at his heart as it always did. It was still the clear high voice that characterized her, but now it had a fullness—a richness. It was hard to imagine that his waif-like little friend with a child's voice was now a woman. Then again, was he not a man?

Philip smiled to himself. At fifteen, he'd been so eager for others to recognize his maturity. He had wanted his adult status recognized at every opportunity. Now that so many more years had passed, he felt more like a child than he had when he was one.

He paused as he stepped between the trees near the pool, his heart jumping into his throat. Dove's cloak hung from a peg driven into the great oak tree within reach. She sat on the same moss-covered log that she'd used as her bench ever since she'd rolled it there while he was off in Oxford. Her long, nearly white hair hung down her back in damp curls, soaking the tunic and breeches beneath it.

Still, he hesitated. Surely, she'd heard him. Why had she not covered? Not since the day of her baptism had he seen any part of her except the rare times her hands were left exposed. If he spoke, she would grab the cloak. Perhaps her own singing had kept her from hearing him. He hadn't tried to be quiet. Perhaps if he crept up behind her and stopped her. After years of respecting her privacy, should they not stop this foolishness? Even at her baptism, he'd tried not to look out of respect.

His conscience wouldn't allow him the stealth-like approach his heart desired. Just a few feet separated them when her hand shot out for her cloak. "Don't." He swallowed hard. In all the years since their last quarrel over it, Philip had never presumed upon their friendship, but now he felt compelled.

"What?"

"Don't put it on, Dove. Please." He took a step.

Her hand stayed frozen in mid-air, but she questioned him again. "Why?"

"Almost nine years I've been your friend. For five of those years, I've tried to remember your face from the one time I saw it clearly. Jacob only had to wait seven years for Rachel."

"Fourteen. Laban was a cheat."

"Are you a cheat?" Inching his way closer, Philip prayed that she wouldn't bolt.

"It's hardly parallel, Philip. I never promised to show myself." Dove's voice held that slight impish lilt that reassured him that she was not angry.

"Now that I am your minister as well as your friend, can you not trust me?" He took two more steps forward, nearly holding his breath to see if she'd bring the cloak closer.

"You truly don't understand, do you?"

Resignation. He hadn't expected resignation in her tone. "Understand what? Obviously I don't."

"Do you know what they say happens if I look in your eyes?" At his silence, she shook her head and continued. "Philip, I've always wanted you to be able to truthfully state that you'd never seen my eyes—never gazed into them."

Understanding dawned. "The possession. You're trying to protect me from the charge of possession." If he took another large step forward, he could touch her shoulder. Would she stiffen? Run? Shroud herself in white again? Risking it all, he reached.

Dove didn't move. She didn't stiffen. A sigh escaped, shoulders slumped. It seemed as if he'd won, but at what cost? Maybe it was enough—for now. His heart battled with his reason until Philip thought he had a perfectly accurate picture of the old man warring with the new. Unsure how to respond, Philip whispered, "Thank you."

"For what?" The words sounded wrung from her by force.

"Trusting me."

"I've always trusted you, Philip. I don't trust the villagers, but you..." Her head dropped lower, hair falling over her shoulders, creating a curtain around her head.

"May I sit?"

Her laughter rang out among the trees, bouncing off the boulders she'd placed around the edge of the pool over the years. "How formal you sound!"

Feeling silly, Philip took her mirth as a "yes" and sat next to her on the log, his arms leaning on his knees, staring in the opposite direction. "I won't look at you until you say I may."

"You shouldn't look at me ever."

"I disagree." His emotions nearly drove him wild. It seemed as if they were carrying on a completely different conversation than the words indicated—one he had only allowed himself to dream of in the wee hours of sleepless nights.

"Philip..."

He took a deep, steadying breath and reached for her hand, covering it completely with his own. "Just tell me one thing."

"What?"

"If your hair was brown, your eyes green, and your skin the color of peaches, would you wish me away as you do now?"

"I don't wish you away, Philip. I just think it best—for you, I mean." Was that a catch in her voice?

He wanted to look at the hand he held, but it seemed as if it would be breaking his word. His other hand, as if an individual entity with its own will apart from Philip's, reached for a lock of her hair, allowing it to slide between his fingers before he dropped it again. "Why have I always imagined your hair coarse and wiry?"

"Why have you ever imagined it at all?"

"You know the answer to that, Dove. I think you've known much longer than I have, even. Broðor Clarke did."

Dove choked out her answer in a whisper that sounded nearly like a gasp. "I have."

"And is it so distasteful to you?" His throat felt as if someone's hands were choking him.

"You know it isn't, Philip. It's just not possible."

"I don't understand." He shook his head. "Regardless, I didn't look. I just wish you didn't hide—"

"I know." She sighed and turned her head toward him.

Something in her tone struck his heart. He was being selfish. He, the minister of Wynnewood—the man chosen by Broðor Clarke to teach the villagers how to live the Word in their lives—was learning lessons from the village outcast. Again. "I won't do it, Dove. I'm sorry."

"Philip—"

"Forgive me, Dove. I need to go. I'm ashamed of myself. Maybe you'd like to have lunch in the clearing? I'll bring the sweet rolls Liam's father sent me."

A shuffling sound followed as he walked toward the trees. She was putting on her cloak already. So it would have to be. He wished that he had the character to be able to set his disappointment aside and stay, but he didn't trust himself. For some reason, today his heart persisted in overcoming his will. He wouldn't do that to her—never again.

"Philip?"

Instinctively, he turned, his eyes meeting hers for a brief moment before he dropped them. She hadn't replaced her cloak after all. "I didn't realize—"

Her footsteps brought her closer until he saw the white of her cloak. Philip began to raise his head when the cloak was thrust toward him. "Why don't you stay and hold that for me?"

"Wha—"

"Didn't your mother ever teach you that it is rude to

talk to someone without looking at them?" She tried to joke, but the words sounded strangled.

With a prayer in his heart and determined to give her an encouraging smile, Philip raised his head.

Shock flooded his face, but Philip was unaware of it. His eyes took in the young woman before him, staring in a most rude, uncouth, and for Dove, frightening way. Tears filled her eyes and spilled down her cheeks, but she met him, gaze for gaze, for several long seconds. At last, unable to bear the apparent horror on his face, Dove dropped her head and turned whispering, "I knew—"

Philip snapped out of his reverie. "Dove—"

"I told you it was a bad idea. I knew you couldn't—that you would try—that—"

"Shh, no listen. I know I stared. I want to apologize, but I can't. I'm not sorry." He waited, unspeaking until her eyes rose to meet his, questioning. "That might not be true. I am sorry that you have lived with such a lie all your life. I am sorry that you don't see what I do. I am sorry that I've known you for so long and never been able to tell you how beautiful you are."

Scornfully, she blurted, "Oh really, Philip—"

"I am quite serious. I've never seen anyone so beautiful in my life." He swallowed the lump that had grown in his throat. "Your father always describes how beautiful your mother was, and he says you look just like her."

At first, he wasn't sure what to think when fresh tears spilled down her cheeks. Unsure, he hugged her and whispered, "What's wrong, Dove? What did I say—do?"

She couldn't answer. In fact, years later each time he asked, the same raw emotions would overwhelm her, stifling her answer. Instead, she buried her face in his chest and clutched at his tunic for support. Something about that was just fine with him.

"Why do people make such a to-do about your eyes? They're pale, to be sure—beautiful, really—but they aren't fearsome."

"Remember, I told you long ago. When I'm angry," she choked out, "they grow darker; Bertha used to say they were a reddish purple. In firelight, they are red and the flames reflect well in them. They say my eyes look like two flames burning."

"That, I want to see."

She raised her eyes to meet his once more. Knowing that this might be his only chance to show her what he had carried in his heart and probably since he'd known her, Philip whispered, "Do you know how I always wanted a wife and family?"

"Yes."

He started to ask the question he most feared the answer to and then grinned. "That was *the* yes, wasn't it?"

Dove's impish grin, the one he'd heard in her voice so many times, teased him. "Yes."

FIN

Books by Chautona Havig

The Rockland Chronicles
Noble Pursuits
Argosy Junction
Thirty Days Hath... (Coming 2012/2013)

The Aggie Series
Ready or Not
For Keeps
Keep Away (coming 2011)

The Annals of Wynnewood
Shadows and Secrets
Cloaked in Secrets
Beneath the Cloak

The Not-So-Fairy Tales

Princess Paisley
Everard (coming 2012)

The adventure began with **Shadows & Secrets** as Philip and Dove began their unusual friendship. New secrets and excitement continued in **Cloaked in Secrets**. Don't miss the books that started it all!

Of all the princesses, in all the kingdoms, of all the lands, in all the world, Princess Paisley of Jackalopany was, by far, the most unique.

A few sheep, an excess of italics, a crusty old King, and a Frogg conspire to ensure Princess Paisley remains the most unique-- and lives happily ever after.

Made in the USA
Charleston, SC
14 December 2011